Reginald Hill

Reginald Hill is a native of Cumbria and a former resident of Yorkshire, the setting for his outstanding crime novels featuring Dalziel and Pascoe, 'the best detective duo on the scene bar none' (*Daily Telegraph*). His writing career began with the publication of *A Clubbable Woman* (1970), which introduced Chief Superintendent Andy Dalziel and DS Peter Pascoe. Their subsequent appearances, together with the adventures of Luton lathe operator turned PI Joe Sixsmith, have confirmed Hill's position as 'the best living male crime writer in the English speaking world' (*Independent*) and won numerous awards, including the Crime Writers' Association Cartier Diamond Dagger for his lifetime contribution to the genre.

The Dalziel and Pascoe novels have now been adapted into a successful BBC television series starring Warren Clarke and Colin Buchanan.

By the same author

Dalziel and Pascoe novels

A CLUBBABLE WOMAN

AN ADVANCEMENT OF LEARNING

RULING PASSION

AN APRIL SHROUD

A PINCH OF SNUFF

A KILLING KINDNESS

DEADHEADS

EXIT LINES

CHILD'S PLAY

UNDER WORLD

BONES AND SILENCE

ONE SMALL STEP

RECALLED TO LIFE

PICTURES OF PERFECTION

ASKING FOR THE MOON

THE WOOD BEYOND

ARMS AND THE WOMEN

DIALOGUES OF THE DEAD

DEATH'S JEST-BOOK

Joe Sixsmith novels

BLOOD SYMPATHY

BORN GUILTY

KILLING THE LAWYERS

SINGING THE SADNESS

FELL OF DARK

THE LONG KILL

DEATH OF A DORMOUSE

DREAM OF DARKNESS

THE ONLY GAME

REGINALD HILL

ON BEULAH HEIGHT

A Dalziel and Pascoe novel

HarperCollins*Publishers*

HarperCollins*Publishers*
77–85 Fulham Palace Road, London W6 8JB

The HarperCollins website address is:
www.**fire**and**water**.com

This paperback reissue 2003

1 3 5 7 9 8 6 4 2

First published in Great Britain
by HarperCollins*Publishers* 1998

A catalogue record for this book
is available from the British Library

ISBN 0 00 649000 X

Set in PostScript Linotype Meridien

Typeset by Rowland Phototypesetting Ltd,
Bury St Edmunds, Suffolk

Printed and bound in Great Britain by
Clays Ltd, St Ives plc

For Allan
a wandering minstrel, he!

Then I saw that there was a way to hell, even from the gates of heaven.

JOHN BUNYAN: *The Pilgrim's Progress*

O where is tinye Hew?
And where is little Lenne?
And where is bonny Lu?
And Menie of the Glenne?
And where's the place of rest –
The ever changing hame?
Is it the gowan's breast,
Or 'neath the bells of faem?

Ay, lu, lan, dil y'u

ANON: *The Gloamyne Buchte*

Wir holen sie ein auf jenen Höh'n
Im Sonnenschein.
Der Tag ist schön auf jenen Höh'n

FRIEDRICH RÜCKERT:
Kindertotenlieder IV

day one
A Happy Rural Seat
of Various View

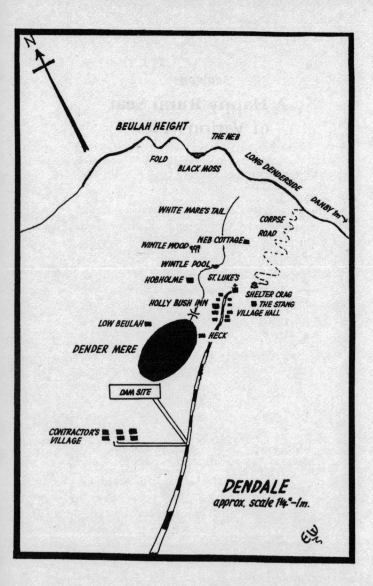

DENDALE
approx. scale 1¼" - 1m.

ONE

BETSY ALLGOOD [PA/WW/4.6.88]

TRANSCRIPT 1
No 2 of 2 copies

The day they drowned Dendale I were seven years old.

I'd been three when government said they could do it, and four when Enquiry came out in favour of Water Board, so I remember nowt of that.

I do remember something that can't have been long after, but. I remember climbing up ladder to our barn loft and my dad catching me there.

'What're you doing up here?' he said. 'Tha knows it's no place for thee.'

I said I were looking for Bonnie, which were a mistake. Dad had no time for animals that didn't earn their keep. Cat's job was keeping rats and mice down, and all that Bonnie ever caught was a few spiders.

'Yon useless object should've been drowned with rest,' he said. 'You come up here again after it and I'll get shut of it, nine lives or not.'

Before I could start mizzling, sound of a machine starting up came through the morning air, not a farm machine but something a lot bigger down at Dale End. I knew there were men working down there, but I didn't understand yet what they were doing.

Dad went to the open hay door and looked out. Low Beulah, our farm, were built on far side of Dender Mere from the village and from up in our loft you got a good view right over our fields

3

to Dale End. All on a sudden, Dad picked me up and swung me on to his shoulders.

'Tek a good look at that land, Betsy,' he said. 'Don't matter a toss now that tha's only a lass. Soon there'll be nowt here for any bugger to work at, save only the fishes.'

I'd no idea what he meant, but it were grand for him to be taking notice of me for a change, and I recall how his bony shoulder dug into my bare legs, and how his coarse springy hair felt in my little fists and how he smelt of sheep and earth and hay.

I think he forgot I were up there till I got a bit uncomfortable and moved. Then he gave a little start and said, 'Things to do still. Nowt stops till all stops.' And he dropped me to the floor with a thump and slid down the ladder. That were typical. Telling me off for being up there one minute then forgetting my existence the next.

I stayed up a long while till Mam started shouting for me. She caught me clambering down the ladder and gave me a clout on my leg and yelled at me for being up there. But I said nowt about Dad 'cos it wouldn't have eased my pain and it would just have got him in bother too.

Time went on. A year maybe. Hard to say. That age a month can seem a minute and a minute a month if you're in trouble. I know I got started at the village school. That's where most of my definite memories start too. But funny enough, I still didn't have any real idea what them men were doing down at Dale End. I think I just got used to them. It seemed like they'd been there almost as long as I had. Then some time in my second year at school, I heard some of the older kids talking about us all moving to St Michael's Primary in Danby. We hated St Michael's.

We just had two teachers, Mrs Winter and Miss Lavery, but they had six or seven and one of them was a man with a black eye-patch and a split cane that he used to beat the children with if they got their sums wrong. At least that's what we'd heard.

I piped up and asked why we had to move there.

'Dost know nowt, Betsy Allgood?' asked Elsie Coe, who was nearly eleven and liked the boys. 'What do you think they're building down the dale? A shopping centre?'

'Nay, fair do's,' said one of her kinder friends. 'She's nobbut a babbie still. They're going to flood all of Dendale, Betsy, so as the smelly townies can have a bath!'

Then Miss Lavery called us in from play. But I went to the drinking fountain first and watched the spurt of water turn rainbow in the sun.

After that I started having nightmares. I'd dream I were woken by Bonnie sitting on my pillow and howling, and all the blankets would be wet, and the bed would be almost floating on the water which were pouring through the window. I'd know it were just a dream, but it didn't stop me being frightened. Dad told me not to be so mardy and Mam said if I knew a dream were just a dream I should try and wake myself up, and sometimes I would, only I wouldn't really have woken up at all and the water would still be there, lapping over my face now, and then I really would wake up screaming.

When Mam realized what were troubling me, she tried to explain it all. She were good at explaining things when she wasn't having one of her bad turns. Nerves, I heard Mrs Telford call it one day when I was playing under the window of the joiner's shop at Stang with Madge. It was Mrs Telford I heard say too that it were a pity Jack Allgood (that's my dad) hadn't got a son, but it didn't help anyone Lizzie (that's my mam) cutting the girl's hair short like a boy's and dressing her in trousers. That was me. I looked in the mirror after that and wondered if mebbe I couldn't grow up to be a boy.

I was saying about my mam explaining things. She told me about the reservoir and how we were all going to be moved over to Danby, and it wouldn't make all that much difference 'cos Dad were such a good tenant, Mr Pontifex had promised him the first farm to come vacant on the rest of his estate over there.

Now the nightmares faded a bit. The idea of moving were more exciting than frightening, except for the thought of that one-eyed teacher with the split cane. Also the weather had turned out far too good for young kids to worry about something in the future. Especially about too much water!

That summer were long and hot, I mean really long and hot, not just a few kids remembering a few sunny days like they lasted forever.

Winter were dry, and spring too, apart from a few showers. After that, nothing. Each day hotter than last. Even up on Beulah Height you couldn't catch a draught, and down in the dale we kept all the windows in the house and school wide open, but nought came in save for the distant durdum of the contractors' machines at Dale End.

Fridays at school was the vicar's morning when Rev Disjohn would come and tell us about the Bible and things. One Friday he read us the story about Noah's Flood and told us that, bad as it seemed for the folks at the time, it all turned out for the best. 'Even for them as got drowned?' cried out Joss Puddle whose dad were landlord at the Holly Bush. Miss Lavery told him not to be cheeky, but Rev Disjohn said it was a good question and we had to remember that God sent the Flood to punish people for being bad. What he wanted to say was that God had a reason for everything, and mebbe all this fuss about the reservoir was God's way of reminding us how important water really was and that we shouldn't take any of his gifts for granted.

When you're seven you don't know that vicars can talk crap. When you get to be fourteen, you know, but.

Slowly day by day the mere's level went down. Even White Mare's Tail shrank till it were more like a white mouse's. White Mare's Tail, in case you don't know, is the force that comes out of the fell near top of Lang Neb. That's the steep fell between us and Danby. It's marked Long Denderside on maps, but no one local ever calls it owt but Lang Neb, that's because if you look at it with your head on one side, it looks like a nose, gradually rising till it drops down sudden to Black Moss col on the edge of Highcross Moor. On the other side it rises up again but more gradual to Beulah Height above our farm. There's two little tops up there and because they look a bit like a mouth, some folk call it the Gob, to match the Neb opposite. But Mrs Winter said we shouldn't call it owt so common when its real name was so lovely, and she read us a bit from this book that Beulah comes into. Joss Puddle said it were dead boring and he thought the Gob were a much better name. But I liked Beulah 'cos it were the same as our farm and besides it sort of belonged to us, seeing as my dad had the fell rights for his sheep up there and he kept the fold between the tops in good repair, which Miss Lavery said was probably older than our farmhouse even.

Any road, no one could deny our side of the valley were much nicer than Lang Neb side, which was really steep with rocks and boulders everywhere. And in the rainy season, while there'd be becks and falls streaking all of the hillsides, on the Neb they just came bursting straight out of fell, like rain from a blocked gutter. Old Tory Simkin used to say there were so many caves running through the Neb, there was more water than rock in it. And he used to tell stories about children falling asleep in the sunshine on the Neb, and being taken into the hill by nixes and such, and never seen again.

But he stopped telling the stories when it really started happening. Children disappearing, I mean.

Jenny Hardcastle were the first. Holidays had just started and we were all splashing around in Wintle Pool where White Mare's Tail hits fell bottom. Usually little ones got told off about playing up there, but now the big pool were so shallow even the smallest could play there safe.

They asked us later what time Jenny left, but kids playing on a summer's day take no heed of time. And they asked if we'd seen anyone around, watching us or owt like that. No one had. I'd seen Benny Lightfoot up the fell a way, but I didn't mention him any more than I'd have mentioned a sheep. Benny were like a sheep, he belonged on the fell, and if you went near him he'd likely run off. So I didn't mention him, not till later, when they asked about him particular.

My friend Madge Telford said that Jenny had told her she was fed up of splashing around in the water all day like a lot of babbies and she were going to Wintle Wood to pick some flowers for her mam. But Madge thought she were really in a huff because she liked to be centre of attention and when Mary Wulfstan turned up we all made a fuss of her.

You couldn't help but like Mary. It weren't just that she were pretty, which she was, with her long blonde hair and lovely smile. But she were no prettier than Jenny, or even Madge, whose hair was the fairest of them all, like the water in the mere when the sun's flat on it. But Mary were just so nice you couldn't help liking her, even though we only saw her in the holidays and at weekends sometimes.

She were my cousin, sort of, and that helped, her mam belonging to the dale and not an offcomer, though they did only use Heck as a holiday house now. Mary's granddad had been my granddad's cousin, Arthur Allgood, who farmed Heck Farm which stood, the house I mean, right at mere's edge just out of bottom end of the village. Mary's mam was Arthur's only child and I daresay were reckoned 'only a girl' like me. But at least she could make herself useful to the farm by getting wed. Next best thing after a farmer son is a farmer son-in-law, if you own the farm, that is. Arthur Allgood owned Heck, but our side of the family were just tenants at Low Beulah, and while a son could inherit a tenancy, a daughter's got no rights.

Not that Mary's mam, Aunt Chloe (she weren't really my aunt, but that's what I called her) married a farmer. She married Mr Wulfstan, who's got his own business, and they sold off most of the Heck land and buildings to Mr Pontifex, but they kept the house for holidays.

Mr Wulfstan were looked up to rather than liked in the dale. He weren't stand-offish, my mam said, just hard to get to know.

But when he had Heck done up to make it more comfortable, and got the cellar properly damp-proofed and had racks set up there to keep his fine wines, he gave as much work locally as he could, and people like Madge's dad, who ran the dale joinery business at Stang with his brother, said he were grand chap.

But I'm forgetting Jenny. Maybe she did go off in a huff because of Mary or maybe that was just Madge making it up, and she really did go off to pick some flowers for her mam. That's where they found the only trace of her, in Wintle Wood. Her blue suntop. She could have been carrying it and just dropped it. We took everything but our pants off when we played in the water in them hot days and we were in no hurry to get dressed again till we got scolded. We ran around the village like little pagans, my mam said.

But that all stopped once police were called in. It was questions questions then and we all got frightened and excited, but mebbe more excited to start with. When sun's shining and everything looks the same as it always did, it's hard for kids to stay frightened for long. Also Jenny were known for a headstrong girl and she'd run off before to her gran's at Danby after falling out with her mam. So mebbe it would turn out she'd run off again. And even when days passed and there were no word of her, most folk thought she could have gone up the Neb and fallen down one of the holes or something. The police had dogs out, sniffing at the suntop, but they never found a trail that led anywhere. That didn't stop Mr Hardcastle going out every day with his collies, yelling and calling. They had two other kids, Jed and June, both younger, but the way he went on, you'd have thought he'd lost everything in the world. My dad said he never were much of a farmer, but now he just didn't bother with Hobholme, that's their farm, though as he were one of Mr Pontifex's tenants like Dad and the place would soon be drowned, I don't suppose it mattered.

As for Mrs Hardcastle, you'd meet her wandering around Wintle Wood, picking great armfuls of flopdocken which was said to be a good plant for bringing lost children back. She had them all over Hobholme and when it were her turn to take care of flowers in the church, she filled that with flopdocken too, which didn't please the vicar, who said it was pagan, but he left them there till it were someone else's turn the following week.

The rest of the dale folk soon settled back to where they were before. Not that folk didn't care, but for us kids with the weather so fine, it were hard for grief to stretch beyond a few days, and the grown-ups were all much busier than we ever knew with making arrangements for the big move out.

It were only a matter of weeks away but that seemed a lifetime to me. I'd picked things up, more than I realized, and a lot more than I really understood. And the older girls like Elsie Coe were always happy to show off how much they knew. She it was who told me that there were big arguments going on about compensation, but it didn't affect me 'cos my dad were only a tenant, and Mr Pontifex had sold Low Beulah and Hobholme along with all the rest of his land in Dendale and up on Highcross Moor long since. Some of the others who owned their own places were fighting hard against the Water Board. Bloody fools, my dad called them. He said once Mr Pontifex sold, there were no hope for the rest and they might as well go along with the miserable old sod. Mam told him not to talk like that about Mr Pontifex, especially as he'd been promised first vacant farm on the Danby side of the Pontifex estate, and she'd heard that Stirps End were likely to be available soon. And Dad said he'd believe it when it happened, the old bugger had sold us out once, what was to stop him doing it again?

He talked really wild sometimes, my dad, especially when he'd been down at the Holly Bush. And Mam would either cry or go really quiet, I mean quiet so you could have burst a balloon against her ear and she'd not have heard. But at least when she were like this I could run around all day in my pants or in nothing at all and she'd not have bothered. Or Dad either.

10

Then Madge, my best friend, got taken. And suddenly things looked very different.

I'd gone round to play with her. Mam took me. She were having one of her good days and even though most folk reckoned that Jenny had just fallen into one of the holes in the Neb, our mams were still a bit careful about letting us wander too far on our own.

The Stang where Mr Telford had his joiner's shop were right at the edge of the village. Even though it were a red-hot day, smoke was pouring from the workshop chimney as usual, though I didn't see anyone in there working. We went up the house and Mrs Telford said to my mam, 'You'll come in and have a cup of tea, Lizzie? Betsy, Madge is down the garden, looking for strawberries, but I reckon the slugs have finished them off.'

I went out through the dairy into the long narrow garden running up to the fellside. I thought I saw someone up there but only for a moment and it probably weren't anyone but Benny Lightfoot. I couldn't see Madge in the garden but there were some big currant bushes halfway down, and I reckoned she must be behind them. I called her name, then walked down past the bushes.

She wasn't there. On the grass by the beds was one strawberry with a bite out of it. Nothing else.

I felt to blame somehow, as if she would have been there if I hadn't gone out to look for her. I didn't go straight back in and tell Mam and Mrs Telford. I sat down on the grass and pretended I was waiting for her coming back, even though I knew she never was. I don't know how I knew it, but I did. And she didn't.

Mebbe if I'd run straight back in they'd have rushed out and caught up with him. Probably not, and no use crying. There was a him *now, no one had any doubt of that.*

Now there were policemen everywhere and all the time. We had our own bobby living in the village. His name was Clark

11

and everyone called him Nobby the Bobby. He was a big fierce-looking man and we all thought he was really important till we saw the way the new lot tret him, specially this great glorrfat one who were in charge of them without uniforms.

They set up shop in the village hall. Mr Wulfstan made a right fuss when he found out. Some folk said he had the wrong of it, seeing what had happened; others said he were quite right, we all wanted this lunatic caught, but that didn't mean letting the police walk all over us.

The reason Mr Wulfstan made a fuss was because of the concert. His firm sponsored the Mid-Yorkshire Dales Summer Music Festival, and he were head of the committee. The festival's centred on Danby. I think that's how he met Aunt Chloe. She liked that sort of music and used to go over to Danby a lot. After they got wed and she inherited Heck, he got this idea of holding one of the concerts in Dendale. They held them all over, but there'd never been one here because there were so few people living in the dale and the road in and out wasn't all that good. The Parish Council had held a public meeting to discuss it the previous year. Some folk, like my dad, said they cared nowt for this sort of music and what were the point of attracting people up the valley when in a year or so there'd be nowt for them to see but a lot of water? This made a lot of folk angry (so I were told) 'cos things hadn't been finally settled and they were still hopeful Mr Pontifex would refuse to sell. Not that that would have made any difference except to drag things out a little longer. But the vote was to accept the concert, specially when Mr Wulfstan said he'd like the school choir to do a turn too.

So the previous year we'd had our first concert. The main singer were from Norway, though he spoke such good English you'd not have known it till you heard his name, which were Arne Krog. He was a friend of Mr Wulfstan's and he stayed at Heck, along with the lady who played the piano for him. Inger Sandel she was called. Arne (everyone called him Arne) was really popular, especially with the girls, being so tall and fair and good looking. Stuff he sang were mainly foreign, which didn't please everyone. He'd come back again this year and he were right disappointed when it looked like there wouldn't be a concert. I was too. I were in the school choir and this year I'd been going to sing a solo.

And most folk in the dale were disappointed as well. The concert were due to take place not long before the big move, and next year there'd be no hall, and no dale, to stage it in.

Then we heard that Mr Wulfstan had persuaded Rev Disjohn to let us use St Luke's instead and you'd have thought we'd won a battle.

But none of this took our minds off Madge's vanishing. Every time you saw police, and we saw them every day, it all came back. All the kids who knew Madge got asked questions by this lady policeman, and me most of all 'cos we were best friends. She were very nice and I didn't mind talking to her. It were a lot better than answering questions Mr Telford kept on asking. I liked Mrs Telford a lot, and Madge's Uncle George, her dad's brother who worked at the joinery with him, he were all right too. But Mr Telford were a bit frightening, mebbe because it was him made the coffins for the dale and wore a black suit at a burying. Madge were like me, an only daughter, with the difference that as far as my dad were concerned, I might as well not have existed, while Madge were like a goddess or a princess or something to Mr Telford. Not that he didn't get angry with her, but that was only because he got so worried about her. Like if she came home late, even if it were just ten minutes after school, he'd tell her he was going to lock her up with the coffins till she learnt obedience. I don't think it would have bothered Madge. Sometimes we used to sneak into the old barn where he stored the coffins, and we'd play around them, even climbing inside sometimes. I'm not saying I'd have liked to be in there by myself, but it would have been better than the belt. Any road, he never did it. When he got his rag back, he usually blamed someone else, like me, for keeping her late. Now he were on at me all the time, looking for someone or something to blame, I suppose. But I think mebbe it was himself he blamed most. 'It 'ud be different if only she'd come back,' he'd say. 'I'd never let her out of my sight.'

But I think like me he knew she were never coming back.

The lady policeman asked me all sorts of questions, like, had Madge ever said anything about any man bothering her? and how did she get on with her dad and her Uncle George? I said no she hadn't, and grand. Then she asked about the afternoon she went missing and had I noticed anyone anywhere near the Telfords' house when I were looking for Madge in the back garden? And I said no. And she said, not even Benny Lighfoot? And I said, oh aye, I think I saw Benny up the fell a way, but nobody paid any heed to Benny. And that was when she asked me about the time we were playing in the water and Jenny went off, had I seen Benny that day too. And I said yes, I thought I had. And she asked why I hadn't mentioned it then, and I explained that I didn't think that seeing Benny counted.

Now no one in the dale believed any harm of Benny Lightfoot and it were thought a right shame when police car went bumping up the track to Neb Cottage, right up under the Neb, where he lived with his gran. Nobby Clark explained that the glorrfat one without a uniform had kept on bothering him to know if there were anyone a bit odd lived local. 'I telt him I didn't know many that wasn't a bit odd,' he said. (This were reckoned a good joke and spread round the dale right quick.) But he'd had to tell him about Benny.

Benny were about nineteen, and I'd heard say he had an accident when young and had a bit of metal in his head, and mebbe this helped make him so shy, especially of lasses. You'd see his long lean figure hanging around village hall when there were a social on, or up by Wintle Wood where the big lads and lasses used to lake around on a fine evening. But once he saw he'd been seen, he'd vanish so quick, you wondered if you'd ever really seen him in the first place. 'Never knew a bugger

14

better named,' folk used to say, and everyone had a right good laugh when they heard that as the police car pulled up at the front of Neb Cottage, Benny went out of the back and took off up the hillside.

One of the bobbies tried to chase him, but there was no point. Once Benny had been persuaded to enter the Danby Tops which is the big fell race out of Danby Show in August. They got him to the start all right and when the gun went, he were off like a whippet and when they turned for home half an hour later at top of the Danby side of Lang Neb, he were half a mile ahead. He came down like a loose boulder, just bouncing from rock to rock, with never another runner in sight. Then he heard crowd cheering and he stopped a couple of hundred feet above the showground on Ligg Common and looked down at all them people.

Next thing he'd turned round and were running back up the fell almost as fast as he came down, and I doubt if he paused till he were over the ridge and back in his gran's cottage in Dendale.

So like I say, most folk just laughed when they heard this 'cos they reckoned it was a waste of time, especially as they were certain it weren't anyone local the police should be looking for, it were some offcomer, and most likely one of the contractors working on the dam.

They'd been round a long time. They'd started work soon as Mr Pontifex had sold them his Dendale estate. They couldn't start on dam proper until the result of the Enquiry, but this made no difference, I heard my dad say later. The Water Board knew they were going to get the result that they wanted, and by the time it came through, they'd laid new drains up on Black Moss between Neb and Beulah Height on Highcross Moor so that what had just been a great bog were now a wide tarn waiting to be spilled down into valley. And at Dale End, they'd cleared the land and put down hardcore tracks for heavy machinery and built cabins for their contractors.

So they'd been around for a long long time by that long hot summer when dam were getting close to being finished and the dale had got used to them. There were odd bits of trouble, but not much. When some chickens got stolen at Christmas and when someone started nicking undies from washing lines, everyone said it must be the contractors, and Nobby Clark went and had a word, but apart from that they weren't any bother. They'd get in the Holly Bush an odd time, but they had their own bar and canteen and games room down at Dale End and seemed to prefer sticking together. But there was one of them who were different. This was a man called Geordie Turnbull.

Geordie wasn't anyone important, he drove one of the big machines that dug up the earth, but he liked to come into the village, drink in the pub, shop in the post office. Everyone liked him, except mebbe for a few of the men who didn't like the way he got on so well with the women.

Even Mrs Winter our old head teacher thought he were grand, and Miss Lavery seemed fair stricken. Few months earlier, Water Board had put on some lectures in the village hall to explain all about the dam, dead boring, I heard my dad say. He stood up and asked questions and it got into a row and he wanted to hit the lecturer but some of the others stopped him even though most agreed with him. Anyway, the Board asked Mrs Winter if they could send a lecturer into the school, and she said no, it would likely just worry the children but if they sent someone we all knew like Geordie Turnbull to explain about the dam, that would be OK.

So Geordie came.

He had a funny way of talking which Miss Lavery said was because he came from Newcastle. He didn't lecture us but just sort of chatted and answered questions. I recall him saying, 'Which of you kiddies ever tried to dam a stream?' And when all the hands went up, he said, 'All right, so tell me, bonnie lads and lasses, what's the best stuff to work with when you're building your dam?' And some said earth, and some said stones, and some said branches. Geordie nodded and said, 'Good answer,' to all of those. Then he said, 'Now here's a hard one. What's the worst stuff of all for your dam?' And while everyone was thinking, Madge yelled out, 'It's the watter!' And Geordie laughed out loud, and we all laughed with him 'cos you had to laugh when he did, and he picked her up and swung her on his shoulders and said, 'Yes it's the watter,' – taking her off – 'the very stuff you're trying to save that fights against you saving it. So when it's hot and dry like now, building a dam's a lot easier than when it's cold and wet. In fact, you might say it's a dam sight easier.' We all laughed again, and even Mrs Winter had to smile.

Then he swung Madge down and gave her a kiss and said if ever she wanted a job moving earth, she just had to come and see Geordie Turnbull.

So it were a great success. And Geordie were even more popular after that. And everyone used to say that it were the well-off folk in their big offices in the city who were responsible for drowning the dale, no use blaming the contractors who were just ordinary working lads trying to earn a living.

But when Madge got took, everything changed. Suddenly we were told not to go anywhere near the site, not to speak to anyone working on the dam, and if anyone tried to talk to us, to run off fast and tell Constable Clark.

And above all we were warned not to talk to Geordie Turnbull. At the talk he gave in the school, no one had been bothered by him putting Madge on his shoulders or giving her a kiss or telling her to come and see him if she wanted a job. Now everyone was talking about it and they wouldn't serve him in the Holly Bush any more, and there was nearly a fight when he wouldn't leave. Then one day we saw him took off in a police car, and everyone was saying they'd got him and he ought to be lynched. Two days later, but, he were back at work, though he never came into village again. But it didn't matter because now there was something new to occupy people's minds.

The bobbies had had no luck getting hold of Benny Lightfoot, *but in the end they got a piece of paper saying they could search his room. Old Mrs Lightfoot said that it'd take more than paper to get in her house and she set the dogs on them, but in the end they did get in, and up in Benny's room they found books with mucky pictures and some of the knickers that had gone missing off clothes lines. I don't think they wanted anyone to know owt of this straight off, but it were all round village in an hour.*

Now they were really hot to catch Benny. They put two men to hide in the old byre alongside Neb Cottage. Everyone said they must be daft to imagine Benny wouldn't be watching them from up the Neb and after couple of days a car bumped up the track and took the men who'd been hiding away. What no one knew was they dropped another man from out the back of the car, and he hid in the byre, and that night when Benny came down to his gran's, he jumped on him. Then he shut both himself and Benny up in the byre and radioed for help, which were just as well. When the others got there, old Mrs Lightfoot were outside byre with her dogs and a shotgun, trying to break down door.

They took Benny away into town, and while everyone were sorry for the old lady, they all hoped this were the end of it. But four or five days later, Benny were back. According to what Nobby Clark said, they'd questioned him and questioned him, but he just kept on saying he'd done no harm, and they had to give him a lawyer, and though they kept hold of him long as they could, in the end they had to let him go.

No one in the dale knew what to think, but all the mams told their kids the same thing: if you see Benny Lightfoot, run like heck. And some of the dads after a few pints in the Holly Bush were all for going up to Neb Cottage and getting things sorted, though my dad said they were a load of idiots who'd pissed their brains out up against the wall. There might have been a fight, but Mr Wulfstan were in the bar with Arne Krog and someone asked what he thought. Folk had a lot of respect for Mr Wulfstan, even though he were an offcomer. He'd married local, he didn't object to hunting and shooting, and he spent his brass in the dale. Above all, he'd fought the Water Board every inch. So they listened when he said they'd got to trust the Law. Best thing they could do was keep the kids in plain view till time came for us all to move out of the dale, which weren't too far away.

It were funny. The more worried folk got about their kids, the less they worried about the dam. In fact some of the mams were saying it would be a blessing to move and get this behind them and start off new somewhere, a long way away from Benny Lightfoot, just as if him and his gran weren't going to have to move too.

Hot weather went on. Mere went down, dam went up. Folk said that with no water to hold in, it weren't really a dam at all, just a big wall, like Hadrian's up north, to keep foreigners out.

Except it hadn't worked. There were two in already. Arne Krog and Inger Sandel.

I knew them quite well 'cos Aunt Chloe often invited me to Heck to play with Mary. Also Arne remembered me from singing in the school choir last year, and when he heard I were singing 'The Ash Grove' solo this year, he asked me to sing it to him one day. I were so pleased I just started right off without waiting for him to start playing the music on the piano. He listened till I finished, then sat down at the piano. It were one of them baby grands, Mr Wulfstan played a bit himself, but he'd really bought it for Mary to practise on during the holidays. Mary didn't like playing very much, she told me. I'd have liked to learn but we didn't have a piano and no hope of getting one. Anyway, Arne played a note and asked me to sing it, then a few more, then he played half a dozen and asked me which was the one that came at the end of the second line of 'The Ash Grove'.

When I told him, he turned to Inger and said, 'You hear that? I think little Betsy could have perfect pitch.'

She just looked at him, blank like, which meant nowt 'cos

19

that was how she usually looked. She could talk English as good as him, only she never bothered unless she had to. As for me, I had no idea what he were talking about but I felt really chuffed that I'd got something that pleased Arne.

This piano at Heck had to be shifted to St Luke's for the concert. There were an old piano in the village hall but it were useless for proper singing, and the one at school weren't much better. If a cat ran up and down keyboard, he'd have made it sound as musical as Miss Lavery when she tried to play it. So it had to be Mr Wulfstan's baby grand.

My dad came to Heck with a trailer pulled by his tractor. He'd brushed most of muck off trailer and put a bit of fresh straw on the boards, so it didn't look too bad. It took Dad and two lads from the village to get the piano out of the house while Aunt Chloe and Arne gave advice. I tried to help, but Dad told me to get out of the bloody way before I tripped someone up. I went and stood by Mary and she held my hand. Her dad never spoke to her like that. If he hadn't seen her for half a day he made more fuss when he got home than my dad had made of me when I came back from hospital after I spent a couple of nights there when I broke my leg.

Mr Wulfstan wasn't there that day. Most days he drove into town to see to his business and this was one of them. We went through the village in a sort of procession, Dad driving the tractor, the lads standing on trailer making sure piano didn't slip, Arne, Inger, Aunt Chloe, Mary and me, walking behind. Folk came to their doors to see what was going off and there was a lot of laughing which hadn't been heard for a bit. No one had forgot about Jenny and Madge, but grieving doesn't pay the rent, as my mam said. Even the policemen who were in the hall looked out and smiled.

Rev Disjohn were waiting at the church. Getting it through the door weren't easy. St Luke's isn't a big fancy building like you see some places. We learned all about it at school. Couple of hundred years back there were no church in Dendale and

20

folk had a long trek over the fell to Danby for services. Worst was when someone died and you had to take the coffin with you. So in the end they built their own church by Shelter Crag at the foot of the fell where they took the bodies out of the coffins and strapped them to ponies that carried them over to Danby. And when they built it they applied same rule as they did to their houses which was, the bigger the door, the bigger the draught.

At last they got it in and set it up. Dad and the farm lads went off with the trailer. Inger sat down at the piano and tried it out. It had had a right jangling, getting it on and off trailer and through that narrow door, and she settled down to retune it. Aunt Chloe said she had some things to do in the village and she'd see us back home. Mary and I asked if we could stay and come back with Arne and Inger and she said all right, so long as we didn't go outside of the church. Arne said he'd keep an eye on us and off Aunt Chloe went. Arne wandered round the church, looking at the wood carvings and such. Rev Disjohn sat in a pew watching Inger at work. I often noticed when she were around he never took his eyes off her. She were too busy to pay any heed to him, playing notes, then fiddling inside the piano. It was dead boring so Mary and I slipped outside to play in the churchyard. You can have a good game of hide and seek there around the gravestones. It's a bit frightening but nice-frightening, so long as the sun's shining and you know that there's grown-ups close by. Not all grown-ups, but. You can still see the old Corpse Road winding up the fellside from Shelter Crag. I were hiding behind a big stone at the bottom end of the churchyard and I could see right up the trail through the lych gate and I glimpsed a figure up there. Like I told the police after, I thought it were Benny Lightfoot but I couldn't be absolutely sure. Then Mary suddenly came round the headstone and grabbed me, frightening me half to death, and I forgot all about it.

Now it were her turn to hide, mine to seek. She were good

at hiding because she could keep still as a mouse and not start giggling like most of us did.

I went right round the church without spotting her. As I passed the door, I heard Arne start singing. Inger must have finished tuning and they were trying it out. I stepped inside to listen.

The words were foreign, but I'd heard him sing it before and he told me what it meant. It's about this man riding in the dark with his young son and the boy sees this sort of elf called the Erlking who calls him away. The father tries to ride faster but it's no use, the Erlking has got his child and when he reaches home the boy is dead. I didn't like it much, it were really frightening, but I had to listen.

Arne saw me in the doorway and all of a sudden he stopped and said, 'No, it's not right. Something's wrong with this place, perhaps it's the acoustics, perhaps you haven't got the piano quite right. I have to go back to the house now. Why don't you play your scales to little Betsy here? She has a better ear than either of us, I think. Let her say what is wrong.'

I recall the words exactly. He were looking straight at me as he spoke and sort of smiling. He had these bright blue eyes, like the sky on one of them sharp winter's days when the sun is shining but the frost never leaves the air.

He picked me up and set me on his shoulder and carried me up the aisle. I remember how cold it felt inside after the hot sun. And I recalled the time Dad put me on his shoulder in the hay loft.

Arne set me down in a pew next to the vicar and ruffled my hair, what there was of it. Then he said, 'See you later,' and smiled at Inger but she didn't smile back, just gave him a funny look and started playing scales as he went out. Every now and then she'd pause and look at me. Sometimes I'd nod, sometimes shake my head. Don't know how I know if something's right or not, I just do.

We must have been there another half hour or more. Finally she were satisfied and we said goodbye to the vicar. He wanted to talk but I could tell Inger weren't interested in him, and we went out of the door. It were like stepping into a hot bath after the cold church, and the bright light made my eyes dazzle.

Then I remembered Mary.

I called her name. Nothing. It were like being at the bottom of Madge's garden again.

Inger called too and Rev Disjohn came out of the church and asked what were up.

'It's nothing,' said Inger. 'I think Mary must have gone back to the house with Arne.'

She said it dead casual, but I saw the way she and the vicar looked at each other that they were worried sick.

I were sick too, but not with worry. Worry's for what you don't know. And I knew Mary were gone.

We hurried back to Heck. Arne were there and Aunt Chloe. I thought she were going to die in front of us when we asked if Mary had come home. I'd heard folk say that someone had gone white as a sheet often enough, but now for the first time I knew what it meant.

Vicar had stopped off at the hall on the way through the village and the police were close behind us.

I told all I could. 'Are you sure it was Lightfoot?' they kept on asking and I kept on saying, 'I think it was.' Then Arne said, 'I think that this young lady has had enough, don't you?' And he put his arm around me and led me out of the house and took me home.

They went searching up the Neb again, with the dogs and everything, just like last time. And just like last time, they came back with nothing.

And they went looking for Benny again, and he weren't to be found either.

His gran said he'd been with her all afternoon till he saw the police cars turning up the track. Then he'd taken off because he couldn't stand any more questioning. No one believed her, at least not about being with her all afternoon.

23

Then Mr Wulfstan came home. He were like a mad thing. He came round to our house and started asking me what had happened. At first he tried to be nice and friendly, but after a bit his voice got louder and he started sounding so fierce that I began to cry. 'What do you mean, you don't know where she was hiding? What do you mean, you think you saw Lightfoot? What do you mean, you stopped playing and went inside to listen to the music?'

By now he'd got a hold of me and I was sobbing my heart out. Then Mam, who'd gone out to make some tea, came rushing back in and asked him what the hell he thought he was doing. I'd never heard her swear before. Mr Wulfstan calmed down and said he were sorry but not sounding like he meant it, then he rushed off without having any tea. We heard later he went up to Neb Cottage and had a big row with old Mrs Lightfoot, and the police had to make him come away, and he told them it were all their fault for letting Lightfoot loose when they had him in their cells, and if anything had happened to Mary he was going to make sure every one of them suffered.

I asked my mam why he were so mad with me. She said, he's not mad with you, he's mad with himself for not taking better care of the thing he loves most in the world. I said, but it's not his fault that Mary got took, and she said, aye, but he thinks it is, and that's why he's running round looking for someone else to blame. And I wondered if my dad would run around like that if I got took. Weeks passed. They didn't find Mary. And they didn't find Benny. The concert was cancelled. Arne and Inger went away. And the day came when we all had to move out of our homes.

I were glad to go. Everyone else had long faces and there were some who were wailing and moaning. Dad went around like he were looking for someone to hit and Mam, who were having one of her bad turns again, could hardly drag herself out of the house. But I sat in the back seat of the car with Bonnie held tight in my arms and bit my cheeks to stop myself smiling. Remember, I were only seven and I thought that grief and guilt and fear were things you could drive away from like houses and barns and fields, leaving them behind you to be drowned.

And when, as we drove down the village street for the last time, the first drops of rain we'd seen in nigh on four months burst on the windscreen, I recalled Rev Disjohn's Friday talk and felt sure that God was once again sending His blessed floods to cleanse a world turned foul by all our sins.

TWO

'And now the sun will rise as bright
As though no horror had touched the night.
The horror affected me alone.
The sunlight illumines everyone.'

'Nice voice,' said Peter Pascoe, his mouth full of quiche.
'Pity about the tuba fanfare.'

'That was a car horn, or can't your tin ear tell the
difference? But no doubt it is Tubby the Tuba leaning on
it.'

'Why do you think I'm bolting my food?' said Pascoe.

'I noticed. Peter, it's Sunday, it's your day off. You
don't have to go.'

He gave her an oddly grave smile and said gently, 'No,
I don't. But I think I will. Give you a chance for a bit of
productive Sabbath-breaking.'

This was a reference to Ellie's writing ambitions,
marked by the presence of a pad and three pens on the
patio by her sunbed.

'Can't concentrate in this heat,' she said. 'Christ, the
fat bastard's going to rouse the whole street!'

The horn was playing variations on the opening motif
of Beethoven's Fifth.

Pascoe, ignoring it, said, 'Never mind. You're probably
famous already, only they haven't told you.'

Ellie had written three novels, all unpublished. The
third script had been with a publisher for three months.
A phone call had brought the assurance that it was being

seriously considered, and with it a hope that was more creatively enervating than any heat.

The doorbell rang. The fat bastard had got out of his car. Pascoe washed the quiche down with a mouthful of wine and stooped to kiss his wife. With Ellie any kiss was a proper kiss. She'd once told him she didn't mind a peck on the cheek but only if she wasn't sitting on it. Now she arched her bikini'd body off the sun lounger and gave him her strenuous tongue.

The doorbell went into the carillon at the end of the '1812' Overture, accompanied by cannon-like blows of the fist against the woodwork.

Reluctantly, Pascoe pulled clear and went into the house. As he passed through the hallway, he grabbed a light cagoule. It hadn't rained for weeks, but Andy Dalziel brought out the boy scout in him.

He opened the door and said, 'Jesus.'

Detective Superintendent Andrew Dalziel, ever full of surprises, was wearing a Hawaiian shirt bright enough to make an eagle blink.

'Always the cock-eyed optimist,' he said, looking at the cagoule. 'Hello, what's yon? I know that tune.'

This beat even the shirt. Like a child catching the strains of the Pied Piper, the Fat Man pushed past Pascoe and headed through the house to the patio where the radio was playing.

'You must not dam up that dark infernal,' sang the strong young mezzo voice. 'But drown it deep in light eternal!'

'Andy,' said Ellie, looking up in surprise. 'Thought you were in a hurry. Time for a drink? Or a slice of quiche?' She reached for the radio switch.

'Nay, leave it. Mahler, isn't it?'

With difficulty, Ellie prevented her gaze meeting her husband's.

'Right,' she said. 'You're a fan?'

'Wouldn't say that. Usually in Kraut, but?'

'True. This is the first time I've heard it in English.'

'So deep in my heart a small flame died. Hail to the joyous morningtide!'

The voice faded. The music wound plangently for another half-minute then it died too.

'Elizabeth Wulfstan singing the first of Mahler's *Kindertotenlieder*, the songs for dead children,' said the announcer. 'A new voice to me, Charmian. Lots of promise, but what an odd choice for a first disc. And in her own translation too, I believe.'

'That's right. And I agree, not many twenty-two-year-olds would want to tackle something like this, but perhaps not many twenty-two-year-olds have a voice with this kind of maturity.'

'Maybe so, but I still think it was a poor choice. There's a straining after effect as if she doesn't trust the music and the words to do their share of the work. More after the break. This is *Coming Out*, your weekend review of the new releases.'

Ellie switched off.

'Andy, you OK?'

The Fat Man was standing rapt, no longer Hamelin child lured away by the piper, but Scottish thane after a chat with the witches.

'Nay, I'm fine. Just feel like someone had walked over my grave, that's all.'

This time the Pascoes' gazes did meet and shared the message, it'd be a bloody long walk!

He went on, 'Yon lass, he said her name was Wulfstan?'

'That's right. She's going to be singing in the Dales Festival. I saw the disc advertised in *The Gramophone*, special mail-order price, so I've got it coming, but I might not have bothered if I'd heard that review first. What do you think, Andy, being an expert? And are you sure you won't have a drink?'

The gentle irony, or the repeated offer, brought Dalziel out of his reverie and for the first time his gaze acknowledged that Ellie was wearing a bikini whose cloth wouldn't have made a collar for his shirt.

'Nay, lass. I know nowt about music. And there's no time for a drink. Sorry to be dragging him off on a Sunday, but.'

He made *dragging off* sound like a physical act.

Ellie was puzzled. Three things which passeth understanding: Dalziel recognizing Mahler; Dalziel refusing a drink; Dalziel not clocking her tits straight off.

'It sounds urgent,' she said.

'Aye, kiddie goes missing, it's always urgent,' he said. 'Where's young Rosie?'

The juxtaposition of ideas was abrupt enough to be disturbing.

Pascoe said quickly, 'She's spending the weekend with a schoolfriend. Zandra with a Zed, would you believe? Zandra Purlingstone?'

There was a teasing interrogative in his tone which Dalziel was on to in a flash.

'Purlingstone? Not Dry-dock Purlingstone's daughter?' he exclaimed.

Derek Purlingstone, General Manager of Mid-Yorks Water plc, the privatized version of the old Water Board, had played down the threat of shortages when this year's drought started by gently mocking the English preoccupation with bathing, adding, 'After all, when you want to clean a boat, you don't put it in a bath, do you? You put it in a dry dock!'

He had learned the hard way that only the sufferers are allowed to make jokes about their pain. Dalziel's surprise rose from the fact that Dry-dock's position and

29

politics made him the kind of man whose company Ellie would normally have avoided like head-lice.

'The same,' said Pascoe. 'Zandra's in Rosie's class at Edengrove and they've elected each other best friend.'

'Oh aye? With all his brass, I'd have thought he'd have gone private. Still, it's reckoned a good school and I suppose it's nice and handy, being right on his doorstep.'

Dalziel spoke without malice, but Pascoe could see that Ellie was feeling provoked. Edengrove Primary, with its excellent reputation and its famous head, Miss Martindale, might lie right on Purlingstone's doorstep, but it was a good four miles north of the Pascoes', while Bullgate Primary was less than a mile south. Ellie had made enquiries. 'Bullgate has many original and unique features,' a friend in the inspectorate told her. 'For instance, during break, they play tiggie with hammers.' After that, she made representations, with the upshot that Rosie went to Edengrove. Even with the shining example of New Labour leadership before her, Ellie felt a little exposed, and as always was ready to counterpunch before the seconds had left the ring.

'If Derek is democratic enough to send his girl to a state school, I don't see why we should try to prove him wrong by refusing to let Rosie make friends with Zandra, do you?' she said challengingly.

Normally, Dalziel would have enjoyed nothing more than winding Ellie Pascoe up. But this morning standing here on this pleasant patio in the warm sunshine, he felt such a longing to subside into a lounger, accept a cold beer and while away the remains of the day in the company of these people he cared for more than he'd ever acknowledge, that he found he had no stomach for even a mock fight.

'Nay, you're right, lass,' he said. 'Being friendly with your little lass would do anyone the power of good. But

I thought her best mate was called Nina or something, not Zandra. T'other night when I rang and Rosie answered, I asked her what she were doing, and she said she were playing at hospitals with her best friend Nina. They fallen out, or what?'

Pascoe laughed and said, 'Nina has many attractions, but she doesn't have a pony and a swimming pool. At least, not a real pony and a real swimming pool. Nina's Rosie's imaginary best friend. Ever since Wieldy gave her this last Christmas, they've been inseparable.'

He went into the living room and emerged with a slim shiny volume which he handed to the Fat Man.

The cover had the title *Nina & the Nix* above a picture of a pool of water in a high-vaulted cave with a scaly humanoid figure, sharp-toothed and with a fringe of beard, reaching over the pool to a small girl with her hands pressed against her ears, and her mouth and eyes rounded in terror. At the bottom it said 'Printed at the Eendale Press'.

'Hey,' said Dalziel. 'Isn't that the outfit run by yon sarky sod our Wieldy took up with?'

'Edwin Digweed. Indeed,' said Pascoe.

'Ten guineas, it says here. I hope the bugger got trade discount! You sure this is meant for kiddies? Picture like that could give the little lass bad dreams.'

He sounds like a disapproving granddad, thought Pascoe.

He said, 'It's Caddy Scudamore who did the illustrations. You remember her?'

'That artist lass?' Dalziel smacked his lips salaciously. 'Like a hot jam doughnut just out of the pan and into the sugar. Lovely.'

It was an image for an Oxford Professor of Poetry to lecture on, thought Ellie as she said primly, 'I tend to agree with you about the illustration, Andy.'

'Come on,' said Pascoe. 'She sees worse in Disney cartoons. It's Nina that bothers me. I had to buy an ice cream for her the other day.'

'That's because you never had an imaginary friend,' laughed Ellie. 'I did, till I was ten. Only children often do.'

'Adults too,' agreed Dalziel. 'The Chief Constable's got several. I'm one of them. What's the story about anyway?'

'About a little girl who gets kidnapped by a nix – that's a kind of water goblin.'

A breeze sprang up from somewhere, hardly strong enough to stir the petals on the roses, but sufficient to run a chilly finger over sun-warmed skin.

'Could have had that drink,' said Dalziel accusingly to Pascoe. 'Too late now. Come on, lad. We've wasted enough time.'

He thrust the book into Ellie's hands and set off through the house.

Pascoe looked down at his wife. She got the impression he was seeking the right words to say something important. But what finally emerged was only, 'See you then. Expect me . . . whenever.'

'I always do,' she said. 'Take care.'

He turned away, paused uncertainly as if in a strange house, then went through the patio door.

She looked after him, troubled. She knew something was wrong and she knew where it had started. The end of last year. A case which had turned personal in a devastating way and which had only just finished progressing through the courts. But when if ever it would finish progressing through her husband's psyche, she did not know. Nor how deeply she ought to probe.

She heard the front door close. She was still holding Rosie's book. She looked down at the cover illustration, then placed the slim volume face down on the floor beside her and switched the radio back on.

The strong young voice of Elizabeth Wulfstan was singing again.

> 'Look on us now for soon we must go from you.
> These eyes that open brightly every morning
> In nights to come as stars will shine upon you.'

THREE

Pascoe sat in the passenger seat of the car with the window wound fully down. The air hit his face like a bomb blast, giving him an excuse to close his eyes while the noise inhibited conversation.

That had been a strange moment back there, when his feet refused to move him through the doorway and his tongue tried to form the words, 'I shan't go.'

But its strangeness was short-lived. Now he knew it had been a defining moment, such as comes when a man stops pretending his chest pains are dyspepsia.

If he'd opted not to go then, he doubted if he would ever have gone again.

He'd known this when Dalziel rang him. He'd known it every morning when he got up and went on duty for the past many weeks.

He was like a priest who'd lost his faith. His sense of responsibility still made him take the services and administer the sacraments, but it was mere automatism maintained in the hope that the loss was temporary.

After all, even though it was faith not good works that got you into the Kingdom, lack of the former was no excuse for giving up the latter, was it?

He smiled to himself. He could still smile. The blacker the comedy, the bigger the laugh, eh? And he had found himself involved in the classic detective black comedy when the impartial investigator of a crime discovers it is his own family, his own history, he is investigating, and ends up arresting himself. Or at least something in himself is arrested. Or rather . . .

No. Metaphors, analogies, parallels, were all ultimately evasive.

The truth was that what he had discovered about his family's past, and present, had filled him with a rage which at first he had scarcely acknowledged to himself. After all, what had rage to do with the liberal, laid-back, logical, caring and controlled Pascoe everyone knew and loved? But it had grown and grown, a poison tree with its roots spreading through every acre of his being, till eventually controlling it and concealing it took up so much of his moral energy, he had no strength for anything else.

He was back with metaphors, and mixing them this time, too.

Simply, then, he had come close from time to time to physical violence, to hitting people, and not just the lippy low-life his job brought him in contact with who would test a saint's patience, but those close around him – not, thank God, his wife and his daughter – but certainly this gross grotesquerie, this tun of lard, sitting next to him.

'You turned Trappist or are you just sulking?' the tun bellowed.

Carefully Pascoe wound up the window.

'Just waiting for you to fill me in, sir,' he said.

'Thought I'd done that,' said Dalziel.

'No, sir. You rang and said that a child had gone missing in Danby and as that meant you'd be driving out of town past my house, you'd pick me up in twenty minutes.'

'Well, there's nowt else. Lorraine Dacre, aged seven, went out for a walk with her dog before her parents got up. Dog's back but she isn't.'

Pascoe pondered this as they crossed the bypass and its caterpillar of traffic crawling eastwards to the sea, then said mildly, 'Not a lot to go at then.'

'You mean, not enough to cock up your cocktails on the patio? Or mebbe you were planning to pop round to Dry-dock's for a dip in his pool.'

'Not much point,' said Pascoe. 'We'll be passing the Chateau Purlingstone shortly and if you peer over his security fence, you'll observe that he's practising what he preaches. The pool is empty. Which is why they've taken the girls to the seaside today. We were asked to join them, but I didn't fancy wall-to-wall traffic. A mistake, I now realize.'

'Don't think I wouldn't have airlifted you out,' growled Dalziel.

'I believe you. But why? OK, a missing child's always serious, but this is still watching-brief time. Chances are she's slipped and crocked her ankle up the dale some-where, or, worse, banged her head. So the local station organizes a search and keeps us posted. Nothing turns up, *then* we get involved on the ground.'

'Aye, normally you're right. But this time the ground's Danby.'

'Meaning?'

'Danbydale's next valley over from Dendale.'

He paused significantly.

Pascoe dredged his mind for a connection and, because they'd just been talking about Dry-dock Purlingstone, came up with water.

'Dendale Reservoir,' he said. 'That was going to solve all our water problems to the millennium. There was an Enquiry, wasn't there? Environmentalists versus the public weal. I wasn't around myself but we've got a book about it, or rather Ellie has. She's into local history and environmental issues. *The Drowning of Dendale*, that's it.

More a coffee-table job than a sociological analysis, I recall . . . Sorry sir. Am I missing the point?'

'You're warm, but not very,' growled the Fat Man, who'd been showing increasing signs of impatience. 'That summer, just afore they flooded Dendale, three little lasses went missing there. We never found their bodies and we never got a result. I know you weren't around, but you must have heard summat of it.'

Meaning, my failures are more famous than other people's triumphs, thought Pascoe.

'I think I heard something,' he said diplomatically. 'But I can't remember much.'

'I remember,' said the Fat Man. 'And the parents, I bet they remember. One of the girls was called Wulfstan. That's what fetched me up short back there when I heard the name.'

'The singer, you mean? Any connection? It can't be a common name.'

'Mebbe. Not a daughter, but. They just had the one. Mary. It nigh on pushed the father over the edge, losing her. He chucked all kinds of shit at us, threatened he'd sue for incompetence and such.'

'Did he have a case?' enquired Pascoe.

Dalziel gave him a cold stare, but Pascoe met it unblinking. Hidden rage had its compensations, one of them being an indifference to threat.

'There were this local in the frame,' said the Fat Man abruptly. 'I never really fancied him, two sheets short of a bog roll, I reckoned, but we pulled him in after the second lassie. Nothing doing, we had to let him go. Then Mary Wulfstan vanished and her old man went bananas.'

'And the local?'

'Benny Lightfoot. He vanished too. Except for one more sighting. Another girl, Betsy Allgood, she got attacked, but that was later, weeks later. Said it were definitely Lightfoot. That did it for most people, especially bloody media. In their eyes we'd had him and we'd let him go.'

'You didn't agree?'

'Or didn't want to. Never easy to say which.'

This admission of weakness was disturbing, like a cough from a coffin.

'So you went looking for him?'

'There were more sightings than Elvis. Someone even spotted him running in the London Marathon on telly. That figured. Lived up to his name, did Benny. Light of head, light of foot. He could fair fly up that fellside. Might as well have flown off it for all we ever found of him. Or into it, the locals reckoned.'

'Sorry?'

'Into the Neb. That's what they call the fell between Dendale and Danby. It's Long Denderside on the map. Full of bloody holes, specially on the Dendale flank. Different kind of rock on the Danby side, don't ask me how. So there's lots of caves and tunnels, most on 'em full of water, save in the drought.'

'Did you search them?'

'Cave rescue team went in after the first girl vanished. And again after the other two. Not a sign. Aye, but they're not Benny Lightfoot, said the locals. Could squeeze through a crack in the pavement, our Benny.'

'And that's where he's been hiding for fifteen years?' mocked Pascoe.

'Doubt it,' said Dalziel, with worrying seriousness. 'But he could have holed up there for a week or so, scavenging at nights for food. Betsy Allgood, that's the one who got away, she said he looked half-starved. And sodden. The drought had broken then. The caves in the Neb would be flooding. I always hoped he'd have gone to sleep down there somewhere and woke up drowned.'

38

The radio crackled before Pascoe could examine this interesting speculation in detail and Central Control spilled out an update on the case.

Lorraine Dacre, aged seven, was the only child of Tony Dacre, thirty, Post Office driver, no criminal record, and Elsie Dacre, née Coe, also no record. Married eight years, residence, 7 Liggside, Danby. Lorraine did not appear on any Social Service or Care Agency list. Sergeant Clark, Danby Section Office, had called in his staff of four constables. Three were up the dale supervising a preliminary search. Back-up services had been alerted and would be mobilized on Superintendent Dalziel's say-so. Sergeant Clark would rendezvous with Superintendent Dalziel at Liggside.

The Fat Man was really reacting strongly to this, thought Pascoe. Old guilt feelings eating that great gut? Or was there something more?

He brooded on this as they ate up the twenty or so miles to Danby. It was a pleasant road, winding through the pieced and plotted agricultural landscape of the Mid-York plain. As summer's height approached, the fields on either side were green and gold with the promise of rich harvest, but on unirrigated set-aside land blotches of umber and ochre showed how far the battle with drought was already engaged. And up ahead where arms of rising ground embraced the dales, and no pipes or channels, sprayers or sprinklers, watered the parching earth, the green of bracken and the glory of heather had been sucked up by the thirsty sun, turning temperate moor to tropical savannah.

'It was like this fifteen years ago,' said Dalziel, breaking in on his thought as though he had spoken it aloud.

'You're thinking heat could be a trigger?' said Pascoe sceptically. 'We've had some good summers since. In fact, if you listen to Derek Purlingstone, the Sahara's had more rain than Mid-Yorkshire in the past ten years.'

'Not like this one. Not for so long,' said Dalziel obstinately.

'And just because there's a drought and Danby is the next valley over from Dendale . . .'

'And the place where most of the Dendale folk were resettled,' added Dalziel. 'And there's one thing more. A sign . . .'

'A sign!' mocked Pascoe. 'Let me guess. Hearing the name Wulfstan on the radio? Is that it? My God, sir, you'll be hearing voices in the bells next!'

'Any more of your cheek, I'll thump you so hard you'll be hearing bells in the voices,' said Dalziel grimly. 'When I say a sign, I mean a sign. Several of them. Clark rang me direct. He knew I'd be interested. Hold on now. There's the first on 'em.'

He slammed on the brake with such violence Pascoe would have been into the windscreen if it hadn't been for his seat belt.

'Jesus,' he gasped.

He couldn't see any reason for the sudden stop. The road stretched emptily ahead under a disused railway bridge. He glanced sideways at the Fat Man and saw his gaze was inclined upwards at an angle suggestive of pious thanksgiving. But his expression held little of piety and it wasn't the heavens his eyes were fixed on but the parapet of the bridge.

Along it someone had sprayed in bright red paint the words BENNY'S BACK!

'Clark says it must have been done last night before the kiddie went missing,' said Dalziel. 'There's a couple more in the town. Coincidence? Sick joke? Mebbe. But folk round here, especially them who came from Dendale, seeing that and hearing about Lorraine, especially folk with young kiddies of their own . . .'

He didn't complete the sentence. He didn't need to. He thinks he's failed once and he's not going to fail again, thought Pascoe.

They drove on in silence.

Pascoe thought of little children. Of daughters. Of his own daughter, Rosie, safe at the seaside.

He found himself thanking God, whom he didn't believe in, for her presumed safety.

And Lorraine Dacre . . . he thought of her waking up on a day like this . . . How could a day like this hold anything but play and pleasure beyond computation for a child?

He prayed that the God he didn't believe in would reproach his disbelief by having the answer waiting in Danby, little Lorraine Dacre safely back home, bewildered by all the trouble she'd caused.

At Pascoe's side, the God he did believe in, Andy Dalziel, was thinking too of answers that awaited them in Danby, and of the little girl waking up perhaps for the last time on a day like this . . .

FOUR

Little Lorraine wakes early, but the sun has woken earlier still.

These are the long summer days which stretch end-lessly through all happy childhoods, when you wake into golden air and fall asleep a thousand adventures later, caressed by a light which even the tightest drawn of curtains can only turn into a gentle dusk.

There is no sound of life in the cottage. This is Sunday, the one day of the week when Mam and Dad allow themselves the luxury of a lie-in.

She gets out of bed, dresses quickly and quietly, then descends to the kitchen where Tig yaps an excited welcome. She hushes him imperiously and he falls silent. He's very well trained; Dad insisted on that. 'Only one thing worse than a disobedient dog, and that's a disobedient daughter,' he said. And Mam, who knows that Lorraine can twist him round her little finger, smiled her secret smile.

A quick breakfast, then up on a stool to withdraw the top bolt of the kitchen door and out into the yard with Tig eager on her heels. No need for the lead. The yard opens right on to the edge of Ligg Common. Well-trodden paths wind through furze and briar till she arrives on the bank of Ligg Beck whose once boisterous waters have been tamed by this parching weather into a barely dimpling trickle.

Never mind. The dried-up beck broadens the path running alongside, slowly climbing high up the dale where there are rabbits for Tig to chase, and butterflies to leap at, and tiny orchids for her to seek, while all around skylarks rocket from their heathy nests to sing their certainty that the sun will always shine and skies be blue forever.

Tony Dacre wakes an hour later. The sun fills the room with its light and warmth. He sits up, recalls it is Sunday, and smiles. His movement has half woken Elsie, his wife, who rolls on her back and opens her eyes a fraction. They sleep naked in this weather. She is slim almost to skinniness and the outline of her light body under the single sheet sets his pulse racing. He bends his lips to hers, but she shakes her head and mouths, 'Tea.' He swings his legs out of bed, stands up and pulls his underpants on. He is no prude, but doesn't think that parents should parade naked in front of their children.

When he reaches the kitchen, a badly hacked loaf, an open jar of raspberry jam, a glass of milk half-finished, and a trail of crumbs to the back door, tell him his precautions were unnecessary. He looks out into the yard. No sign of Lorraine. He shakes his head and smiles. Then he makes some tea and takes two cupfuls upstairs.

Elsie sits up in bed to drink it. From time to time he glances sideways, taking in her small dark-nippled breasts, checking the level of her tea. Finally it is finished.

She leans across him to put the cup on his bedside table. As she straightens up, he catches her in his arms. She smiles up at him. He says, 'All that money I wasted buying you gin when I could have had you for a cup of tea!'

They make love. Afterwards he sings in the bathroom as he shaves. When he comes back into the bedroom she has gone downstairs. He gets dressed and follows.

She frowns and says, 'Lorraine's had her breakfast.'

'Aye, I know.'

43

'I don't like her using that bread knife. It's really sharp. And standing on a stool to unlock the door. We'll have to talk to her, Tony.'

'I will. I will,' he promises.

She shakes her head in exasperation and says, 'No, I'll do it.'

They have breakfast. It's still only half-past nine. The Sunday papers arrive. He sits in the living room, reading the sports page. Outside in the street he can hear the sound of girls' voices. After a while he stands up and goes to the front door.

The girls are playing a skipping game. Two of them are swinging a long rope. The others come running in at one end, skip their way to the other, then duck out making violent falling gestures.

Skippers and swingers alike keep up a constant chant.

> One foot! Two foot! Black foot! White foot!
> Three foot! Four foot! Left foot! Right foot!
> No one runs as fast as Benny Lightfoot!
> OUT GOES SHE!

Tony calls out, 'Sally!'

Sally Breen, a stout little girl who lives two doors up, says, 'Yes, Mr Dacre?'

'You seen our Lorraine?'

'No, Mr Dacre.'

'Anyone seen her?'

The chanting fades away as the girls look at each other. They shake their heads.

Tony goes back into the house. Elsie is upstairs making the beds. He calls up the stairway, 'Just going for a stroll, luv. I want a word with old Joe about the bowling club.'

He goes out of the back door, through the yard, across the common. He's been walking with his daughter often enough to know her favourite route. Soon he is by the dried-up beck and climbing steadily along its bank up the dale.

After a while, when he is sure he is out of earshot of Liggside, he starts calling her name.

'Lorraine! Lorraine!'

For a long time there is nothing. Then he hears a distant bark. Tremulous with relief he presses on, over a fold of land. Ahead he sees Tig, alone, and limping badly, coming towards him.

Oh, now the skylarks like aery spies sing *She's here! she's hurt! she's here! she's hurt!* and the dancing butterflies spell out the message *She's gone forever.*

He stoops by the injured dog and asks, 'Where is she, Tig? SEEK!'

But the animal just cringes away from him as though fearful of a blow.

He rushes on. For half an hour he ranges the fellside, seeking and shouting. Finally, because hope here is dying, he invents hope elsewhere and heads back down the slope. Tig has remained where they met. He picks him up, ignoring the animal's yelp of pain.

'She'll be back home by now, just you wait and see, boy,' he says. 'Just you wait and see.'

But he knows in his heart that Lorraine would never have left Tig alone and injured up the dale.

Back home, Elsie, already growing concerned, without yet acknowledging the nature of her concern, goes through the motions of preparing Sunday lunch as though, by refusing to vary her routine, she can force events back into their usual course.

When the door bursts open and Tony appears, the dog in his arms, demanding, 'Is she back?' she turns pale as the flour on her hands.

All the windows of the house are open to move the heavy air. Out in the road the girls are still at their game.

And as husband and wife lock gazes across the kitchen table, each willing the other to smile and say that everything's right, the words of the skipping chant come drifting between them.

> One foot! Two foot! Black foot! White foot!
> Three foot! Four foot! Left foot! Right foot!
> No one runs as fast as Benny Lightfoot!
> OUT GOES SHE!

FIVE

Danby, according to a recent *Evening Post* feature, was that rarest of things, a rural success story.

Bucking the usual trend to depopulation and decline, new development, led by the establishment of a Science and Business Park on its southern edge, had swollen the place from large village to small town.

It ain't pretty but it works, thought Pascoe as they drove past the entrance to the Park on one side of the road and the entrance to a large supermarket backed by a new housing estate on the other.

It takes more than the march of modernity to modify the English provincial sabbath, however, and the town's old centre was as quiet as a *pueblo* during siesta. Even the folk sitting outside the three pubs they passed with no more than a faint longing sigh from Dalziel looked like figures engraved on an urn.

The main sign of activity they saw was a man scrubbing furiously at a shop window on which, despite his efforts, the words BENNY'S BACK! remained stubbornly visible, and another man obliterating the same words with black paint on a gable end.

Neither of the detectives said anything till open countryside – moorland now, not pastoral – began to open up ahead once more.

'This Liggside's right on the edge, is it?' asked Pascoe.

'Aye. Next to Ligg Common. Ligg Beck runs right down the valley. Yon's the Neb.'

The sun laid it all out before them like a holiday slide.

Danbydale rose ahead, due north to start with, then curving north-east. The Neb rose steeply to the west. The road they were on continued up the lower eastern arm of the dale, its white curves clear as bones on a beach.

'Next left, if I recall right,' said Dalziel.

He did, of course. Lost in a Mid-Yorkshire mist with an Ordnance Survey cartographer, a champion orienteer, and Andy Dalziel, Pascoe knew which one he'd follow.

Liggside was a small terrace of grey cottages fronting the pavement. No problem spotting number 7. There was a police car parked outside and a uniformed constable at the door, with two small groups of onlookers standing a decent distance (about ten feet in Mid-Yorkshire) on either side.

The constable moved forward as Dalziel double-parked, probably to remonstrate, but happily for his health, recognition dawned in time and he opened the car door for them with a commissionaire's flourish.

Pascoe got out, stretched, and took in the scene. The cottages were small and unprepossessing, but solid, not mean, and the builder had been proud enough of them to mark the completion by carving the date in the central lintel: 1860. The year Mahler was born. Dalziel's unexpected recognition of the *Kindertotenlied* brought the name to his mind. He doubted if the event had made much of a stir in Danby. What great event did occupy the minds of the first inhabitants of Liggside? American Civil War . . . no, that was 1861. How about Garibaldi's Redshirts taking Sicily? Probably the Italian's name never meant much more to most native Danbians than a jacket or a biscuit. Or was he being patronizingly elitist? Who should know better than he that there was no way of knowing what your ancestors knew?

What he did know was that his mental ramblings were an attempt to distance himself from the depth of pain and fear he knew awaited them beyond the matt-brown door with its bright brass letter box and its rudded step. Where a lost child was concerned, not even rage was strong enough to block that out.

The constable opened the house door and spoke softly. A moment later a uniformed sergeant Pascoe recognized as Clark, i/c Danby sub-station, appeared. He didn't speak but just shook his head to confirm that nothing had changed. Dalziel pushed past him and Pascoe followed.

The small living room was crowded with people, all female, but there was no problem spotting the pale face of the missing child's mother. She was sitting curled up almost foetally at the end of a white vinyl sofa. She seemed to be leaning away from, rather than into, the attempted embrace of a large blonde woman whose torso looked better suited to the lifting of weights than the offering of comfort.

Dalziel's entrance drew all eyes. They looked for hope and, getting none, acknowledged its absence by dropping their focus from his face to his shirt.

'Who the hell's this clown?' demanded the blonde in a smoke-roughened voice.

Clark said, 'Detective Superintendent Dalziel, Head of CID.'

'Is that right? And he comes out here at a time like this dressed like a frigging fairground tent?'

It was an image that made up in comprehensiveness what it lacked in detail.

Dalziel ignored her, and crouched with surprising suppleness before the pale-faced woman.

'Mrs Dacre, Elsie,' he said. 'I came soon as I got word. I didn't waste time changing.'

The eyes, mere glints in dark holes, rose to look at him.

'Who gives a toss what you're wearing. Can you find her?'

What do you say now, old miracle worker? wondered Pascoe.

'I'll do everything in my power,' said Dalziel.

'And what's that then?' demanded the blonde. 'Just what are you doing, eh?'

Dalziel rose and said, 'Sergeant Clark, let's have a bit of space here. Everyone out please. Let's have some air.'

The blonde's body language said quite clearly that she wasn't about to move, but Dalziel took the wind out of her sails by saying, 'Not you, Mrs Coe. You hold still, if Elsie wants you.'

'How the hell do you know my name?' she demanded.

It was indeed a puzzling question, but not beyond all conjecture. Coe was Elsie Dacre's maiden name, and an older woman who had assumed the office of chief comforter without either a family resemblance or the look of a bosom friend was likely to be an in-law.

Dalziel just looked at her blankly, not about to spoil that impression of omniscience which made people tell him the truth, or at least feel so nervous, it showed when they tried to hide it.

'Right Sergeant,' he said, as Clark closed the door after the last of the departing women. 'So what's going off?'

'I've got my lads up the dale . . .'

'Three. That's how many he's got,' interposed Mrs Coe scornfully.

'Tony – that's Mr Dacre – naturally wanted to get back up there looking and a bunch of locals were keen to help, so I thought it best to make sure they had some supervision,' Clark went on.

Dalziel nodded approvingly. The more disorganized and amateur an early search was, the harder it made any later fine-tooth combing whose object was to find clues to an abduction, or murder.

'Quite right,' he said. 'Little lass could easily have

turned her ankle and be sitting up the dale waiting for someone to fetch her.'

Such breezy optimism clearly got up Mrs Coe's nose, but she kept her mouth shut. It was Elsie Dacre who responded violently, though so quietly to start with that at first the violence almost went unnoticed.

'No need for all this soft soap, Mr Dalziel,' she said. 'We all know what this is about, don't we? We all know.'

'Sorry, luv, I'm just trying to . . .'

'I know what you're trying to do, and I know what you'll be doing next. But it didn't do any good last time, did it? So what's changed, mister? You tell me that. What's bloody changed!'

Now the woman's voice was at full throttle, her eyes blazing, her face contorted with anger and fear.

'Nay, lass, listen,' said Dalziel intensely. 'It's early doors, too early to be talking of last time. God knows, I understand how that'll be in your mind, it's in mine too, but I'll keep it at the back of my mind long as I can. I won't rush to meet summat like that, and you shouldn't either.'

'You remember me then?' said Mrs Dacre, peering at Dalziel closely as if there was comfort to be fixed in the Fat Man's memory.

'Aye, do I. When I heard your maiden name I thought, that could be one of the Coes from over in Dendale. You were the youngest, weren't you?'

'I were eleven when it started. I remember those days, hot days like now, and all us kids going round in fear of our lives. I thought I'd never forget. But you do forget, don't you. Or at least, like you say, you put it so far at the back of your mind it's like forgetting . . . and you grow up and start feeling safe, and you have a kiddie of your own, and you never let yourself think . . . but that's where you're wrong, mister! If I hadn't kept it in the back

of my mind, if I'd kept it at the front where it belongs
. . . something like that's too important . . . too bloody
terrible . . . to keep at the back of . . .'

She broke down in a flood of tears and her sister-in-law
embraced her irresistibly. Then the door opened and an
older woman came in. This time the family resemblance
was unmistakable. She said, 'Elsie, I was down at Sandra's
. . . I've just heard . . .'

'Oh, Mam,' cried Elsie Dacre.

Her sister-in-law was thrust aside and she embraced
her mother as though she could crush hope and comfort
out of her.

Dalziel said, 'Mrs Coe, why don't you make us all a
cup of tea?'

The three policemen and the blonde woman went
into the kitchen. It was just as well. It was full of steam
from a kettle hissing explosively on a high gas ring. Mrs
Coe grabbed a tea towel, used it as a mitt to remove the
kettle.

'Should make a grand cuppa,' said Dalziel. 'Needs to be
really hot. Mrs Coe, what do you reckon to Tony Dacre?'

'What kind of question's that?' demanded the woman.

'Simple one. How do you feel about your brother-
in-law?'

'Why're you asking, is what I want to know.'

'Don't act stupid. You know why I'm asking. If I can
eliminate him from my enquiries, then I won't have to
take this house to pieces.'

Honesty is not only the best policy, it's also sometimes
the best form of police brutality, thought Pascoe, watching
as shock slackened the woman's solid features.

Dalziel went on, 'Afore you start yelling at me, think
on, missus. You want me to have to start asking that poor
woman if her man works on a short fuse or has got any
special interest in his own daughter? You're not daft, you

know these things happen. So just tell me, is there owt I ought to know about Tony Dacre?'

The woman found her voice.

'No, there bloody isn't. I don't like him all that much, but that's personal. As for Lorraine, he worships that little lass, I mean like a father should. In fact, if you ask me, he spoils her rotten, and if she set fire to the house he'd not lose his temper with her. Jesus, I'd not have your job for a thousand pounds. Aren't things bad enough here without you looking for something even filthier in it?'

Her tone was vehement, but she managed to control the sound level to keep it in the kitchen.

'Grand,' said Dalziel with a friendly smile. 'Bring the tea through when it's mashed, eh?'

He went out, pulling the door shut behind him. Behind it, Pascoe noticed for the first time, was a dog basket. Lying in it was a small mongrel dog, somewhere between a spaniel and a terrier. Its eyes were open but it didn't move. Pascoe stooped over it and now its ears went back and it growled deep in its throat. Pascoe responded with soothing noises and though its eyes remained wary, it accepted a scratch between the ears. But when his hand strayed down to its shoulder, it snarled threateningly and he straightened up quickly.

'Anyone sent for the vet?' he enquired.

Mrs Coe said, 'For crying out loud, my niece is missing out there and all you're worried about is the sodding dog!'

The sergeant replied, 'Not that I know of. I mean, with everything else . . .'

'Do it now, will you? I don't like to see an animal in pain, but just as important, I want to know how it got its injuries.'

'Oh aye. I didn't think, sir,' said Clark guiltily. 'I'll get on to it right away.'

The woman, who'd busied herself mashing the tea,

pushed past them angrily. Clark, following her, paused at the door and said, 'Owt else I should have thought of, sir?'

'Unless Lorraine turns up OK in the next half hour or so, this thing's going to explode into a major enquiry. We'll need an incident room. Somewhere with plenty of space and not too far away. Any ideas?'

The sergeant's broad features contorted with thought, then he said, 'There's St Michael's Hall. It's shared between the church and the primary school and it's just a step away . . .'

'Sounds fine. Now get that vet. Good job you thought of it before the super, eh?'

He smiled as he spoke and after a moment Clark smiled back, then left.

One thing about Dalziel, thought Pascoe. He provides solid ground to build a good working relationship with the troops.

He opened the back door of the kitchen which led into a small, tidily kept yard with a patch of lawn and a wooden shed. He stepped out into the balmy air and opened the shed door. Some gardening tools, an old pushchair, and a child's bike.

Carefully controlling his thoughts, he next went to the yard door and unlatched it. He found himself looking across an area of worn and parched grassland scattered with clumps of furze whose bright yellow flowers threw back defiance at the blazing sun. This had to be Ligg Common with beyond it the long sweep of Danbydale rising northwards to Highcross Moor.

Sunlight eats up distance and the head of the valley looked barely a half-hour's stroll away, while the long ridge of the Neb stood within range of an outfielder with a good arm. He let his gaze cross to the valley's opposite lower arm and here caught the glint of the sun on the glass of a descending car, and suddenly its tininess gave a proper perspective to the view.

There was a huge acreage of countryside out there, more than a few dozen men could search properly in a long day. And when you added to the outdoors all the buildings and barns and byres from the outskirts of the town to the farmed limits of the fell, then what lay in prospect was a massive operation.

He stood and felt the sun probe beneath his mop of light brown hair and beneath the surface of his fair skin. A few more minutes of this and he'd turn pink and peel like a new potato, while another hour or so would beat his brain into that state of sun-drunk insensibility he usually experienced on Mediterranean beach holidays while Ellie by his side only grew browner and browner and fitter and fitter.

Sometimes insensibility was the more desirable fate.

'You taken root or wha'?'

He turned and saw Dalziel in the yard doorway.

'Just thinking, sir. Anything happened?'

'No. She's quieter now. Much better with her mam than yon sister-in-law. Where's Clark? I want to ask him about Dennis Coe, the brother.'

'Mrs Coe's husband?'

'We'll make a detective of you yet. Six or seven years older than Elsie, if I recall. We'll need to take a close look at him.'

'Why? Was he in the frame fifteen years back?' asked Pascoe, thinking that Dalziel's coup with Mrs Coe's name was looking a pretty simple conjuring trick now.

'Missing kids, every sod old enough to have a stiff cock ends up in the frame. He'd be eighteen or thereabout. Bad age. And all the kids who went missing were blonde and he wed himself a blonde . . .'

'Come on!' said Pascoe. 'You reach any further and

you'll be in the X-files. In any case, I'd say Mrs Coe's colour comes straight out of a bottle.'

'So he married dark but let her know he preferred blondes. OK, stop flaring your nostrils else you'll get house martins building. One thing you can't argue with, he's Lorraine's uncle, and uncles rate high in the statistics for this kind of thing.'

Pascoe shook his head and said dully, 'Mrs Coe said she'd not have our job for a thousand pounds. She's way out. Sometimes a million's not enough for the way we have to look at things.'

'Talking of looking, what's yon?'

The Fat Man was staring north. Over the distant horizon the heat haze had coalesced into something thicker.

'Never a cloud, is it?' said Dalziel.

'Not of rain,' said Pascoe. 'I'd say smoke. Slightest spark starts a grass fire this weather.'

'Best make sure some other bugger's noticed,' said Dalziel.

He pulled out his mobile, dialled, spoke and listened.

'Aye,' he said, switching off. 'They know. It's a big one. And not the only one either. Brigade's on full alert and they're using our uniformed too, which isn't good news for us if we have to hit the red button.'

'When?' said Pascoe. 'You don't think that there's . . .'

He was interrupted by Sergeant Clark from the doorway.

'Excuse me, sir, but Mr Douglas the vet's here. We got him on his mobile coming back from a farm call.'

'Vet?' said Dalziel to Pascoe. 'What's up? Feeling badly?'

In the kitchen they found a broad-built grey-bearded man kneeling down by the dog basket. His examination of the mongrel produced the odd rumbling growl but nothing as menacing as the snarl provoked by Pascoe's inexpert probe.

Finally he stood up and turned his attention to the humans.

'Peter Pascoe, DCI,' said Pascoe, offering his hand. 'And this is Superintendent Dalziel.'

'We've met,' said Douglas shortly. His voice had a Scots burr.

'Aye, what fettle, Dixie?' said Dalziel. 'So, what's the damage?'

'Shoulder and ribcage badly bruised. I don't think there's a fracture, but he needs an X-ray to be sure. Possibility of internal injury. I think it's best in all the circumstances if I take him back to the surgery with me. Any news of the wee lassie?'

'Not yet,' said Pascoe. 'These injuries, what do you think caused them?'

'No accident, that's for sure,' said the vet flatly. 'If I had to guess, I'd say someone had given the poor beast a good kicking. Good day to you.'

Gently he lifted the dog from the basket and went out of the kitchen.

'Good man, that,' said Sergeant Clark approvingly. 'Really worries about sick animals.'

'Aye, well, he supports Raith Rovers,' said Dalziel. 'So someone gave the dog a kicking. That's enough to get the show on the road. Good thinking to have the beast checked out.'

Pascoe said, 'Yes. Well done, Sergeant Clark. So what do you want me to do, sir? Call in the troops and set up an incident room?'

'Aye, best go by the book,' said Dalziel without enthusiasm. 'Any suggestions, Sergeant? As far as I recall, your Section Office isn't big enough to swing a punch in.'

'St Michael's Hall, sir,' said Clark with brisk efficiency.

'Doubles as assembly hall and gym for the primary school and as a community centre. I've spoken on the phone with Mrs Shimmings the school head. You'll likely remember her, sir. She were in Dendale, like me. Miss Lavery, she was then. She's really upset. Says she'll go to the school now to be on hand in case we need her help, talking about the little girl and such.'

Dalziel looked at him reflectively and said, 'Well done, Sergeant. You're thinking so far ahead, you'll end up telling fortunes. OK, Peter, off you go. Tell 'em I want someone from uniformed who knows left from right to head up the search team. Maggie Burroughs'll do nicely. And we'll need a canteen van. It'll be thirsty work tramping round them fells. And an information caravan for the Common. I'll be here to see they get themselves sorted. Any questions?'

'No, sir,' said Pascoe. 'Lead on, Sergeant.'

Clark went out. As Pascoe followed, Dalziel's voice brought him to a halt.

'Word of advice, lad,' he said.

'Always welcome,' said Pascoe.

'Glad to hear it. So listen in. You do Nobby Clark a favour, don't let him pay you back in beer. Make sure you work the bugger's arse off. All right?'

Not just a conjuring trick, thought Pascoe. He really does know everything.

'Yes, sir,' he said. 'Right off its haunches.'

SIX

St Michael's Primary, like Danby itself, had grown.

The original stone building, apparently modelled on the old church from which it took its name, had sprouted several unbecoming modern extensions which compensated in airiness for what they lacked in beauty. The Hall, standing between the church and the school, was clearly designed by the same hand and even had a belfry and stained-glass windows through which filtered a dim religious light to illumine a spacious lofty interior with a stage at one end and a small gallery at the other.

Pascoe wrinkled his nose as the musty smell set up resonances both of lessons in the gym and of amateur dramatics in draughty village halls. Not that the entertainments on offer here were totally amateur. Among the notice board's 'Forthcoming Attractions' he saw a poster for the opening concert of the eighteenth Mid-Yorkshire Dales Music Festival due to take place the following Wednesday and consisting of a song recital by Elizabeth Wulfstan, mezzo-soprano, and Arne Krog, baritone.

That name again. He recalled the strong young voice singing mournfully, *And now the sun will rise as bright/As though no horror had touched the night . . .*

The heat wave looked set for many more days, perhaps weeks, but he doubted if there'd be any more bright dawning for the Dacres.

For Christ's sake! he admonished himself. Don't rush to embrace the worst.

'This will do nicely,' he said to Clark, and got on his

mobile. He'd already set the operation in motion back at Liggside and this was merely to confirm the location. ETA of the first reinforcements was given as thirty minutes.

'I'll go and have a word with Mrs Shimmings,' he said. 'You OK, Sergeant?'

The man was pale and drawn, as if he'd been exposed to biting winds on a winter's day.

'Yes, fine. Sorry. It's just being here at the school, the incident room . . . suddenly it's really happening. I think up till now I've been trying to pretend it were different from last time, over in Dendale, I mean. Not that it wasn't the same then to start with, telling ourselves that at worst there'd been an accident and little Jenny Hardcastle 'ud be found or manage to get back herself . . .'

'Then you'll know how these things work,' said Pascoe harshly. 'One thing we'll need to get sorted quickly is this Benny business. Someone's responsible for these graffiti. We need to find out who, then we can start asking why. Any ideas?'

'I'm working on it,' said Clark. 'Has to be a stupid joke and a lousy coincidence, hasn't it, sir? I mean, it were done last night and Lorraine didn't vanish till this morning. And the perp wouldn't do it in advance, would he?'

'Less chance of being caught,' said Pascoe.

'But that 'ud mean the whole thing were planned!'

'And that's worse than impulse? Well, you're right. Worse for us, I mean. Impulse leaves traces, plans cover them up. Either way, we need the spray artist.'

'Yes, sir,' said Clark. 'Sir . . .'

'Yes?' prompted Pascoe.

'Benny. Benny Lightfoot. Anything you know that I don't? I mean, there could be information that reached HQ but you felt best not to pass on down here, for fear of opening old wounds . . .'

'You mean, could Benny *really* be back?' said Pascoe

60

grimly. 'From what I've heard, I doubt it. But the very fact that you can ask shows how important it is to finger this joker's collar. Get to it.'

He walked across the playground to the school. He could see the figure of the head teacher at the window of a classroom he guessed would be Lorraine's. She'd been standing at the main entrance when they arrived, but after a brief exchange, he'd cut the conversation short and headed into the hall.

Now he joined her in the classroom and said, 'Sorry about that, Mrs Shimmings, but I had to get things rolling.'

'That's O K,' she said. 'I know how these things work.'

He recalled then that like Clark, she too had been here before. Looking at her closely, he detected the same symptoms of re-entry to a nightmare she thought she'd left behind.

She was a slimly built woman with greying chestnut hair and candid brown eyes. Late forties. Thirty-plus when Dendale died.

She said, 'So you think the worst?'

'We *prepare* for the worst,' said Pascoe gently. 'Tell me about Lorraine.'

'She was . . . *is* a bright, intelligent child, a little what they used to call old-fashioned in some ways. It doesn't surprise me to hear that she got up early and decided to take her dog for a walk all by herself. It's not that she's a solitary child. On the contrary, she's extremely sociable and has many friends. But she never has any difficulty performing tasks by herself and on occasion, if given a choice, she will opt for the solitary rather than the communal activity.'

After the initial slip, she had kept determinedly, almost pedantically to the present tense. As she talked, Pascoe let his gaze wander round the classroom. Bringing up

61

Rosie had honed his professional eye to the school environment. Now he found himself assessing the quality of wall displays, the evidence of thought and order, the use of material that was stimulating aesthetically, intellectually, mathematically. In this classroom everything looked good. This teacher hadn't shot away on Friday afternoon but had stayed behind after the children had gone, to refine their efforts at tidying up and make sure the room was perfectly prepared for Monday morning. This teacher, he guessed, was going to be devastated when she discovered what had happened to one of her pupils.

He said, 'Would she go off with a stranger?'

'Someone offering her sweets in the street, asking her to get into a car, no way,' said Mrs Shimmings. 'But you say she'd gone up the dale for a walk? Things are different up there, Mr Pascoe. Do you do any walking yourself?'

'A little,' said Pascoe, thinking of Ellie cajoling her rebellious husband and daughter into completing the Three Peaks Walk last spring.

'Then you'll know that, in the street if a complete stranger says "Hello" to you, you think there's something wrong with him, but up there on the hills if you meet anyone, you automatically exchange greetings, sometimes even stop and have a chat. *Not* to say something would be the odd thing. Yes, I think that nowadays we've all got our children trained to regard strangers with the utmost suspicion, but they learn by example more than precept, and out in the country the example they get is of strangers being greeted almost like old acquaintance.'

'So she might stop and talk.'

'She wouldn't be surprised if someone spoke to her and she wouldn't run. Indeed, up there, what would be the point? Didn't she have her dog with her, though?'

'Dogs are an over-rated form of protection,' said Pascoe. 'Unless they're so big and fierce, you wouldn't let a little girl take it out alone anyway. This one may have tried. It got badly kicked about for its pains. Any of these Lorraine's?'

He was looking at a display of paintings with the general heading 'My Family'.

Even as he asked, he saw the neatly printed label LOR-RAINE'S FAMILY under a picture of a man and a woman and a dog. The human figures were of roughly equal size, both with broad slice-of-melon smiles. The dog was, relatively, the size of a Shetland pony. Psychologists would probably say this meant she had no hang-ups with either parent, but was really crazy about Tig. Just what you'd hope to find in a seven-year-old girl. He recalled his own sinking feeling a little while back when, without comment, Ellie had shown him a painting of Rosie's which had her standing there like the fifty-foot woman and himself a mere black blob in a car moving away fast.

'Happy family?' he said.

'Very happy. I've known the mother since she was a girl.'

'Of course. You used to teach in Dendale back before they built the reservoir, I gather.'

'That's right. Like everyone else, I had to move out. Part of the price of progress.'

'But in the end, some people were probably glad to go, even to see the valley under water?' he probed.

'You think Lorraine's disappearance may have something to do with what happened back then?'

'You tell me, Mrs Shimmings,' said Pascoe. 'I wasn't around then. You've heard about these painted signs? "Benny's Back"?'

She nodded.

'So, could he be back? And if so, where's he been? I heard he was a bit simple.'

'He could have been living with people who don't ask

questions or make judgements,' she offered. 'Like these New Age travellers. Anyway, Benny wasn't simple. In fact, he was very bright.'

'I'm sorry. I was told he'd had an accident . . . something about a plate in his head . . .'

'Oh, that,' she said dismissively. 'I taught Benny both before and after that accident, Mr Pascoe. And he was just as sharp after it as before. But he was always different, and folk in Yorkshire confuse *different* with *daft* just as readily as anywhere else. No, he wasn't simple, but he was . . . fey, I think that's the word. I taught him till he was old enough to go to the secondary. That meant taking the bus out of the dale and he wasn't keen. But his father told him to go and do his best, and Benny paid a lot of heed to Saul, his dad. Then, when Benny was twelve, Saul Lightfoot died.'

'How?' asked Pascoe. The policeman's question.

'He drowned. He was a fine athletic man,' said Mrs Shimmings, with what a romantic observer might have called a faraway look in her eyes. 'He used to go swimming in the mere. He was a good strong swimmer, but they think he got tangled up with a submerged tree branch. It devastated poor Benny. The family all lived with old Mrs Lightfoot, Benny's gran, in Neb Cottage. It must have been a tight squeeze, there were three kids: Benny, and his younger brother and sister, Barnabas and Deborah. But it worked all right as long as Saul was around. He was that sort of man. Charismatic, I suppose they'd say nowadays. Or what the young girls would call a hunk.'

Pascoe smiled and glanced surreptitiously at his watch. Local history was fine, but he had responsibilities in the here and now which wouldn't wait.

'I'm sorry, I'm holding you back,' said Mrs Shimmings. He'd forgotten she was a head teacher with an eye long trained for the tell-tale minutiae of behaviour.

'Nothing I can do till my men arrive,' he assured her. 'Please, carry on.'

'Well, Marion, that's Benny's mother, and old Mrs Lightfoot never really got on. She wasn't a country lass, Saul had met her at a dance in town, and now with him gone, there was nothing to keep her in Dendale. It was no surprise when she got a job in town and took the children off. Benny came back from time to time to see his gran. I gathered he wasn't happy. Not that he spoke much to anyone, he was becoming more and more withdrawn. Then it seems his mother met up with a new man. He moved in. I think that ultimately they got married, but only because they'd decided to emigrate – Australia, I think it was – and being married made things easier. Benny didn't want to go. The night before they were due to leave, he took off and came to his gran's. Marion came looking for him. He refused point-blank to go back with her and old Mrs Lightfoot said he could stay with her. So that's what happened. I daresay there were a great number of other things said that shouldn't have been said. Net result was the family left and Benny settled in at Neb Cottage. As far as I can make out, he dropped right out of school. The truancy officer came round several times, and the Social Services, but at the first sight of anyone vaguely official, indeed anyone he didn't recognize, Benny would take off up the Neb, and in the end they more or less gave up, though I'm sure they found some face-saving formula to regularize the situation.'

'How do you regularize truancy?' wondered Pascoe.

'You don't. Time does that,' said Mrs Shimmings. 'I think they must have heaved a mighty sigh of relief in the Education Office when Benny passed his sixteenth birthday. But the psychological damage was done. Benny was wary, elusive, introverted, solitary, devoid of social skills – in other words, in the eyes of most people, plain simple.'

'And could he have been responsible for the disappearances?' he asked.

'Sex is a strong mover in young men,' she said. 'But before the attack on Betsy Allgood, I had serious reservations. After that, however . . .'

She shook her head. 'You were quite right what you said before. In the end, I think a lot of folk were glad to get out of Dendale, glad to see it go under water. The more biblically inclined saw it as a repeat of the Genesis flood, aimed at drowning out wickedness.'

'Nice thought,' said Pascoe. 'But wickedness is a strong swimmer. And how did you feel, Mrs Shimmings?'

It seemed an innocent enough question, but to his distress he saw her eyes fill with tears, even though she turned away quickly to hide them and went to the teacher's desk.

'Funny,' she said. 'While I was waiting for you, I went into our little library and this was the book I picked out.'

She took a book from the desktop and held it up so he could see the title.

It was *The Drowning of Dendale*.

'I know it,' said Pascoe. 'My wife has a copy.'

It was, as he recalled, a coffee-table book, square-shaped and consisting mainly of photos with very little text. It was in two parts, the first entitled 'The Dale', the second 'The Drowning'. The first photograph was a panorama of the whole dale, bathed in evening light. And the epigraph under the subtitle was *A happy rural seat of various view*.

'Paradise Lost,' said Mrs Shimmings. 'That's how I felt, Mr Pascoe. It may have been spoilt, but it was still like leaving Paradise.'

A horn blew outside. Glad of a diversion from this

highly charged and, he hoped, totally irrelevant display of emotion, Pascoe went to the window.

They were arriving, all kinds of vehicles bearing everything necessary for the Centre. Furniture, telephones, radios, computers, catering equipment, and of course personnel. Must be like this in a war, he thought. Before a Big Push. Like Passchendaele. So much hustle and bustle, so many men and machines, failure must have seemed inconceivable. But they had failed, many many thousands of them needlessly killed, one of them his namesake, his great-grandfather, not drowning in mud or shattered by shell-fire, but tied to a post and shot by British bullets . . .

He said, 'We'll talk again later, Mrs Shimmings,' and went out to take control.

SEVEN

'I often think they've only gone out walking,
And soon they'll come homewards all laughing and talking.
The weather's bright! Don't look so pale.
They've only gone for a hike updale.'

'So what's this? Narcissism, or the artist's response to just criticism?'

Elizabeth Wulfstan pressed the pause button on her zapper and turned her head to look at the man who'd just come in.

The years had been good to Arne Krog. Into his forties now, his unlined open face framed in a shock of golden hair and a fringe of matching beard kept him looking more like Hollywood's idea of a sexy young ski-instructor than anyone's idea of a middle-aged baritone. And if, in terms of reputation and reward, the years had not been quite so generous, he made sure it didn't show.

She said, 'Most of what you said was right. Makes you happy, does it?'

She spoke with a strong Yorkshire inflexion which came as a surprise to those who knew her by her singing voice alone.

'It makes me happy that you have seen your error. Never mind. It will be a collector's disc when you are old and famous. Perhaps then, to be contrary, you will make your last recording of songs best suited to a young, fresh voice. But preferably in the language in which they were written.'

'I wanted folk to understand them,' she said.

'Then give them a translation to read, not yourself one to sing. Language is important. I should have thought someone so devoted to her own native woodnotes wild would have understood that.'

'Don't see why I should have to speak like you just to please some posh wankers,' she said.

She smiled briefly as she spoke. Her face with its regular features, dark unblinking eyes, and heavy patina of pale make-up, all framed in shoulder-length ash blonde hair, had a slightly menacing mask-like quality till she smiled, when it lit to a remote beauty, like an Arctic landscape touched by a fitful sun. She was five nine or ten, and looked even taller in the black top and lycra slacks which clung to her slim figure.

Krog's eyes took this in appreciatively, but his mind was still on the music.

'So you will change your programme for the opening concert?' he said. 'Good. Inger will be pleased too. The transcription for piano has never been one she liked.'

'She talks to you, does she?' said Elizabeth. 'That must be nice. But chuffed as I'd be to please our Inger, it's too late to change.'

'Three days,' he said impatiently. 'You have the repertoire and I will help all I can.'

'Thanks,' she said sincerely. 'And I'd really like your help to get them right. But as for changing, I mean it's too late in here.'

She touched her breastbone.

He looked exasperated and said, 'Why are you so obsessed with singing these songs?'

'Why're you so bothered that I'm singing them?'

He said, 'I do not feel that, in the circumstances, they are appropriate.'

'Circumstances?' She looked around in mock bewilderment. They were in the elegant high-ceilinged lounge of the Wulfstans' town house. French windows opened on to a long sunlit garden. Faintly audible were the rumbles of organ music under the soaring line of young voices in choir. If they'd stepped outside they could have seen a very little distance to the east the massive towers of the cathedral whose gargoyled rain-spouts seemed to be growing ever longer tongues in this unending drought.

'Didn't think you got circumstances in places like this,' said Elizabeth.

'You know what I mean. Walter and Chloe . . .'

'If Walter wanted to complain, he's had the chance and he's got the voice,' she interrupted.

'And Chloe?'

'Oh aye. Chloe. You still fucking her?'

For a moment shock time-warped him to his early forties.

'What the hell are you talking about?' he demanded, keeping his voice low.

'Come on, Arne. That's one English word no one needs translating. Been going on a long time, hasn't it? Or should I say, off and on? All that travelling around you do. Must be great comfort to her you don't let yourself get out of practice, but. Like singing. You need to keep at your scales.'

He had recovered now and said with a reasonable effort at lightness, 'You shouldn't believe all the chorus-line gossip you hear, my dear.'

'Chorus line? Oh aye, I could give Chloe enough names to sing the *Messiah*.'

He said softly, 'What's the point of this, Elizabeth? What do you want?'

'Want? Can't think of owt I want. But what I don't want is Walter getting hurt. Or Chloe.'

'That is very . . . filial of you. But you work very hard at that role, don't you? The loving, and beloved, daughter. Though in the end, alas, as with all our roles, the paint and wigs must come off, and we have to face ourselves again.'

He spoke with venom, but she only grinned and said, 'You sound like you got out the wrong side of bed. And you were up bloody early too. Man of your age needs his sleep, Arne.'

'How do you know how early I got up? Am I under twenty-four hour surveillance then?'

'Woke with the light myself, being a country lass,' she said. 'Heard your car.'

'It could have been someone else's.'

'No. You're the only bugger who changes up three times between here and end of the street.'

He shrugged and said, 'I was restless, the light woke me also. I wanted to go for a walk, but not where I'd be surrounded by houses.'

'Oh aye? See anyone you know?'

He fingered the soft hair of his beard into a point beneath the chin and said, 'So early in the day I hardly saw anyone.'

She said, 'Give us a knock next time, mebbe I'll come with you. Listen, now you're here, couple of things in the Mahler you can help me with.'

He shook his head wonderingly and said, 'You are incredible. I tell you, I think you made a mistake to sing these songs on your first recording and that you will be making another to sing them at the concert. You ignore my advice. You make outrageous accusations, and now you want me to help you to do what I do not think you should be doing anyway!'

'This isn't personal, Arne. This is about technique,' she said, sounding puzzled he couldn't make the distinction.

'I might think you're a bit of a prick, but I've always rated you a good tutor. Mebbe that's what you should have gone in for instead of performing. Now listen, I'm a bit worried about my phrasing here.'

She pressed her zapper and the song resumed.

> 'Oh, yes, they've only gone out walking,
> Returning now, all laughing and talking.
> Don't look so pale! The weather's bright.
> They've only gone to climb up Beulah Height.'

'You hear the problem?' she said, pressing pause again.

'Why did you say up Beulah Height?' he demanded. 'That is not a proper translation. The German says *auf jenen Höh'n.*'

'All right, keep your hair on. Let's say *on yonder height*, that keeps the scansion,' she said impatiently. 'Now *listen*, will you?'

She started to play the song again. This time Krog concentrated all his attention on her voice, so much so that he didn't realize the door had opened till Elizabeth said, 'Chloe, what's the matter? What's happened?'

Chloe Wulfstan, heavier now than she'd been fifteen years before, but little changed in feature apart from a not unbecoming pouchiness under the chin, had come into the room and was leaning against the back of a sofa and swaying gently. 'I've been listening to the local news,' she said. 'It's happening again.'

Krog went to her and put his arm round her shoulders. At his touch she let go of the sofa and leaned all her weight into his body so that he had to support her with both arms. His eyes met Elizabeth's neutral gaze and he gave a small shrug as if to say, so what am I supposed to do?

'What's happening again?' asked the younger woman in a flat, calm voice. 'What have you heard?'

'There's a child gone missing,' said Chloe. 'A little girl. Up the dale above Danby.'

Now the man's gaze met Elizabeth's once more. This time it conveyed as little message as hers.

And around them the rich young voice wound its plaintive line;

'Ahead of us they've gone out walking
But shan't be returning all laughing and talking.'

EIGHT

Ellie Pascoe was ready for fame. She had long rehearsed her responses to the media seagulls who come flocking after the trawlers of talent. For the literary journalist doing in-depth articles for the posh papers she had prepared many wise and wonderful observations about life and art and the price of fish and flesh, all couched in periods so elegant, improvement would be impossible and abbreviation a crime.

For the smart-arses of radio and television she had sharpened a quiverful of witty put-downs that would make them sorry they'd ever tried to fuck with Ellie Pascoe!

And for her friends she had woven a robe of ironic modesty which would make them all marvel that someone revealed as so very much *different* could contrive to remain so very much *the same*.

She'd even mapped out a History of Eng. Lit. account of her creative development.

Her first novel, which she steadfastly refused to allow to be published, but whose discovery in her posthumous papers was the literary event of 2040 – no make that 2060 – is the typical autobiographical, egocentric, picaresque work by which genius so often announces its arrival on the world stage. Much of it is ingenuous, even jejune, but already the discerning eye can pick out that insight, observation and eloquence which are the marks of her maturity.

Her second novel, which after much pressure and considerable revision, she allowed to appear at the height of her fame, is the story of a young woman of academic bent who marries a soldier and finds herself trying to survive in a world of action, authority and male attitudes which is completely foreign to her. The autobiographical elements here are much more under control. She has not merely regurgitated her experience, but first digested it then used it to produce a fine piece of . . . art.

(That metaphor needed a bit of work, she told herself, grinning.)

But it is in her third novel, which exploded her name to the top of the best-seller lists, that the voice of the mature artist – assured, amused, amusing, passionate, compassionate, compelling and melismatic – is heard for the first time in all its glory . . .

After Peter had left that Sunday morning, she lay in the sun for a while, playing the fame-game in her mind, but found that it quickly palled. If it ever did happen, she guessed it would be very unlike this. Reviewers, interviewers, and programme makers might be the poor relatives at the great Banquet of Literature, but one tidbit they were always guaranteed was the Last Word.

So finally her thoughts turned to where she had been trying to avoid turning them – to Peter.

She knew – had known for some time – that something was going on inside him that he wasn't talking about. He wasn't a reticent man. They shared most things. She knew all the facts of the case which had thrown up the devastating truth about his family history. They had talked about them at great length, and the talk had lulled her into a belief that the wounds she knew he had suffered would heal, were already healing, and only needed time for the process to complete. She was sure he had thought so too. But he'd been wrong, and for some reason was not yet able to admit to her the nature of his wrongness.

So far she hadn't pressed. But she would. As wife, as

lover, as friend, she was entitled to know. Or, failing those, she could always claim the inalienable right of the Great Novelist to stick her nose into other people's minds.

The thought made her pick up her notebook and pen and start considering the jottings she'd made for her next opus. But looked at with these personal concerns running around inside her head, and this sun beating down on its outside, the jottings seemed a load of crap.

Dissatisfied, she got up and went into the house in search of something that would really stretch her mind. All that she could come up with was a pile of long neglected ironing. She switched the radio on and set to work.

It was, she discovered (though she would not have dreamt of admitting it outside the cool depths of the confessional which, as a devout atheist, she was unlikely ever to plumb anyway), a not unpleasant way of passing a mindless hour or so. From time to time she went outside again to give herself another shot of ultraviolet, followed by another slurp of iced apple juice, while the local radio station burbled amiably and aimlessly on. She even ironed some bed sheets with great care. Normally her attitude to sheets was that, as one night's use creased them like W. H. Auden's face, what was the point in doing much more than show them a hot iron threateningly? But Rosie, she guessed, would have been sleeping on Jill Purlingstone's smooth and crisp sheets last night, and while the Pascoe house might not be able to compete by way of swimming pools and ponies, in this one respect, on this one occasion, her daughter would not feel deprived.

The radio kept her up to date with reports of the marvellous weather and how the incredible British public were finding intelligent ways of enjoying it. Like starting fires on the moors or sitting in crawling traffic queues on the roads to and from the coast.

Finally, with the ironing finished and the apple juice

replaced by a long gin and tonic, she sat down calm of mind, all passion spent, at about six o'clock, just in time to hear a report of a major traffic accident on the main coast road.

There was an information number for anxious listeners. She tried it, found it engaged, tried the Purlingstones' number, got an answering machine, tried the emergency number again, still engaged, slammed down the phone in irritation and as if in reaction it snarled back at her.

She snatched it up and snapped, 'Yes?'

'Hi. It's me,' said Pascoe. 'You heard about the accident?'

'Yes. Oh God, what's happened? Is it serious? Where . . .'

'Hold it!' said Pascoe. 'It's OK. I'm just ringing to say I got on to the co-ordinator soon as I heard the news. No Purlingstones involved, no kids of Rosie's age. So no need to worry.'

'Thank God,' said Ellie. 'Thank God. But there were people hurt . . .'

'Four fatalities, several serious injuries. But don't start feeling guilty about feeling relieved. Keeping things simple is the one way to survive.'

'That what you're doing, love?' she asked. 'How's it going? No mention of developments on the news.'

'That's because there are none. We've got a couple of dog teams out on the fell now and as many men as we've been able to drum up with all this other stuff. You've heard about the fires? God, *people*. I'm going to join the Lord's Day Observance Society and vote for making it an offence to travel further than half a mile from home on a Sunday.'

Beneath his jocularity she easily detected the depression.

She said, 'Those poor people. How're they taking it?'

His memory played a picture of Elsie Dacre's wafery face, of Tony Dacre who'd finally come down off the hillside, his legs rubbery with grief and hunger and fatigue. He said, 'Like something's been switched off. Like the air they breathe is tinged with chlorine. Like they're dead and are just looking for a spot to drop in.'

'So what happens now?'

'Keep looking till dark. Start again in the morning. A few other things ongoing.'

Nothing he had much hope in or wanted to talk about. She tried to think of something comforting to say and was admitting failure when the doorbell rang and she heard the letter box rattle and Rosie's voice crying impatiently, 'Mummy! Mummy! It's me. We're home again. Mummy!'

'Peter, Rosie's back,' she said.

'Thought I could hear those dulcet tones,' he said.

'I'd better go before she breaks the door down.'

'Give her my love. Take me when you see me.'

When she opened the door, Rosie burst in crying, 'Mummy, look at me, I'm going to be brown as you. We had five ice creams and three picnics and Uncle Derek's car blows really cold air and I can beat Zandra at back-stroke.'

Ellie caught her, hugged her and swung her high. I remember when I was like that, she thought. So much to tell, that vocal cords seemed inadequate and what you really need is some form of optical-fibre communication able to carry thousands of messages at once.

Derek Purlingstone was smiling at her on the doorstep. He was a tall Italianately handsome man in his mid-thirties but looking six or seven years younger. His origins were humble – his father had been a Yorkshire coal miner – but he wore the badges of wealth – the Armani shirt, the Gucci watch – as if they'd been tossed into his cradle.

She smiled back and said, '*Three* picnics. That sounds a bit excessive.'

'No, we had a breakfast picnic and a lunch picnic and a tea picnic and we drove through a fire . . .'

'A fire? You were near the accident?' she said to Purlingstone, alarmed.

He said, 'You mean the pile-up on the main road? I heard it on the news. No, we used the back road, bit longer, damn sight quicker. The fire was up on Highcross Moor as we came back. Lot of smoke, no danger, though there seemed to be a lot of police activity round Danby.'

'Yes. Peter's there. There's a child gone missing, a little girl.'

He made a concerned face, then smiled again.

'Well, lovely to see you, Ellie, especially so much of you.'

His tone was theatrically lecherous and his gaze ran over her bikini'd body in a parody of bold lust. Ellie recalled a sentence from some psycho-pop book she'd read recently: *To conceal the unconcealable, we pretend that we're pretending it.* Purlingstone was what her mother would have called 'a terrible flirt'. Ellie had no problem dealing with it, but sometimes wondered how close it came to sexual harassment when aimed at younger women in subordinate positions at his office.

Despite this, and despite his fat-cat job in a privatized industry, she quite liked the guy and was very fond of his wife, Jill, who dressed at Marks and Sparks and had insisted that little Zandra went to Edengrove Junior rather than, as she put it, 'some Dothegirls Hall where you pay through the nose for monogrammed knickers.'

'No time for a drink?' she said.

'Sorry, but better get back. Zandra's feeling a bit under par. Too much sun, I expect. She's got her mum's fair skin, not like us Latin types who can pour on the olive oil and let it sizzle, eh?'

The hot gaze again, then his hand snaked out and for a second she thought he was reaching for her breast, but all he did was ruffle Rosie's short black hair before moving off to the Mercedes estate whose colour coincidentally matched the shade of his jeans. Coincidentally? thought Ellie. Bastard's probably got a colour co-ordinated car for all his fancy outfits. Miaou. Envy wasn't her usual bag, and really she was quite fond of Derek. It was just that in this weather it would be rather nice to have some form of in-car air-conditioning a touch more sophisticated than the draught through the rust holes in her own mobile oven.

Rosie's voice broke through her thoughts, crying, 'Mummy, you're not listening!'

'Yes, I am, dear. Well, I am now. Come and sit down and tell me all about it. I'm sorry Zandra's not well.'

'Oh, she'll be all right,' said the girl dismissively. 'I want to tell Daddy all about it too.'

'And he'll want to hear,' said Ellie. 'So I'm afraid you'll have to tell it all again when he comes home.'

The prospect of having a second captive audience was clearly not displeasing. Rosie's day now spilled out in a stream-of-consciousness spate in which sensations and emotions drowned out details of time and place. The only downbeats were that Zandra had started feeling poorly on the way home and that Rosie had lost her cross. The Purlingstones were Catholic and Zandra wore a tiny crucifix round her neck on a fine silver chain. Rosie had indicated that her life would not be complete without one. Ellie, on more grounds than she cared to enumerate, had told her, no way! But when her daughter with considerable ingenuity had 'borrowed' a dagger-shaped earring from Ellie's jewel box, threaded a piece of blue ribbon through it and hung it round her neck as a cross, neither of her parents had felt able to take it away.

Ellie made a note to hide the other one of the pair, then felt guilty. Was she thinking like this because of her genuine opposition to all forms of revealed religion? Or did it have anything to do with her mixed feelings of great delight that her daughter had apparently had the best time of her life, and small resentment that she could have had it despite her own absence?

Someone else was absent too, she noted. It had been interesting to observe over the past couple of weeks how reality in the shape of Zandra had edged out fiction in the form of Nina.

She said casually, 'Nina wasn't there then?'

'No,' said Rosie dismissively. 'The nix got her again. Can I have a cold drink? I'm a bit hot.'

So much for imaginary friendship, thought Ellie. Now you're here, now you're back in the story book!

She said, 'No wonder you're hot after a day like that. Let's see what we've got in the fridge, then I'll rub some of my after-sun lotion on just to make sure you don't start peeling like an old onion. OK?'

'OK. Will Daddy be home before I go to sleep?'

She yawned as she spoke. The effort of telling her tale seemed to have drained all the energy from her.

'I doubt it,' said Ellie. 'From the look of you, I think we'll be lucky to get you into bed before you go to sleep.'

'But he will be coming home soon as he finds the little girl?'

Oh, shit. Something else to remember from her own childhood, how sharp her ears had been to pick up and note down scraps of adult conversation.

She recalled Peter's description of the missing child's parents – *like something's been switched off* – and another line came into her mind: *so deep in my heart a small flame died*.

She put her arms round Rosie and hugged her so hard the child gasped.

'Sorry,' said Ellie. 'Let's go find that cold drink.'

NINE

They are long, the days of midsummer, and usually their beauty lies in their length, with sunlight and warmth apparently unending and giving those able to relax a taste of that eternal bliss which was ours before the Great Banker in the Sky repossessed our first home and garden.

It was not so for the police working in Danby. There was not even that sense of growing urgency which the approach of night usually brings to a search team, that resentment at having the operation interrupted by several hours of darkness. From somewhere a dullness had stolen upon them, a feeling of futility. It sprang, Pascoe guessed, from the community's close links with Dendale, from a common memory of what had happened there fifteen years ago, and from the link made in so many minds between the three Dendale children who had vanished without trace and Lorraine Dacre.

On the surface, Andy Dalziel fought against it, but in some ways it seemed to Pascoe he was a major contributor to it. It wasn't that he gave the impression of a lack of urgency and involvement. On the contrary, he seemed to be more personally involved in this case than in any other Pascoe could recall. It was just that somehow he seemed to feel the whole physical and bureaucratic structure of the investigation – the search parties, the incident room, the house-to-house – was some kind of going-through-the-motions gesture, serving only as a sop to public morale.

For Pascoe, the machine was a comfort. It collected scraps of information, some negative, such as, this patch of ground or that outhouse had been searched and nothing had been found; some positive. You put these scraps in place, and joined them together carefully like the numbered dots in a child's drawing book, and eventually with luck a recognizable shape emerged.

He wished Wieldy was here. When it came to making sense out of joined-up dots, no one came close to Sergeant Wield. But he and his partner were away for the weekend on a book-buying expedition in the Borders. At least that was what the partner, Edwin Digweed, antiquarian bookseller, was doing. Wield's interest in books began and stopped with the works of H. Rider Haggard. He, as Andy Dalziel with instinctive salaciousness had put it when told of the sergeant's non-availability, was just along for the ride.

About eight o'clock, Dalziel appeared in the incident room and told Pascoe he'd given instructions for the search to be wound down for the night.

'Still a couple of hours of daylight,' said Pascoe, slightly surprised.

'We're short-handed,' said Dalziel. 'And knackered. They'll miss things in the dusk, start thinking of home, stop for a quiet drag, next thing we've got another grass fire down here and everyone's up all night. I've called in on the Dacres, let them know.'

'How'd they take it?'

'How do you think?' snarled the Fat Man. Then relenting, he added, 'I pushed the no-news-good-news line. Never say die till you've got a body that has.'

'But you don't feel like that, sir?' probed Pascoe. 'From the start you've been sure she's gone for good.'

'Have I? Aye. Happen I have. Show me I'm wrong, lad, and I'll give you a big wet kiss.'

Nobly, in face of such a threat, Pascoe persisted. 'It could be abduction. There's still some car sightings unaccounted for.'

This was straw-grasping stuff. All early-morning vehicle sightings had been eliminated except for three. A local farmer had seen a blue car heading up the Highcross Moor road at what he termed a dangerous speed; several people had noticed a white saloon parked on the edge of Ligg Common; and Mrs Martin, a short-sighted lady who'd gone early into St Michael's Church to carry out her flower-arranging duties, thought she'd heard a vehicle going up the Corpse Road.'

'The Corpse Road?' Dalziel echoed.

'That's right. It's what they call the old track . . .'

'. . . that runs over the Neb into Dendale, the one they used for bringing their dead 'uns across to St Mick's for burying before they got their own church,' completed Dalziel. 'Don't come the local historian with me, lad; I'm a sodding expert.'

He scratched his chin thoughtfully, then said, 'Tell you what, fancy a walk? It'll do you good, you're looking a bit peaky.'

'A walk . . . ? But where . . . ?'

'You'll see. Come on.'

Outside, the Fat Man plunged briefly into the boot of his car, from which he emerged with a small knapsack which he tossed to Pascoe.

'You carry it up. I'll carry it down.'

'Up?' said Pascoe uneasily.

'Aye. Up.'

He led the way through a small gateway into the churchyard, through the green and grey lichened tomb-stones, past the church and out of the lych gate on the far side. A pleasant green track stretched ahead running between old elms and yews. At least it was pleasant for the first thirty yards or so, then it began to grow more rocky and steep.

'Anything that came up here would need four-wheel drive. Or a tractor maybe,' panted Pascoe. 'Ground's too hard to leave any traces.'

'Well, thank you, Natty Bumppo,' said Dalziel. 'What's been here then? Herd of cows in gum-boots?'

In a small clearing just off the track where the trees had thinned out considerably, he pointed to the crushed grass and powdered earth in parts of which tyre tracks were clearly visible.

'Yes, well, OK,' said Pascoe. 'There's been something up here. Well spotted, sir.'

He turned away and took a couple of steps back down the track.

'Hey, sunshine, what's your hurry? We've not got there yet.'

He looked back to see that Dalziel was still heading uphill where the track emerged from the trees and began to wind across the open fellside.

'But why . . . ? I thought you were just . . . Oh, sod it!' said Pascoe, and followed.

In fact, the track meandered fairly gently up the fellside, worn there over centuries by the heavy feet of all those sad processions – and also, he reassured himself as the melancholy vision threatened to overwhelm him, by their presumably much lighter feet, tripping merrily back to Dendale after the wake.

At least, being the eastern flank of the Neb, it was out of reach of the declining sun, though he managed to produce sweat enough by the time he laboured up to the sunlit ridge.

'Forty-five minutes,' said Dalziel, sitting at his ease against a boulder. 'I'd have thought a fit young shag like you 'ud have done it in half an hour.'

86

Pascoe sagged to the ground beside him, trying not to pant too audibly.

'Gi's the sack then,' said the Fat Man.

Pascoe wriggled it off his shoulders and handed it over. Then he turned his attention to Dendale.

It was only now, looking down, that he realized how much of a real frontier the Neb must have seemed to the old dalesmen. The fell on this side was much steeper and the sinuous curves of the Corpse Road on the Danby side turned into sharp zigzags beneath him. Also, while Danby had one foot and half its soul in the great fertile agricultural plain of Mid-Yorkshire, the narrow glaciated valley of Dendale belonged completely to the county's wild moorlands.

It was, he supposed, this wildness and steep enclosure which had made the dale so attractive to the grey suits in search of a reservoir site. He knew nothing of their search and final selection, but guessed it contained much that was unedifying, with references to the greater good of the greater number and the difficulties of making omelettes without breaking eggs flowing like hot lava, destroying all lives and homes that lay in its path.

Doubtless there'd been an Enquiry. There always was. Some linguistic archaeologist of the next age, putting together a lexicon of late twentieth-century usage would probably conclude that the space between choosing a site and starting work on it was for some arcane reason called 'The Public Enquiry'.

So the inevitable had happened and the valley had changed. Beyond recognition? Possibly. Beyond redemption? Probably. In one sense it was wilder now than before, because human beings no longer lived and worked here.

But the stamp of man's presence was visible beyond disguise in the shape of the long curve of the dam wall.

Nature, though, is a tough cookie. Through his art man tries to perfect her, and through his science to control her. But always she will shrug her shoulders and be herself again.

So here it was, the famous reservoir, built out of public money for the public weal in the days when privatization of public utilities was still a lurid gleam in a pair of demon eyes. Now of course it was a key feature in the master plan by which Mid-Yorkshire Water plc hoped to keep its consumers (sorry; customers) wet and its shareholders wealthy for the next hundred years.

And Nature, simply by opening her great red eye in the sky for a couple of months, had set all the plans at nought.

Around the dark waters of the reservoir ran a broad pale fillet of washed rock and baked mud across which ran the lines of ancient walls and on which stood piles of shaped and faced stone showing where bits of the drowned village had come gasping up for air again.

'You want this beer or not?' said Dalziel.

Pascoe turned to find the Fat Man was proffering a can of bitter.

'Well, I carried it up,' said Pascoe. 'I might as well carry it down.'

He took a long satisfying pull. Dalziel meanwhile had put down his own can and extracted from the knapsack a pair of binoculars with which he was scanning the valley.

What else did I lug up here? wondered Pascoe. A kitchen sink?

'This is where it all started, lad,' said Dalziel. 'This is what I wanted you to see.'

'Thank you for the thought, sir,' said Pascoe. 'Is there anything in particular I should be looking at, or is it just the general aesthetic I should be drinking in?'

'Is that what they call irony?' wondered Dalziel. 'That's

sarcasm for intellectuals, isn't it? Lost me. I just want you to have some idea what it used to be like down there, what it must have felt like fifteen years back when they were told they had to get out. I reckon it pushed one of the buggers over the edge. Now I know you think I've been brushing my teeth in home-brew or something, but if I'm going to be tret like a half-wit, I'd like to be tret like a half-wit by some half-wit who's got half an idea what I'm talking about. You with me, lad?'

'Trying to be, sir.'

'That the best you can do?'

'I've always felt that if Satan took me up to a high place, I'd be inclined to go along with most anything he said till I got down safe,' said Pascoe. 'So fire away. Give me a guided tour.'

'No need,' said Dalziel. 'I've got a map. It was in the file. I've got the rest of the file down in the car. You can take it home tonight and have a good read. Here.'

He passed over a sheet of cartridge paper. Pascoe looked at it and smiled.

'I recognize this fair hand, surely? Yes, there they are, the magic initials E.W.'

'Aye, it's one of Wieldy's. Thing you've got to remember is that what he's marked as houses are nowt but piles of rubble down there.'

'Was that the action of the water?' wondered Pascoe.

'No. The Water Board bulldozed them. They reckoned if they left buildings standing underwater, they'd be paying off sub-aqua freaks' widows for evermore. Even the houses that weren't going to be submerged they knocked down. Didn't want anyone trying to sneak back and take possession.'

Pascoe studied the map. Dalziel passed him the glasses.

'Start at the main body of the village,' said Dalziel. 'If you follow the Corpse Road down, you'll see it ends at a bloody great rock. Shelter Crag, that is. So called 'cos that's where they used to lay their dead 'uns, all wrapped up nice and cold for their trip over the hill to St Mick's. When they got their own church, that seemed obvious place to build it, and that's what that big pile of stones was.'

Slowly Dalziel guided Pascoe round the ruined valley with the care and precision of a courier who'd made the trip too often ever to forget. The main body of the village was easy enough to sort out once he'd got the church located. In any case, its relicts were substantial enough to be immediately obvious. Buildings which had stood apart weren't so easily identified. Hobholme, the farm where the first girl had lived, wasn't too difficult, but the Stang, site of the dale joinery, seemed to have been scattered far and wide. Heck, the Wulfstans' house, had re-emerged as a substantial promontory of stones running out from the new shore to the edge of the shrinking mere, and on the far side it was easy to spot the long rounded hillock alongside which had stood Low Beulah, the home of the girl who had survived.

But Neb Cottage, home of prime suspect Benny Lightfoot, and scene of that last attack, perhaps because it was high enough up the fell not to have spent the last fifteen years under water, was very hard to spot. Perhaps, like the man himself, it had re-entered the earth from which its stones had been prised.

He didn't share this fancy with the Fat Man but swung the glasses to bring the dam wall into view.

Somewhere there was a valley – the Lake District was it? – whose naive inhabitants according to legend built a wall to keep the cuckoo in and so enjoy spring forever. Here the purpose had been scientifically sounder, but not all that much more successful. With two-thirds of its footing in dried-up clay and the middle third lapped by sun-flecked wavelets that wouldn't have swamped a matchbox, the dam wall looked as awkward as a rugger forward at a ballet school.

He ran his gaze up the gentle concavity of its front to the balustraded parapet. There was someone there, a man, strolling along, very much at his ease. From this distance and angle it was hard to get much impression of his face, but he was tall with long black hair brushed straight back.

'Someone down there,' said Pascoe.

'Oh aye? Bit earlier and likely you'd have seen dozens. Local historians, bird-watchers, nebby hikers. No way the Water Board can keep them away without mounting an armed guard,' said Dalziel. 'Let's have a shufti.'

He took the glasses, scanned the dam, then lowered them.

'Gone, else you're having visions. Someone up on Beulah Height, though.'

He'd raised his glasses to the saddled crest of the opposite fell.

'Beulah Height. And Low Beulah. Someone must have been pretty optimistic,' mused Pascoe.

'Am I supposed to ask why?' demanded Dalziel. 'Well, no need, clever-clogs. ''Thou shalt be called Hephzibah and thy land Beulah.'' Isaiah sixty-two: four. And *Pilgrim's Progress*, last stop afore heaven, the Land of Beulah ''where the sun shineth night and day''. Got that just about right. Mind you, there's some as say it comes originally from Anglo-Saxon. *Beorh-loca* or some such. Means hill enclosure. There's the remains of some old hill-fort up there, dating from Stone Age times they reckon. Some time later on, farmers used the stones to make a sheepfold under the saddle, so they could be right.'

'You haven't been going to evening classes, have you, sir?' asked Pascoe, amazed.

'You ain't heard nothing yet. Could be it's the fold itself gives the name. *Bought* or *bucht* is a fold and *law*'s a hill.'

'That makes *Height* a touch tautologous, doesn't it?' said Pascoe. 'And it all sounds a bit Scottish, anyway.'

'Do you not think we sent missionaries down to civilize you buggers?' said Dalziel, referring to his own paternal heritage. 'Any road, there's others still who say it's really *Baler* Height, *bale* meaning fire, 'cos this is where they lit the beacon to warn of the Armada in 1588. You likely got taught that at college, or were they not allowed to learn you about times when we used to whup the dagoes and such?'

Ducking the provocation, and slightly miffed at having their usual cultural roles reversed, Pascoe said, 'And Low Beulah? They lit a beacon to warn the ducks, perhaps?'

'Don't be daft. A low's one of them burial mounds. Yon little hillock next to where the farm was is likely one of them.'

Pascoe knew when he was beaten.

'I'm impressed,' he said. 'You really did your home-work fifteen years back.'

'Aye. Whatever there were to know about Dendale, I learnt by heart,' said Dalziel heavily. 'And you know what? Like all them dates and such I learnt at school, it did me no fucking good whatsoever.'

He pushed himself to his feet and stood there, glower-ing into Dendale, looking to Pascoe's imagination like some Roman general sent to tame a rebellious province, who'd discovered that in terrain like this against foes like these, classical infantry tactics were no sodding good.

But he'd find a way. They – Roman generals and Andy Dalziels – always did.

Except of course in this case he was looking into the wrong valley.

As if in response to this critical thought, Dalziel said, 'I know what's down there is old stuff, lad. And what's down in Danby is a new case. But there's one thing I learnt fifteen year back that chimes useful to me now.'

'What's that, sir?' asked Pascoe dutifully.

'I learnt that in this place in this kind of weather, the bastard who took that first lass didn't stop, mebbe couldn't stop, till he'd taken two more and had a go at taking another. That's why I brought you up here, to try to get it into your noddle. Some things you can't learn out of books. But take the Dendale file home with you for home-work anyway. I'll test you on it tomorrow.'

'Will I be kept in if I fail?' asked Pascoe.

'With this one, I think we'll all be kept in long after the bell goes,' said Dalziel. 'Now let's be getting back down while it's still light enough to see how far we've got to fall.'

He strode ahead down the Corpse Road.

Pascoe took a last look across the dale. The setting sun filled the fold bowl between the two tops of Beulah Height with a pool of gold. *Last stop afore heaven*. On a night like this you could believe it.

'Oy!'

'Coming,' he called.

And he followed his great leader into the darkness.

day two
Nina and the Nix

NINA AND THE NIX

PRINTED AT THE EENDALE PRESS

EDITOR'S FOREWORD

We came from water and if the Greenhouse theorists are right, to water we shall probably return.

It accounts for 72% of the earth's surface and 60% of a man's body.

In places under permanent threat of drought, like Arabia Deserta and Mid-Yorkshire, it brings riches to some and death to others.

And over the centuries man has peopled it with a whole range of elemental creatures, mermaids, undines, naiads, neriads, krakens, kelpies, and many more, all suited to the particular age and culture which spawned them.

Here in Mid-Yorkshire the most common hydromythic entity is the nix.

The nix stands midway between the English pixie and the Scandinavian nicor.

In some tales it figures as a sort of brownie, generally benevolent in its relation with humanity. In others it is much closer to its Norse cousin which emerges from its watery lair by night to devour human prey. The Grendel monsters in the Beowulf saga are a form of nicor.

The present tale I heard many years ago from the lips of old Tory Simkin of Dendale, now sadly taken from us, both man and valley. It troubles me to think how much of the past we have lost while modern technology preserves in electronic perpetuity the idiocies of our own age (of all that have ever been perhaps the most deserving of oblivion). I thank God there are a few superannuated fools like myself who think it worthwhile to record the old stories before they are lost forever.

If this be vanity or blasphemy, then behold a vain

blasphemer from whom you may obtain further copies of this book and information about other publications of The Eendale Press at Enscombe, Eendale, Mid-Yorkshire.

EDWIN DIGWEED

NINA AND THE NIX

Once there were a nix lived by a pool in a cave under a hill.

For food he et whatever swam in his pool or crawled in the mud around it.

Only friend he had were a bat that hung upside down high in the roof of his cave, though often when it spoke to him its little squeaky voice seemed to come from somewhere high in the roof of his own head.

If nix wanted to go out, he usually waited till night. But sometimes he'd hear voices of kiddies playing in village far below and he'd sneak out in the daytime and find a shady place in the hillside where he could watch them.

Best of all were when they played in the pond on the village green and splashed each other, and ran around shouting, their shining faces and white limbs all dripping with water.

The one he liked watching most were called Nina. Her hair was as blonde as his was black and her skin as smooth as his was scaly.

Came a summer when sun shone so warm and sky stayed so cloudless that not even thought of seeing Nina could 'tice nix out into that heat and that brightness. He sat tight in his dark dank cave waiting for weather to change. But it didn't change and after a week or so he noticed when he knelt to take a drink that the water in his pool were further away than it used to be.

Day followed dry day. Sun burnt so hot, nix could feel its stuffy heat even down here in his cave. And without a drop of rain to slip through the cracks in the hillside and fill up his pool, the level got lower and lower. Soon the creatures that lived in it, and them as lived in the muddy edge which was getting bigger and bigger and drier and drier, began to die. And soon the nix began to feel very hungry.

'You going to sit there moping till you fade away?' said bat.

'Don't see what else I can do,' said nix.

'You can find some food,' said bat.

'I've looked and I've looked and there's nowt left to feed me,' said nix.

'I weren't thinking of feeding thee,' said bat. 'I were thinking of feeding the pool.'

'Eh?' said nix.

'Have you not noticed? Yon pond in the village hasn't got much smaller. And you know why that is?'

'No,' said nix.

'It's because of them juicy young lasses always splashing about in it,' said bat. 'Get yourself one of them, and you'd soon see pool filling up again.'

So nix went up to the surface to take a look for himself. It were so bright and hot he could only stay up there for half a minute, but it were long enough to see that bat was right. The village pond were still full of water, and the little kids were still splashing around in it.

Back down he came to his cave and he said, 'So you're right, but it's not much help. How am I going to get one of them to come down here? They're all shut up in their homes at night, and if I go out during the day, I'll shrivel up and die.'

'Then she'll have to come to you,' said bat. 'Go out tonight and gather all the prettiest flowers you can find, and plant them all around the entrance to the cave. Then just sit and wait.'

So that night the nix stole out and went far and wide over hill and dale, uprooting all the flowers he could find, moon daisies and stepmothers, Aaron's rod and bedstraw, but no flopdocken, for that's a flower nixes and their kind cannot abide. And he planted them all around the mouth of his cave.

Next morning, Nina went for a walk up the hill afore the sun got too hot. She wanted to pick some flowers for her mam, but there weren't very many because the heat had dried up all the ground and baked it so hard that even the grass was brown. Then suddenly she spotted this hollow in the hillside so full of flowers it looked like a garden. She made haste to get there and started picking the brightest blooms when a voice said, 'What do you think you're up to, little girl? Do you always steal flowers from other folks's gardens?'

'Oh, I'm so sorry,' cried Nina. 'I didn't realize this was anybody's garden.'

'Well, you realize now,' said the voice.

She couldn't see who was speaking but the voice seemed to be coming out of this hole in the hillside. So she went to it and said timidly, 'I really am sorry. I'll put them down here, shall I?'

'Nay, now they're picked, you might as well keep them,' said the voice.

'That's right kind of you,' said Nina. 'But won't you come out into your garden where I can see you?'

'Nay, lass. I can't bear this heat,' said the voice. 'In fact, I were just making myself a jug of iced lemonade. Would you like to try a glass?'

Now Nina was very hot and thirsty indeed and she said eagerly, 'Yes please.'

'Right, I'll pour you one. Just step inside and help yourself.'

So she pushed past the flowers which fringed the entrance to the tunnel leading down to the cave and stepped inside.

Next moment she felt herself seized by her long blonde hair which she was wearing in two pigtails and before she could scream she was dragged right down into the bowels of the earth.

There she lay in the foul-smelling dark, sobbing her heart out.

Finally she ran out of tears and rubbed her eyes and sat up to take a look around.

Outside, sun were so bright, a little bit of light filtered down the entrance tunnel. By its dim glow she saw she were in a cave. The ground were strewn with rocks and stuff. In the middle of the cave was a small, foul-smelling pool, and on its edge sat this thing.

101

Its body was long and scaly, its fingers and toes were webbed with long curved nails, its face was gaunt and hollow, its nose hooked, its chin pointed and fringed with sharp spikes of beard, its eyes deep-set and staring, and its mouth twisted in a mockery of a smile showing sharp white teeth as it spoke.

'How do, Nina,' it said.

'How do, Nix,' she answered in a very low voice.

'You know who I am then?' said nix.

'Aye. My mam's told me about you,' said Nina.

What her mam had told her was never go up the fell on her lone else the wicked nix that lived beneath it might steal her.

Now she wished with all her might that she'd taken heed!

'Then it's nice of you to come visiting, Nina,' said nix.

'It's nice of you to have me,' said Nina politely like she'd been taught. 'But please, I'd like to go home now, it's nearly time for my dinner.'

'It's long past time for mine,' snapped nix. Then, smiling his terrible smile again, he went on, 'Tell you what, Nina. It's so hot, why don't you have a little swim afore you go?'

Nina looked at the dreadful pool and shook her head.

'No, thank you,' she said. 'My dad says I'm never to go swimming by myself, only when there's someone bigger around to take care of me.'

'Never fear,' said nix, standing up. 'I'm bigger and I'll take care of thee.'

He came round the pool towards her. At that moment a voice came drifting down the tunnel from far above.

'Nina! Nina!' it cried.

'It's Dad!' cried Nina. 'I'm coming. I'm coming.'

And she set off to run up the tunnel, but she'd only gone a little way when those terrible hands caught at her ankles and dragged her screaming back down.

Far above she could still hear her dad's voice, but now it was fading and soon it was far away, then she couldn't hear it at all.

She lay on the edge of the pool with the nix towering over her.

'Just wait till my dad gets a hold of you,' she sobbed. 'He'll pull your neck like a chicken's for the pot.'

'He'll have to catch me first,' laughed nix. 'Now let's go for this swim.'

Nina looked up at him and saw he were strong enough to make her do whatever he wanted her to do. No use fighting then. What was it her mam used to say? God made men strong but he made us clever. Why use fists when you can use your noddle? And her dad were always boasting she were bright as a button.

Well, now was time to see just how bright a button she really was.

'All right,' said Nina. 'But I'll need to tidy up first.'

She stood up and began brushing off her dress, which had got all dusty when the nix dragged her down the tunnel. Then she took the ribbons out of her pigtails and unplaited her hair and combed it with her fingers so that it tumbled over her shoulders like a fall of bright water.

And all the while nix watched her with eyes like hot coals.

'There,' said Nina. 'I'm ready. But you'll need to jump in with me to help me to swim.'

'Take care, Nix,' squeaked bat. 'They're sly as spiders, these lasses.'

But nix wasn't listening. His eyes and his thoughts were fixed entirely on Nina.

She took his hand in hers and made him stand alongside her on a big rock at the edge of the pool.

And she said, 'I'll count up to three and then we'll jump together. All right?'

'All right,' said nix.

'One,' said Nina.

'And two,' said Nina.

'And three,' said Nina.

And they jumped.

Only, as nix jumped forward into the pool, Nina let go his hand and jumped backwards on to the ground.

Then she turned and ran as fast as she'd ever run in her life up the tunnel.

It only took nix a second to realize her trick.

Then, screaming with rage and dripping foul-smelling mud and water, he dragged himself from the pool and set out after her.

Oh, she were fast, but he were faster.

She didn't dare waste time looking back, but she could hear him behind her, his sharp nails screeling against the rock like hard chalk on a shiny slate, his stinking breath panting like Bert the blacksmith's bellows.

Her long hair streamed behind her and she felt it touched by his outstretched hand. Faster then she ran, and faster, till she felt it no more. But still he was close and her strength was failing. Now she felt the hand again, this time close enough to get a hold of a tress.

She felt the grip tighten, she felt her hair being twisted to make the grip firmer, above her she could see the ring of bright light that marked the end of the tunnel.

But it was too late. He had her hair fast now. He was pulling her to a stop. It was too late.

She stretched out her arms to the light and screamed, 'Daddy! Daddy!'

And just as she gave up hope and knew she were about to be dragged back down to the depths, she felt her hands seized.

For a moment she was stretched taut as a rope in the tug-o'-war at the village sports. Then, just as in the tug-o'-war when it seems the two teams are so evenly matched they must hold each other there for ever, suddenly one side will find the strength for one last pull and the other will go sprawling helpless on the ground, so Nina felt the pull above increase, the pull behind slacken.

And next moment she was out on the hillside in the bright golden sunlight, lying on the grass at her father's feet.

Oh, how they hugged and kissed, and nothing was said to scold her or remind her she'd disobeyed.

When they were done hugging and kissing, her dad rolled a huge boulder across the entrance to the cave.

'There,' he said. 'That'll keep yon nix where he belongs.

Now, let's be getting you home to your mam. Let's take her some flowers to brighten the house.'

So they set to, and picked moon daisies and stepmothers, Aaron's rod and bedstraw, and on their way home they found a bank covered with flopdocken, which the nixes hate, and them they picked also.

And very soon after, when Nina's Mam went to the back of her cottage and looked anxiously up the hillside, her heart jumped with joy as she saw her man and her little lass coming downhill towards her with their eyes bright as star-shine, their voices raised in a merry catch, and their arms full of flowers.

TWO

Monday dawned, the sun rising into the inevitable blue sky with the radiant serenity of Alexander entering a conquered province.

Its soundless reveille against the leaded light of Corpse Cottage in Enscombe did not disturb the deep slumber of Edwin Digweed, antiquarian bookseller and founder of the Eendale Press, but not for nothing had Edgar Wield been nicknamed by a previous lover, Macumazahn, He Who Sleeps With His Eyes Open.

He answered the summons immediately, taking care to make as little noise as possible. Edwin was not at his best if woken too early, one of the many adjustment-necessitating discoveries made during their first year together.

Downstairs, Wield brewed his morning coffee (two spoons of instant and three of white sugar in boiling milk, not the cafetière of freshly ground Colombian Edwin insisted on at all times of day) then went on his morning visit.

This took him via the churchyard into the grounds of Old Hall, home of the Guillemard family, by permission squires of Enscombe for nearly a thousand years. Falling on hard times, the family had been preserved by the acumen of its present commercial head, Gertrude (known, misleadingly, as Girlie), who had lured visitors to the estate by all manner of attractions, including a Children's Animal Park. Here, in pens or roaming free as their nature required, could be found calves, lambs, kids, piglets, fowl (domestic and game), dormice, harvest mice, field mice, and a rat called Guy. But it was not on any of these that Wield was making his morning call.

He made for a lofty oak which held the remains of a tree house in its fork and whistled gently.

Instantly a small figure appeared and dropped with scarcely more than a token touch to trunk or branch the thirty feet into his arms.

'Morning Monte,' said Wield. 'What fettle?'

Monte was a monkey; a marmoset, the local vet had informed him when he'd taken the animal for a comprehensive check – a necessary precaution in view of its origins. For Monte was an escapee from a pharmaceutical research lab who'd taken refuge in Wield's car. The sergeant had smuggled it out, assuring himself this was a decision postponed, not a decision made.

It had been the first real test of his new relationship. Edwin Digweed, though fond enough of animals, made it clear that he had no intention of sharing his home with a free-roaming primate. 'A *ménage à trois* may have its attractions,' he said. 'A *ménagerie à trois* has none.'

There had been a moment, as Wield's unblinking eyes in that unreadable face regarded him calculatingly, that Digweed had recalled an anecdote told of John Huston. Required by his current mistress to choose between herself and a pet monkey of peculiarly disgusting habits, the film director had thought for thirty seconds, then said, 'The chimp stays.'

Digweed held his breath, suddenly fearful that his world might be about to dissolve beneath his feet.

But what Wield had said was, 'He's not going back there. He escaped.'

Hiding his relief, Digweed exclaimed, 'He ... it ... is a monkey, not the Count of bloody Monte Cristo. All right, we can't send him . . . it . . . back to that place, but the proper place for him . . . it . . . is a zoo.'

'Monte. That's what we'll call him,' said Wield. 'As for the zoo, I know just the spot.'

He'd taken Monte to see Girlie Guillemard. Much impressed by the little animal, and having established he was marginally less inclined to bite, scratch or otherwise assault ill-behaved children than herself, she'd offered him refuge in the Animal Park.

The move had worked surprisingly well. Wield visited every morning he could, bearing gifts of peanuts and fruit. There'd been an early crisis when duty had prevented his visit for nearly a week. Finally, Monte had gone looking for him at Corpse Cottage. Finding only Edwin there, asleep in bed, Monte had awoken him, presumably to make enquiries, by pushing up his eyelids.

'Naturally, my first thought was, I'm being raped by an ape,' said the bookseller. 'So I lay back and thought of Africa.'

Now Wield gently removed the beast from his head where it was searching diligently for nits. He regarded the little animal with great affection. He'd tried to explain to Edwin that it wasn't just sentimentality. In fact, of all the decisions he'd made as a gay man, of all the small steps he'd taken towards his present state of 'outness', none – not even his acceptance of Digweed's suggestion that they set up house together – seemed more significant than his rescue of Monte.

It had been theft, no matter how you looked at it. It had put his career on the line. Would he have done it before he took up with Edwin? He doubted it. It was as if his own pool of contentment had filled to such an unanticipated level there was a constant overspill which could no more let him ignore the monkey's plight last

November than his sense of duty could have permitted him to steal it a year earlier.

Edwin, who, as he listened to his partner's untypically hesitant self-analysis, had been preparing *huevos a la flamenca*, remarked acidly, 'Do let me know when you go soft on unborn chickens.' Thereafter, however, whenever Monte came searching for the absent Wield, he was greeted with great kindness and given a lift back to Old Hall.

Dalziel did not know, at least not officially, about Monte. 'Keep it that way,' advised Pascoe, who'd got the full story, 'else some day when you think you're out of reach, he'll use the beast to track you down.'

The previous day, the Fat Man had had to rely on the telephone. When Wield and Digweed got back from their book-buying foray into the Borders, the former had found what the latter called an HMV message on the answering machine. After a terse outline of the situation, Wield had been invited with satirical courtesy to put in an appearance at the incident room in Danby first thing the following morning, weather and social calendar permitting.

It was not a prospect that pleased. Wield, too, remembered Dendale. Like the Fat Man said, it wasn't your collars kept you awake, it was the ones that got away, and Dendale rated high on that insomniac list. OK, Danby was different, thriving, pushing up from village to township, nowhere near as enclosed, and certainly not doomed the way Dendale had been. But it was just a couple of miles west, just a short walk over the Corpse Road . . .

'But a man's gotta do . . . something,' said Wield. 'Don't crap on too many kids, kid. See you.'

He threw the monkey up into the lower branches of the oak and walked away.

Half an hour later, as he freewheeled his old Thunderbird down the track from Corpse Cottage in order not to disturb Edwin, he was still thinking how pleasant it would be to be still lying abed on such a morning as this. But Danby called. And Dalziel.

He switched on the ignition and kicked the starter and, as the engine roared into life, he cried to a surprised cat on the hunt for early birds, 'Hi-yo Silver. Away!'

In the Pascoe household, too, there was reluctance at all levels.

Pascoe himself, after rising early and settling down to read the Dendale file, had fallen asleep in his chair, and wasn't aroused till Ellie started the morning bustle of getting Rosie ready for school.

His first instinct as he bestirred himself ere well awake was to rush off unshaven and unfed, but Ellie's cooler counsel had brought him to his senses and when he rang St Michael's Hall at Danby and was assured by the duty officer that the only thing disturbing the peace was the approaching roar of Sergeant Wield's motorbike, he had relaxed in the certainty that on the ground organization was in the best possible hands.

So he had sat down to the relatively rare pleasure of taking breakfast with his daughter.

It did not seem to be a pleasure shared. Rosie blinked her eyes irritably against the sun streaming in through the kitchen window and announced, 'I'm feeling badly.'

Her parents exchanged glances. Peter, left in sole charge some weeks earlier, had been targeted by his daughter at breakfast with little sighs and sobs as she bravely forced her branflakes down, till, always a soft target, he had caved in and said, 'Are you feeling badly or something?'

'Yes,' she'd replied. 'I'm feeling very badly.'

'Then perhaps you'd better not go to school,' he'd replied, secretly glad of an excuse to keep her at home all day with him.

In the event, by halfway through the morning she'd recollected that her class was going out on a bird-spotting expedition that afternoon, so made a rapid recovery and nobly insisted it would be wrong of her to remain at home under false pretences.

But the phrase, 'I'm feeling badly,' was thereafter used as a formula to unlock her father's heart when necessary.

Ellie Pascoe, however, was made of sterner stuff.

'I told you to keep your sunhat on yesterday,' she said indifferently.

'I did,' retorted Rosie. 'All the time.'

'Of course you did,' said Pascoe. 'Even when you were swimming underwater.'

'Don't be silly,' she snapped. 'It would float away. Do I *have* to go to school?'

'Oh, I think so,' he said. 'I think I saw Nina waiting at the gate for you just now.'

'No, you didn't. I told you. She got taken again. By the nix. I saw her get taken.'

Pascoe looked at Ellie, who made an I-forgot-to-mention-it face.

'Perhaps her dad's rescued her again,' he said.

'Not yet he won't have. It was only yesterday. You'll be sorry if I get taken too.'

Not so much a conversation-stopper as a heart-stopper.

'Well, try to hang around as long as you can,' he said lightly. 'It's the same for me too, you know. I'd rather stay at home.'

'Not the same,' she said sullenly. 'You haven't got a stiff neck.'

'And you have? Like the people of Israel,' he laughed. 'We should have called you Rose of Sharon.'

Being a curious child, she usually insisted on explanations of jokes she didn't understand, but this morning all she did was repeat with great irritation, 'Don't be silly.'

'I'll try not to,' said Pascoe, rising. 'See you tonight.'

Her skin was warm to his kiss.

At the front door he said, 'She does look a bit flushed.'

'You would too if you'd been running around in the sun all day,' said Ellie.

'I was,' he said. 'And no doubt will be again.'

'Well, keep your sunhat on,' said Ellie, determinedly cheerful. She had listened to his weary account of the day's frustrations when he got home the previous night, held him close for a while, then poured him a large whisky and talked brightly about Rosie's trip to the seaside. At first he thought her motive was purely distraction, but after a while he became aware that it was her own mind she was distracting too, from her unbearable empathy with Elsie Dacre. So he had switched on the TV allegedly in search of the news and instead had got a late-night discussion on the growing problem of juvenile runaways. A psychiatrist called Paula Appleby whose strong opinions, linguistic fluency and photogenic features had got her elected 'the thinking man's thinking woman' was saying, 'When a child disappears, rather than simply looking *for* the child, we should be looking *at* first the parents, who are often the cause, then the police, who are more likely to be part of the problem than its solution.'

'Time for bed,' Pascoe had said, switching off.

Now he looked up at the perfectly laid blue wash of the sky and guessed that hours earlier the Dacres' dark-rimmed, sleepless eyes had watched it pale from black to grey and then to pink and gold, and sought in the returning light and the rising birdsong some hint of that freshness and hope that had always been there before, but was now nowhere to be found.

And then his mind's eye ran up the Corpse Road and over the sun-rimmed Neb and looked down into Dendale still filling with pearly light.

It seemed to him that he saw far below a shadowy figure who peered up towards the fell's gilded rim, then threw up its arms in welcome or derision, before slipping silent and naked into the still dark waters of the mere.

Daylight visions now, he thought. Were they better or worse than waking in the dark and still smelling the mud of Passchendaele?

'Peter!' said Ellie in a tone that told him she'd spoken his name already.

'Sorry,' he said. 'Miles away.'

'Yes, I've noticed. Peter, don't you think . . .'

But the moment wasn't ripe. A voice said, 'Lovely morning again, sod it!' and they saw the postman coming up the drive. He handed Pascoe two packages, one small, one large. Both were addressed to Ellie, but when he proffered them, she took the small one and ignored the other.

'Oh, good,' she said, tearing it open. 'That Mahler disc.'

'*Songs for Dead Children*. Just the stuff for a summer's day,' he said, taking it from her hand and replacing it with the other package which bore a well-known publisher's logo. 'What about this?'

'If I want cheering up, I'll listen to Mahler,' she said.

'Perhaps they've just sent your script back to ask you to make a few minor revisions?' he offered.

'Bollocks,' said Ellie. 'I've got these Braille-sensitive fingers. They can read "get stuffed" through six layers of wrapping. Weird design.'

She was determined not to talk about the novel. He looked down at the disc which bore a silhouette

113

drawing of a girl's or cherub's profile, spouting a line of music. He found himself thinking of Dendale, though the connection seemed slight. Then he spotted what it was. In the bottom right corner, as on the map from the Dendale file, were the initials E.W. Not of course Edgar Wield this time, but, as was confirmed when he turned the disc over and read the small print on the back, Elizabeth Wulfstan.

'Does the translation, sings the songs, designs the cover; I wonder if she plays the instruments in the orchestra?' he said.

'Very likely. Some people get all the talent, which is why there's so little left over for the rest,' said Ellie, dispiritedly.

'It'll happen, love. Really. You've got more writing talent in your little finger than any of those London creeps licking each other's bums in the Sunday reviews,' he said loyally, putting his arms round her.

They clung together as if he were going back to the Front after all too short a leave.

Then he got into his car and drove away.

THREE

'How many times?' said Father Kerrigan.

'Five.'

'Jesus! With the same fellow, was it?'

'Yes, Father,' said Detective Constable Shirley Novello indignantly.

'And on the Sabbath, too.'

'Does that make it worse?'

'It doesn't make it any better. Five times. It's this hot weather I blame. Is he one of mine? Don't tell me. I'll recognize him by the weary way he walks. And this is why I didn't see you in church yesterday? You were too busy fornicating.'

'No, Father. I told you. We went off to the seaside for the day, and it just sort of happened.'

'No, my girl. *Once* it just sort of happens, *five times* takes enthusiasm.'

It wasn't easy, thought Novello as she left the church a little later, being a modern woman, a Roman Catholic, and a Detective Constable all at the same time. They got in each other's way. To the soul sisters, a good screw was 'exuberating in your own sexuality'; to the holy father it was the sin of fornication. As for her job, there were times when it required her to behave in ways equally offensive to both the sisterhood and the Fatherhood.

She arrived at the Danby incident room five minutes late. No sign of Dalziel (thank you for that at least, God); or Pascoe. But Wield was there.

'Sorry, Sarge,' she said. 'Went to confession.'

Somehow telling a lie in these circumstances didn't seem on.

'Hope you got it on tape,' said Wield.

A joke? She made a guess and smiled.

'You weren't here yesterday? Me neither. Get up to speed, then I'd like you to take a closer look at these three car sightings.'

'Super around?'

'Up the dale with DI Burroughs and the search team.'

'And Mr Pascoe?'

'Along shortly. He's checking the shop.'

An excuse for lateness? They covered each other's backs, these two.

The thought must have showed. Wield said, 'Or mebbe he's at confession too. Takes longer as you get older, they say.'

Another joke? He was in an odd mood today. She found herself a computer screen and went to work.

Three cars. In the early stages of a case like this when you went in mob-handed, with rough-terrain search teams, house-to-house enquiries, media appeals, etc. etc., what you rapidly got was a vast amount of clutter. Which is why the better part of investigation was elimination. (Pascoe.) Not easy. Probably by the time she sorted out these three, there'd be several others reported. Sunday was a bad day for witnesses. People went off for the day, didn't get back till late. There'd be huge gaps in yesterday's house-to-house. Not her problem. Yet.

She plotted her car sightings on the map. The closest, not a sighting but a hearing, was on the Corpse Road. Someone had added a note, *evidence of parking two hundred yards up track: 4WD?* Not much point pursuing the flower arranger. On the other hand . . . she looked at her watch, then rose and headed out, whistling a hymn tune which caused Sergeant Wield to wonder if

116

too much religion might be getting in the way of her work.

The hymn was in fact 'In Life's Earnest Morning', but its present occasion was secular. Novello had once lodged with a dog-owning family. The dog, a well-trained poodle, had signalled its need to go out every morning by a loud yapping to which her landlord, equally well trained, had responded by singing, 'In life's earnest morning, When our hope is high, Comes thy voice in summons, Not to be put by,' as he got the lead and headed for the door.

She headed past the church and sat on a stone at the foot of the Corpse Road. After only five minutes her faith was rewarded. A springer spaniel came running down the track, stopped dead when it saw her, then approached cautiously. She reached out her hand and spoke to it softly and finally it allowed her to scratch its head.

It was followed a few moments later by a breathless, thickset woman in loose cotton slacks and a pink suntop.

'There you are, Zebedee,' she said. 'It's all right. He won't bite.'

'Me neither,' said Novello.

She stood up and introduced herself. The woman gave her name as Janet Dickens, Mrs, and said she lived about ten minutes' walk away.

'Is this about that little girl?' she asked. 'That's really dreadful. We were away all day yesterday across at my sister's near Harrogate – we go alternate Sundays and they come here – but I heard it on the news when we got back.'

'Did you take Zebedee for his walk before you went?' asked Novello.

'Oh yes. No way he'll let me get away without his morning stroll.'

'And you always come here.'

'That's right. He gets quite uppity if I try to take him anywhere else.'

'Good. I wonder if you noticed a vehicle up this track yesterday morning,' said Novello.

'A vehicle? Oh, you mean the Discovery? Yes, it was there again. Why? You don't think . . . ?'

'No, we don't think anything,' said Novello firmly. 'This is just one of several vehicles we need to check out for elimination purposes. This vehicle was a Land Rover Discovery, you say?'

'That's right. Green. Local, it had the Mid-Yorkshire letters, and this year's registration, and one of the numbers was a six, I think, but I'm sorry, I can't recall the others.'

'You've done very well,' said Novello, making notes. 'But you said "again". *It was there again*. What did you mean?'

'Oh, I've seen it four or five times in the past couple of weeks. That's how I remember as much as I do about the number, I suppose; I'm so scatter-brained, if I'd just seen it once, I'd likely have told you it was a yellow Porsche with an 007 number plate. What will you do now? Put out some kind of alert?'

'Nothing as dramatic as that, Mrs Dickens,' said Novello.

It took a couple of minutes to persuade Mrs Dickens that she wasn't about to conjure up the Flying Squad and a pack of bloodhounds. Finally, assurances that as they'd missed her yesterday, the house-to-house team would probably be on her doorstep this very moment, got her on her way.

Novello returned to the Hall. Wield was nowhere to be seen, so she passed her information to Control and asked for a list of possibilities. Then, with one down, and feeling hot for hunches, she went in pursuit of another.

The two people reporting the white car at the edge of Ligg Common had been vague and contradictory. One described it as small, another as quite big. The first opined it might have been a Ford Escort, the second was certain it was some sort of Vauxhall but couldn't say which.

But there'd been a third sighting even vaguer, picked up during house-to-house, Mrs Joy Kendrick who'd been driving by the common early and thought she'd noticed a car and it could've been white, but she wasn't absolutely sure as the kids were being fractious in the back because they didn't like being left with their gran for the day, which was the purpose of the journey.

Novello had noticed children beginning to arrive for school as she went out to the Corpse Road. On her return, the numbers had grown considerably. Because of the constant coming and going of police vehicles from the incident centre next door, a line of crowd-control barriers had been set up to reinforce the low wall which divided the playground from the hall forecourt, and the naturally curious kids were pressing thick against them. There were a lot of adults there too. After yesterday's news, parents who'd normally just drop their kids off, or even let them walk there under their own steam, were taking extra precautions.

As Novello re-emerged from the Centre, a couple of teachers were going along the barrier urging the children to go into the school. Novello entered the playground and approached one of them showing her warrant card.

'I'm Dora Shimmings, head teacher,' said the woman. 'Look, I arranged with Mr Pascoe yesterday that any general questioning of the children in Lorraine's class wouldn't be done until we'd got the school day under way in as normal a fashion as possible.'

She spoke with a quiet authority that made Novello glad she wasn't about to contradict her.

'It's not that,' she said reassuringly. 'I just wanted to know if Joy Kendrick was one of your parents.'

'Very much so. We have all three of hers. But none of them is in Lorraine's class.'

'What age are they?'

'The twins are six and Simon's eight. There they are now.'

Novello turned. A harassed-looking woman with loose blonde hair bobbing around her shoulders with all the vigour but none of the gloss of a shampoo ad was shepherding a trio of children through the gate – twin girls who, contrary to the usual image of close love and special understanding, seemed each ambitious to achieve uniqueness by kicking shit out of the other, and an older boy, Simon, looking as bored and aloof as only an eight-year-old with twin sisters can.

'I'd like to meet them. It'll only take a few seconds,' promised Novello.

Unlike most police promises, this one was just about kept.

After the introduction, Novello said, 'Mrs Kendrick, when you talked to the officer who called at your house yesterday, did he talk to the children?'

'No. They weren't there, were they? I didn't pick them up till seven.'

'Of course not. Simon, your mum says there was a white car parked by the common as you drove past yesterday morning. You didn't happen to notice it, did you?'

'Yeah,' he said. It wasn't an uninterested or ill-mannered monosyllable. Children, Novello recalled, tended to answer questions asked them, unlike adults who were always reaching for your reasons for asking.

'So what kind was it?'

'Saab 900 cabriolet.'

'Did you notice the number?'

'No, but it was the latest model.'

That was that. She thanked the boy and his mother, who had been holding the twins apart like a pair of over-psyched contenders in a title fight, and now she continued dragging them towards the school entrance.

'Clever,' said Mrs Shimmings.

'Lucky,' said Novello. 'I could have got a boy whose sole obsession was football. So why did Mrs K dump the kids on Gran all day yesterday, I wonder? Nothing to do with the case, just idle curiosity.'

'Boyfriend,' said Mrs Shimmings laconically. 'Kendrick took off last year. Joy's got herself a man, but Simon hates him. And you can't have good sex with a protest meeting going on outside your bedroom door, can you?'

'Never tried it,' said Novello with a grin.

She went back to the Hall. Still no sign of Wield. No reply yet from Control to her query about the Discovery. She ought to give someone what she'd got, but she couldn't see anyone she altogether trusted to make sure the credit stayed with herself. Many of her male colleagues, even those not quite so chauvinist as to think a woman's place was in the kitchen, had no problem with thinking it was in the background. What man, compli-mented on his appearance, says, 'My wife chose the tie, ironed the suit, washed the shirt and starched the collar and cuffs?'

Anyway, she was hot, she was on a roll. Two down, one to go.

She went in search of Geoff Draycott of Wornock Farm who'd seen the blue estate speeding up the Highcross Moor road.

FOUR

There were two men scrubbing away at the BENNY'S BACK! graffiti on the railway bridge as Pascoe drove beneath it.

They didn't seem to be making much progress. Perhaps they would scrub and scrub till finally they wore out the solid stonework and nothing remained but the red letters hanging in the air.

An idle fancy, or a symptom? Reading the Dendale file earlier that morning, before his mind took refuge in sleep, he had found himself reluctant to engage with the facts as presented, or indeed *any* facts as presented, preferring to slip sideways into surreal imaginings. There had been a time when life seemed a smooth learning curve, a steady progress from childish frivolity through youthful impetuosity to mature certainty, which would occur somewhere in early middle age, whenever that was, but you'd recognize it by waking one morning and being aware that you'd stopped feeling nervous about making after-dinner speeches, you really believed the political opinions you aired at dinner parties, you no longer felt impelled to tie your left shoelace before your right to avoid bad luck, and you didn't have to read the instruction book every time you programmed the video.

Well, that was out, that was a sunlit plateau he knew now he was never going to reach. This, for what it was worth, was *it*. Not a steady climb but an aimless wandering along the mazy paths of the wildwood. Sometimes the pleasure of a sunlit glade or a crystal stream;

sometimes the terror of a falling tree or snarlings and crashings in the undergrowth; and sometimes the path winding you back to your starting place, except that it never looked the same.

Did he think he was unique? Dr Pottle his tame shrink, had asked him. Or did he believe that everyone felt like this?

'Neither,' he replied. 'I'm sure many people don't feel like this, but I'm equally sure I'm not unique.'

'Bang goes religion and politics,' said Pottle. 'It could be you're in the right job, after all.'

But it didn't feel like it. Curious how, as Ellie seemed (outwardly at least) increasingly resigned to the ambiguities of his work, he himself (inwardly at least) was finding them more and more troublesome.

A lost child. A dead child, that was how Dalziel saw it, he could tell. He felt the agony of her parents. And through his climb to the rim of the Neb, and his reading of the Dendale file, he felt the agony of all those other parents who'd seen their children go out and never saw them return.

But his empathy didn't make him want to toil tirelessly at the task of catching this man, this monster, who was responsible for these disappearings. No, all he wanted was to go home and stay home and hold eternal vigil over his own child. The world forgetting, by the world forgot. Cultivate your own garden. There is no such thing as society.

Which, he told himself sternly, was like rubbing away the solid stonework and leaving the red letters dancing in the empty air.

His introspective musings had got him through Danby on autopilot and he found he was outside St Michael's Hall. Near the main door was an empty parking space marked DCI. He smiled. As anticipated, Wield had things under control.

Inside he found a scene of well-ordered activity. The detective sergeant, regimental in front of the troops, stood up and said, 'Good morning, sir.'

'Morning,' said Pascoe, thinking that probably even machines in a factory ran more smoothly when Wieldy showed his face. Not that his face was smooth. In fact it was possible to theorize that his penchant for organization was a reaction to having features that looked like creation a parsec after the Big Bang.

'Nice to see a hive of industry,' he went on. 'Got everything we need?'

'Except the fridge, and that's coming,' said Wield.

'Fridge? You expecting samples?'

'For cold drinks,' said the sergeant. 'I can do you a coffee, but. And there's a note for you from Nobby Clark. I saw him when I arrived. He were very insistent I gave it to you direct. Think you've made a conquest there.'

This was said with a straight face, or in Wield's case a crooked one, which in terms of inscrutability came to the same thing. But it also came as close to a bit of gay badinage as Pascoe had ever detected in the sergeant.

He opened the envelope. It contained a piece of paper bearing the name JED HARDCASTLE.

'That it?' said Pascoe. 'No message?'

'He said something about paint,' said Wield, handing over a mug of coffee. 'I got the feeling he wanted to give you something you could pull out of your hat.'

'God save me from the gratitude of the simple-hearted,' said Pascoe. 'What am I expected to do? Tell Andy I've worked out the graffiti artist is called Jed Hardcastle, only I don't know who he is or where he lives or *anything* about him?'

'Son of Cedric and Molly Hardcastle,' said Wield. 'Brother of Jenny, first lass to go missing in Dendale. Present address, Stirps End Farm, Danby.'

'Oh, *that* Jed Hardcastle,' said Pascoe with slight irritation, mainly at himself for not having made the link even though he'd just read the Dendale file a couple of hours earlier. God, his mind was really refusing to engage with the facts.

He sipped his coffee and said, 'So, another link with last time.'

'Last time?'

'Dendale.'

'Oh aye. That's official is it? Dendale was last time?'

'The Fat Man seems to think so. He's had me reading the file. He even marched me up to the top of the Corpse Road last night.'

'Did he now? That sounds pretty official.'

'You don't sound like it makes you happy.'

'I think it's a bit soon to be talking of *this time* and *last time*, that's all.'

'What about this fellow Lightfoot?' insisted Pascoe. 'You must have met him. What did you reckon? I gather some folk thought he was the village idiot, but I've heard that in fact he was pretty bright.'

'Oh, he was bright enough,' said Wield. 'But there was something about him. Like he came from another world.'

This was untypically imprecise for the sergeant.

Pascoe said, 'What do you mean, other world? Heaven? Hell? Jupiter? Wales?'

'Not as far removed as that,' said Wield. 'No, his other world was . . . Dendale.'

'I don't get you,' said Pascoe. 'OK, that's where he lived, and I know that he was so upset when his mother decided to emigrate that he ran off to his gran's. But lots of people like where they are so much it would take dynamite to shift them.'

'It did take dynamite to shift them out of Dendale, remember?' said Wield. 'OK, for most of them, it was an uprooting, but the roots would take again in similar soil. The majority of them resettled over here around Danby and from all accounts they've settled in very well. But the odd one . . . well, since I've been living in Enscombe, I've got a different perspective on how folk relate to the place they call home. There's none of us there would want to leave. I feel like that and I've not been living there long enough to shit my own weight, as they say. But I've met some people, like the Tokes – you recall the Tokes? – that I reckon you couldn't uproot, only break off at ground level.'

The Tokes were a mother and son living in Enscombe who'd figured in the case which brought Wield and Edwin Digweed together.

'Yes, I remember the Tokes,' said Pascoe. 'Lightfoot was like that?'

'To some extent. You know how folk say, "I belong to such a place." Just a figure of speech usually, but with Lightfoot, like with Toke, it really means what it says. The place owns them. For better or worse. For good or evil.'

'Hold on, Wieldy,' said Pascoe. 'You're stealing my lines. I'm the one who goes all metaphysical, right? You're Mr Microchip, the man with the pointy ears.'

Wield scratched one of the organs which, though certainly irregular, were hardly pointed.

'Just goes to show what country life can do to you, doesn't it?' he said.

Like Shirley Novello earlier, Pascoe found it hard to tell if the sergeant was altogether joking, but he laughed anyway. There were enough uncertainties in life without admitting the possibility that your Rock of Ages might after all turn out to be soft-centred.

He said, 'But I agree with you about sticking to *this time*. Let's work with what we've got. There were some car sightings unaccounted for . . .'

'I've got Novello working on them,' said Wield. 'In fact, this came through for her a couple of minutes ago. Presumably it's to do with the sightings, but she's not around to tell me what.'

'Yes, she is,' said Pascoe, who'd just seen Novello come through the door. He glanced at the sheet of paper Wield had handed him as she approached. It was a list of green Land Rover Discoverys registered locally in the past year.

'Morning, Shirley,' he said.

Dalziel called her Ivor. Pascoe had made sure no one else did. Eccentric leaders were for following not imitating, else the *Victory* would have been full of one-eyed sailors.

'Morning, sir,' she said, looking a touch anxiously at the list in his hand. Pascoe guessed she'd have liked to get to it before Wield so she could have presented it with her interpretation all ready. Like Clark, she was still at the stage where she thought rabbits plucked from hats impressed the brass. Unlike Clark, she'd probably grow out of it. Her face, while not conventionally good-looking, was full of character and intelligence. She'd settled down well since joining the department a few months back, but she was still on guard. Perhaps that was a permanent condition of service for women in the police force, thought Pascoe. Or was that too easy? Was there something more he could be doing to assure her that here in Mid-Yorkshire at least there wasn't anyone lurking in the shadows, waiting for the chance to chop her off at the knees?

'So you're making progress,' he said, handing her the list.

Glancing at it as she spoke, she explained how she had got the information, then went on to the Saab cabriolet, and finally to the moving car on the Highcross Moor road.

She led them to the wall map to illustrate her findings here.

'Geoff Draycott, thirty-two, married, tenant at Wornock Farm, that's here. He was out in this field, here, about half eight, quarter to nine, when he saw this car heading up the road away from town. It was moving very fast, which was what drew his attention. Mind you, he seems to think everything that uses that road moves too fast. It seems it's been improved considerably in the last ten years as the Science and Business Park developed and a lot of the people there began to use it as a quick way of heading north to join up with the arterial here, instead of heading south and east. But improvement hasn't extended to fencing, and Draycott reckons he loses a couple of sheep a year because of speeding cars and lorries.'

'Must have been pretty powerful if it was speeding,' said Wield, looking at the contours.

'He says it was a big estate, blue, but he couldn't identify the make and was at the wrong angle to get any numbers. He did say he thought that it might have stopped up here.'

She pointed to a high bend of the road marked on the map with the viewpoint symbol.

'There's a bit of hardstanding. It's a popular place for picnics. He caught the flash of sun on a glass up there just a little later, but he can't be sure it was the same car.'

'Bit early for a picnic,' said Wield. 'Owt else?'

'Not on any of these. But when I caught up with Draycott, he was driving a red Ford pick-up. Popular vehicle with farmers, I spotted another three as I drove around. And I got to wondering if some of the folk round here who got asked about car sightings mightn't have bothered to mention these, or other farm vehicles, because they're so familiar they're almost invisible. Like the postman in the Chesterton story.'

One for me? thought Pascoe, amused. He hoped she was bright enough not to have tried it out on Andy Dalziel, whose response would probably have been . . .

'Postman? On a Sunday? Now that *is* odd.'

They turned. There he was. Sometimes he came roaring in like a steam locomotive, sometimes he rolled up, soft as a hearse, which, today, clad in a suit black enough to please an undertaker and a shirt white enough to make a shroud, he might have been following.

'No, sir, the Father Brown story . . .' said Novello, flustered into the error of explanation.

'Father Brown? I thought you were one of Father Kerrigan's flock. Not been head-hunted, have you?'

Time for a rescue act.

Pascoe said, 'Shirley was just trying out an idea on us, sir. And very interesting it was, too. But let's make a start on what we've got first, shall we?'

He gave Dalziel a digest of Novello's findings. The Fat Man was dismissive.

'A blue estate, speeding? Overtake their tractor, bloody farmers think you're speeding. And if he wants to get away so quick, what's he stop up the hill for? And this white Saab, right out in the open, weren't it? At the edge of the common for all to see. Not what you'd call furtive, is it?'

'The Discovery was quite well hidden,' said Pascoe.

'Except for anyone walking their dog past it,' said Dalziel. 'Told you it 'ud be a four-wheel drive last night, didn't I?'

'I think, to be strictly accurate, I told you that,' said Pascoe, thinking, he doesn't want to be bothered with any of this. His mind's fixated on Benny bloody Lightfoot. 'But we do have a list of names and we're going to need to check them . . .'

'Aye, aye, shove up the overtime bill,' said Dalziel gloomily. 'Desperate Dan's going to love me.'

This from one to whom police budgets and the affection of his Chief Constable were matters of equal indifference rang false as a politician's indignation.

'One in there might interest you, sir,' said Wield.

He jabbed his finger at the bottom of the sheet. Pascoe looked over the Fat Man's shoulder.

Walter Wulfstan.

That name again. Pascoe's eyes strayed to the poster still visible on one of the few parts of the notice board not yet covered up by constabulary paper.

The opening concert of the Mid-Yorkshire Dales Music Festival, Elizabeth Wulfstan singing *Kindertotenlieder.* Songs for Dead Children. Not the most diplomatic of programmes for this place at this time.

It occurred to him that *this place* was literally this place. Had anyone told the Festival people that their opening venue had been commandeered?

Observing Dalziel for the second time in two days apparently rapt at the appearance of this name from the past, Pascoe voiced his concern to Wield.

'The secretary of the Parish Council was round first thing this morning,' the sergeant said. 'I told him he could certainly cancel everything this week. Next week, we'd have to wait and see.'

'He wouldn't be pleased.'

'Oddly enough, his words were, Mr Wulfstan wouldn't be pleased. Seems he's chair of the Music Festival committee.'

'He's back at that again, is he?' said Dalziel, who never let rapture obstruct eavesdropping.

'Back?' said Pascoe.

'He dropped out of Yorkshire after Dendale. Seemed to uproot himself completely. Sold up his house in town,

130

handed over the on-site running of the business to his partners, and set himself up down south as their international sales manager, running across Europe, oiling the wheels, that sort of thing. Speaks good Frog and Kraut, they say. Must have done all right. Seven, eight years back, the company needs more space and builds on a greenfield site outside Danby. That was the start of yon Science and Business Park thing. Lots of Euro-lolly, they say, most of it down to Wulfstan. And eventually he moves back to town. Bought a house "in the bell". Holy-clerk Street.'

'In the bell' referred to the top price area round the cathedral.

'Very nice,' said Pascoe.

'Keep doing the Lottery,' said Dalziel. 'Ivor, get on the phone to Wulfstan's firm at the Business Park, will you? See if he's there. If he is, I'll just pop round and have a word.'

'There are other names on the list, sir,' said Pascoe.

'Nay, it'll be his,' said Dalziel dismissively. 'What's up, lass? Tha does know how to work a phone?'

Novello, who hadn't moved, said, 'What's the firm's name, sir?'

'Oh aye. Summat weird. Helioponics, that's it. Helioponics. You need six O-levels to know what it means.'

'Sounds to me like a nonce word, by analogy with hydroponics,' said Pascoe.

'Nonce, eh? Well, them perverts do have a language of their own.'

Wield came in before this could get silly and said, 'I think they started off making domestic solar panels, but now they're into all kinds of alternative energy sources and applications.'

'My God, Wieldy, you got shares, or what?'

Wield looked blank, which was easy. In fact it was

Edwin who had Helioponic shares. Financial openness was part of their unwritten partnership agreement. 'If you know how poor I am,' Digweed had said, 'you will not be forever expecting me to pay half of all those expensive foreign holidays your crooked friends doubtless subsidize for you in their Bermudan villas.'

'Sir,' said Novello from the phone. 'Mr Wulfstan *was* at the Park, but he's just headed back to town. Seems he's had to call an emergency committee meeting, something about the Music Festival needing a new location?'

'Must be mellowing,' said Dalziel. 'In the old days he'd have come round here and given us all a rollocking. Right, that's me. I'm off to put myself on Any Other Business. Pete, what are you up to?'

'I need to see Clark. He might have a line on the spray-can artist.'

'Oh aye? Well, he's up the dale with Maggie Burroughs. I've just been up there. She's got the search well organized, so try not to give the impression you're double-checking her. I know how heavy-footed you can be. Wieldy, you keep things steady here till George Headingley shows his ugly face, then see if you can find something useful to do. That everything?'

'Sir, shall I stick with these car sightings? I've got a couple of ideas,' said Novello.

'Ideas? Nice young lass like you shouldn't be having ideas,' said Dalziel. 'Nay, they'll keep. That's why red herrings are red, to preserve them. Anyone talked to the kiddies in Lorraine's class yet?'

'Not yet,' said Wield. 'Mrs Shimmings wanted to get the school routine going first.'

'I doubt if there'll be owt there, but someone had better do it. That's the job for you, Ivor. Off you go, chop chop.'

Novello turned swiftly and moved away through the door before her resentment could show.

'She did well,' Pascoe observed neutrally.

'She did her job,' growled Dalziel.

Pascoe glanced at Wield, who rubbed his chin.

'Jesus wept,' said the Fat Man.

He went to an open window and bellowed, 'Ivor!'

The woman turned.

'You did well,' shouted Dalziel.

Then, turning back to face the others, he said, 'There. Can't bear the thought of having you two looking at me all day like I'd drowned your kitten. Now can we all go off and do what we get paid to do, or would you like a big wet kiss from mother to help you on your way?'

FIVE

Rosie Pascoe was having a bad day at school.

She'd looked for Zandra as soon as she got into the yard, but she was nowhere to be found, and Miss Turner, their class teacher, told her that Mrs Purlingstone had phoned to say that Zandra was poorly and wouldn't be coming in.

At least that had meant she was able to hold the floor alone with her tales of treats and adventures at the seaside. But by playtime, as the heat of the day built up, she found her usual energy lacking and was content to stand aside from the intricate whirl of playground games.

All the voices seemed distant, like the TV with the sound turned low, and the playing children moved before her like figures on that small screen. It wasn't an unpleasant sensation, this distancing. Indeed it was the kind of mood in which she usually most easily made contact with her friend Nina. But there was no sign of her today, and then she remembered that Nina had been taken by the nix again and was probably still being held captive in his cave.

Out of the corner of her eye she glimpsed a figure beyond the high wire mesh which bounded the playground. Her heart full of hope she went towards it. The bright sunlight dazzled her, in fact she'd been irritated by bright light all day, and she couldn't see clearly, but as she got close she knew it wasn't Nina, and when she blinked she found there was no one there at all, and she was left clinging to the mesh like a marmoset in a cage.

Someone touched her shoulder and she turned quickly.

It was Miss Turner. She was a small woman, a lot shorter than Mummy, but somehow today she seemed to loom very high.

'Play's over, Rosie,' she said in a voice with the same distant, unreal quality. 'It's time to come inside.'

Some miles to the north, Shirley Novello was having a bad time in school too. She didn't mind kids, but she wasn't mad about them. And she did mind the assumption that her gender automatically meant she was the best person to talk to Lorraine's classmates, particularly when she felt she was doing an OK job on the car enquiry. But she had more sense than to complain, not in the middle of a missing child case. Here, if you were told it would help to wrestle in mud, you wrestled in mud.

Not that there was much chance of finding any mud to wrestle in. All the windows of the school were wide open, but a feather resting on a sill had as much chance of moving as on a dead man's lips.

The children were lethargic, partly because of the heat, partly because the initial charge of excitement at the police presence had faded, leaving them increasingly aware of the reason for it. Mrs Shimmings and Miss Blake, the class teacher, did their best to divert and distract, but they too were weighed down by their more specific fears for their lost pupil and, despite their best efforts, some of this filtered through.

Very little was forthcoming. Some of Lorraine's friends said that Lorraine had a 'secret place' up Ligg Beck, but when pressed as to its whereabouts, they looked at Novello like she was brain dead and said, 'We don't know. It was a secret!' Finally she pushed too hard and provoked a squall of sobbing from one girl which quickly spread to others, and the interview was over.

'I'll keep talking to them,' promised Mrs Shimmings as they walked down the corridor together. 'It's no use pressing with children this age. You've got to let things come in their own good time.'

Great, thought Novello. But you don't have to answer to a bunch of men who aren't all that impressed even when you've got something positive to report!

By 'bunch of men' she meant, of course, Dalziel and Pascoe, and to a lesser extent, Wield. On joining CID she'd quickly sussed out that what mattered most to an ambitious officer was how you rated with the terrible trio.

She'd observed with interest but without comment how her male colleagues reacted. Dalziel put the fear of God into them. His wrath was like being run over by a Centurion tank. On the other hand, going into battle, there's nothing an infantryman likes more than advancing behind a Centurion tank.

Pascoe was rated OK. Lots of concern for the troops. He'd long outlived his early disadvantage of a degree. Indeed, most of them would never even think about it if it wasn't for the Fat Man's occasional weighty witticisms.

And Wield was . . . Wield. Unreadable as a Chinese encyclopaedia, but containing everything a cop needed to know. There were stories about his private life which might have washed away another man's career. But against that unyielding crag, they broke and vanished back into the sea.

Word was that when Dalziel spoke, you obeyed; when Pascoe spoke, you listened; when Wield spoke, you took notes.

But Novello had come to see them rather differently.

The rumours about Wield she ignored. It was so clear to her he was gay that she couldn't understand the need for whisperings. He was a good cop and she could learn a lot from him. But, she guessed, he was also a cop who'd made a conscious decision to stay at sergeant rather than risk the greater exposure of higher rank. This she could understand, but had no intention of taking as a role model.

Pascoe. At first she'd liked him. He'd been welcoming, helpful, protective when she joined the squad. He still was. But when she'd talked about this with Maggie Burroughs who'd helped her a lot in her transfer to CID, the inspector had said, 'Watch out for the friendlies. They're sometimes the worst.' And when a few minutes after she started talking to the kids, Pascoe had stuck his head into the classroom and asked for a quick word with Mrs Shimmings, all his apologetic smile had said to her was that what he was doing was beyond debate far more important than what she was doing.

Which left Dalziel. A tank was just a machine, but a machine needs someone to run it. A mechanic. Or God. Jokes were made about the Holy Trinity, usually with Pascoe as Son and Wield as Holy Ghost. Novello as a sort of good Catholic favoured Pascoe as Holy Ghost. But big Andy Dalziel was beyond all dispute the Almighty. Get up his nose, and the best you could hope was a big sneeze might carry you a long way away. It was a small comfort to know no one was immune. Even that Spiritus Sanctus, Peter Pascoe, came in for a fair share of crap. So, *I believe in Andy Dalziel* was the first and last clause of the CID creed. But faith without works didn't get you into heaven and even though the fat prophet had forecast that talking to kids was a waste of time, he'd probably still expect some form of result.

It was therefore with relief that she found only Wield in the incident centre. He was poring over a thick file. In his hand was a can of mineral water.

He said, 'The fridge has turned up. Help yourself.'

Gratefully she took a can of lemonade. She would have liked to put it under her T-shirt and roll it around but she instinctively avoided anything which would draw her male colleagues' attention to her sex. Even Wield's.

Perhaps, she thought, we have a lot in common.

'Any luck?' he asked without looking up.

'Not much. Some talk of Lorraine having a secret place up Ligg Beck, but none of them knows where.'

'Well, they wouldn't, being a secret,' said Wield with a childlike logic she recognized. He closed the file. Upside down she read DENDALE.

She said, 'Nothing from the search team, Sarge?'

'Not a sign.'

'So it could be she's long gone.'

'Super seems to reckon they're still around here.'

She noticed the *they*. He noticed her noticing but didn't correct it.

'What do *you* think, Sarge?' she asked.

He stared at her reflectively. His eyes, she noticed for the first time, were rather beautiful, circles of Mediterranean blue round a dark grey centre set on a field of pristine white with not a red vein to be seen. It was like finding jewels in a ruin.

He said, 'I think you've got a notion you'd like to let out. Something to do with yon blue estate is my guess.'

This was opening enough. She went across to the wall map and said, 'The Highcross Moor road's got no turn-offs except a few farm tracks for four and a half miles till it swings east and joins the main road here. There's a pub, the Highcross Inn, at the junction. What I'd like to do is check out all the farms along the road and the pub too, to see if anyone else noticed the blue estate.'

It sounded pretty feeble now it was out. She was glad it wasn't the Fat Man she was talking to.

Wield said, 'We've had men out at all those farms.'

'Yes, Sarge. But they'll have been searching barns, out-buildings, stables and such. I'd be asking a specific question about a specific car.'

'You've got a feeling about this blue estate, haven't you?'

'Sort of,' she admitted reluctantly.

'You won anything on the National Lottery?' he enquired.

'Ten pound.'

'Not enough to retire on if Mr Dalziel catches you running around following hunches,' said Wield. 'But as I can't think of anything else for you to do, off you go. Keep in close contact though. And you get buzzed to come back here, no mucking about saying reception's bad because of the hills, that sort of crap. You come running. OK?'

'OK, Sarge. Thanks.'

And turning quickly before he could change his mind, she hurried out into the sweaty embrace of the panting sun.

As she got into her car she saw DI George Headingley's gleaming Lada turn into the car park. She sent her beat-up Golf roaring past him with a casual wave. George had always had a reputation as a careful man, but as retirement loomed closer, carefulness became an obsession. Privately, not a penny was spent unnecessarily and it was rumoured he'd worked out to the hour if not the minute the best time to take his pension. Professionally, he did everything by the book, and if the book didn't tell him what to do, he did what he thought would please the Chief Constable and Andy Dalziel, not necessarily in that order.

No way if he'd arrived ten minutes earlier would she have been heading out on a hunch. 'Make us a cup of tea, Shirl,' he would have said. 'Then you can take care of answering the phone till the Super gets back.'

But now, with one mighty bound, she was free. She gunned the car up the rising road, wound down the window and pulled up her T-shirt to let the cooling draught play upon her burning skin.

She didn't stop till she reached the high bend where Geoff Draycott thought the blue estate might have halted. Recognizing that a lot of people would be tempted to stop here for the view, the Council when they improved the road in response to Danby's growing prosperity had put down some hardstanding to make a small informal car park complete with rubbish bin.

Are we the only race in the world, she wondered, who if they visit a place of great natural beauty where there *isn't* a rubbish bin, would just dump their litter all over the ground?

She got out of the car and viewed the view. It was worth looking at in every direction. She had a pair of binoculars with her and through them she scanned the peaceful roofs of Danby, grey and blue slated, red, yellow, brown and ochre tiled, basking and baking far below. Then she followed the winding line of Ligg Beck up the valley. She began to feel her good feeling drain out of her as she reached a police Range Rover and remembered why she was here.

She picked out Maggie Burroughs wearing a very unofficial straw sun bonnet as she pored over a map on the open tailgate and talked into a radio. And standing a little apart in deep conversation with Sergeant Clark was Peter Pascoe, shirt-sleeved, his fair skin pinking, looking very like a twenties young gent out on a walking tour.

She continued her sweep up the valley, moving over the double line of searchers advancing slowly a half mile ahead of the Range Rover, till the slight eastwards twist put the valley head out of her vision.

And finally she came full circle and looked at the closest section, that which fell away immediately beneath her feet.

Now this *was* interesting. The valley narrowed the further up it you went, and this plus the location of the viewpoint on a spur of ground meant that the deep gash which marked the beck's course in the upper reaches was relatively close here. Of course the tucks and folds of the terrain meant a lot remained hidden. But a man standing up here and glimpsing a child walking along the path beside the ghyll, say at that point *there*, would have no problem moving down the valley flank, far less steep on this side than on the Neb, and cutting her off, say *there*.

She lowered the glasses and studied the scene without them. Now it all looked a lot further off. Well, it would, wouldn't it? But no reason someone stopping here shouldn't have a pair of binoculars. And with them it would be all too easy to establish that what you were looking at was one small girl, alone, except for one equally small dog . . .

All theory, of course. Not to be paraded naked before the sceptical gaze of the Holy Trinity. But clothe it with a couple of relevant facts . . .

She scanned the ground at the edge of the hardstanding in hope of seeing something to show that someone had headed down the slope. Rapidly she realized it was not a very profitable way of spending her time. She was no Chingachgook to read in bent and heather who had passed this way and when. Also probably every kid in every family who'd ever stopped here had run a little way down the fellside.

She went to the car, found a pair of plastic gloves, and removed the inner liner of the rubbish bin. It was packed full. This would have been a popular stopping place yesterday as the day wore on, and the presence of a Sunday tabloid on the top indicated it hadn't been emptied since. She tipped the contents on to the ground and began to sift through the lower strata. From her convent school Latin lessons the word *haruspex* popped into her mind; a soothsayer who based his prognostications on the entrails of animals. Good name for those FBI investigators she'd read about who specialized in the interpretation of trash. Could be Scotland Yard or MI5 had a few too, but it didn't rate high in the Mid-Yorkshire training programme. Possibly an expert could have made much of the food containers and wrappings which made up the greater part of the rubbish, but Novello concentrated on the rest and after a few minutes she had isolated a lithium 3V battery of the type used in some cameras, an empty Marlboro Lights cigarette packet, two Sunday papers (one broadsheet, one tabloid), a broken earring, and a tissue with a brown stain that might be blood.

These she bagged separately. The rest she replaced in the plastic liner, which she sealed with tape and placed in the boot of her car. She had no real hope that any of it would have anything to do with the case, but if it did, she didn't want to have to tell Dalziel that the rest of the potential evidence was in some municipal tip.

Now she scanned her map. There were four farms worth visiting. Her hopes were high. She felt things were going well.

A couple of hours later, things were grinding to a halt. Finding the farms was easy. Finding all the folk who might have been around on Sunday morning was less so. Soon, as she tramped across tussocky heather and grazed her knees and elbows clambering over drystone walls, all that was left of the famous 'feeling' was aching muscles and the beginnings of a heat rash under her arms.

But she was determined that whatever other accusation might be aimed at her, half-heartedness wasn't going to be on the agenda. Thoroughness, an old teacher had once told her, was its own reward. Which was just as well as by the time she crossed off the last farm, she had to acknowledge she had reaped no other.

So finally she came down to the Highcross Inn.

SIX

There was a RESIDENTS PARKING ONLY sign at either end of Holyclerk Street.

Dalziel nipped into a spot ahead of an old lady who scanned his screen furiously for sight of a resident's disc, found none, started to get out of her car to remonstrate, glimpsed that huge face regarding her with a Buddha's benevolence, felt her road rage evaporate, and drove on.

Had she followed her first instinct and dropped a lighted match into his petrol tank, Holyclerk Street would not have been surprised. There was very little of human emotion and appetite it hadn't seen during its long history.

Its name pointed its link with the great cathedral which loomed over the human dwellings like an ocean-going liner over a fleet of bumboats. It stood 'within the bell', which meant that anyone living here could set out at a brisk pace on the first note of any summons and guarantee being in his place by the last. Nowadays a house 'within the bell' usually cost at least 20 per cent more than a comparable house without, but it was not always thus.

The original medieval street containing the seminary from which it derived its name had by the reign of Queen Anne fallen almost completely into disrepair and disrepute. The timbered buildings had developed such alarming lists and been so often patched and propped, they looked like a file of drunken veterans staggering home from a very hard war. No person of wealth or standing would have dreamt of occupying one, and they had declined to low taverns, verminous lodging houses, and brothels.

That such a civic sore should pustulate within pissing distance of the cathedral was regarded by many good burghers as an offence against both God and Man. But as a substantial number of the said good burghers actually owned the houses and shared in their profits, Man delayed so long in providing a remedy that God grew impatient, and one dark September night, having first ensured the wind was in the right quarter, He tripped a drunken punk and her geriatric jo as they climbed the stairway to her reechy bed and sent their link flying like a meteor through a hole in the rotten boards down into the cellar where it landed in an open cask of illicit brandy.

The resultant fire left an ashen scar which for many years was regarded as lively evidence of the wrath of the living God, but when a combination of shanty town and Paddy's Market looked to be developing there, the City Fathers this time pre-empted the deity by sweeping the area clean of undesirables and initiating a building programme of dwellings fit for dignitaries of the Church.

It was these elegant residences that now lay before Dalziel's unimpressed eye. He knew little of medieval history and eighteenth-century fires, but he could look back to a period when the well-to-do had demonstrated their well-to-do-ness by migrating to the Green Belt, leaving the likes of Holyclerk Street to fragment into student flats and fly-by-night offices. But the Church had flexed its financial muscle (this was before its Commissioners had demonstrated their inability to serve either God or Mammon by losing several millions), purchased and refurbished, then made a killing when a hugely successful tele-adaptation of the Barchester novels cast a romantic glow over cathedral closes and made living 'within the bell' once more the thing.

The sun was laying its golden blade right down the centre of the street so there was no shade to be found. Dalziel thought of following the example of the owner of the white cabriolet parked in front of him which had been left with its top down and its expensive hi-fi equipment on open offer. Surely in these ecclesiastic surroundings such confidence was justified? He wound his window down an air-admitting fraction, walked a step or two away, remembered the Church Commissioners, and returned to wind the window up as far as it would go.

This second passing of the white cabriolet registered that it was a Saab 900, the property of a national car-hire company. He checked the Resident's parking disc. It was marked *temporary* and the address on it was 41 Holyclerk Street. The Wulfstan house.

Glancing up at the cathedral tower, he nodded appreciatively and moved on.

At number 41 he leaned on the bellpush a measured second then stepped back and waited.

In its previous posh manifestation he'd guess this street's doors had been opened by uniformed maids, but nowadays domestic servants were pretty thin on the ground, if only because the kind of people who needed the work weren't prepared to kow-tow to the kind of prats who needed the servants.

He recognized instantly the woman who opened the door though it was fifteen years since they had met.

And Chloe Wulfstan's face showed that she recognized him.

'Mr Dalziel,' she said.

Age hadn't changed her much. In fact she looked a lot younger than last time he'd seen her, but that wasn't so surprising. Then, the news of her daughter's disappearance

146

not only drained the blood from her face but also melted the flesh from her bones. But he had never seen her cry, and somehow he knew that she hadn't cried in private either. All her energy had gone to holding herself together even at the expense of locking everything inside.

No point in mucking about.

He said, 'I'm sorry to trouble you, Mrs Wulfstan. You'll have heard about this lass who's gone missing from Danby?'

'It was on the radio,' she said. 'And in this morning's paper. Is there any news?'

The voice was level, conventionally polite, as if he were the vicar being invited to take tea. Fifteen years back he recalled that she'd still retained a trace of the accent of her birth and upbringing on Heck Farm; educated, yes, but enough there to remind you that she was a Mid-Yorkshire lass. Now that had entirely gone. She could have been presenting *Woman's Hour*.

Over her shoulder he could see a hallway hung with prints of musical cartoons. Down a broad staircase drifted the tinkle of a piano and a woman's voice singing.

'When your mother dear to my door draws near,
And my thoughts all centre there to see her enter
Not on her sweet face first off falls my gaze
But a little past her . . .'

There was the sound of discord as if someone had banged a hand down on the piano keys and a man's voice said, 'No, no. Too much too soon. At this point he is still trying to be matter of fact, still trying to be rational about his own irrational behaviour.'

That voice. He thought he recognized it. Both voices in fact. The woman's was the lass he'd heard singing on the radio at Pascoe's the previous morning. Same bloody set of songs too. His memory took him back to the first

147

time he'd heard them ... He wrenched it back to the other voice, the man's. That rather too perfect English. Surely it was the Turnip. Despite Wield's frequent reminders that Arne Krog was a Norwegian, not a Swede, Dalziel had persisted in his awful joke. Poncy sod had once dared correct his English, and Dalziel was an unforgiving God.

'Mr Dalziel?' said Chloe Wulfstan.

He realized he hadn't answered her question.

'No. No news,' he said.

'I'm sorry for it,' she said. 'How are ... no, I needn't ask.'

'How're the parents?' he concluded. 'Just like you'd expect. You'd likely know the mother. Came from Dendale. Elsie Coe afore she married.'

'Margaret Coe's girl? Oh, God. Margaret was very ill last year. Her recovery seemed a miracle. Now I wonder if it wasn't a curse. Is that a wicked thing to say, Mr Dalziel?'

He shrugged impassively, denying the inclination rather than the qualification to judge.

She went on, in a curious reflective tone. 'I got used to thinking wicked things, you know. When I saw their sympathetic faces, women like Margaret Coe, I used to think: inside you're really glad it's me, not you, glad it's my Mary who's gone, not your Elsie or ...'

She stopped as if someone had alerted her to her hostessly duties and said, briskly, 'Is it Walter you want to see, Mr Dalziel? He is here, but he's in the middle of a meeting about the Music Festival. They have to find a new location for the opening concert ... but of course, you'd know that. I'm being very rude keeping you on the doorstep. Do come inside. I'll let him know you're here.'

He advanced into the hallway. It was a relief to be out

of the sun's direct rays, but even with all the windows open, its heat walked in with him.

You'd have thought a bugger into solar power would have installed air-conditioning, grumbled Dalziel.

Chloe Wulfstan knocked gently on a door, opened it and slipped inside.

In his brief glimpse into the room which looked like an old-fashioned oak-panelled study, Dalziel saw three people, one full face, one in profile, and one just the back of a head above an armchair. But it was the back of the head that he focused on. He felt something inside him tighten for a second, his stomach, his heart, it wasn't possible to be anatomically precise, but it was the kind of feeling he couldn't recollect having had for a long long time.

The door opened again and Mrs Wulfstan came out. The piano had started again upstairs.

> 'But a little past her seeking something after
> There where your own dear features would appear
> Lit with love and laughter . . .'

The woman in the chair had turned her head and was peering towards the doorway. Their gazes met. Then the door closed.

'If you can give him just a minute,' said Chloe Wulfstan apologetically. 'He should be able to bring the meeting to a close, then the other committee members won't have to hang around waiting for Walter to return. In here, if you please.'

She led him into a drawing room at the back of the house with French windows wide open on to a long garden whose lawn showed the effect of the drought.

'One is tempted, of course,' she said following his gaze. 'But I'm afraid that we've all become water-vigilantes, and if anyone thought our lawn was looking a little too green . . . Quite right too, I suppose. But when I think that we gave up Dendale to provide a sure supply for the future . . . it makes you think, doesn't it?'

Her tone was now bright, polite and light.

'It does that,' he said. 'Reservoir's right down. Do you ever go back to take a look, Mrs Wulfstan?'

'No,' she said. 'I never do, Mr Dalziel.'

He studied her for a moment, pulling at his heavy lower lip. It came across as a sceptical assessing stare, but in fact his eyes were seeing another face completely.

'Would you like a glass of something cold?' asked Chloe Wulfstan.

'What? Oh aye, that 'ud be nice,' he said. 'By the by, there's a car outside, white Saab, got a visitor's parking disc . . .'

'That's Arne's. You remember Arne? Arne Krog, the singer. He's staying with us during the festival. And Inger. His accompanist. She's here, too.'

'Well, she would be. Accompanying him,' said Dalziel. He smiled to show he was attempting a joke but she just looked faintly puzzled, then left the room.

Old habits die hard and Dalziel immediately started wandering round, glancing at the papers on an open bureau, trying the odd drawer, but his heart wasn't in it. Upstairs the piano had fallen silent again and there'd been another spate of raised voices. Suddenly the door burst open and a tall slim woman strode into the room. She was wearing black cotton trousers and a black T-shirt which accentuated the whiteness of her skin and the paleness of her long ash blonde hair. She stopped dead at the sight of Dalziel and regarded him impassively out of slate-grey eyes which somehow looked ageless by comparison with the rest of her which looked early twenties.

He put the voice and place together and said, 'How do, Miss Wulfstan. I'm Detective Superintendent Dalziel.'

If he'd expected his prescience to impress, he was disappointed. If anything, she seemed amused, a faint smile touching her long still face like a sunstart on a mountain tarn.

'How do, Superintendent. You being tekken care of, or have you just brok in?'

For a second he thought she was taking the piss by imitating his accent. Before he could decide between the put-down oblique (*throat sore from too much singing, luv?*) and the put-down direct (*happen you'll make a nice grown-up woman when your mind catches up with your tits*), another woman came into the room, blonde also, but shorter, more solidly built, and about twenty years older.

She said, 'Are we finished? If so, I shall go and sunbathe.'

'Not much point asking me, luv. I'm not the one making all the durdum. You'd best ask the lord and master. Him that knows it all!'

The Yorkshire accent remained in place. So, not a piss-taking exercise after all. Dalziel felt grateful he hadn't spoken, but only mildly. Embarrassment didn't rate high on his list of pains and punishments.

'Arne will help as long as you want help,' replied the other woman.

This one was Inger Sandel, the pianist. She'd put on a bit of weight in fifteen years and he might not have recognized the face. But the voice with its flat Scandinavian accent triggered his memory. Not that she'd spoken much all those years back. It had nothing to do with use of a foreign language. In fact, the accent apart, her English was excellent. It was simply that she never said more than the situation warranted. Perhaps she saved her expressive energies up for her playing, but even here she had opted for being an accompanist. In his head, the voice belonging to the face glimpsed through the open door said, 'In *Lieder* recitals, the pianist and the singer are equal partners.' But to Andy Dalziel an accompanist was still someone who thumped a guiding rhythm while the boys in the bar roared out their love of Annie Laurie or their loathing of Adolf Hitler.

'Help!' exclaimed Elizabeth Wulfstan. 'You call non-stop carping *help*, do you?'

There was little heat in her voice. She made it sound like a real question.

'I think you are lucky to have someone with Arne's experience to advise you,' said Inger, very matter-of-fact.

'You reckon? Well if he's so fucking good, why's he not singing at La fucking Scala?'

'Because Mid-Yorkshire is so much cooler than Milano at this time of year, or at least it used to be,' said Arne Krog, timing his arrival with a perfection Dalziel guessed came from listening in the hallway for a good cue. Wanker. But there was no denying the Turnip had aged well. Bit heavier all round, but still the same easy movement, the same regular good-looking features with that faint trace of private amusement round the mouth which had once pissed Dalziel off.

At sight of the fat detective now, however, the face became entirely serious and he advanced with hand out-stretched, saying, 'Mr Dalziel, how are you? It's been a long time.'

They shook hands.

'Nice to see you too, Mr Krog,' said Dalziel. 'I'm only sorry about the circumstances. You'll likely have heard there's a little lass been missing from Danby since yesterday morning? We're talking to possible witnesses.'

'And you have come to see me?' said Krog, nodding as if in confirmation of something half-expected. 'Yes, of course, I was at Danby yesterday, but I do not think I can be of help. But please, ask your questions. Perhaps I saw something and did not realize the significance.'

Dalziel was unimpressed by this openness. Leaving your car in full view near a crime scene could as easily be evidence of impulse as innocence, and while you might keep quiet initially in the hope you hadn't been spotted, once you got a hint that you had, you got your admission in quick.

He said, 'Happen you did. You parked on the edge of Ligg Common, right?'

He'd made an instant decision to question him in front of the other two. That made it more casual, less threatening. Also it provided an audience who knew him a lot better than Dalziel did, and while there was little chance of such a seasoned performer getting stage fright, if he resorted to any bits of stage business, they might notice and react.

Neither of the women offered to leave the room, nor did they disguise their interest in what the men were saying.

'That's right.'

'Why?'

Many people would have shown, or pretended, puzzlement, obliging him to be more precise. Krog didn't.

'I felt restless yesterday morning, hemmed in by the heat and the city. So I went for a drive in the country. I felt like a walk, somewhere where the air was fresh and I could be alone, so that if I opened my lungs and sang a few scales, I would frighten nobody except perhaps the sheep. I chose Danby because I know the countryside round there. I have sung often in St Michael's Hall during previous festivals and I always like to take a stroll by myself before I perform.'

That was pretty comprehensive, thought Dalziel.

He glanced at Elizabeth Wulfstan. Something about her

that bothered him. Mebbe it was just those old eyes in that young face.

He said, 'How about you, luv? Do you like a walk afore you perform?'

She shook her head.

'Not me. On wi' the motley and over the plonk,' she said.

'And you, Miss?'

This to Sandel.

'No. I take exercise for necessity, not for recreation,' she said.

He returned his attention to Krog.

'So where did your walk take you?'

'Across the common, to the right, the east that would be? I'm not so hot on points of the compass.'

'Aye. East. Not up the beck path, then?'

'No. I had thought of going up the beck, but when I got out of the car and realized how warm it was, I decided to head in this other direction. There is farmland over there, with trees, no big woods, just some copses, but at least they provide some shade. The little girl went up the beck path, did she? I wish now I had done so too. Perhaps if I had . . .'

Chloe Wulfstan had come back into the room, bearing Dalziel's cold drink. As she handed it to him, behind her back Krog made a little gesture of the head, inviting Dalziel to continue his interrogation out of her presence.

Ignoring the gesture, Dalziel sipped the freshly pressed lemonade and said, 'That's grand, luv. So you saw nowt, Mr Krog?'

'Of course I saw sky and earth and trees, and I heard birds and sheep and insects. But I did not see or hear any other person that I recall. I'm sorry.'

'That's OK. You'd see the Neb too, of course.'

'What?'

154

First time he didn't appear fully briefed.

'The Neb. Being on the other side of the valley, you'd not be able to avoid looking over at it, I'd have thought. You didn't think of strolling up there along the Corpse Road, say, and taking a look down into Dendale?'

He was still speaking over Mrs Wulfstan's shoulder. Her eyes were fixed unblinkingly on his face.

'No, I did not,' said Krog angrily. 'I have told you what I did, Mr Dalziel. If you have any more questions to ask, I think that common courtesy, if not common decency, requires that you ask them elsewhere.'

'By gum, I reckon tha talks better English than a lot of us natives, Mr Krog,' said Dalziel. He caught Elizabeth Wulfstan's eye as he spoke and fluttered a gentle wink her way. That got him that faint, brief smile again.

Chloe Wulfstan said, 'If you're done here, Superintendent, Walter's meeting is over. He thought you might prefer to talk to him in private, so if you care to go into the study . . .'

'Thanks, luv,' said Dalziel. He finished his lemonade, handed her the glass, nodded pleasantly at the other two women and went out of the door.

Arne Krog followed.

'You are seeing Walter about the Danby girl, too?' he asked.

'Happen,' said Dalziel.

'Do you really think it has something to do with Dendale all those years ago?'

'Any reason it should have, Mr Krog?'

'I drove to Danby yesterday morning, remember? I saw those words painted on the old railway bridge,' said Krog sombrely. 'At the time I thought little of it. Graffiti these days is like advertising. You see the signs without registering the message, not consciously, anyway. But later, when I heard . . .'

'Mustn't jump to conclusions,' said Dalziel with the kindly authority of one who in his time had jumped to more amazing conclusions than Red Rum.

'You are right, of course. But please, I beg you, think of Chloe, Mrs Wulfstan. In this house we try to avoid mention of anything which might remind her of that dreadful time.'

He let the note of accusation sound loud and clear.

'Very noble,' said Dalziel. 'But a waste of time.'

'I'm sorry?'

'You don't imagine a day's gone by in the last fifteen years without her thinking of her daughter, do you, Mr Krog?' said Dalziel. 'Thing like that, just waking up each morning reminds her of it.'

He spoke with great force and Krog looked at him curiously.

'And you too, Superintendent. I think you have thought of it.'

'Oh aye. But not every day. And not like her. I just lost a suspect, not a daughter.'

'I think perhaps if you had, you would not have lost your suspect also,' said Krog, making a sharp chopping movement with his right hand.

'For a foreigner, you're not so bloody daft, Mr Krog,' said Andy Dalziel.

SEVEN

Peter Pascoe, being as Ellie put it not exactly a New Man but certainly a one-careful-lady-owner, genuine-low-mileage, full-service-record-available kind of used man, had tried his hardest to like Inspector Maggie Burroughs, but he couldn't quite manage it. That she was efficient was beyond doubt. That she had become a sort of unofficial shop steward for all Mid-Yorkshire's women officers was most commendable, given the number of female high fliers who adopted the Thatcher principle of *I'm aboard, pull up the gangplank*! That she was sociable, reasonable, and desirable, was generally agreed.

And yet . . . and yet . . .

'I don't think I'd have taken to her even if she'd been a fellow,' Pascoe told his wife in an effort to assure her that this was not a gender issue.

He was a little taken aback when Ellie's response was to hover between screaming with rage and laughter. Happily she had opted for the latter even when he compounded his unwitting condescension by adding, 'No, no, I assure you, I really do see her as the future of the Force . . .'

'Exactly. And like most men approaching an interesting age, the last thing you can look at with any equanimity is the future.'

Perhaps she was right. But certainly not in every respect.

Because one identifiable factor in, but uncitable reason for, his dislike of Burroughs was that he'd detected she didn't care for Ellie, and that, especially in another woman, showed a deficiency of judgement beyond forgiveness or repair.

Unlike Dalziel, who let dislike show like buttocks through torn trousers, Pascoe hid his behind smiling affability.

'Hi, Maggie,' he said. 'How's it going?'

'Not a damn thing so far,' she said. 'I'm beginning to agree with the locals that she's not here.'

'Car, you reckon? That's what Shirley Novello is plugging. Not to any great effect, mind you.'

He made a wry face to dissociate himself from the Fat Man's put-down of the DC, but Maggie Burroughs was shaking her head.

'No, not a car, but ghosts and ghoulies and things that go bump in the night, or the morning in this case. They're all convinced this Benny guy's got her, and it's catching. What's the official line on that, sir? I mean, it is all bollocks, isn't it?'

'Benny is to Danby what Freddy was to Elm Street,' said Pascoe. 'A legend based on a terrible reality.'

He saw her hide a smile and guessed he must have sounded a touch portentous.

'Just make sure every inch of ground gets covered,' he said abruptly. 'Sergeant Clark around?'

'Yes. Using his local knowledge to singularly little effect,' said Burroughs scornfully.

'He's a good man,' said Pascoe. 'You know he was the resident constable over in Dendale when it all happened fifteen years ago?'

'I doubt if there's anyone over the age of two he hasn't told that,' said Burroughs. 'He's hanging around somewhere.'

Advice formed in his mind. *Make friends unless you feel strong enough to make enemies.* But he kept it to himself.

Perhaps she was tomorrow's version of Andy Dalziel. His own philosophy was, *You don't have to suffer fools gladly, but for a lot of the time it makes sense to suffer quietly*. In any case, he didn't think Clark was a fool, just the kind of steady, stolid, old-fashioned sergeant a go-getter like Burroughs would see as a dinosaur.

He found Clark pulling on a cigarette in the stingy shade of a clump of furze.

He dropped the butt-end guiltily at Pascoe's approach and ground it under his heel.

'Make sure it's out,' said Pascoe. 'I'd rather you destroyed your lungs than set fire to the fellside. So, tell me about Jed Hardcastle.'

'Oh aye. Jed. Thing you should know is, Jed's the youngest of the Hardcastles out of Dendale . . .'

'Yes, yes, and he lives at Stirps End and he's got a sister, June, and they don't get on with their dad, I know all that stuff,' said Pascoe impatiently. 'What I want from you is why you think he's responsible for the graffiti.'

He'd got his information from Mrs Shimmings, never suspecting how much his interruption had pissed off Shirley Novello.

'Jed Hardcastle?' the head teacher had said. 'Yes, I know him well. His eldest sister was one of the Dendale girls, but you'll know that.'

'Yes,' said Pascoe. 'Tell me about Jed.'

'Well, he was the youngest of the three Hardcastle children, only two years old when they moved over here, so he did all his schooling in Danby.'

'So the move can't have had much effect on him?' said Pascoe.

'Growing up in a family where a child's gone missing must have had an effect, I imagine,' she said quietly. 'And in the Hardcastle family, there'd not be much doubt about it. None of the other kids were ever allowed to forget what happened to Jenny. Cedric blamed himself for not keeping a closer eye on her, and in reaction he brought up June, her young sister, like she was going to be Empress of China. She couldn't do anything without close supervision. Didn't matter so much when she was a child, but when she got to be a teenager . . . well, you know what teenage girls are like.'

'I'm looking forward to finding out,' said Pascoe. 'My girl's seven.'

'Then be warned. At seven, June was a quiet biddable child, but by the time she got to fifteen, she'd had rebellion bred into her. One day she took off to town. They found her and brought her back. She waited a year then took off again, this time to London. It took months, but finally they made contact with her. But she's not coming back, she's made that quite clear.'

'And Jed?'

'The same story but different. He suffered both ways. From over protection when he should have been learning how to flex his wings. And from the Yorkshire farmer's assumption that an only son will follow in his father's footsteps when he's dead, but till that time he'll act as unpaid, unprivileged farm labourer. It didn't help that Jed's a slightly built lad, and quite sensitive. To be told that your dead sister was a better help about the place when she was half your age can't be very encouraging.'

'But he didn't follow his sister to the bright lights?'

'No. He got into a bit of bother, nothing serious, teenage vandalism, that sort of stuff. And life round the farm was one long slanging match with his father, so I gather. Heaven knows how it might have ended, but Mr Pontifex – it's one of his farms that Cedric leases – saw the way the wind was blowing and took young Jed under his wing, gave him a job helping round the estate office. Like I say, he's bright, picks things up quickly, could do well in the right environment.'

'Which isn't mucking out byres?'

'Especially not with your father telling you how useless you are all the time,' agreed Mrs Shimmings.

'And he still lives at home?'

'That was the main aim of the exercise,' she said. 'One thing everyone agrees on. If Jed leaves home too, his mother will either kill herself or her husband before next quarter day.'

No doubt he could have got some of this from Clark, but when it came to psychological profiling of the young of Danby, he preferred Mrs Shimming's keener professional eye.

Clark said, 'After we talked yesterday, I made out a list of possibles. We'd had a bit of bother with these spray-can jokers a while back and I'd tracked it back to a bunch of half a dozen of 'em . . .'

'But not Hardcastle,' said Pascoe. 'I ran his name through the computer. Nothing known.'

'Not enough evidence to go to court, so I dealt with it myself,' said Clark, making a small chopping gesture with his big right hand. Pascoe regarded him blankly. The mythology that there'd been a time when a clip round the ear from your friendly local bobby produced good upstanding citizens was not one he subscribed to, though he had to admit that healthy terror at the approach of Fat Andy did seem to have a temporarily salutary effect.

'So you had a short list. How come you picked out Hardcastle?'

'Made enquiries,' said Clark vaguely. 'Three of the lads I spoke to pointed the finger at Jed and his mate, Vernon Kittle.'

He didn't make the gesture this time, but Pascoe could

imagine the nature of the enquiries. What was more important was the reliability of the replies.

'This Kittle, anything known?'

'Bit of juvenile. Thinks he's a hard case. Impresses Jed, but not many others.'

'So why didn't you do something about this last night?' asked Pascoe.

'Sunday. Every bugger's off doing something, so it took me till last night to get hold of most on 'em.'

'Even so . . .'

'And Jed weren't home,' continued Clark. 'Went off to the seaside with Kittle and a couple of birds in Kittle's van. Molly, that's Mrs Hardcastle, she said there was no telling when he'd get back. Lads . . . well, you know. So I thought I might as well leave it till morning and pass it on to you.'

So he'd been right. A gift to pay him back for protecting the sergeant from the wrath of Dalziel the previous day. They didn't like to be beholden, these Yorkshiremen. And they didn't like to be treated as fools, as Maggie Burroughs might find out to her cost some day.

He said, 'Tell me, Nobby, all this stuff about Dendale, what do you reckon? Waste of time or could it lead somewhere?'

The sergeant hesitated, almost visibly weighing up the implications of the new intimacy implied by use of his nickname.

Then he said, 'Happen it could. But I hope not.'

'Why not? If it turns out there's a connection, we could solve four mysteries for the price of one.'

'Mebbe. But what if we're just waking a lot of sleeping dogs for nowt? Folk were just about getting to be able to think of Dendale without just thinking about them poor lasses. That were terrible, but life's full of terrible things, and they shouldn't be let spoil everything that's lovely.'

He spoke defiantly, as though anticipating objection or more probably mockery for his fancy words.

'And Dendale was lovely, was it?' said Pascoe.

'Oh, yes. It were a grand place, full of grand folk. Oh, we had our bad 'uns, and we had our ups and downs, but nought we couldn't sort ourselves. I'd have been happy to see my time out there, I tell you, promotion or not.'

He spoke with a fervour that made Pascoe smile.

'You make it sound like Paradise,' he said.

'Well, if it weren't Paradise, it were right next door to it, and as near as I'm like to get,' said Clark. 'Then it all got spoilt. From the moment Mr Pontifex sold his land, that's how most people saw it.'

'So what does that make Mr Pontifex? The serpent? Or just poor gullible Eve?'

He'd gone too far with his light ironic touch, he saw instantly. Your Yorkshireman enjoys a bit of broad sarcasm but is rightly suspicious that light irony conceals the worm of patronage.

'Be able to see for yourself,' the sergeant said gruffly. 'Jed works for him, so the Grange is where we'll need to go if you want to talk to the lad.'

'Oh, I do, I do,' said Pascoe. 'Lead on.'

The Grange turned out to be a pleasant surprise, not the grim granite block of Yorkshire baronial he'd been expecting, but a long low Elizabethan house in mellow York stone.

The estate office occupied what looked like a converted stables. No sign that anyone here rode anything more lively than the big blue Daimler standing before the house.

They parked in the shade of some old yew trees and walked across the yard towards the office. Its door opened as they approached and a man came out. He was silver-haired, rising seventy, with a narrow, rather supercilious face. He carried a walking stick with a handle in the shape of a fox cast in silver, a perfect match for his hair; and in fact the stick did seem to be for effect rather than need as he came to meet them with a bouncy sprightly step.

'Sergeant Clark,' he said. 'This is a terrible business. Have I the pleasure of addressing Superintendent Dalziel?'

A man who can believe that can believe anything, was the reply which sprang to Pascoe's mind but fortunately didn't make it any further.

'No, sir. Detective Chief Inspector Pascoe. Mr Dalziel sends his compliments but is detained in town.'

A smile broke out on the man's face, changing its whole caste.

'Not the mode of speech my spies have led me to expect from Mr Dalziel,' he said. 'And now I look more closely at you, I see that neither are you the mode of man. My apologies. I really must learn to hold my fire.'

He had come very close and taken Pascoe's hand. Now Pascoe understood the cause of that screwed-up, apparently supercilious expression. The man was dreadfully short-sighted. Presumably the stick was for detecting obstacles on unfamiliar terrain.

Clark had taken a few steps towards the office. He paused and looked at Pascoe enquiringly. Pascoe gave him a slight nod and he went inside.

'So tell me, Mr Pascoe, is there any news?' asked Pontifex.

'I'm afraid not,' said Pascoe. 'We can only hope.'

'And pray,' said the man. 'I have heard that locally they are speaking of the man Lightfoot that so many blamed for the Dendale disappearances. Surely there can be nothing in this?'

Pascoe had heard the word *surely* spoken with more conviction.

He said, 'At the moment, sir, we are keeping a completely open mind.'

The man had released his hand but was still standing uncomfortably close. Pascoe turned as though to look at the house, using this as an excuse to step away.

'Lovely old building,' he said appreciatively. 'Elizabethan?'

'At its core. With later additions but always in the style.'

'You're lucky to have had such tasteful ancestors,' said Pascoe.

'Not really. The Pontifex connection only dates back to my father whose eagerness to modernize the interior probably did more damage to the structure than anything in the previous four hundred years.'

'So he bought the estate, did he?'

'Such as it was in the late twenties. Chap who owned it went under in the Depression. Too many bad guesses. My father moved in and set about expanding. Anything that came up, he bought, which was how he came to own a good number of farms over in Dendale. But not enough to form a viable whole. An estate to be workable needs to have unity, to be contained within a common boundary. There were too many gaps across in Dendale. If the dam hadn't come up, they would have had to be sold anyway.'

Pascoe got a sense of hearing an excuse well rehearsed and often repeated. He guessed that in the eyes of some what was simply sequence – Pontifex selling, the dam being built, and the children disappearing – had become a chain of cause and effect. But it was surprising to find a presumably level-headed businessman affected by such idle chatter.

'Sir, he's gone.'

It was Clark who'd emerged from the office.

'Gone? Where?'

'Estate manager says he saw us out of the window and next thing he knew, the lad had vanished.'

'Was it Jed you wanted to see?' said Pontifex, sounding relieved. 'Any particular reason?'

'Just checking with everyone to see if they noticed anyone strange wandering around yesterday, sir,' Pascoe prevaricated.

'Of course. One of your chaps called. Wasn't able to help him, I'm afraid. You've seen how unreliable my eyesight is.'

Did he want an affidavit? wondered Pascoe.

He shook hands and took his leave. As he walked back to the cars, he asked Clark, 'Pontifex got any family?'

'Daughter. He's divorced. Wife got custody.'

'So he lives here alone. Does he help a lot of lads or is Jed Hardcastle unique?'

Clark shot him a disapproving glance.

'Nothing of *that*,' he said with distaste. 'There's never been a sniff of *that*.'

'I wasn't suggesting *that*,' protested Pascoe. Or was I? From the sound of it, *that* was still a stonable offence round Danby. Better warn Wieldy!

'I reckon truth is that Mr Pontifex feels he owes the Hardcastles something,' continued Clark. 'Lot of folk would agree. I mean, mebbe if he'd not sold his land . . .'

'But there'd have been a compulsory purchase order, wouldn't there?' objected Pascoe.

'Lot of difference between compulsion and profit,' said Clark with Old Testament sternness.

'You think he might be to blame in some degree, then,' said Pascoe curiously.

'Well, if it were someone local like Benny Lightfoot took them lasses, it could be that finding himself sold up and moved out triggered something off in him that might else have laid buried till his dying day.'

From Old Testament sentence to modern psycho-babble! Which was not to deny the possibility that there could be something in it. There'd been no such suggestion in the file, though. Fifteen years ago, offender profiling had been the job of a police artist, and even today in certain parts of Yorkshire it was an art practised by consenting officers in private.

Pascoe asked, 'Was the Lightfoot cottage part of Pontifex's estate?'

'No. Belonged to old Mrs Lightfoot, Benny's gran. Way it was, her husband had it as a tied cottage from Heck when Arthur Allgood were farming there. When old Lightfoot died, his son Saul took it over on the same tie.'

'That's Benny's father, the one who drowned?'

'You keep your lugs open,' said Clark, admiring again. 'That's right. After he died and Marion fell out with the old lady and took her kids off back to town, everyone thought Arthur would soon have her out of Neb Cottage to make way for a new man. But before he could do it, lo and behold, he snuffed it too! A hundred years ago I reckon they'd have had the old girl down for a witch.'

'But what difference did that make? The cottage would still be tied.'

'Oh aye. But now it belonged to Chloe Allgood, Arthur's daughter, her that married Mr Wulfstan. They wanted to hang on to Heck for a holiday place, but the rest of the farm they were happy to sell. Naturally, Mr Pontifex's agent were round there in a flash.'

'But Pontifex didn't get Neb Cottage?'

'No, he didn't. Turned out the old lady had got hold of Chloe right after her dad's funeral and talked her into selling her the cottage. No one knows where the money came from – word was that she'd had a bit of insurance on her man and put it all into a bigger insurance on her son. Well, she knew that long as Saul were alive, she'd be OK, but if owt happened to him, she'd be in trouble.'

'Bright lady,' said Pascoe.

'Oh aye. You had to get up early in the morning to reach market before Mr Pontifex,' said Clark, laughing. 'I gather he weren't best pleased when he found he weren't getting Neb Cottage along with the rest of the Heck holdings.'

'So what happened when Pontifex decided to sell up to the Water Board?'

'That were the finish, really. Most as owned their own places caved in and sold. Mr Wulfstan at Heck made a fuss, but it didn't get him anywhere. Only old Mrs Lightfoot held out to the end and they'd have had to send the bailiffs in to drag her out if she hadn't been taken ill with a stroke. It was all too much for her, they reckoned, the move and all that business about Benny. So they carried her off in an ambulance and 'dozed the cottage quick as maybe. It was a right shame, her ending her time in the dale like that. Something else on Mr Pontifex's conscience, they reckoned.'

'People blamed him, did they?'

'Aye. For everything. The move. And the vanishings. They were linked in people's minds, you see. And in Mr Pontifex's, too. That's why he gave Ced Hardcastle Stirps End, which by all accounts had been as good as promised to Jack Allgood who were twice the farmer Cedric ever was. And it didn't stop there. Like I say, when he saw what was happening between Jed and his father, he stepped in and gave the boy a job in his office.'

'After all those years?' said Pascoe. 'Now that's a tender conscience.'

'Aye, in some folks it's like game. Longer it hangs, tenderer it gets.'

Pascoe smiled and said, 'Ever thought of writing for *The Archers*, Sergeant? They pay good money for lines like that.'

They had reached their cars and were standing in the shade of a tall yew tree. It was pleasantly cool here out of the skull-drilling rays of the relentless sun.

'So whither away, Sergeant?'

'Sir?' Puzzled.

'It's your patch. I'm sure round here the word is that fear wists not to evade as Clark wists to pursue.'

'*Sir*?' The monosyllable now bewildered.

'Where will we find the lad?' Pascoe spelled it out.

'He'll have gone home, won't he? Where else?' said Clark confidently. 'You all right, sir?'

Pascoe had suddenly reached out to rest his hand against the rough bark of the yew tree.

'Fine,' he said. 'Someone must have walked across my grave. That's what comes of standing under this church-yard tree.'

He moved briskly towards his car. He looked pale.

Clark said anxiously, 'You sure, sir?'

'Yes, I'm fine,' said Pascoe with some irritation. 'And there's work to do. Just lead the way to Stirps End with all the majestic instancy you can muster, Sergeant!'

EIGHT

Ellie Pascoe was breaking the speed limit even before she got out of her own short driveway. She knew it was stupid, and by great effort of will got to braking distance of thirty miles per hour by the end of the street. It was only four miles to the school and the difference between driving like normal and driving like a lunatic was significant only in the soul.

Miss Martindale greeted her with a face as placidly reassuring as her voice on the phone had been.

'Nothing to worry about, Mrs Pascoe,' she said. 'Miss Turner thought she seemed a little bit *distant*, that was how she put it. Reluctant to get on with anything, and downright snappy if pressed. We all have days like that, days when we'd rather spend time inside ourselves than face outside demands. Happens to me all the time. Then Miss Turner noticed Rosie was a bit hot and flushed. Probably only the start of a summer cold. Getting hot and then cooling off all the time makes children susceptible. No real problem, but better nipped in the bud with half an aspirin and the rest of the day in bed.'

The soothing flow of words relaxed Ellie, even though she recognized that this was what they were meant to do. Miss Martindale was a bright young woman. No; more than that; Ellie knew a lot of bright young women, but Martindale was one of the rare breed she felt her own genius rebuked by. Not that they were in competition, but on the rare occasions when they did lock horns, it was always Ellie who found herself giving ground.

She tried to explain this to Peter, who'd said, 'Whatever she's taking, I wonder if she'll give me the name of her supplier?'

Rosie was sitting on the edge of the bed in the small medical room watched over by the school's massively maternal secretary. When she saw her mother, she said accusingly, 'I told you you shouldn't have made me go to school this morning.'

Thanks a bunch, kid, thought Ellie.

She gave her a hug, then examined her closely. Her face certainly looked a bit flushed.

'Not feeling so good, darling?' she said, trying to keep it matter of fact. 'Bed's the best place for you. Let's get you home.'

She thanked Miss Martindale who smiled reassuringly, but from the secretary, who clearly had her down as the kind of mother who sent her ailing child to school rather than spoil her own social life, all she got was an accusing glare. Ellie responded with a sweet smile. OK, the head might have the Indian sign on her, but she wasn't going to kow-tow to a sodding typist.

On the way home she chatted brightly, but Rosie hardly responded. In the house, Ellie said, 'Straight to bed, I think. Then I'll bring you a nice cool drink, shall I?'

Rosie nodded and let her mother unbutton her dress, something which in recent months had brought a fierce, *I can do that myself*!

Ellie made her comfortable in bed then went down to the kitchen and poured a glass of home-made lemonade. Then she poured another. Sick-bed circumstances demanded a bit of indulgence.

'Here we are, darling,' she said. 'I brought one for Nina, too, in case she got thirsty.'

'Don't you ever listen?' demanded Rosie. 'I've told you

a hundred times. Nina's back in the nix's cave. I saw her get taken.'

The flash of spirit was momentarily reasssuring, but it seemed to wear the little girl out. She took only a single sip of the drink, then sank back into her pillow.

'I'll leave it for her anyway,' said Ellie cheerfully. 'She might like it after her daddy rescues her.'

'Don't be silly,' muttered Rosie. 'That was last time.'

'Last time?' said Ellie, smoothing the single sheet over the slight body. 'But there's only been one time, hasn't there, darling?'

For a moment, Rosie regarded her with a role-reversing expression in which affection was mixed with exasperation. Then she closed her eyes.

Ellie went downstairs. Worth bothering the doctor with? she wondered. While ready to go to the barricades for her rights under the NHS, she'd always been resolved not to turn into one of those mothers who demanded antibiotics for every bilious attack.

She made herself a cup of tea and went into the lounge. The CD player was switched on with the pause light showing. She'd been listening to her new Mahler disc when Martindale rang.

The larger package remained unopened.

Few things are better suited to putting literary ambition in perspective than bringing a sick child home, so this seemed a good time to take her bumps.

She ripped open the package and took out her script. There was a letter attached.

. . . shows promise, but in the present climate . . . hard times for fiction . . . much regret . . . blah blah . . .

The signature was an indecipherable scrawl. Couldn't blame them, she thought. Assassination must be a real danger in that job. Even she, perspective and all, felt the sharp pang of rejection. Perhaps I'm simply barking up

the wrong tree? Who the hell wants to read about the
angst-ridden life of a late twentieth-century woman when
it's just like their own? Perhaps I should have a stab at
something completely different . . . a historical, maybe?
She'd always felt a bit guilty about her fondness for historical fiction, regarding it as pure escapism from life's
earnest realities. But sod it, letters like this were an aspect
of earnest reality she'd be only too glad to escape from!

Moodily she picked up the CD zapper and pressed the
restart button.

> 'At last I think I see the explanation
> Of those dark flames in many glances burning.'

It was the second of the *Kindertotenlieder*. She relaxed
and let the rich young voice wash over her.

> 'I could not guess, lost in the obfuscation
> Of blinding fate . . .'

Obfuscation! Not a pretty word. But she sympathized
with the translator. Unlike a lot of the multi-inflected
Continental languages, English wasn't rich in feminine
rhymes and they often ran the risk of sounding faintly
comic. Not here though, not with the tragic power of this
music setting the agenda.

> '. . . even then your gaze was homeward turning,
> Back to the source of all illumination.'

What made a composer choose to set one poem rather
than another to music? In the brief introduction to the
songs, she'd read that Alma Mahler had strongly resisted
her husband's obsession with these poems of loss, superstitiously fearing he might be tempting fate to attack his
own family. OK, so it was irrational, but Ellie could sym-
pathize, recalling her own impulse to break all traffic laws

to get to Edengrove, despite Miss Martindale's assurance that there was nothing to worry about.

And there wasn't, was there? Not if Miss Martindale said there wasn't. Despite all her efforts to avoid the stereotype, she'd ended up as another silly, over-anxious mother, like Alma Mahler . . . Except that Alma had been right, hadn't she? How she must have looked back on her fears and wished she'd protested even more vehemently when, a couple of years later, their eldest daughter died of scarlet fever.

> 'These eyes that open brightly every morning
> In nights to come as stars will shine upon you.'

And that's meant to be a consolation? She zapped off the melancholy orchestral coda, reached for the telephone and started dialling Jill Purlingstone's number.

NINE

The Highcross Inn had once occupied a premier site where coachmen, drovers, horse riders, and foot travellers about to start the long haul over the moor to Danby took on sustenance, while those who'd completed the passage in the other direction treated themselves to congratulatory refreshment.

The internal combustion engine had changed all that. What had been effortful was now easy and most travellers using the moor road were simply taking a shortcut to its junction with the busy north–south arterial.

Externally, apart from the signs advertising GOOD GRUB, DEEP PAN PIZZA, and a mention in some obscure guide written by some equally obscure journalist posing as a North Country expert despite the fact that he'd moved from Yorkshire to London at the age of eighteen and only returned twice for family funerals, the inn had changed little in two and a half centuries. In fact some of the flaking paint looked as if it might be original, but that could be down to the long hot summer.

Inside, though, things *were* different. Inside, it had presumably once looked like what an old country pub looks like. Then some keg-head brewer had decided it needed to look like what some flouncy designer thought an old country pub ought to look like. Out had gone the real and particular, in had come the ersatz and anonymous, and now a steady drinker might require to step outside from time to time to remind himself where he was steadily drinking.

Novello quite liked it. She was young, and a townie, and this to her was what pubs usually looked like. She sat at the bar and ordered herself a lager and blackcurrant. At her initiation into the Mid-Yorkshire CID's home pub, the Black Bull, she'd been foolish enough to request this mixture when invited to name her poison. The kind of great silence had fallen which usually only follows the opening of the seventh seal. Dalziel had fixed her with a look which confirmed the rumour that as a uniformed PC his number had been 666. Then some friendly angel had loosened her wits and her tongue, and she'd said, 'But if it's not really poison you're offering, I'll have a pint of best.'

Pascoe had got it for her, murmuring as he handed it over, 'Your principles may be in tatters, but at least your soul is safe.'

The pub was almost empty. The woman behind the bar had time to chat. She was middle-aged, size sixteen, most of it muscle presumably developed from a life of pulling pumps and carting crates. The conviviality of her broad handsome face faded into inevitable wariness when Novello produced her warrant card. But when she mentioned the nature of her enquiries, indignation replaced all, and the woman said, 'I'd castrate the bastards without anaesthetic. Then hang them by what's left! How can I help, luv?'

Novello went at it obliquely. All she had was a blue estate, and she'd prefer to get anything there was to be got without too much prompting. Eagerness to co-operate could sometimes be as frustrating as reluctance to speak.

First she got personal details. This was Bella Postle-thwaite, joint tenant with her husband Jack. They'd been here five years and relied mainly on passing trade to scrape a living.

'There's not much local trade – I mean, look around

outside – not exactly crowded with houses, is it? And you couldn't exercise an ant on the profit margins the Brewery allows us. Bastards. Them's some more I'd like to see hanging high.'

She was a very pendentious lady. Novello moved on to Sunday morning. She'd been up early. Jack had a bit of a lie-in. No, she'd noticed nowt out of the ordinary. What about the ordinary, then? Well, the ordinary was bugger all, not to put too fine a point on it. Couple of tractors. Other traffic? A bit on the main road. Not much, being Sunday, but there was always some. And on the moor road? Yes, there had been a car. She'd been out front watering her tubs while they were still in the shade, and this car had been turning out of the moor road on to the main road. Just came up and turned; there was a stop sign, but you could see a long way down the main road and there was so little traffic on Sunday, you didn't need to halt. Kind of car? Don't be daft, luv! All the bloody same to me. Colour then. Blue, she thought. Definitely blue.

At this point her husband appeared. He was as thin as his wife was broad, angular, almost lupine. Jack Spratt and his wife. Introduced and put in the picture, he immediately poured scorn on any hope of getting useful information from Bella on the subject of motor vehicles.

'She can tell our Cavalier from the brewery wagon and that's about it,' he averred.

His wife, though willing enough to admit her deficiencies voluntarily, was not disposed to have them trumpeted by one who didn't have enough spare flesh on him to merit the description 'better half'.

'At least I were up and about, not pigging it in my bed like some I could name,' she said indignantly. 'Mebbe if you hadn't spent most of Saturday night supping our profits, you'd have been lively enough to be able to help this lass instead of slagging me off.'

Novello, though young in years, was old enough in experience to know that marital arguments have their long-established scripts which, once started, are very hard to stop.

She said loudly and firmly, 'So it wasn't a Cavalier then. Was it bigger?'

'Yes, bigger,' said Bella, glaring defiantly at her husband.

'A lot bigger? Like a van maybe?'

'No. Too many windows.'

'A sort of jeep, then. You know, a Land Rover like the farmers use? Fairly high?'

'No! It were more like one of them long things, like a funeral car, sort of thing. Like what Geordie Turnbull drives.'

This last was aimed at her husband. Signalling a truce by appealing to his expertise perhaps? Didn't sound like that somehow. More like a sly shot from a hidden gun.

'Oh aye, you'd remember that all right,' Postlethwaite spat out viciously.

'What kind of vehicle does this Mr Turnbull drive?' asked Novello quickly before his six-gun could clear leather.

'A Volvo estate,' said the man. 'Aye, and it's blue.'

'Blue? Light blue? Dark blue?' demanded Novello.

'Light blue.'

'And this vehicle you saw, Mrs Postlethwaite, was that light or dark?'

'Lightish,' admitted the woman, meeting her husband's glare with a matching anger. 'But it weren't Geordie's.'

'How'd you know?' jeered Postlethwaite. 'All you'll have studied close is his roof from the inside.'

To hell with guns, this was hand-to-hand fighting with bayonets! Bella drew in a deep breath and looked ready to go for the jugular. Then she caught Novello's pleading gaze and decided to postpone the pleasure till she had him alone.

With a promissory glare at her husband, she said, 'If I had a mind like thine, I'd grow mushrooms in it. And I know for a fact this couldn't have been Geordie's car, 'cos there were a kiddie in the back.'

She didn't realize what she was saying until she'd said it, and in that moment the script changed from long-running soap to tragic drama.

Ten minutes later, Novello was on her mobile, talking to Wield in St Michael's Hall.

He listened with an intensity she could feel over the air and when she'd finished, he asked, 'How do you rate this Bella?'

'No good on car makes. Fair on colours. I tried her with some cars passing on the main road. Not what you'd call an artist's eye, but she could tell blue from black, grey, and green.'

'And the kiddie?'

'Just a glimpse. Little blonde girl looking out of the back window.'

'Frightened? Distressed? Waving? Or what?'

'Just looking. She didn't get a look at anyone else in the car, can't say if there was anyone but the driver. But even though it was just a glimpse, she's certain about the girl.'

'Didn't mention her straight off, but.'

'No reason to. I didn't want to risk leading her.'

Novello described her interrogation stratagem.

'Nice,' said Wield. 'And this guy, Turnbull. Anything there?'

'She's adamant it wasn't his car.'

'But it was her mentioned him first.'

'Only to wind up her husband. Way I read it is, this Turnbull drops in fairly regularly and has a nice line in chat she enjoys. Maybe they've got something going, or maybe she just gets fed up of jealous Jack's innuendo. Either way, I'd guess he's a red herring. Bella may not know makes, but she insists this car was a lot newer and cleaner looking than Turnbull's.'

'They've got these things called car washes,' said Wield. 'Couldn't she just be trying to get him off the hook she thinks she's put him on?'

He's doing the devil's disciple bit, thought Novello. Making me double check my conclusions.

She said carefully, 'I've heard her going on about what she'd do to child molesters. No way can I see her protecting anyone suspected of that.'

'But if she's certain in her own mind this Turnbull couldn't be our man . . . There's men banged up for multiple murder who've got mothers and lovers protesting their innocence.'

'You think I should give him a look,' said Novello, uncertain whether to feel resentful or not.

'You know where he lives?'

'Oh yes. Jealous Jack is very much of your mind, Sarge, and he insisted on giving me clear directions. Turnbull has a contracting business in Bixford on the coast road, about ten miles. He lives next to the yard, but if he's not there, Jack says it'll be easy to find him. Just look for bulldozers with GEORDIE TURNBULL painted on them in big red letters, crawling along, holding up bloody traffic . . .'

Novello had lapsed into what she thought was a rather good impression of the publican's bitter snarl, but Wield clearly didn't rate the act.

'What was that you said?' he interrupted. '*Geordie* Turnbull?'

'That's right.'

'Hold on.'

Silence. Had the Fat Man turned up? The silence stretched. She thought of suggesting they got a tape to play when they put you on hold. 'The Gendarmes' Duet'? Too obvious. Judy Garland singing 'The Man That Got Away'? Her grandfather had been very partial to Garland. She was indifferent, but knew all the songs off by heart from hearing them blasted out of his old record player. Now approaching eighty, his taste was turning back to the Italian music of his childhood . . .

'You there?'

'Yes, Sarge.'

'Don't move, I'm coming to join you.'

His voice gave away as little as his face, but Novello detected an underlying excitement which filled her head with speculation. She reckoned that if Wield were juggling eggs as his lottery number came up, he'd never crack a shell. So for him to be excited . . .

She felt she'd done all that was to be done at present with the Postlethwaites, so she took her drink to a bench on the shady side of the pub and sat there trying to separate in her mind her real concern for the missing child and her imagined advancement if she should be the one who cracked it.

When Wield arrived, he said to her, 'I'm going over it all again with them.'

'Sure,' she said. 'That's OK, Sarge.'

'I'm not telling you so's not to hurt your feelings,' he said. 'I'm telling you so I can be sure you'll be listening close instead of feeling hard done to.'

He went through it all again. When he was finished he said, 'Thank you both very much. You've been very helpful.'

They left Wield's car and drove in hers. She drove north on the main road without being told, watching for the sign pointing east to Bixford.

He said, 'So what do you think? Hear anything you missed first time?'

'She was a bit more positive about shape and things. And also how bright and shiny it looked. Didn't sound much like an old Volvo.'

'Like I said before, mebbe she was trying to make it sound as little like an old Volvo as possible.'

'Could be, Sarge. But if it had been a car she knew well, wouldn't she have recognized it straight off? Also, her husband . . .'

She paused to marshal her thoughts. Wield didn't prompt, but waited patiently for her to resume.

'I got the impression that he'd really like this Turnbull to be in bother with the police, but even though he resents the man, he can't bring himself to believe he'd be in this kind of bother. Maybe he just can't see how anyone who'd fancy someone like Bella could also fancy little children.'

'That the way you feel?'

'Instinctively, yeah. But I've not had enough experience to know if my instinct's got anything to do with reality. Anyway, I'm really curious to meet this Turnbull.'

'Why's that?' asked Wield.

'Because you are, Sarge. Do I get to hear why?'

'Simple,' said Wield. 'Fifteen year back when we were investigating the Dendale disappearances, one of the men we questioned was called Geordie Turnbull. He was a bulldozer driver on the dam site.'

Novello whistled. It was one of many men sounds she had learned to produce as part of her work camouflage. Giggles, screams, anything which could be designated 'girlish' were out. She had a good ear and had rapidly mastered, which is to say, mistressed, a whole range of intonation, accent, and rhythm. She'd even managed – like that old politician, whatshername? – to drop her voice half an octave. Indeed, she'd overcooked it and reached a sexy huskiness which was counterproductive so had headed back up a couple of tones.

'But you didn't keep him in the frame?' she said.

'He stayed in the bottom left-hand corner, so to speak. Nothing to prove he couldn't have been around at the possible times, but even less to suggest he was. Only reason he got picked up in the first place was locals pointing the finger.'

'He wasn't liked then?'

'He were one of the best liked men I ever met,' said Wield. 'Everyone – men, women, kids, even jealous husbands – thought he were grand. But when trouble hit, it were loyalty not liking that mattered. The locals wanted to believe it were an outsider, not one of their own.'

'God,' she said with all the superiority of a townie in her early twenties for a rustic of any age. 'Closed places, closed minds, eh?'

'Sorry?'

'Communities like Dendale,' she explained. 'They must get to be so inbred and inward-looking, it's no wonder dreadful things happen.'

'Sort of deserve it, you mean?'

There was nothing in his voice to suggest anything but polite interest, but she recalled that Wield was now living out in the sticks up some valley or other.

'No, of course not,' she said, trying to recover. 'It's just that, like you say, any isolated community will tend to close ranks, blame the outsider. It's human nature.'

'Yes it is. It's also human nature to want your life to be as lovely as the place you're spending it in.'

This came as close to a personal statement as she'd

ever heard from Wield. Amazing that it was the kind of quote they'd love in *Hello!* magazine.

'You sound like you were fond of Dendale, Sarge,' she pressed.

'Fond? Aye. It were a place a man could have got fond of,' he said. 'Even doing what we were doing. You can't always be looking at the sun and seeing eclipses, can you?'

Better and better. I should have a tape recorder! she thought.

'You mean, like, we're always looking at the dark side of things.'

'Something like that. I recall a day . . .'

She waited. After a while she realized it wasn't a tape recorder she needed but a mind reader.

. . . a day when lost for anything else to do, he'd walked off up the fell towards Beulah Height, justifying his absenteeism by following a team of dog handlers, whose animals were sweeping ever wider in their search for any trace of the missing girls.

It was early evening – the sun still two or three hours from completing its long summer circuit, but already giving that special gloaming light which invests everything it touches with magic – and as he climbed higher from the dale floor he felt the burden of the case slip slowly from his shoulders.

Standing on the higher of the two peaks of Beulah with his back to Dendale, he looked out over a tumble of hills and moorland. He could see far but not clearly. The heat smudged the sharp lines of the horizon into a drowsy golden mist and it was possible for a man to think he could walk off into that golden haze and by some ancient process of absorption, become part of it. Even when, attracted by the baa-ing of sheep and barking of dogs, he turned and looked down, he was still able for a while to keep that feeling. Between the two tops a craggy rock face about ten feet deep fell to a relatively level area of turf which had been turned into a sheepfold by the erection of a semicircular dry-stone wall. Wield, who had read the tourist books about Dendale as assiduously as his master in their desperate search for anything which might throw light on what had happened here, knew that the stones forming the wall had probably been used in the prehistoric hill-fort which had once stood on the Height. The fold was full of sheep at the moment and they and the collies belonging to the man who'd brought them there were getting agitated at the approach of the search dogs.

For a while, though, it was possible to let the image of the shepherd with his long carved crook, and the sound of the sheep and the dogs, blend into his sense of something that had been before, and would be long after, this present trouble.

Then one of the search dogs and one of the collies launched themselves in a brief but noisy skirmish, the shepherd and the handler shouted and dragged them apart, and Wield too felt himself dragged back to here and now.

By the time he descended to the fold, the searchers had moved on. In an effort to re-establish his previous mood, he'd greeted the shepherd cheerfully.

'Lovely day again, Mr Allgood,' he said. 'Right kind of weather to be up here doing this job, I should think.'

He knew everyone in the dale by sight and name now. This was Jack Allgood from Low Beulah, a whipcord thin man with skin tanned dark brown by wind and weather, and a black unblinking gaze which gave promise of assessing the exact value of sheep or of a man in a very few seconds.

'That's what you think, is it?' retorted Allgood. 'I'm supposed to be grateful, am I? Mebbe you should stick to your own job, Sergeant, though you don't seem to be so hot at that either.'

The man had a reputation for being a prickly customer, but this seemed unprovoked.

'Sorry if I've said owt to offend you,' said Wield mildly.

'Aye, well, not your fault, I suppose. Reason I'm getting my sheep ready for bringing down this time of year is they've all got to go. Aye, that's right. What did you think? That we'd be dragged out of our houses but all the stock would just stay here to take care of itself?'

'No. I'm sorry. It must be hard. Leaving somewhere like this. Your home. All of it.'

For a moment the two men stood looking down at the valley bottom – the village with its church and inn, the scattered farms, the mere blue with reflected sky. And then their eyes dropped down to the dam site with its moving machines, its cluster of prefabs, and the wall itself, almost complete now.

'Aye,' said Allgood. 'Hard.'

He turned back to his sheep and Wield set off down the fellside, the sun still as warm, the day still as bright, the view still as fair, but with every step he felt the burden reassembling on his shoulders . . .

'Sarge?' prompted Novello. 'You were saying?'

'Next right's the turn to Bixford,' said Wield. 'Slow down else you'll miss it.'

TEN

'Mr Dalziel,' said Walter Wulfstan. 'It's been a long time.'

He didn't make it sound *too* long, thought Dalziel.

They shook hands and took stock of each other. Wulfstan saw a man little changed from the crop-headed overweight creature he had once publicly castigated as gross, disgusting and incompetent. Dalziel found recognition harder. Fifteen years ago he had first known this man as a lean energetic go-getter with an expensive tan, bright impatient eyes and a shock of black hair. News of his daughter's disappearance had hit him like a hurricane blast hitting a pine. He had bent, then seemingly recovered, pain, rage, and a desperate hope energizing him into a hyperbolical parody of his normal self. But it had been the false brightness of a Christmas tree and all these years on nothing remained but dried-up needles and dying wood. The hair was gone, the skin was grey and stretched so tight across the skull that his nose and ears seemed disproportionately large and his eyes glinted from deep caverns. Perhaps in an effort at concealment or compensation, he had grown a spikey fringe of moustacheless beard. It didn't help.

'So, let's get to it,' said Wulfstan, remaining standing himself and not inviting Dalziel to sit. 'I'm very busy and this necessity of finding a new venue for the opening concert has already taken up time I could ill spare.'

'Sorry about that, sir, but in the circumstances . . .'

He let his voice tail off.

Wulfstan said, 'I'm sorry, is that a sentence?'

If the bugger wants to play hard, let's play hard, thought Dalziel.

'I mean, in the circumstances, which are that a child's gone missing and we need a base to organize the hunt for her, I'd have thought mebbe, seeing what you went through, you'd have been a bit sympathetic. Sir,' said Dalziel.

Wulfstan said softly, 'Naturally, when I hear that parents have lost a daughter and are relying on you and your colleagues to recover her, I am deeply sympathetic, Superintendent.'

Nice one, thought Dalziel appreciatively. His instinct was to hit back but his experience was that, if you lay down submissively, your antagonist often decided it was all over, got careless and exposed his soft underbelly. So he sighed, scratched his breast-bone raucously, and sat down in an armchair.

'If she's still alive we want to find her quick,' he said. 'We need all the help we can get.'

Wulfstan stood quite still for a moment, then pulled up an elegant but uncomfortable-looking wheelback chair and sat directly in front of the Fat Man.

'Ask what you need to ask,' he said.

'Where were you yesterday morning between, say, seven o'clock and ten o'clock?'

'You know already. I presume someone noticed my car.'

'I know where the vehicle was, sir, but that's not the same as knowing you were in charge of it.'

Wulfstan nodded acknowledgement of the point and said, 'I parked my Discovery by the Corpse Road not far from St Michael's at about eight thirty. I then went for a walk and returned to the car shortly after ten.'

'By yourself?'

'That's right.'

'And where'd you walk?'

'Up the Corpse Road to the col and back the same way.'

'That's thirty, thirty-five minutes up and twenty back. What about the rest of the time, sir?'

Wulfstan said flatly, 'I stood on the col and looked down into Dendale.'

The question, 'At anything in particular?' rose in Dalziel's throat, but he kept it there. The man was trying to co-operate.

'Up, down, or standing still, you see anyone else, sir?'

Wulfstan bowed his head forward and rested the index finger of each hand against his brow. It was a conventional enough 'thinking' pose, but in this man it gave an impression of absolute focus.

'There were a couple of cars in Dendale,' he said finally. 'Parked by the dam. Some people were walking from one of them. Tourists, I expect. The drought has caused a lot of interest as the ruins of the village start showing through. On the track itself, up and down, I saw no one. I'm sorry.'

He made as if to rise. End of interview. He thinks, thought Dalziel, making himself more comfortable in the armchair.

'You often walk up the Corpse Road, sir?' he asked.

'Often? What is often?'

'Witness who spotted your car says she'd noticed it several times in the past couple of weeks.'

'Not surprising. My firm has a research unit and display centre at the Danby Science Park and when I'm out there I frequently take the opportunity to stretch my legs.'

'Nowt better than a bit of exercise,' said Dalziel, patting his gut with all the complacency of Arnold Schwarzenegger flexing his biceps. 'Sunday yesterday, but.'

'I know. I trained as an engineer, Superintendent, and one of the first things they taught us was the days of the week,' said Wulfstan acerbically. 'Has Sabbath breaking been reinstated as an actionable offence in Yorkshire?'

'No, sir. Just wondered about you going to work on a Sunday, and so early. You did say that's why you went to Danby; because of your business, not just to take a walk?'

'Yes, I did. And that's what I've been doing on and off for many years, Superintendent, as you can check, though why you should want to, I cannot imagine. Running the business takes up so much of my time, it is easy to lose sight of what makes the business run. I am an engineer first, a businessman second. In my work, as in yours, it is easy to let yourself be lifted out of your proper sphere of competence.'

Like Traffic you mean, thought Dalziel.

He rose, smiling.

'Well, thanks for your help, sir. One thing, but. You obviously knew about the missing lass, through the papers and having to change your concert venue and all. And you knew you'd been out there Sunday morning. Did you never think it might be an idea to give us a bell, just in case your vehicle had been noticed and we were spending time trying to eliminate it?'

Wulfstan stood up and said, 'You are right, Mr Dalziel. I should have done. But knowing the questions you would ask, and knowing that nothing I said could assist you in any way, I felt that contacting you would simply be a waste of both our times. As it has proved, I fear.'

'Wouldn't say that, sir. Wouldn't say that at all,' said Dalziel, offering his hand.

He gave him a masonic handshake just for a laugh. He liked people to think the worst of him because then the best often came as an unpleasant surprise.

'Tell Mrs Wulfstan thanks for the drink. Hope the concert goes OK,' he said at the front door. 'Have you found somewhere else, by the by? Thought mebbe you'd use the church.'

This echo of what had happened in Dendale produced no perceivable reaction.

'Unfortunately, St Michael's has an intolerable acoustic,' said Wulfstan. 'But religion may still come to our aid. There's an old chapel which is a possibility.'

'Chapel?' said Dalziel doubtfully. 'From what I know of chapel folk, I should have thought this concert of thine would have been a bit too frivolous.'

'Mahler, frivolous? Hardly. But profane, perhaps. However, happily, for us that is, the chapel is no longer used for worship. The sect that built it – the Beulah Baptists, I believe they were called – died out in this area before the war.'

'Beulah?' said Dalziel. 'Like in *Pilgrim's Progress*?'

'You've read it?' said Wulfstan, keeping his surprise just this side of insulting. 'Then you will recall that from the Land of Beulah the pilgrims were summoned to go over the river into Paradise, for some an easy, for others a perilous passage.'

'But they all got there just the same,' said Dalziel. ' "When they tasted of the water over which they were to go, they thought it tasted a little bitterish to the palate, but it proved sweeter when it was down." Bit like Guinness.'

'Indeed. Well, it seems these Mid-Yorkshire Beulah Baptists, taking their example from Bunyan's text, went in for a form of total immersion which involved converts passing from one side of a river to the other. The river they used locally was the Strake, which, as you may know, is moderately deep and extremely fast flowing. The candidates for baptism were therefore aided by a pair of Elders known, from the book, as Shining Ones. Unfortunately, at one ceremony in the late thirties, the river was in such spate that not even the strength of the Shining Ones was able to withstand it, and they and their baptismal candidate, a ten-year-old boy, were swept away and drowned. Local revulsion was so great that the sect withered away after that. I'm surprised you have not heard of the case. The police were accounted much to blame for their incompetence in allowing such a dangerous activity to persist. But perhaps with only one child dying, it was not reckoned a failure to mark down in the annals.'

Dalziel, who had been wondering if the revelation of shared acquaintance with *The Pilgrim's Progress* had modified Wulfstan's attitude to him, realized that he'd got it wrong. But a soft answer turned away wrath.

'And you reckon this chapel might do?' he said.

'Local memory avers that as a place to sing in it had no equal. Whether it can be rendered usable in so short a space remains to be seen. For some years now it's been rented by a local joiner for use as a workshop. You may recall him. Joe Telford from Dendale.'

Oh, shit. He didn't let up, did he? Dalziel, for whom the study of revenge and immortal hate was among his favourite hobbies, almost admired the man.

'Telford,' he echoed, playing along. 'Him whose daughter . . .'

'That's right, Mr Dalziel. "Him whose daughter." Telford moved his business to Danby, but by all accounts his heart was never in it. It was his brother, George – you remember him? – who held things together. Joe became increasingly reclusive. His marriage suffered. Eventually his wife could take no more. She went off. With George.'

He spoke flatly with a lack of emphasis that was more emphatic than a direct accusation that this tragedy too was down to police incompetence.

'That must have been a shaker,' said Dalziel.

'They say Joe hardly noticed.'

'And the business?'

'Joe does nothing but a bit of odd-jobbing now, I believe. But he still has a lease on the Beulah Chapel. If he's agreeable, and we can get his junk moved, the place cleaned up and certificated by the fire-officer in forty-eight hours, then we can go ahead. As a voluntary and amateur body, we have to rely on ourselves to do most of the work, so if I've seemed a little impatient . . .'

The ghost of an apology. Funny how folk imagined they had the power to give, and he the thin skin to take, offence.

'Nay, I know all about pressure,' said Dalziel.

They shook hands. Level on points. But Dalziel knew in his heart that no matter what happened in his encounters with this man, he could never count himself the winner. Mary Wulfstan had been the last of the Dendale girls to go. By then he'd been on the spot for long enough to have taken care of that. You've got a strong suspect and you're running out of time, break the bugger's leg rather than let him loose. He remembered with affection the old boss who'd given him that advice. Perhaps if he'd contrived an 'accident' as Benny Lightfoot was brought up from the cells to be released, Mary Wulfstan would still be alive . . .

He put the thought out of his mind and let it be replaced by another as he was escorted to the front door.

Driving into and through Danby yesterday morning, Wulfstan must have seen the BENNY'S BACK! signs. Why'd he not mentioned them?

It was worth asking perhaps. He turned. The door was almost closed, but he did nothing to prevent it closing. His gaze had brushed across his car parked a little way down the street, and all desire to resume his interrogation fled.

There was a figure standing by it looking towards him.

He blinked against the dazzle of the sun, and felt a surge of heat up his body which had nothing to do with the weather.

It was the woman he'd glimpsed in Wulfstan's committee meeting. The woman to whom he owed his tenuous acquaintance with Mahler. And much much more.

She watched his approach with a faint smile on her full lips.

'How do, Andy?' she said. 'What fettle?'

Her imitation of his speech mode was unmistakable, but, unlike Elizabeth Wulfstan's wrongly suspected mockery, unresentable. Piss-taking between lovers, even ex-lovers, was an expression of intimacy, of true affection.

'Nowt wrong wi' me that the sight of you plus two pints of best can't put right, Cap,' he said.

Amanda Marvell, known to her friends as Cap, let her smile blossom fully and held out her hand.

'Then let's go and complete the medication, shall we?' she said.

ELEVEN

Stirps End Farm lay in the sun like an old ship on a sandbank, lapped around by thistled meadows and surging fell. Everything about the farmhouse and its yard said, 'We have lost, you have won, leave us be, here to rot, washed by rain, parched by sun. Trouble us not and we'll not trouble thee.'

They pushed open a gate hanging off its hinges, though they could as easily have stepped through the dry-stone wall at several places where its fallen stones lay cradled in nettles.

'Don't know much about farming,' said Pascoe. 'But this looks like second-division stuff.'

'Cedric were always a make-do-and-mend kind of farmer,' replied Clark. 'But recent years, he's just stuck to making do.'

'And you reckon Pontifex gave him the tenancy out of guilt?' said Pascoe, looking round with distaste at the rusting relics of agricultural machinery which littered the yard. 'Lot of guilt to put up with this for fifteen years.'

'Lose a kid, what's fifteen years?' said Clark.

Pascoe felt reproved. Out of the barn, which was a continuation of the house and seemed to lean against it for mutual support, a man had emerged and was standing in the dark rhomboid of its warped doorway, regarding them with weary hostility.

'What you after, Nobby?' he demanded.

His voice was harsh and grating, as if from long disuse.

He was unageable without expert medical testimony, anything between forty and sixty, with a sharp nose, hollow cheeks, and a salt-and-pepper stubbled chin indicating an early beard or a very late shaving. He was broad in the shoulder and the hip, but the frayed and patched boiler suit he wore hung loosely on him, giving the impression of a big man who'd somehow collapsed in on himself.

'How do, Cedric. This here's Chief Inspector Pascoe. We'd like a word with Jed.'

'At work, if that's what you can call it,' said Hardcastle. 'You'd think there was nowt to do round here.'

It would take a great leap of the imagination, or no imagination at all, to think that, thought Pascoe.

'No, he's here, Sergeant,' said a woman's voice.

In the doorway of the farmhouse a woman had appeared. She was small and neat and had been baking. Her hands were floured and she wore a dark blue apron over a grey dress. Her long hair was tied up in a square of blue silk, giving a wimpled effect. Indeed, with her grey dress and above all a stillness of body and softness of voice which seemed to reflect some deep calm within, she could have passed for a nun.

'How do, Mrs Hardcastle,' said Clark. 'All right if we come in?'

Pascoe noted the formality of their exchange, contrasting with the use of first names man to man. But he got the impression that there was little correlation between form of address and warmth of feeling here. On the contrary.

It was a relief to step out of the hot dung-scented air of the yard into the cool interior, but the contrast didn't stop at temperature. Here was no sign of neglect. Everything was neat and cherished. The old oak furniture glowed with that depth which only comes from an age of loving polishing, and brass candlesticks shone on the long wooden mantelshelf flanking almost religiously a large head-and-shoulders photograph of a young girl. Other pictures of the same child were visible; in the nook by the fireplace where in old times a saltbox would have stood, and on each of two low windowsills, which also held vases of wild flowers among which Pascoe recognized foxgloves and hawk's-beard, glowing like candles lit to light a lost sailor home.

'You'll take a glass of lemon barley against the warm?' said the woman.

'Can't think of anything I'd like more,' said Pascoe.

She called, 'Jed. Visitors,' up the stone stair which rose at one end of the long low-beamed room, then went out into the kitchen.

For a few moments there was no sound. Then, just as Mrs Hardcastle returned bearing a tray with glasses and a pot jug, footsteps clattered down the stairs and a young man erupted into the room.

He had nothing of his father's wariness or mother's calm, but emanated nervous energy even when he stood still, which was not often. He was slightly built, dressed in a black T-shirt and the kind of tight-fitting jeans which gave a male profile once only enjoyed by aficionados of the ballet. What happened if you got excited? wondered Pascoe.

'Yeah?' said the youth, staring defiantly at Clark.

'Nice to see you, too, Jed,' said the sergeant. 'Couple of questions we'd like to ask. About Saturday night.'

The youngster's stare had moved round to Pascoe who was drinking his lemon barley and finding it as cool and refreshing as a thirsty cop could desire.

'Who's this? Your minder?'

Trying too hard to sound big, thought Pascoe. Especially for a boy who hadn't run any further from the estate

197

office than home. It had been his intention to stand back and let Clark's local knowledge have room to play. But with the weak it was often familiarity that gave strength, and Clark's most effective interrogatory weapon, which seemed to be a clip round the ear, could hardly be used in present company.

He stepped closer to the youth and said pleasantly, 'I'm Detective Chief Inspector Pascoe. I'm making enquiries into the disappearance of a young girl yesterday morning. How old are you, Jed?'

'Seventeen, just turned.' He shot an enigmatically accusing glance at his mother then went on 'You gonna send me a card or something?'

'No,' said Pascoe equably. 'Just want to check you're an adult in the eyes of the law. That way we don't need to bother your parents to accompany you down to the station. Sergeant, bring him.'

He turned away. Mrs Hardcastle looked like he'd just condemned her son to death. Her husband stood in the doorway, his features working angrily. Even Clark looked shell-shocked.

Pascoe halted his progress to the door, turned back and said, 'Of course, if you answer a couple of questions here, we may not need to trouble you further. Who actually did the spraying? It's always interesting to see if the stories match. Was it you or Kittle?'

It worked. The boy said, 'You been talking to Vern? What's he say?'

Pascoe smiled enigmatically and said, 'Well, you know Vern.'

'What the hell's this mad bugger on about?'

Hardcastle senior had found his voice at last.

Pascoe said, 'I'm talking about the words BENNY'S BACK, sprayed by your son and his mate on the old railway bridge and various other sites around the village.

And in view of the fact that Lorraine Dacre went missing yesterday morning, I'm interested to know why he sprayed them.'

'It had nowt to do with that,' protested the boy. 'We did it Saturday night. We knew nowt about the Dacre lass then.'

'So why'd you do it?' demanded Pascoe. 'Just got an urge, did you? Thought it would be funny? Maybe seeing those words put the idea of taking the girl in someone's mind. Maybe it put it in your mind or Vernon's mind . . .'

'No!' screamed the boy. 'I did it 'cos I've had it up to here with Benny fucking Lightfoot. He's been around this house all my life. Take a look around, see if you can find a picture of me or our June. No, there's nowt but our Jenny who got took by Benny Lightfoot all them years ago. We even have a cake for her on her birthday, candles and all, can you believe that? Well, it were my birthday on Saturday and I tret myself to a long lie-in and I got up at dinner time, thinking there'd be presents and cards like, and a special meal, and what did I find? I found bugger all! I found Mam sitting there trembling and Dad raging like a mad thing, and you know why? She'd been out and seen Benny Lightfoot! My birthday, and all I get is – "He's back, Benny's back!" So I took off out and later I was having a few beers with Vern and he said, "Well, if he's back, let's tell the whole fucking world, see if we can't spoil some other fucker's birthday."'

'So you decided to do some spraying? Good thinking,' said Pascoe.

The youth was trembling with the emotion of his outburst, but his mother looked to be in a worse state.

She said, 'Oh, Jed, I'm sorry . . . I'm really sorry . . .'

Pascoe said, 'Mrs Hardcastle, I need to ask . . .' but Clark had moved past him, almost shouldered him aside and, taking the woman by the arm, he said, 'I'll see to this, sir,' and steered her into the kitchen.

Interesting, thought Pascoe.

He turned to the elder Hardcastle and said, 'Did you see Lightfoot, too, sir?'

'No!' spat the man. 'Do you think I'd have seen him and not tore his throat out? But I always knew he'd be back. I've been saying for years, it's not over, not yet, not by a long chalk. Them as thought they were safe, they all looked church solemn and said how sorry they were, but all the time they were thinking, "Thank God it was yours not mine, thank God I've got away safe." It's Elsie Dacre's kid that's gone, isn't it? Elsie Coe as was. She were a girl herself back then when it happened and I recall her dad saying he'd see nowt happened to his lass even if it meant keeping her in shackles. But it has happened, hasn't it? It has!'

'We don't know what's happened, sir. But we need to look into every possibility.'

He turned to the boy. No defiance or even anger there any more, just a lost child's face with tears swelling at the eyes.

Hardcastle was right. Whatever the truth about Lightfoot's return, it hadn't been over, not for this boy and his runaway sister, because it would never be over for their parents.

He said gently, 'You've been very silly, Jed, and I may need to talk to you again. Meanwhile, hadn't you best get back to work?'

The boy nodded gratefully, then pushed by his father without a word.

Happy families, thought Pascoe.

He went into the kitchen. Clark had had his innings. He found the sergeant sitting close to Mrs Hardcastle at a long kitchen table, scrubbed almost white by generations of strong country women.

At sight of him, Clark stood up and said, 'Thanks then, Mrs Hardcastle. I'll be in touch. Take care.'

Pascoe let himself be steered out of the house. In the yard he stopped and said mildly, 'Right, Sergeant. Now persuade me that I shouldn't be back in there, questioning Mrs Hardcastle for myself.'

'She's told me all she knows,' said Clark.

'Tell me, then.'

'She went out on Saturday morning to gather some bilberries. Bilberry pie is a favourite of Jed's and she wanted to make one for his birthday. The best place for them round here is high up the far side of the dale where it gets the morning sun. She went over there, and went higher and higher and finally got to the ridge. She says she had a fancy to look down into Dendale 'cos she'd heard about the village showing up again with the drought, but she'd not cared to take a look so far. And when she did look down she saw more than she bargained for. She saw Benny Lightfoot down there, wandering around close by where Neb Cottage used to be.'

'So what did she do?'

'Just stood and looked till he looked up the fellside towards her. He were a good way off, but she says she saw him smile. Then she dropped all her berries and turned and ran down the fell all the way home.'

'When she says he was wandering around, she means walking? On his feet? Not floating over the ground?'

Clark took a deep breath and said, 'She's not daft, sir. She's been through what would have broke a lot of women, but she's still got all her wits.'

'And her eyesight? Has she still got that?'

'I've not heard her complain. And she doesn't wear glasses.'

'Perhaps she should. How old did Lightfoot look?'

'Sorry?'

'Was he the same age as last time she saw him, or did he look fifteen years older?'

'Don't know, sir. Didn't ask.'

Pascoe shook his head irritably. The cooling effect of the shadowy interior plus the lemon barley was rapidly being evaporated by the uncomfortably warm air.

'You know I'm going to have to talk to her, don't you?' he said. 'I'm going to need a properly witnessed statement.'

'Yes, sir. But not now, sir.' Clark's voice was pleading.

'Forgive me for being personal,' said Pascoe, 'but you haven't got something going with Mrs Hardcastle, have you?'

'No,' exclaimed Clark. Then, more softly. 'No, not now. Once, a long time since, there was . . . something. But she had three kiddies, it didn't seem right, even though her and Cedric . . . well, who knows what might have happened? What did happen was little Jenny got took. And that was that. Some women might have got out after that. She saw it as a kind of judgement. And the way it hit Cedric, she knew she'd never leave him, come what might. She told me, no need really, I could see it . . . So now we're Sergeant Clark and Mrs Hardcastle. But I'll not see any harm come to her, sir. No matter what.'

He spoke defiantly.

'I'm pleased to hear it,' said Pascoe. 'Look, it's probably best we see her down at the hall, when Mr Dalziel's back. Get back in there and tell her we'll need to see her down there in, say, two hours. That should give us time to get hold of the super.'

'I'll ask her, sir.'

'You *tell* her,' said Pascoe fiercely. 'Middle of an investigation like this is no time for personal feelings, Sergeant.'

Was Clark going to turn out to be a liability? he wondered. It was what he was coming to think of as the Dendale effect. Bit like Gulf War syndrome; hard to define, but impossible to deny once you'd met a few of those suffering from it. Including perhaps the Fat Man himself.

He would prefer to believe Dendale was irrelevant, but all roads seemed to lead back there and till he saw a signpost pointing definitely in another direction, perhaps he ought to follow, if only to confirm a dead end.

He said, 'Sergeant.'

Clark, moving slowly back to the farmhouse, turned to show an unhappy face and said, 'Sir?'

'This fellow, Benny Lightfoot, who was he close to?'

'No bugger,' said Clark. 'A right loner.'

'So if he did come back, there's nowhere special he'd head?'

'Only Dendale, and there's nowt there for him now, not even with the drought. All the buildings got 'dozed down before they flooded the dale, including Neb Cottage where he lived with his gran.'

'His gran. You said she had a stroke. What exactly happened to her?' asked Pascoe.

'She dug her heels in, said they'd have to carry her out of her cottage, and that's what they had to do,' said Clark. 'She'd barricaded herself in. I went up there to try to talk some sense into her and I saw her through the window lying on the floor. Another few hours, I reckon she'd have snuffed it.'

'Lucky you were so conscientious,' said Pascoe.

'I'm not sure she saw it that way,' said Clark. 'I went to see her in hospital and she didn't exactly seem grateful.'

'Did she recover?'

'Depends who was talking to her,' said Clark with a reminiscent grin. 'Any official questions about Benny and she'd lost the power of speech and memory. She was certainly a bit confused and had trouble with finding the right words, but she was soon well enough to be a right trouble to the nurses. They'd have discharged her a lot sooner, only they had to find a place for her to go. She couldn't look after herself, you see. Even after she got most of her speech back, she was partially paralysed down one side. So it had to be nursing home and she led the Social Services a merry dance when they started making suggestions.'

'But in the end she went?'

'No. A niece turned up. Lived somewhere near Sheffield. Said she'd take her. And that's the last anyone round here saw of her.'

'So she could be still alive,' said Pascoe.

'She'd be getting on, but she's the kind who'd stay alive forever if she thought folk were expecting her to die.'

'Can't remember the niece's name, can you?'

'No. But they might still have a record down at Social Services.'

'Depends who was running the case,' said Pascoe unoptimistically.

'I can tell you that. Lass name of Plowright.'

'You don't mean Jeannie Plowright who's head of Social Services at County Hall now?' said Pascoe, hope reviving.

'Aye, she's done right well,' said Clark. 'I thought she would. Anyone who could survive dealing with old Mrs Lightfoot was always going to make it right to the top!'

He went into the house. Pascoe took out his mobile and dialled.

'County Hall.'

'Social Services. Ms Plowright, please.'

A pause, unfilled (thank God) by soothing music. Then a man's voice.

'Hello?'

'Is Jeannie there, please?'

'Sorry, she's out. Can I help?'

'No. When will she be back?'

'Not till late this afternoon, maybe early evening. Look, if it's about . . .'

'It's not about anything you can help with,' said Pascoe. 'Can you make sure she gets a message?'

'I expect so, but listen . . .'

'No. You listen. Carefully. My name is Pascoe. Detective Chief Inspector Pascoe. Tell Ms Plowright I shall call to see her in her office at nine o'clock tomorrow morning. This is urgent and confidential police business, OK? Subject of meeting: Mrs Agnes Lightfoot, formerly of Neb Cottage, Dendale. You got that? Good. Thank you.'

He rang off. If you see me coming, better step aside, he thought. Bullying Clark for having personal feelings. Now riding roughshod over some poor devil whose name or status I didn't even bother to find out. Another fifteen stone and I'll be indistinguishable from Dalziel!

The phone rang.

'Hello!' he barked.

'Peter, it's me. Listen, don't worry, but Rosie wasn't well at school and Miss Martindale sent for me and I brought her home and I thought it was just too much sun or something, then I got to thinking about Zandra so I rang Jill and she said Zandra was a lot worse, and she'd got the doctor there so I started getting a bit concerned and rang Doctor Truman and he's here now and he says he'd like Rosie to go to hospital for some tests . . . Peter, can you get there soon . . . please . . .'

He'd never heard Ellie like this before. The world reeled as if the great ocean of heathery moor had decided to shrug its shoulders and ease Stirps End Farm off its sandbank.

Then all went still again.

He said, 'I'm on my way.'

So much for hard cases, he thought. So much for slagging people off for letting personal feelings get in the way. Dalziel was right. If there was a god, he dearly loved a joke.

'Sergeant Clark!' he roared.

And set off at a run towards the car.

TWELVE

When Wield and Novello reached Bixford, there was no need to ask for direction.

Towering over the sign extending Bixford's welcome to careful drivers was a hoarding proclaiming the imminence of GEORDIE TURNBULL (DEMOLITION & EXCAVATION) LTD.

It stood inside a high wire-link security fence running round a site of about an acre. At its centre stood a bungalow on one side of which was parked a bright yellow bulldozer bearing Turnbull's name in fiery red and on the other a light blue Volvo estate.

It bore not a trace of dirt or dust and sparkled in the sunlight.

Novello drove in through the open gate and parked next to the Volvo.

Wield got out and walked slowly around the estate car, peering in through the gleaming windows. Novello went up to the bungalow and pressed the bell push. After a short delay the door opened. A short stout man appeared, dressed in khaki shorts, a string vest, and espadrilles. His coarse blonde hair was standing on end and he was yawning and rubbing his eyes, as though just roused from sleep. But his yawn stopped and his eyes brightened and a welcoming smile spread like dawn across his round and ruddy face as he clocked Novello.

'Hello, there,' he said. 'Just having a nap, but this is worth waking up for. And what can I do for you, bonny lass?'

Geordie was more than just a version of George then. The ripple of the Tyne was in his speech.

'Mr Turnbull, is it?' she asked, noticing that his bare muscular arms were covered with a light golden down which seemed to reflect the warmth of the sun.

'Aye, it is. Will you come inside out of this blessed heat and slake your thirst on a can of lager? Or lemonade, if you've come to talk to me about Jesus.'

She found herself smiling back.

It was remarkable. In the space of a few seconds, Turnbull had made the transition from fat disgusting middle-aged slob to pleasant amusing cuddly koala. It was partly the radiance of his smile, partly the undisguised, non-threatening, wholly flattering admiration of his regard, but perhaps largely the readiness with which he offered refreshment before finding out what her business was. The Englishman on his doorstep is by nature a suspicious creature, always anticipating the worst. Novello knocked on a lot of doors in her job. She didn't look very menacing and not at all (she hoped) like a cop. But the usual response ranged from neutrally guarded to downright hostile, and that was before she identified herself.

Now she produced her warrant card and said, 'Detective Constable Novello. Could we have a little chat, Mr Turnbull?'

One eyebrow flickered up comically, but otherwise there was no change to the sunny welcome of his expression as he said, 'It'll be the lemonade then, pet? Come on through.'

And then there was a change, like the shadow of a thin high cloud moving swiftly over a golden landscape, passing almost before you saw it.

'Mr Turnbull.'

Wield had come up behind her. Turnbull recognized him, of that she was sure. And the recognition had not been pleasing to him. Interesting to see if the man admitted old acquaintance or played hard to get.

But even as the thought formed in her mind, Turnbull's smile had turned up a kilowatt and he was saying, 'It's Mr Wield, isn't it? Aye, of course it is. Two of a kind, you and me, Sergeant. Once seen, never forgotten.'

It should have been offensive, but it didn't come out that way, just one guy confident that appearance didn't matter to another he flattered by including him in the same club.

Wield took the outstretched hand and said, 'Long time since Dendale.'

'You're right. But always seems like yesterday, something like that,' said Turnbull, solemn suddenly. 'Come away in. Cooler inside.'

It was, partly because of the shade, but also on account of a portable air-conditioning unit standing in the corner of the living room. Turnbull was unmarried, Novello had established that from Bella. But this interior didn't look to be suffering from the absence of a woman's touch. Why should it? Man like this probably had a waiting list of local ladies queuing to cook, clean and generally mollycoddle. The idea should have caused a pang of indignation. Instead she found herself straightening an antimacassar before she sat down in the chair he offered.

Come on, Novello, she warned herself. This guy's old enough to be your father. She made herself start looking at things like a cop again. He read the *Daily Mirror*. There was no sign of any other reading matter in the room. The furniture was old but not antique, and the woodwork had that nice glow which comes from frequent polishing – that female touch again? Also perhaps evidenced by the richly gleaming brass urn filled with fresh fern standing in front of the fireplace. Probably the ladies of the parish had a roster, taking turns to do the church flowers before coming on to sort out Mr Turnbull. There I go again! she thought. Concentrate. The fireplace, now that was interesting. Handsome, Victorian, rather too large for the room and certainly not coeval with it.

Turnbull had gone into the kitchen and now returned bearing a tray with a jug of iced lemonade and three glasses. There'd been a pint pot and a can of bitter on a coffee table when they came in, but he'd taken these with him. Wanting to keep a clear head?

'Cheers,' he said, raising his glass. 'Now what can I do you for, Mr Wield?'

'Business bad?' said Wield.

'Eh?'

'Finding you home in the middle of the day. The 'dozer outside.'

'Oh no,' said Turnbull. 'The other way round, I'm glad to say. Things ticking away so nicely the boss can afford to leave his lads to it while he catches up on a bit of paperwork.'

Wield's gaze flicked to the *Daily Mirror*.

Turnbull laughed and said, 'Not that paper. You caught me in my tea break. No, you should see my office.'

'Thanks,' said Wield, standing up. 'Which way?'

Turnbull looked momentarily nonplussed to have his remark taken literally, but he got to his feet and led the way out of the room.

The office was in what had probably been the bunga-low's second bedroom. Not much use for a second bed-room here, Novello guessed. She somehow doubted if Turnbull's house guests necessitated much extra laun-dering of bed linen. Trouble was, more she thought of him as a 'ladies' man', the harder it was to see him as a child molester.

'Do you have someone to run your office, Mr Turnbull?' she asked.

'Christ, yes. Too much for a simple soul like me. I've got this lovely lady who keeps me straight.'

'I can imagine. Not here today?'

'No. I gave her the day off,' said Turnbull.

Novello forced herself not to glance significantly at Wield. Giving the help a holiday the day after the abduction . . . *possible* abduction . . . that had to be, could be, might be significant.

'Local, is she?' asked Novello.

'Very,' said Turnbull. Then he laughed that infectious laugh it was so hard not to join in. 'I bet you're thinking "dollybird", bonny lass? Well, I did think of getting one of those, but I could foresee all sorts of problems. Never mix business and pleasure, as the bishop said to the prioress. Then I struck lucky. Mrs Quartermain. Sixty-five. Widowed. Loves work. And she lives just down the road, in the vicarage.'

'The vicarage?'

'That's right, pet. She's the vicar's mam. He's glad to get her out of his hair, I'm glad to get her into mine. But I let him have her back when he's got anything special on. It's the old folks' outing today. They'd not get out of the village if it wasn't for Ma Quartermain.'

He grinned at her, inviting her to join in his amusement even though what joke there was was on her. She found herself smiling back, then tried to hide it by looking to see how Wield was reacting to this by-play.

He wasn't. He had been taking a slow stroll around the room, studying the filing cabinet, bulletin board, fax machine, copier, with which it was crowded though not cluttered. This was a very well-organized business. The business of a very well-organized man. Able to sort out his innermost life and urges with the same degree of precision? wondered the sergeant, who knew all about such things.

'Very impressive,' he said finally. 'You've done well, Mr Turnbull. You didn't have your own business when you were working on the Dendale dam, did you?'

Dendale. Second mention. And again it seemed to cast a gloom on Turnbull's natural spirits. But it would, wouldn't it? On anyone's who'd been there. Jesus, this guy's got me working for the defence already! thought Novello.

'No, I was driving for old Tommy Tiplake back then. Sort of junior partner, really. Meaning, I stuck with him in the bad times. No family of his own, old Tommy, or not any he bothered with, and we got on so well that I took over when he had to retire. I've been very lucky. Done nothing to deserve it, but I thank God every day for all His blessings.'

They had returned to the living room as he talked and he gave Novello a waggle of the eyebrows as she sat down again, which said clear as speech that he rated her high among the aforementioned blessings.

'Didn't know you were a religious man,' said Wield.

'Comes with age, I expect, Mr Wield. Well, it's a good each-way bet, isn't it? Maybe that's why I employ the vicar's mother.'

'So with all this religious feeling, you'd be at church on Sunday morning?' said Wield.

'As a matter of fact, I was,' said Turnbull. 'Why're you asking, Mr Wield?'

You know why we're asking, thought Novello. It's been on the news. In the paper. In the *Daily Mirror*. Or perhaps you knew before that . . .

It was an afterthought. A professional coda. She must fight against this submission to charm which got employers leaving businesses to him and vicars passing over their mothers to work for him, and God knows what else . . .

'Which service?' asked Wield.

'Matins.'

'That's eleven o'clock, right?'

'Right.'

'And before that?'

'Before? Let me see . . .'

He screwed up his brow in a parody of remembrance.

'I got up about nine. I remember Alistair Cooke's *Letter From America* was on the radio as I shaved. Then I made myself some coffee and toast and sat with it outside round the back because it was getting hot already, and I read the Sunday paper. That would take me up till about nine forty-five, I expect. That enough for you, Mr Wield, or do you want more?'

There was an undertone of anger there now which he couldn't disguise. Or perhaps he could have disguised it perfectly well but just wasn't bothering. Or perhaps he wasn't angry at all.

'You were by yourself? You didn't see anyone? No one saw you?'

'Not till I went out to church,' said Turnbull.

'How far's the church?'

'The other side of the village, about a mile.'

'So you walk there?'

'Sometimes. Depends on the weather and what I'm doing afterwards.'

'And yesterday?'

'I drove there. I was picking up a friend, heading out for a day on the coast after the service.'

'You always leave your car out front where it is now?'

'Not always. Sometimes I put it in the garage.'

'And Saturday night?'

A hesitation. Would it be so hard to remember? Perhaps, like Novello, he was working out where Wield was going with this. And like her, getting there.

'In the garage,' he said.

Which meant that if, say, the newspaper boy recalled that when he delivered the paper sometime before nine o'clock the car hadn't been visible, it signified nothing.

She looked at Wield. She knew, indeed had first-hand experience of, his reputation for thoroughness. He wasn't going to let this go till he had checked out everyone in the area who might have noticed Turnbull driving away from his house early on Sunday morning. Correction; she thought. Till *I* have checked them all out! Great.

Turnbull was on his feet. He went out of the room and they heard him dialling a number on the phone in the narrow hallway.

'Dickie,' he said. 'Geordie Turnbull. Yeah, not bad, considering. Considering I've got company. The police. No, no trouble, but I think I'd like you down here to hold me hand. Soon as you can. Thanks, bonnie lad.'

He came back in and said, 'Dick Hoddle, my solicitor, is going to join us, Mr Wield. Hope you don't mind?'

'It's your house,' said Wield indifferently.

'Yes, and I'm staying in it,' said Turnbull. 'That's why I want Dickie here. One thing we should get straight, Mr Wield. I've no intention of letting you take me over to Danby to help you with your enquiries. Not without I'm under arrest.'

'You asked me before what this was about,' said Wield. 'Seems like you knew all the time.'

'Oh, I knew all right, bonnie lad. Only I couldna believe it. You lot have done this to me once before, remember? I couldn't really believe you were going to do it again, but you are, aren't you?'

'We're going to pursue all possible lines of enquiry into the disappearance of Lorraine Dacre, yes,' said Wield.

'You do that. And I hope you find the bastard responsible. But you people track your muddy boots through people's lives and never think about the mess you leave behind. I'm not going anywhere there'll be cameras and reporters. Anything you want from me, you'll get here, else you'll not get it at all.'

'Fine,' said Wield. 'Here's where we want to be. To start with, I appreciate your co-operation, Mr Turnbull. We'll need to search your premises. And examine your car. Is that agreeable to you?'

'Do I have a choice?'

'Oh, yes. Between sooner or later,' said Wield.

'Go ahead,' said Turnbull, tossing his car keys on to the floor in front of Novello. 'Do what you bloody well like. You always did.'

He spoke with a good deal of bitterness, but it was diluted by something else, thought Novello as she picked up the keys. Something which had been there almost from the start. Something very like . . . relief?

But relief at what? That finally his crimes were catching up with him? Or perhaps simply relief that something he'd feared was actually under way?

She went out to the car.

Wield walked round the room whistling, not very tunefully, 'A Wandering Minstrel, I'. Music for him began with Gilbert and ended with Sullivan.

'Nice room, Mr Turnbull,' he said when he completed the circuit and rejoined the other in front of the fireplace.

'Like I say, I've been lucky. And people have been good to me. Tommy Tiplake. And all the folk round here. They'll speak for me, Mr Wield.'

It was almost an appeal, and Wield was almost affected.

'Nice to have friends,' he said. 'Grand old fireplace, that.'

'Yes.'

'Bit big for here, mebbe. And it looks, don't know how, familiar.'

215

'Grand memory you've got there,' complimented Turnbull. 'It came out of the Holly Bush in Dendale. The snug bar, remember? Don't worry. It was paid for. Tommy and the other demolition men did a deal with the Water Board for any bits and pieces they fancied. It'll be in their records.'

'I'm sure it will,' said Wield. 'Better for something like that to find a good home than end up in pieces at the bottom of the mere, eh?'

There was a moment of shared nostalgia for a past through which progress had ploughed its six-lane highway.

Then, from the doorway, Novello said, 'Sarge.'

He went out. She showed him a pair of evidence bags. In one was a child's pink-and-white trainer. In the other a blue silk ribbon tied in a bow.

'The ribbon was down the back seat,' she said. 'The trainer was buried beneath a whole pile of stuff in the boot.'

Wield stood in silent thought. Novello guessed what the thought was. Confront Turnbull with their discovery now, or wait till they'd tried to get an identification from the Dacres?

Problem was solved by the appearance of the man in the doorway.

'What's that you've got there, bonnie lass?' he asked.

He sounded unconcerned. Perhaps in the circumstances too unconcerned, thought Novello. Wield ignored him.

'Get on the radio ... no, make that the phone,' he said. 'Tell them what's going off and say I'd like a search team and forensic down here s.a.p.'

Then finally he turned his attention to the man and began to intone, 'George Robert Turnbull, I must caution you ...'

THIRTEEN

Andy Dalziel and Cap Marvell sat facing each other in the snug of the Book and Candle. The snug lived up to its name, having room for no more than half a dozen chairs and two narrow tables under one of which their knees met; indeed, more than met, had to interlock, but Dalziel's apologetic grunt having provoked nothing more than an ironic smile, he relaxed and enjoyed the contact.

The pub wasn't one he used often, its location 'in the bell' and its ultra respectable ambience, marked by the absence of game machines, pool tables and muzak, making it unsuitable for most of a CID man's professional encounters. But, as it was a pub and as it was on his patch, he knew it, and was known in it, and the landlord had shown no surprise either at Dalziel's order of three pints of best and a spritzer, or his request that the snug should be regarded as closed for the next half hour.

The first pint hadn't touched the sides and the second was in sad decline before he opened the conversation.

'Missed you,' he said abruptly.

Cap Marvell laughed out loud.

'Would you like to try that again, Andy, and this time see if you can make it sound a bit less like some errant schoolboy's reluctant confession to self-abuse?'

He took another long pull at his pint, then growled, 'Mebbe I didn't miss you all that much.'

She squeezed his leg between her knees and said, 'Well, I've missed you more than I would have believed possible.'

The admission provoked a feeling in him which he didn't altogether recognize.

While trying to identify it, he said surlily, 'Your choice.'

'No,' she said calmly. 'There was no choice. Not then.'

'So why're you here now?'

'Because now there may be.'

'And?'

'And if there is, I'll choose.'

'Mebbe you should wait till you're asked,' he said. He had identified the feeling as embarrassed delight. It bothered him somewhat. He'd be blushing next!

'Oh no. That's a cop-out. All the important choices are made in advance of their occasion.'

He sat looking at her, recognizing now it wasn't just the handsome face, the sturdy body and the big knockers he'd missed, but her humour, her independence and the no-crap way she put things, a quality sometimes obscured, sometimes underlined by her posh accent. That was all that obviously remained of her previous life in which, barely out of finishing school, she had married into the lower reaches of the peerage, given birth to a son, and watched him (as closely as nannies and boarding school permitted) grow up into a young Army officer who was reported missing, believed dead, in the Falklands War.

This had been her epiphanic experience, forcing her to a review of her life which not even the news that her son was in fact heroically alive could reverse. There had followed, in not too rapid succession, disaffection from high society, divorce, deconstruction of all previous moral certainties, dissipation, dedication to a series of radical causes; and finally, Dalziel.

They had met when an animal rights group she was leader of had been involved in a murder investigation. Separated by a few years, several class-strata, and a moon river of attitudes, they had nevertheless felt a mutual attraction strong enough to bridge all gaps until her demand for trust and his need for professional certainties had required a bridge too far.

Now this chance encounter seemed to offer the possibility that this missing bridge could be put in place after all.

She said, 'So while we're choosing, let's chat. What brought you to Walter's house? Didn't I read that you're in charge of this missing child case?'

So she took note of his name in the papers. He was pleased but hid it.

'That's right. His car were spotted parked near where she lived . . . lives. The Turnip's too.'

'Sorry?'

'Krog. The Swede.'

'Norwegian, I think. But hardly polite, anyway.'

'Polite? Mebbe it were some other bugger you missed.'

'Could be. So you wanted to see them. Walter and the . . . and Krog?'

'Aye. For elimination.'

'Thought you sent sergeants to do that.'

This was a reference to his use of Wield to interview her when things got hot.

'Not when it's someone like Wulfstan,' he said.

'Andy, you're not suggesting the rich and powerful get treated better than poor plebs?' she mocked.

His brow creased like a field furrowed by a drunken ploughboy. She'd not have said that if she knew the Wulfstans' history.

'How well do you know them, the Wulfstans?' he asked.

'Not well. The wife, hardly at all. Walter, only as chair of the festival committee. When I settled down here a few years back, I started going to concerts locally and made a few friends in musical circles – not people who overlapped with my other activities, I hasten to add, before you start asking for names. A particular friend was on the committee. When her job required her to leave the district, she recommended me to take her place, and that was how I got to know Walter.'

'Oh aye? And he was impressed by your experience of organizing pickets and demos and illegal raids on private premises, was he?'

'I keep my life pretty well compartmentalized, Andy,' she said. 'Poke holes in dykes and trouble comes pouring through, as you and I found out. This is my first year on the committee, so I'm still feeling my way.'

'Thought you'd have been in charge by now.'

'Not much chance of that,' she smiled. 'It's so well organized there's very little to do. This change of venue is our first real crisis and Walter seems to have got that well under control.'

'So I gather. You'll be off to Danby to shift furniture, then?'

'Not today. But I've offered my services tomorrow, if needed. Walter runs a tight ship, no skivers need apply. But that's really all I know about him. No use trying to pump me for more, Superintendent.'

'I'm not,' said Dalziel. 'I reckon I know all I need. Probably best you know it too, in case you feel like letting on you're a friend of mine.'

She started to make a joke of this, saw his face, and stopped. Her expression turned dark as his as he told her about the Dendale disappearances.

'Those poor people . . . I remember how I felt when they told me Piers was missing . . .'

'Can't understand how you didn't read about it,' he said, half accusing.

'Maybe I did. But, Andy, fifteen years back I had other

things on my mind. Now I see why you're giving Walter the softly softly treatment. Poor man. But that explains why they adopted.'

'Elizabeth? Aye, you're right, she's not theirs. You managed to winkle that out even though you say you hardly know the Wulfstans, did you? Well, like they say, once a snout, always a snout.'

This ungallant comment was in fact a further reminder of their old intimacy, referring to a time when she'd been the source of some useful information.

'No, I did not winkle it out,' she said firmly. 'It was volunteered to me, and certainly not by the Wulfstans or anyone up here. By one of those coincidences which can hardly be part of a divine plan as they keep on throwing us together, I have a friend in London, Beryl Blakiston, who happens to be head of the school that Elizabeth attended for a while.'

'Bugger me,' he said admiringly. 'With you upper-class lot, who needs the Internet?'

She regarded him narrowly, suspecting that his acquaintance with the Internet was as vague as hers with the arcana of tactics in the front row of a rugby scrum. But she'd learnt it was dangerous to challenge without certainties, and went on, 'I lunched with Beryl in the spring. Exchanging notes, I mentioned my new respon-sibilities as a member of the festival committee – it comforts her to hear I keep a couple of toes on the strait and narrow – and she said, was this Wulfstan I mentioned the father of the singer? And I said, yes, because I knew that Elizabeth was pencilled in for this year's festival. End of story.'

He took a long swallow which brought the end of the second pint a lot closer.

'Bollocks,' he said.

'I'm sorry?'

'First off, you've already let on that your mate Beryl

told you the lass were adopted. And second, with a couple of g and t's in your belly and a bottle of burgundy on the table, there's no way a pair of likely lasses like you two were going to let go of any interesting subject until well chewed.'

'Why do you designate someone you haven't met a likely lass?'

''Cos you'd not keep on meeting her for lunch else. So what did she say?'

Cap Marvell fixed him with a cool assessing gaze and said, 'Andy, this isn't official, I hope? A drink with an old friend is one thing, but if this is turning into an interrogation, I want my solicitor playing gooseberry.'

He looked hurt.

'Nay, lass, I've told you, only reason I came round to see Wulfstan myself was because of what happened way back. Routine enquiry. He's not in the frame. All I'm doing here is making polite conversation till I see which side up the toast is going to fall. If you like, we can talk about the England cricket team. Or the government. Makes you weep, doesn't it?'

'The government?'

'Don't be daft. I don't waste tears on yon prancers.'

She laughed and said, 'OK. I believe you, Andy. So, what Beryl told me was that Elizabeth was an adopted child and that there'd been some trouble with her early on, but she'd settled down ...'

'Trouble?' interrupted Dalziel. 'I like trouble. Tell me about it.'

'Beryl didn't go into detail. There is such a thing as professional discretion, even after a bottle of burgundy. But I got the impression that it was a question of expectations unsatisfied; the girl's of her adoptive parents, theirs of their adopted child. It was serious enough to require the services of a psychologist, or psychiatrist, I'm not sure which. But in the end it all worked out, mainly, Beryl surmised, because of the girl's burgeoning musical talent. Which, of course, was the main occasion and topic of our discussion.'

'Burgeoning,' said Dalziel dreamily. 'I love it when you talk fancy. Even when I don't understand half you're saying.'

'I'm saying that through her singing, Elizabeth discovered a sense of her own value, and also a belief that her adoptive parents valued her. After that, it was possible for her to get back to normal development.'

'Normal? Like the way she talks?'

'The accent you mean? I'm surprised you think there's anything abnormal about that, Andy,' she said with wide-eyed innocence.

'Ha ha. It's all right for an ignorant tyke like me, but a lass brought up by the Wulfstans, going to fancy schools and colleges down south, she talks like that out of choice. You've only got to hear her sing to know that.'

'You've heard her sing?'

'Aye. On the wireless. Yon dreary stuff you used to play.'

'Yon dreary stuff,' she echoed. 'Is this a portmanteau term to cover all my collection? Or did you have some particular piece of dreariness in mind?'

'It were one of them songs about dead children. Mahler. Only it were in English, and she didn't sing it with a Yorkie accent.'

'Ah, her *Kindertotenlieder* disc. I've heard it. Very interesting.'

The Fat Man laughed.

'Don't much like it, eh?'

'Why do you say that?'

'I've got this lad, Peter Pascoe – you'll likely recall him; Ellie Pascoe's man – he's sort of cultured, degree and such.

I've tried to squeeze it out of him, but it's like malaria, once you've had it, it stays in the blood, and you never know when you're going to start shaking. Well, I've noticed with him, and buggers like him, whenever they don't much like summat, but it's not polite or fashionable to say it's crap, what they say is, it's very interesting.'

Cap Marvell smiled and said, 'How you do pin us butterflies down, Andy. But you're right. I didn't care much for the translation, and I didn't think her voice was yet ready for those particular songs.'

'So why'd she choose them? More to the point, why'd the record company let her choose them?'

'Her reasons, I can't guess at. But the recording company . . . well, it's a very minor label, too small to catch anyone really big, so they concentrate on young hopefuls, get them to sign up for three or four discs, and hope by the time they get to the third or fourth some of them will have made it to stardom. Elizabeth has great potential. After the concert, she's heading for Rome where she's been taken on by Claudia Alberini, one of the top voice coaches in Europe. I suspect she dug her heels in and told the record company she wasn't going to sign unless she started with the *Kindertotenlieder* and they decided it was a risk worth taking. Particularly when she said she wanted to do them in her own translation.'

'Why'd that help?'

'It's a talking point. Anything that rouses interest and gets exposure is OK. You still can't make it unless you're good, but if you're good and marketable, then you hit the heights a lot quicker. Nigel Kennedy was a good example back in the eighties.'

'Didn't he start speaking funny too?'

'Yes he did. And you could be right,' said Cap. 'Beryl reckoned she went on speaking like this at school just to make a statement of individuality; you know, "I might

224

be adopted but I'm not dependent on anyone." But of course, now she's starting on her career, she might see it as a marketing image thing. I don't know. Like I say, I don't really know the girl at all. But singing the cycle on Wednesday doesn't look like a good choice.'

'Because of Lorraine Dacre, you mean?'

'Indeed. Also musically. I've never heard them without the original orchestral accompaniment. Sandel's a fine pianist, but they're bound to lose something.'

A phone rang. It took Dalziel a second to realize it was in his own pocket.

'Bloody hell,' he said. 'Can't escape these things even in the bog. Hello! Wieldy, what's amiss? Hold on. I can hardly hear you.'

He stood up, said to Cap, 'I've marked my drink,' and went out of the snug.

When he returned, she said, 'You weren't long. I've hardly touched your beer.'

He finished the second pint, looked sadly at the third and said, 'I've got to go.'

'Still business before pleasure,' she said.

'This business,' he said sombrely. 'Someone's been picked up. Just for questioning, nothing definite, but I need to be there. Sorry.'

'Of course, you've got to go,' she said. 'Andy . . .'

She hesitated. She'd anticipated having more time for negotiation about a possible future meeting before they parted. She hadn't yet made up her mind how she wanted to play it, but now wasn't the time to prevaricate.

'Andy, there's still a lot to say,' she went on. 'Promise you'll ring. Or better still, call round. I've always got plenty of tofu in the fridge.'

This reminder of her vegetarianism brought a wan smile.

'It's a date,' he said. 'See you.'

He hurried out, leaving for possibly the first time in his life an untouched pint on the table.

She drew it to her and took a sip.

Not a gap bridged, she thought. But certainly a bridge commenced, even if it consisted only of pontoons, lifting and shifting in currents and tides, and promising only the most perilous of passages for each to the other's distant shore.

FOURTEEN

The first hospital gate Pascoe reached had an EXIT ONLY sign.

Pascoe turned in and roared up the drive towards the looming grey building.

There was a parking space vacant next to the main entrance. It was marked CHIEF EXEC. Pascoe swung into it, narrowly missing a reversing Jag XJS. He got out, slammed his door shut and set off running. Through the Jag's open window a man called angrily, 'Hey you. That's my spot.'

Over his shoulder, Pascoe called, 'Fuck you!' without slackening his pace.

He'd been here before, knew the layout well. Ignoring the lift, he ran up the stairs to the third floor. It required no effort. Far from panting, it was as if his body had given up the need for breathing. There was a waiting room at the end of the children's ward. Through the open door he saw Ellie. He went in and she came to his arms.

He said, 'How is she?'

'They're doing tests. They think it might be meningitis.'

'Oh, Christ. Where is she?'

'First left, but they say we should wait till they tell us . . .'

'Tell us what? That it's too late?'

'Peter, please. Derek and Jill are here . . .'

For the first time he noticed the Purlingstones, clinging together on a sofa. The man tried a smile which made as

227

little impression on his tense face as a damp match on concrete.

Pascoe didn't even try.

Breaking away from Ellie's grasp, he went out of the waiting room and straight through the first door on the left.

It was a small side ward with only two beds. In one he saw the blonde head of little Zandra Purlingstone. In the other, Rosie.

There were doctors and nurses standing round. Ignoring them, he went to the bedside and took his daughter's hand.

'Rosie, love,' he said. 'It's Daddy. I'm here, darling. I'm here.'

For a fraction of a second it seemed to him the eyelashes flickered and those dark almost black eyes registered recognition. Then they vanished, and there was nothing to show that she was even breathing.

Someone had him by the arm. A voice was saying, 'Please, you must go. You have to wait outside. Please, let us do our job.'

Then Ellie's voice saying, 'Come on, Peter. For Rosie's sake, come on.'

He was back in the corridor. The door closed. His daughter vanished from his sight.

He said to Ellie, 'She recognized me. She really did. Just for a second. She knows I'm here. She'll be all right.'

'Yes,' said Ellie. 'Of course she will.'

Two men were coming along the corridor. One wore the hospital security uniform, the other an elegantly cut lightweight linen suit.

The suit said, 'That's the fellow. Damn cheek.'

The uniform said, 'Excuse me, sir, but Mr Lillyhowe says you've left your car in his reserved place.'

Pascoe looked at them blankly for a long moment then said slowly, 'I'm not sure . . .'

'Well, I'm absolutely sure,' snapped the suit. 'It was you. And you swore at me . . .'

'No,' said Pascoe, balling his fist. 'I mean, I'm not sure which of you to hit first.'

The suit took a step back, the uniform a half-step.

Ellie moved swiftly into the space created.

'For God's sake,' she said crisply to the suit. 'Our daughter's in there . . .'

The crispness faded, crumbled. She took a deep breath and tried again.

'Our daughter's in . . . Rosie's in . . .'

To her surprise she found the world had run out of words. And out of space except that little room which held her daughter's life. And above all it had run out of time.

She sat in a waiting room, staring at a poster which proclaimed the comforts of the Patients' Charter. Peter was there too, but after a few fruitless attempts they made no effort to speak. Why speak when all the words were done? The Purlingstones weren't there. Perhaps they were in another room like this one. Perhaps they were taking a miraculously recovered Zandra home. Either way, she didn't care. Their grief, their joy was nothing to her. Not now. Not in this helpless, hopeless, endless now.

Something happened. A noise. Peter's mobile phone. Was time starting again?

He put it to his ear. Mouthed something at her. Dee. Ell. Dalziel. Fat Andy. She remembered him as in a dream, so surfeit swell'd, so old, and so profane. Peter was saying to her, 'You OK?' She nodded. Why not? He said, 'I'll go outside.'

In the corridor, Pascoe put the phone to his ear again, a gesture somewhat superfluous with Dalziel bellowing full blast, 'Hello! HELLO! You there? Sod this bloody useless thing.'

'Yes, I'm here,' said Pascoe.

'Oh aye? Where's here? Down a sodding coal mine?'

'At the Central Hospital,' said Pascoe. 'Rosie's here. They say she may have meningitis.'

There was a silence, then the sound of a tremendous crash, as from a fist hitting something hard, and Dalziel's voice declared savagely, 'I'll not thole it!'

Who, or what, he was addressing was unclear. Another silence, much briefer, then he spoke again in his more everyday matter-of-fact tone.

'Pete, she'll be OK. Right little toughie that one, like her mam. She'll make it, no bother.'

It was completely illogical, but somehow the blunt assurance, with its absence of breathless sympathy and request for details, did more for Pascoe's spirits than all the medical staff's qualified reassurances.

He said, 'Thank you. She's . . . unconscious.'

He found he couldn't say *in a coma*.

'Best thing,' said Dalziel with a Harley Street certainty. 'Time out to build up strength. Pete, listen, owt I can do, owt at all . . .'

Again, no conventional offer of help, this. Pascoe guessed that if he hinted the hospital wasn't doing enough, the Chief Executive would find himself in an interview room, being made an offer he couldn't refuse.

'That's good of you,' he said. 'Was there some special reason you were ringing, sir?'

'No, nowt. Well, in fact we've got someone in the frame. I'm on my way to Danby now. Likely it'll be nowt. Listen, Pete, forget the job . . . well, no need to tell you that. But is there owt you were doing that I should know about and no other bugger can tell me?'

'Don't think so,' said Pascoe. 'Nobby Clark can fill you

in on . . . oh, hang on, I've made an appointment to see Jeannie Plowright at Social Services at nine tomorrow morning. It's about Mrs Lightfoot, the grandmother. There's stories about Benny being seen, Clark's got details, and I thought the old lady's the only person he'd want to make contact with, if she's alive, which I doubt, and if he's here, which I doubt even more. Straw clutching. Probably simplest to cancel it, if you've got a better straw to clutch.'

'No, we'll leave it till I see how things are looking. Pete, I'll be in touch. Remember, owt I can do. Luv to Ellie. Tell her . . .'

For once the Dalziel word-hoard seemed to be empty.

'Yes,' said Pascoe. 'I'll tell her.'

He stood for a moment, reluctant to move, as if the clocks had stopped and his movement would start them ticking again. A nurse passed him, paused, looked back and said, 'Excuse me, sir, no mobiles in here. They can set up interference.'

'Interference?' said Pascoe. 'Yes. Of course. Sorry.'

He went back into the waiting room and put his arm round Ellie's shoulders.

'Andy sends his best. He says she'll be OK.'

'He does? Oh, good. That's it then. Let's all go home.'

'Come on,' he chided. 'Who'd you rather have being optimistic? The Pope or Fat Andy?'

She managed the ghost of a smile and said, 'Point taken.'

'There's a coffee machine on the next floor, look, it says so here. Let's head down there and treat ourselves.'

'Suppose something happens . . .'

'It'll only take a minute. Better than sitting here . . . anything's better . . . Everything's going to be fine, love. Uncle Andy's promised, remember?'

The door opened. A woman came in. They knew her

name was Curtis. She was the paediatric consultant.

She came straight to the point.

'She's very ill. I'm afraid we can now confirm it's meningitis.'

'What kind?' demanded Ellie.

'Bacterial.'

The worst kind. Even if he hadn't known that, Pascoe could have guessed from Ellie's expression.

He put his arm round her, but she twisted away. She was looking for someone to hit out at just as he had been with the chief executive and the security man.

He said, 'Ellie.'

She turned on him and yelled: 'What price Uncle Andy now, eh? What price the fat bastard now?'

FIFTEEN

Edgar Wield was feeling quite pleased with himself. He'd got the search under way at Bixford and transported Geordie Turnbull to Danby without so far attracting the attention of any of the flock of carrion crows who called themselves reporters. Downside was that Turnbull's solicitor was also here, closeted in the station's one small interview room with his client.

Then Nobby Clark arrived and told him about Pascoe. No details. Just that Rosie was in hospital. Wield felt sick. The Pascoes were special to him, the nearest thing to family left for him in this country since his sister emigrated. Edwin . . . Edwin was different. Closer, yes. But more important? No; just differently so. He looked at the phone. He could ring up and find out what had happened. But he hesitated. He tried to work out why. Fear at what he might hear? That certainly. But something more . . . He probed, and was bewildered to find something that looked like guilt. For what? Was he mean-spirited enough to resent this intrusion on his new-found personal happiness? That would be cause enough to make him feel guilty. He hoped to God it wasn't. But if not that, what? He probed deeper, saw more clearly, still didn't believe it. Then had to. He felt responsible. It was an extension of his feelings about this lost child case. Some cynical, self-despising element at the centre of his psyche did not believe he was meant for happiness and was therefore sure that whatever he got of it could only be procured by subtraction from someone else's store. It was an absurdity, an egotism in its way as disgusting as selfish vanity. But he still hesitated to pick up the phone. It was as if by doing so he would acknowledge creating whatever monstrous news awaited his enquiry.

'Super's just driven into the yard,' said Clark, coming into the office and anxiously checking out his appearance in the glass-fronted photo of the Queen.

Fear of Dalziel was a healthy condition, but belief that he was appeasable by gleaming brass, polished boots, or any other kind of bullshit meant that you had more than average cause to be afraid, thought Wield, glad of the diversion.

He went out to the yard and saw the Fat Man sitting in his car as if reluctant to get out. The sergeant approached and opened the door like a commissionaire.

'How do, sir,' he said. 'Got some bad news. Clark says the DCI's . . .'

'I've spoken to him. They reckon it could be meningitis. She's in a coma.'

There it was. The worst. No, not quite the worst. That still lay ahead . . . perhaps awaiting his phone call . . .

He said, 'Oh, shit.'

'Aye, that about sums it up. Nowt we can do about it, but, so let's get on with the job.'

He climbed out of the car. Wield, undeceived by this display of stoic indifference, fixed his gaze on the vehicle's dashboard which was cracked in half.

'Having trouble, sir?'

'Aye,' said Dalziel, rubbing his left hand. 'Speedo got stuck, so I gave it a whack.'

'Hope I never get stuck,' murmured Wield, closing the door gently.

'Hope you're going to get started,' said Dalziel. 'Turnbull. From the top.'

Wield was the Schubert of report makers, compressing

into little space what others would have struggled to express in symphonies. Even the fact that the greater part of his mind was struggling to accommodate the news about Rosie Pascoe didn't inhibit the flow and in the short walk from the car park to the station office, where sight of Dalziel sent Sergeant Clark snapping to attention, he brought the Fat Man up to strength.

Mention of Turnbull's solicitor made Dalziel smile. He liked it when suspects ran crying to their briefs.

'Dick Hoddle? Nose goes one way, teeth go t'other?'

'That's the one.'

'Bit rich for the likes of Geordie Turnbull, I'd've thought.'

'He's done well, sir. His old boss left him the business or something.'

'Need to be something like that,' said Dalziel. 'Didn't strike me as the kind to save up his bawbees. So what do you reckon, Wieldy?'

'Turnbull's co-operating like a lamb,' said the sergeant. 'OK, he called up Hoddle, but in the circs, who wouldn't? Waived his right to be present during the search of his premises. Hoddle wasn't happy, but Geordie said something like, if it was a drugs bust, it 'ud be different, everyone knew the cops were capable of planting shit all over the place, but not even Mid-Yorks CID was going to fit someone up in a case like this.'

Dalziel, unoffended, said, 'He's not so daft. This trainer and the ribbon from the car . . . ?'

'Novello's taken them round to show the parents. They're not an exact match with the description of what the little girl was likely wearing, but not a million miles off.'

'And Turnbull says . . . ?'

'Seems he often has kids in his car. Does a lot locally, ferrying folk about, kids to football matches, that sort of thing. But not just kids. Old folk, disabled, all sorts. He's well liked.'

'So was the Duke of Windsor,' said Dalziel. 'You've still not told me what you reckon.'

'Same as in Dendale. I reckon everyone who knows him, even the odd husband who doesn't like him, would be amazed if he turned out to be our man,' said Wield. 'And I reckon I would too. Which means he's either very, very clever, or we should be looking somewhere else.'

'Oh aye? Any suggestions where?'

Wield took a deep breath and said, 'Mebbe you'd best talk to Sergeant Clark, sir.'

'I will, when he's recovered from his fit. Can you hear me, Sergeant, or is it rigor mortis?'

Clark, who on the better-safe-than-sorry principle had opted to remain in a sort of half attention posture, let his muscles relax.

'Right, lad. I gather you've got some ghost stories to tell me. Off you go.'

Clark had few of Wield's narrative skills and Dalziel let his impatience show.

'So Mrs Hardcastle that everyone reckons has gone a bit doolally with grief has started seeing things? Sounds like it's her doctor she should be talking to, not hard-worked coppers. You don't agree, lad?'

Clark, who lacked the guile to conceal his resentment of Dalziel's dismissive remarks about Molly Hardcastle, said, 'I think she saw summat, sir.'

'Summat?' Dalziel spat out the word like a cocktail cherry found lurking in a single malt. 'You mean, summat like a sheep? Or a bush? Or summat?'

The sergeant was saved from a possible test to destruction by the entrance of Shirley Novello.

'Ivor, make me day. Tell us the Dacres have given us a positive on the stuff you found in Turnbull's car.'

'The trainer, a definite no,' she said. 'But the ribbon, a maybe. Lorraine liked ribbons, collected them, did swops with friends, so she ended up with a whole boxful. No way of saying what was in there and which she took out that morning. The hair on the one from Turnbull's car's our best bet. They'll be checking that against samples taken from the girl's bedroom. But that's going to take a little while.'

'Bloody marvellous,' groaned Dalziel. 'Which leaves me with a ferret down my trousers.'

Meaning, Shirley guessed, that if he kept Turnbull too long, he'd start biting, and if he let him go too soon, he'd be out of sight down the nearest hole.

The Fat Man was regarding her broodingly.

'It was you got on to Turnbull in the first place, right?'

'With Sergeant Wield's help,' she said cautiously.

'No. Credit where it's due. You did well. Again.'

He didn't make it sound like something he expected her to make a habit of.

'So, what do you reckon to this Turnbull? He were reckoned a bit of a masher back in Dendale. So what's the female view. Still got it, has he?'

'He's . . . attractive,' she said. 'Not physically, I mean, not his appearance, but he's got . . . charm.'

'Charm?' Dalziel savoured the word. 'Would kids like him?'

'Oh, yes. I think so.'

'And could he like kids?'

'Sexually? I don't know. I'd have said he was pretty well focused on mature women, preferably those who were safely married and were happy to have a fling without wanting to rock the boat . . .'

'But?' said Dalziel, who could spot buts the butters didn't know they were butting.

Novello hesitated then flung caution to the winds.

'But it could be a double bluff. Or not bluff, meaning not conscious. He could chase women because he doesn't want to admit to himself that he really wants to chase little girls . . .'

The look on Dalziel's face made her wish she could whistle the winds back.

He said, 'Well thank you, Mrs Freud. You been at the communion wine, or you got half the ghost of a reason for spouting this crap?'

She said defiantly, 'He's worried about something, I can tell.'

To her ears, it sounded far weaker and wafflier than what she'd said before, but to her surprise, Dalziel nodded almost approvingly and said, 'Well, that's something. Wieldy?'

'Aye. I'd say so, too,' said the sergeant.

Novello felt like kissing him. Perhaps he'd turn into a frog?

'Right then, let's go and have a chat afore Hoddle starts ringing the Home Office.'

'Shall I come?' said Novello hopefully.

Dalziel thought, then shook his head.

'No,' he said. 'No distractions.' Then, observing the look of disappointment which this time she could not disguise, he condescended to explain. 'This Turnbull, I recall him and I know his sort. Women make 'em sparkle. Can't help it. Hang him upside down over a tub of maggots and bring a woman into the room and he'd feel better. I don't want him feeling better. I want him feeling bloody terrified! Come on, Wieldy. And don't forget the maggots!'

And Novello, watching them go, felt almost sorry for Geordie Turnbull.

*   *   *

Three hours later, Dalziel was feeling sorry for no one but himself. Also he had a lousy headache.

It was called Dick Hoddle and it wouldn't go away, not unless it took Geordie Turnbull with it.

It didn't help that the interview room made the Book and Candle snug (which he remembered with great longing) look like the Albert Hall. Its one window wouldn't open (the result of paint and rust rather than security) and even with the door left ajar, the temperature in there would have cooked meringues.

Hoddle was clearly a meticulous man. Every hour on the hour he made a case for the interview to end, in progressively stronger terms. This was his third.

'My client has been co-operative beyond the call of civility in each and all of its principal senses . . .'

He paused, as if inviting Dalziel to demand definition, but the Fat Man didn't oblige. There had been a time before tape recorders became a fixed feature of interview rooms when he might have offered to push each and all of the lawyer's crooked teeth down his crooked throat if he didn't belt up and let his client speak for himself. Not that that would have been altogether fair, as Turnbull on several occasions had volunteered answers against his brief's advice. But Dalziel wasn't feeling altogether fair, just altogether pissed off.

'. . . and as it became clear to me, as a reasonable man, a good two hours ago that he had no case to answer, I can only assume that even your good self must by now have reached the same conclusion. You are, of course, entitled to hang on to him for twenty-four hours from the time of his arrest . . .'

'And another twelve on top of that, if I give the word,' interjected Dalziel.

'Indeed. But admit it, Superintendent, there is no prospect that you are going to be able to charge my client with anything, so any attempt to prolong the agony might appear merely malicious and would certainly add weight to any case Mr Turnbull might already be contemplating for police harassment and false arrest.'

'No,' said Geordie Turnbull firmly. 'There'll be nothing of that. Once I'm free of here, I'll be happy not to have any contact with the law in any form for the next fifteen years.'

Dalziel noted the time span, tried to hear it as an admission that his urge to kill had gone off and wouldn't be returning for another decade and a half, failed, and scratched his lower chin so vigorously the sound-level needle on the recorder jumped.

The door opened behind him. He looked round. It was Wield, who'd been summoned out a few minutes earlier by Novello. Not an easy face to read, but to Dalziel's expert eye he didn't look like he'd just ridden from Aix to Ghent.

At least it gave him a temporary out. He suspended the interview, flicked off the machine and went out into the corridor.

'Cheer me up,' he invited.

'They do a nice pint round the corner at the Queen's Head,' said Wield with a sympathetic glance at the Fat Man's sweat-beaded brow.

'And that's it?'

'If it's cheer you want, sir. Word from Forensic. That hair on the ribbon, definitely not Lorraine's. And so far nothing else in the car which suggests she's ever been in it. Same with the stuff Novello got from that rubbish bin.'

'Shit,' said Dalziel.

'You really fancy him for it, do you, sir?'

'When you're in the clag, you fancy whatever you've got, as the gravedigger said to the corpse. God, I hate that bastard. I'd really like to bang him up and throw away the key.'

'Turnbull?' said Wield, surprised.

'No! Hoddle, his sodding brief. Any more good news?'

'Not from Bixford. If Turnbull stood for MP, he'd get elected. The ladies think he's lovely, the men think he's a grand chap so long as it's not their particular lady he's chatting up. The vicar's ready to pawn the church silver if dear Geordie needs bail. And his congregation would rather trust their kids with Geordie Turnbull than with Dr Barnado.'

'Oh aye? It'll be a different tale once word starts getting around and the tongues start wagging. These Christians can forgive owt save innocence. You think he's innocent, Wieldy?'

Wield shrugged and said, 'Makes no difference, does it? Without we've got a lot more, or even a little more, I think we're flummoxed. How about you, sir?'

'I don't know,' said the Fat Man. 'There's summat there that doesn't smell right . . . he's not mad enough, maybe that's it. Hoddle's threatening all kinds of false arrest shit, but Turnbull's being all laid-back and forgiving. And he's from Newcastle! When them buggers finish telling you how many times they won the Cup, they start listing all the bad offside decisions against them since 1893.'

'Doubt that'll stand up in court, sir,' said Wield.

'Happen not. Owt from Burroughs?'

'Not a thing. They've been right up the valley and back down again. She's waiting to be told what to do next.'

Dalziel pondered, his great face brooding like God's over a tricky piece of epeirogeny.

'We'll get 'em off the fell,' he said finally. 'Hit the buildings again. I want every farmhouse, barn, byre, pig-sty, hen-coop, garden shed, outside privy, every bloody thing turned upside down. She's close, Wieldy. I feel it.'

It would have taken a brave man in search of a medal to point out he'd felt much the same back in Dendale all those years ago, and Wield, though no coward, was equally no pot hunter.

He said, 'And Turnbull, sir? Does he walk?'

'Don't be bloody daft! Whatever Hoddle says, he's not leaving here till the twenty-four hours are up. No bugger's going to say I let a possible child killer loose afore I were forced to, not this time.'

'No, sir. Novello were wondering if mebbe now things have been going on so long, she could sit in . . .'

'No,' said Dalziel irritably. 'Besides what I said before, bring a new face in now and Hoddle will be abso-bloody-lutely certain he's got us on the run. Tell her to take the Dendale file and learn it by heart. Tomorrow morning, nine o'clock, Peter had an appointment with yon Plow-right woman who runs Social Services. Thought he might get a line on old Mrs Lightfoot who's probably dead, but if she's not, then she's the one Benny would want to find if he came back, which I don't believe. Ivor can go along instead.'

'Sounds like a waste of time,' said Wield.

'Better a DC's time than a DCI's,' said Dalziel. 'Think of the money we'll save. Any word of the little lass, by the way?'

'I rang the hospital,' said Wield in a flat voice which concealed the effort of will even that call had required. 'No change.'

He still hadn't been able to bring himself to try and contact Pascoe direct. That needed to be face-to-face contact, he told himself. But he wasn't sure he believed himself.

'Life's a bastard, eh, Wieldy?' said Dalziel wearily.

'Yes, sir. And then we die,' said Edgar Wield.

And so the second day of the Lorraine Dacre enquiry draws to an end.

As the shadows lengthen, her parents, unable now to bear any company but their own, sit together holding hands in the tiny living room of their cottage, neither of them deriving any comfort from their contact except for the possibility of giving it to the other. Hope has died in both their hearts and all that remains is the concealment of despair.

Between Peter and Ellie Pascoe, too, there is a silence born of a secret, but the secret here is not the death of hope but its survival. Life without Rosie is unimaginable, so they refuse to imagine it. Like primitives in a cave, they watch darkness running towards them across the fells and know it holds danger, but know also that tomorrow the sun will rise again and make all things well.

And Rosie Pascoe?

Rosie Pascoe is in the nix's cave.

It's dark down here, but a little light filters down the long winding tunnel leading to the entrance. Gradually her eyes begin to adjust and shapes and textures begin to rise out of the darkness.

She is on the edge of a small pool of black water. At least, at first it seems dull black, but as she peers into it, a little of the light from that sunlit world far above runs across its surface, polishing it as it passes, so that the blackness shines like a mirror held up to the night sky.

In that dark mirror she sees the roof of the cave, soaring high above, like the ceiling of a great old cathedral. And up there something moves, not much, just enough to catch her eye.

It is a bat, hanging upside down at the topmost point of that high ceiling.

Rosie shivers and lets her gaze move across the pool to its far margin. And there in its black mirror she sees another face, bright shining eyes, sharp prying nose, a lantern jaw fringed with jagged whiskers, and teeth like a length of ripsaw in the smile-parodying mouth.

She cries out and raises her terrified gaze from the reflection to the reality.

It is the nix himself, crouched opposite on the far bank of the pool. Seeing that he has her attention, the nix slowly raises his left hand and with a long thin finger tapering to a long sharp nail, he beckons to her.

Rosie shakes her head.

The nix stands up straight. Crouched, he had seemed frog-like; a large frog it is true, but with the comforting promise of a frog's awkward movement out of the water. Now he straightens into a tall thin man whose long legs have brought him halfway round the pool before fear, which has locked her muscles, becomes terror, which releases them, and she scrambles away from him over the stones and bones which litter the floor of the cave.

Her first thought, for despite everything she's still thinking, is to keep the water between them, and for a while she succeeds. But her young limbs are growing tired, and on her third circuit of the pool, it seems that the thin light spilling through the entrance tunnel is brightening to a golden glow as if that distant sun is shining directly on its mouth in the grey fellside far above.

The way is long and hard, she knows, and very steep. In a straight race she doubts if she would have much chance against those long skinny legs. But the call of the sun is too strong.

She breaks away and heads into the tunnel.

How rocky the ground is! How full of twists and turns the passage! How low the ceiling!

She comforts herself with the thought that what is awkward for her must be very difficult indeed for the nix, but when she risks a glance back she sees him crouched low and squat once more, not like a frog this time, but scuttling along like a huge spider.

The sight gives her new strength. Also the growing brightness which has in it now not just the light but the warmth of the sun.

She turns another bend. Still far above her but now clearly visible she glimpses the tiny circle of blue sky. And as she looks, the blue becomes a frame round a familiar face and she hears a familiar voice crying her name.

'Rosie. Rosie.'

'Daddy! Daddy!' she calls back, and strives towards him.

But the scuttling noise behind is very close now. She feels those bony fingers tighten round her ankles, she feels those rapier nails digging into her flesh.

And she sees the circle of blue shrink to a pinhole then vanish altogether as the nix drags her back down to his gloomy cavern and his black and fathomless pool.

day three
The Drowning of Dendale

ONE

Once it started raining, it rained like it were bent on catching up in a week for all the dry weather we'd had over the past months.

That first day was a real cloudburst, then it settled into a steady downpour, sometimes slackening for a while but never really stopping. Back in Dendale we heard they were finishing off the clearing-up job, shifting any big stuff left, sorting out the electrics and such, and when that were all done, they bulldozed the buildings. Seems it didn't matter whether they were going to be drowned or not, the Board didn't want owt left standing to tempt folk to explore either under the water or out of it.

So school, pub, church, houses, barns, byres, everything were knocked flat in preparation for flooding the dale. The dam was nigh on finished, the becks were full bubble, the Neb was spouting water like a leaky bucket and White Mare's Tail was wagging full force again, so that Dender Mere was nearly up to its old flood level, and high on Black Moss col twixt the Neb and Beulah the new tarn were broadening and deepening ready for its release into the valley below.

All this I picked up the usual way kids pick things up, by hanging around grown-ups with mouth shut and lugs open. No chance of seeing any of it for myself. I'd been warned like all the rest of us not to go anywhere near Dendale. Partly, it were that our mams and dads were still feart of Benny Lightfoot or the nix or whoever had taken the three girls. Partly, I think they knew how much it would hurt them to see their old homes flattened and drowned, and reckoned it would be just as bad or worse for us kids.

In my case, they were dead wrong. I really liked it in Danby. I settled in real quick. And when school started in September, I found that Mr Shimmings, the teacher with the eye-patch, hadn't got it any more. He'd only been wearing it 'cos he'd hurt his eye in an accident and needed to cover it up till it mended. And he didn't have a split cane, but only a walking stick to help with the limp he'd got from the same accident. In fact, he were really nice, and him and Miss Lavery got on right well.

I forgot to mention, Miss Lavery had got taken on at St Michael's Primary, and though I weren't in her class any more, she always stopped and had a word with me when we met.

There were lots of the old Dendale faces around. Mr Hardcastle, like my dad, were working for Mr Pontifex on his estate. The Telford brothers had set up their joinery business in Danby, though I heard tell it were mainly Madge's Uncle George doing the work, as Joe (that's her dad) didn't seem able to keep set on anything. The Wulfstans had moved back to town and then sold up there and moved off down to London. Nobody saw owt of Aunt Chloe again, but Mr Wulfstan's works were up here and he was still around, and there were stories of him being seen wandering around the fells like he was still hoping to find some trace of Mary. Also, there was talk of his lawyers suing the police for not doing their job properly, but nowt came of it.

As for Benny Lightfoot, he'd gone without trace. His gran made a right durdum about leaving the dale, and barred herself in Neb Cottage when time came. They went up there to try and talk her out, but when there was no sign of her, they broke in and found she'd had a seizure with all the excitement, so she'd been taken off to hospital. She'd have likely ended up in a home if some niece down near Sheffield hadn't said she'd take her in and look after her.

All this seeped into my head the usual way, but none of it bothered me. Dendale and hot weather, and Jenny and Madge and Mary being taken seemed miles and years away. We had a cottage quite near the school, right on the edge of Danby, and though it might have seemed like living in the country to a townie, for me after Low Beulah, it were like being in the middle of a city, with different people and different sights all round me every day.

I think change did Mam good at first, too. She seemed a lot livelier and made some new friends and even went out with them now and then. Dad were better too for a bit. He were shepherd overseer for Mr Pontifex and I heard Mam tell someone if he kept his nose clean and his lip buttoned, he should get Stirps End Farm when present tenant retired which were expected next Lady Day or midsummer at latest. Dad used to say he didn't know if there were much point in starting all over, and I knew he were thinking of me being only a lass. And mebbe that's why them days I didn't much mind having my hair cut short and nearly always wearing dungarees or jeans, 'cos I thought that mebbe I'd do for a boy and be able to take on the farm.

Sounds stupid, I know, but that's what I thought. And I tried not to think at all about Dendale, and like I say, soon it seemed as far away as London, and I'd not have dreamt of going back if it hadn't been for Bonnie.

The move seemed to have bothered Bonnie most of all and if it hadn't been that it hardly ever stopped raining, I doubt he'd have come in our new house at all. He wandered around, all restless. If I shut him in a room with me, he wanted to be out. And if I shut him out, he wanted to be back in. And whatever he wanted, he yelled till he got it, and this really got on Dad's nerves. He'd never liked Bonnie, anyway, so I did my best to keep them out of each other's way.

Then this night it all went wrong. Dad came into the kitchen through the back door and Bonnie shot between his legs, almost tripping him.

He swore and lashed out with his boot, catching Bonnie right in the ribs.

The cat let out a screech and shot through the open door. I screamed too and Mam came in to see what was going off.

'It's Bonnie,' I sobbed. 'Dad kicked him and he's run away.'

'Is that right?' Mam demanded.

'Bloody useless animal,' said Dad. 'Good for nothing. If I never see it again, it'll be too soon. Anything that can't earn its keep isn't bloody well worth keeping.'

This made me cry even more, and not just for Bonnie.

Mam tried to comfort me by saying Bonnie would be back once he realized he were just getting soaking wet outside. And even Dad, who mebbe felt a bit guilty, said it would be all right, Bonnie would be back under his feet in the morning.

But he wasn't. No sign of him.

I cried all through breakfast and all the way to school. No one noticed at first, we were all so wet, a few tears made no difference. It were a really foul day, rain hissing down so hard it came straight back up again, filling the air with curling mist so's you couldn't see across playground. But once we got inside and dried off, my friends soon spotted I were crying and asked me what was wrong. My girlfriends were all dead nice, but one of the boys, Joss Puddle whose dad had had the Holly Bush in Dendale, said, 'Don't know why you're bubbling. I know where he'll be. He'll have gone home.'

'Well, he hasn't, stupid,' I said. 'That's what I've just been telling you. He hasn't come home.'

'I don't mean Danby home, I mean his old home, his real home. So who's stupid now?' he retorted. 'And I'll tell you summat else. If he's gone back to Low Beulah, he'll likely get drowned 'cos they're letting loose Black Moss today.'

I thought about this all through the morning till break. The more I thought, the more I reckoned Joss were right. Bonnie had been fretting ever since the move. Where else would he run after Dad had kicked him but back to Dendale? At morning break, I told Joss to tell teacher I'd gone off home with a bellyache.

Looking back, I know what I set out to do were daft. Chances of finding Bonnie even if he had set out back to Low Beulah were rotten. Chances of me slipping and breaking a leg were a lot better. But I had this picture of Bonnie sitting down by the mere all forlorn and this big wall of water rushing down from Black Moss and sweeping him away.

So I set off up the Corpse Road to Dendale.

It were a steep climb out of Danby, but I were strong for my age and the path were so well worn, I had no problem following it even when the mist swirled close. Rain never let up, and soon I was sodden through, but it weren't a cold rain with the wind coming from the south, and I was moving fast as I could, so that kept me warm inside.

As I came over the ridge of the Neb, I could hear White Mare's Tail thundering but there were another noise I didn't recognize. It wasn't till I got halfway down into the dale and suddenly the mist opened up like it does that I saw where it came from.

Down from Black Moss what had used to be a whole lot of becklets streaking the hillside like silver threads had knit together into a great tumbling force. It rushed straight down fellside into the valley bottom where it joined with White Mare's Beck and went roaring down to the mere.

Already the mere itself were fuller than I'd ever seen it even in the old spring floods. Its old shape were gone and it were covering fields and walls which ran along its edges and lapping about ruins of houses like Heck which had stood close.

I stood there and felt . . . I don't know what I felt. I were looking at place I'd spent most of my little life and not recognizing it. It were like looking in mirror and seeing someone else there.

Through the mist, I could just make out on far side of the mere the round hillock close by where Low Beulah had stood. Then it vanished, and in no time at all I could hardly see more than a couple of steps in front of me again. But it were easy enough to follow Corpse Road down to Shelter Crag. Now I was scrambling around on blocks of stone from buildings that had been knocked down and it were hard to tell just where I was. I were trying to get to the little hump-back bridge over White Mare's Beck which would take me on to the road round mere and so up to Low Beulah, but when I reached edge of the beck, or river as it were now, I realized how daft I'd been. Bridge would have gone, if it hadn't been knocked down it would be underwater now. I were so wet, I thought of wading over, but I could see it were too deep, and any road it moved so fast I'd have been knocked off my feet.

I stood there shouting Bonnie! Bonnie! over the water for a while. Then it struck me. If I couldn't get over, neither could a cat. One thing Bonnie hated was getting wet. He'd be really miserable just being out in the rain, no way he'd try to swim across a river.

So what would he do? Try and find shelter, I told myself.

I felt a bit happier now. Water was rising fast, but not so fast it could catch a cat, and though the new river were running strong, it were a long way short of the huge wave rushing down the dale I'd seen in my fancy.

So I started calling 'Bonnie! Bonnie!' and went wandering off up what were left of the village. The rain was harder now and it seemed to stot up from ground to join the mist so that you could really feel it like stroking your face and arms and legs as you moved along. It were a funny feeling, but I were so wet now that I didn't mind it, in fact I think I might have quite enjoyed it if I hadn't been so worried about Bonnie. I couldn't see a thing, but I thought as long as I were going uphill I couldn't come to much harm, and all the time I kept on shouting his name.

And then I heard him miaowing back.

I knew right off there were summat wrong. I know all the sounds Bonnie makes, and the kind of yell he gives when he's hungry and wants his supper, or when you've left him shut up for a long time and he's narked with you, is a lot different from the noise he makes when he's scared.

I thought, mebbe he's hurt himself, and I shouted again, and he shouted back, and I went towards the noise.

First thing I saw was this big pile of stones. Then I heard Bonnie again and I saw his eyes, two slivers of green glistening in the dark. But they were quite high up and I thought he must be standing on this pile of stones. Then above his eyes I saw something else, a paleness in the air, and another pair of eyes, and I took a step closer and saw that someone was holding Bonnie tight against his chest.

And at the same time I realized the pile of stones was all that was left of Neb Cottage and the man holding Bonnie was Benny Lightfoot.

He said, 'Is that you, Betsy Allgood?'

His voice were low and unearthly, and his face so thin and his eyes so staring, he looked just like one of the nixes I recall seeing in an old picture book. I'd never been so scared before, nor since. But he had Bonnie and I knew that nixes ate any beasts they took, lambs or dogs, or cats.

So I said, 'Yes, it is.'

He said, 'And you've come calling for me,' sort of wonderingly.

I said, 'No, I were calling for my cat.' Then seeing how he'd made his mistake, I went on, 'He's Bonnie. That's what I were calling. Bonnie, not Benny.'

'Bonnie not Benny,' he echoed. Then he sort of smiled, and he said, 'Never mind, you're here now, Betsy Allgood. Come here.'

'No, I don't want to,' I said.

'You mean, you don't want your cat?'

He held Bonnie up in both hands and he must have squeezed or something, because Bonnie let out a squawk of pain. I didn't decide to do anything, I just found myself walking towards him.

He were standing higher than I was, being up the fell and also on one of the stones from the cottage, and he held Bonnie out towards me. I reached up to take him, but just as my fingers were almost touching his fur, Benny pulled him back with one hand and with the other he grabbed me by the arm.

I started screaming, and he pulled me closer to him, his fingers so tight around my flesh, I thought he were going to snap the bone. His face came down close to mine and I could feel his breath on my face, his cold wet lips against my neck, as he spoke in a horrible, breathless whisper, 'Listen, listen, little Betsy. I don't want to hurt you, all I want you to do is . . .'

Then, because I were twisting so hard to get away, he must have slackened his grip on Bonnie, and Bonnie shot up into the air and caught with his claws at Benny's face to stop himself falling.

Now it were Benny's turn to scream. He let go of me to grab at the cat, but Bonnie was already dropping to the ground, and I stooped down and scooped him up. Benny made another grab for me, I felt his fingers touch my hair, but it were so short and so wet, he couldn't get any grip, and then I was running away fast as I could with Bonnie in my arms.

How far I ran, I don't know. Not all that far. The ground was damp and skiddy and covered with rocks and I soon tripped and fell. I could feel my ankle hurting, so I didn't try to get up but rolled over under a big boulder and lay there, panting so hard I thought I must be heard half a mile away. But slowly my breathing eased, and Bonnie tight against my chest seemed to know that it wasn't a good idea to make a lot of noise, and eventually I could hear the hiss of the rain once more, and the thunder of White Mare's Tail, and the roar of the new force tumbling down from Black Moss.

There were other sounds too, movings, shiftings, breathings, which could have been Benny looking for me, so I closed my eyes and lay there quiet as I could and tried to say my prayers like the Rev Disjohn had taught me. But I couldn't say them in my mind and I didn't dare say them out loud for fear of sharp ears out there listening for me. In the end I think I fell asleep. Or mebbe I started to die. Mebbe it's the same. One moment you're here, next you're nowhere.

Then suddenly I were plucked from that peaceful darkness by arms seizing me close and a voice crying in my ear. For a second, I struggled wildly, thinking that Benny had got me again. Then the smell of the body I was pressed against and the sound of the voice in my ears told me it was my dad who'd got a hold of me, and I pressed close as I could, and I knew everything was going to be all right now. I thought everything was going to be all right forever.

TWO

On the third day of the Lorraine Dacre enquiry, Shirley Novello woke up feeling pissed off.

The feeling hit her a good minute before she'd struggled far enough out of the clutches of sleep to identify its source. Feelings were like that. Sometimes she woke up happy and lay there luxuriating in mindless joy till finally her waking brain reminded her what she was happy about.

Now she opened her eyes, saw the inevitable bright sunlight spilling in through the thin cotton curtains, yawned, and remembered.

Andy Dalziel, the Pol Pot of Mid-Yorkshire, the thinking woman's Kong, had told her off to keep Peter Pascoe's appointment with Ms Jeannie fucking Plowright, Head of Social Services, this morning.

She tried to tell herself she should be flattered to be handed the DCI's assignment, but all she could feel was pissed. Like yesterday. She'd done all the hard work on the cars, then she'd been shoved off into the school to talk to the kiddywinks. She'd dragged herself back from that by persuading Wield that it was worth asking questions about the blue estate the whole length of the Highcross Moor road. He'd gone along with it, more, she guessed, because he couldn't think of anything better for her to do than in expectation it would be worth doing. Well, she'd proved him wrong. Result, they had a suspect. OK, no one seemed very hopeful, but no one had come up with anyone better. Turnbull was for the time being the focal point of the enquiry. The clock was ticking. He would have to be released later today if nothing concrete emerged. But that gave them several more hours to hammer away. She ought to be there, helping with the hammering. Instead of which, she was pushed out to the periphery again, all because these pathetic men were scared something from a fifteen-year-old cock-up might come back to haunt them.

Unfair, she told herself. She'd spent a good part of last night studying the Dendale file. The photos of those three little blonde-haired girls had gripped her throat like a cold hand and she'd had to pour herself a drink. There'd been a photo of the fourth girl, too, Betsy Allgood, the one who got away, a strange little chubby-faced creature, with cropped black hair, more like a boy than a girl, except for those wide watchful eyes which seemed to belong to some creature of the night. What had become of her? Had the experience of being attacked by Lightfoot left its mark on her soul forever? Or had the resilience of childhood been powerful enough to shrug it off, leaving her free to go forward unscathed?

Whatever, yes, if she'd been engaged in such a case and not brought it to a satisfactory conclusion, then she too might find it haunting her dreams for the rest of her life. In fact, if they didn't get a result in the Lorraine Dacre enquiry, perhaps fifteen years from now . . .

She pushed the thought away. They were going to get a result. And if the memory of Dendale made the Fat Man even more determined to get his man, that was all to the good.

But this concern with old Mrs Lightfoot was surely clutching at straws. She was old and sick fifteen years ago. She was almost certainly long dead. God rest her soul, she added, crossing herself. Police work meant you had to become hardened to death in the physical sense, able to look at all sorts and conditions of corpse without spewing your guts. She was becoming better at that. But she was determined to avoid that parallel and irreversible hardening of the emotional and spiritual response.

Now the reason why the DCI couldn't keep his own appointment rose to the surface of her mind and with it a surge of guilt at her own resentment.

She slipped out of bed, dropped on her knees before the ghastly picture of the Blessed Virgin her mother had bought at Lourdes and made her promise to hang on her bedroom wall, presumably as the only form of prophylactic a good Catholic girl ought to use, and said a quick prayer of intercession for the Pascoe girl. Then she rose and looked at herself in the mirror.

A wreck, she judged herself. So fucking what? Even a wrecked policewoman would shine among the tatty-bag-smock-and-no-make-up freaks who haunted the offices of Social Services!

It came as a shock at nine o'clock to find herself facing a tall slender woman in a Gucci-clone suit.

And she clearly came as a disappointment to the Head of Social Services.

'I was expecting DCI Pascoe,' said Plowright.

And looking forward to him, thought Novello. The sexy face of policing!

'He couldn't make it,' she said, and explained why.

'Oh, God, that's terrible,' said Plowright, concern shining through with a force which must have reassured many clients ready to be alienated by her appearance. She made a note on a pad, then became briskly professional.

'So how can I help? The message said something about Mrs Lightfoot from Dendale.'

Novello explained. She thought she'd been equally briskly professional but when she'd finished, the social worker said, 'And you think it's a waste of time?'

Shit, thought Novello. Memo to self; Plowright's job, like her own, required sensitivity to sub-texts, and she'd been a lot longer at it.

She tried for a misunderstanding. 'Sorry, I know how busy you are . . .'

'Not my time. Yours,' smiled Plowright, pulling out a gold cigarette case and proffering it. Novello shook her head. Smoking was one form of male CID camouflage she had steadfastly resisted. Plowright lit up without any of the now almost compulsory do-you-mind? gestures. Well, it was her office.

'But Peter, DCI Pascoe, presumably didn't think it a waste of his time,' the woman continued.

'Mr Pascoe's a very thorough man,' said Novello, determined to retake the high ground. 'He likes to eliminate the possible, no matter how improbable. So, can you help, Mrs Plowright?'

'Call me Jeannie,' said the woman. 'Yes, I think I can. It's a long time ago, but fortunately we tend to horde our records. I became involved with Agnes, that's old Mrs Lightfoot, after she'd recovered from her stroke sufficiently to be moved out of hospital. Things weren't quite so bad in the NHS back then, but already there was a growing shortage of beds, and hospital managers were particularly keen to avoid becoming long-term minders of the elderly infirm.'

'So Agnes was no longer in need of treatment?'

'She was in need of care,' said Plowright. 'No way could she go back to looking after herself. Mentally she was back to full strength, but she couldn't walk unaided and had limited use of her left hand and arm. No further physical improvement was expected, so the hospital

261

turned to us. Our job . . . *my* job was either to get her a nursing home place or find some member of her family able and willing to look after her. The latter didn't seem a possibility.'

'Why?'

'Because her son was dead, her daughter-in-law had remarried and gone to Australia, and her designated next of kin was her grandson, Benny, and nobody knew where he was, but I daresay you know all about that.'

'So what happened?' asked Novello, ignoring the dig.

'I set about finding her a place in one of our approved nursing homes. Agnes didn't co-operate. There were forms to be filled in, details to check, all the usual bureaucracy. She just refused to answer questions or write her signature. And then her niece turned up.'

'How did that come about?'

'I'd come across her name and address in Agnes's papers, such as they were. One of her old acquaintances from Dendale who came to see her told me that this Winifred Fleck was Agnes's niece. They exchanged Christmas cards because that was what relatives did, but there was no love lost between them. I'd gone through the motions of writing to her anyway, because, like Peter Pascoe, I believe in eliminating the possible no matter how apparently improbable.'

She smiled as she said this, presumably to show it was a joke not a crack. Novello gave a token smile back to show she didn't much care which, and said, 'But in this case the improbable possible came good, right?'

'That's right. Mrs Winifred Fleck turned up at the hospital one day, had a chat with Agnes, then informed the authorities that she would be taking her aunt home to live with her.'

'Nice caring lady,' said Novello approvingly.

'She looked to have the qualifications. She'd worked

as a care assistant in a nursing home, so she knew the kind of thing that was involved.'

'But you didn't like her?' said Novello, not displeased to show Jeannie Plowright that she wasn't the only one able to pick up a nuance.

'Not a lot. But that means nothing. I can't say I was exactly in love with old Agnes, either. You had to admire her will and her independence, but in her eyes I was an authority figure, and she didn't go out of her way to show her best side to authority figures. Anyway, she was *compos mentis*, so even if the niece had just served time for beating up patients in the geriatric ward, there was nothing I could have done to prevent Agnes moving in with her once she indicated this was what she wanted.'

'Which it was?'

'She said so, signed all the hospital discharge papers, didn't bother to thank anyone, was helped into a car by Winifred, and that was that.'

'And you heard nothing more?'

'I passed on the papers to the appropriate Social Services office down in Sheffield and checked with them a couple of weeks later. They said everything was fine, Mrs Fleck was taking her new responsibility seriously, and she'd applied for all the grants and allowances and so on.'

'And that was evidence she was taking it seriously?' said Novello.

'Not in itself, but it gave the Social Service department allotting the funds a right of access and inspection. We don't just pour our largesse with unstinting hand and no follow-up, you know.'

'No. Sorry. You heard anything since?'

'No. I've enough on my own plate without examining other people's kitchens.'

'Of course not. Though you have climbed a bit higher up the tree,' said Novello.

'From which the view may be better, you mean?' Plowright grinned. 'Depends which way you're looking. I'm sure you'll find out for yourself one day. Are we done?'

'When you give me Mrs Fleck's address.'

It was already typed on a sheet of non-official paper.

Winifred Fleck, 9 Branwell Close, Hattersley, Sheffield (South).

As Novello folded it carefully and put it in her shoulder bag, she thought, this woman must have been up at the crack to dig out those old files and prepare herself so thoroughly for the interview. Would she have been quite so conscientious and co-operative if she'd known it was the tweenie who was coming and not the young master?

Miaou! she added guiltily.

She stood up, offered her hand, and said, 'Thank you for being so helpful.'

'Is that what I've been? You've changed your mind about it being a waste of your time then?'

She spoke very seriously and for a second Novello floundered between courteous dishonesty and honest discourtesy.

Then Jeannie Plowright laughed out loud and said, 'Don't worry, my dear. Peter sometimes lets the mask slip, too. I hope we meet again soon.'

Novello went down the stairs fast and furious.

Bloody patronizing cow! At least you knew where you were with a man, even if it was in the gutter being kicked.

By the time she reached the ground floor, she'd cooled down a bit. Perhaps it was her own fault. She knew that she approached Inspector Maggie Burroughs with a sort of aggressive caution lest it should seem she was expecting some special sisterhood treatment. Not that she was averse to getting it, but she didn't want to look like she was expecting it. Maybe this defiant I'll-do-it-my-way attitude had coloured her approach to Jeannie Plowright.

I'll do it my way! Odd choice of song for an advanced feminist.

Bit like Marie Antoinette comforting herself by whistling the Marseillaise!

That made her smile away the remnants of her resentment and she went in search of a phone, humming Ol' Blue Balls' hymn.

Through to Danby Section Office, she asked for Wield and, when he came on, she reported the interview crisply, using lessons learned from his book.

'So what do I do now, Sarge?' she asked when she'd finished.

He hesitated, then said, 'Well, the super's in with Turnbull at the moment . . .'

'Anything happening there?' she asked.

'Not a lot,' said Wield. 'When the clock stops ticking, I reckon he'll walk free. Look, I think you should follow this thing up, even if it's just to make sure it's a cold trail. I'll clear it with Sheffield so's you don't get arrested for impersonating a police officer.'

'If you say so, Sarge,' she said despondently.

'Believe me, I wish I were coming with you,' said Wield. 'This isn't going to be a good place to be when Geordie heads for home.'

Was he just being kind? she asked herself as she got into her car. Or did he mean it?

Bit of both, she guessed.

But she couldn't rid herself of the feeling that she was moving away from the real centre of things as she headed south.

THREE

Peter Pascoe had watched the sun rise from the roof of the hospital.

'OK,' he said, applauding slowly. 'You're so fucking clever, let's see what you can do for my daughter.'

He heard a noise behind him and turned to see Jill Purlingstone sitting on the parapet, leaning back against the anti-suicide mesh, smoking a cigarette. He guessed she'd deliberately shuffled her feet or something to let him know he was overheard. Not that he gave a toss.

He said, 'Looks like being a nice day.'

She said, 'In our house, the wet days are the nice ones.'

She looked totally wrecked.

He said, 'Didn't know you smoked.'

'I gave up when I found I was pregnant.'

Superstitiously he thought, then this is a bad time to start again.

She said, defensively as if he'd spoken, 'I need something, and getting smashed didn't seem a good idea.'

'It has its attractions, though,' said Pascoe.

He liked Jill. She was so determinedly down-to-earth in face of all temptations to soar. She and her husband came from the same lower middle class background, but their new-found wealth (no myth this; the salaries and share options of all the Mid-Yorkshire Water directors had been frequently listed in the local press in various articles critical of their performance) had changed her very little. Derek Purlingstone, on the other hand, had recreated himself, either deliberately or instinctively, and was now a perfect son-of-privilege clone.

Pascoe, Ellie and Jill had spent the night at the hospital. There was a limited supply of 'guest' beds, and the pressure had been for the men to go home, the women to stay. Purlingstone had let himself be persuaded. Pascoe hadn't even listened. 'No,' he'd said, and walked away.

'Sunday was such a nice day,' said Jill. 'You know, one of those perfect days.'

Why the hell was she talking about Sunday? wondered Pascoe. Then he got it and wished he hadn't. She was looking for fragments to shore against her ruin, and Sunday, the last day before the illness struck, was being retouched into a picture of perfection.

'Everything went so right, you know how it sometimes does,' she continued, after she'd lit a new cigarette from her old one. 'We got up early, packed the car; I was setting the table for breakfast when Derek said, no, don't bother with that, we'll eat on the way, so we just chucked everything in, milk, cornflakes, orange juice, rolls, the lot, and we stopped after a while and had a picnic breakfast, sitting on the grass, and we saw an eagle through Derek's glasses, well, it wasn't an eagle really, Derek said it was a peregrine but the girls were so excited at seeing an eagle it seemed a shame to disillusion them, and you could see for miles, miles, I'd have been happy just to spend the whole day there, but the others were so keen to get on, and they were right, we hardly saw any traffic along the back roads and we got this lovely spot in the dunes . . .'

'I think I'd better head back,' said Pascoe. 'Let Ellie take a rest.'

He saw from her face he'd been more abrupt than he intended, but he couldn't stand here letting a watch over the living turn into a wake for the dead.

Or was it just that this day she was reshaping was a day he had no part in? How far back would he need to go in search of such a perfect day, a day he had spent entirely with his family without any interruption of work? Or why blame work? Interruption from himself, his own preoccupations, his own hang-ups? In fact, even when he was with Rosie, was most enjoying her company, wasn't there something of selfishness even in that, a use of her energy and joy as therapy for his own beleaguered mind . . . ?

He raced down the stairs as if running from something. The anger inside which had been his companion for so long now had an object, or rather a twin object – the world in which his daughter could fall so desperately ill, and himself for letting it happen. But there was still no way he could let it out. He reached his right hand in the air as if it had somehow escaped and he was trying to claw it back inside of him.

A figure was standing on the landing below looking up at him. Embarrassed, he tried to pretend he was doing a one-armed yawn. Then he saw who it was and stopped bothering.

'Wieldy!' he said. 'What brings you here?'

This was probably the stupidest question he'd ever asked, but it didn't matter because now he had reached the landing and he did not resist as his impetus took him into the other's waiting embrace.

They held on to each other for a long moment, then Wield broke away and said, 'I saw Ellie. She said she thought you'd be up on the roof. Pete, I'm sorry I didn't get last night . . .'

'Christ, you must have left last night to get here so early this morning.'

'Yeah, well, I'm an early riser. Ellie says there's no change.'

'No, but there was definitely something last night. Ellie was out of the room and I was talking to Rosie and just for a moment I thought she was going to come out of it . . . I wasn't imagining it, really I wasn't . . . she definitely reacted . . .'

'That's great,' said Wield. 'Listen, everyone's . . . well, you know. Andy's really cut up.'

'Yes. We spoke on the phone. He sounded . . . angry. Which was how I felt. Still do. I've been feeling angry for a long time now, you know, a sort of generalized anger at . . . things. What I had at home was my refuge from that. Now I've got something specific to be angry about, but it's taken my refuge too . . .' He rubbed his hand over his thin, pale face, and had a sudden certainty that that other Peter Pascoe had made the same gesture as he waited for the light to break for the last time on that grey morning in 1917.

'Pete, listen, I almost didn't come, don't ask me why, it was stupid, I felt scared . . .'

'That's O K. I hate these places, too,' Pascoe assured him.

'No. Look, only reason I'm mentioning it is, now I'm glad. Because I think it will be all right. Since I got here, that's how I've felt. I'd not say it else.'

They stood and looked at each other for a moment, then, embarrassed, looked away.

Pascoe said, 'Thanks, Wieldy. How're things going, anyway – with the case, I mean? Andy said something about you bringing in a possible.'

'Aye. Fellow called Geordie Turnbull. Has a contracting business. If you read the Dendale file, you might recall he was a possible back then too. So, big coincidence, but I doubt if it's going to come to anything this time either.'

'No. Pity,' said Pascoe, unable to drum up a great deal

of interest. Then, ashamed, he said, 'Do you know if Andy did anything about my appointment with Jeannie Plowright this morning?'

'Aye. He's put Novello on it.'

Pascoe smiled wanly.

'Oh, well. It wasn't such a good idea anyway.'

'Sounds a bit sexist, that,' said Wield.

'No, she's a good cop. I just think Andy would have gone himself if he'd felt there was the faintest hope of turning anything up.'

'Andy's going to be too busy turning the thumbscrews at Danby, which is where I'm on my way to.'

'You've taken the long way round. Thanks a lot, Wieldy.'

'Aye, well. I'll keep in touch. Keep your chin up. Cheers.'

'Cheers.'

He touched the younger man's arm then turned and walked away.

Pascoe watched him go. There had been comfort in the contact, no denying it. But now he was alone again, looking for something to blame. What had he narrowed it down to as he ran down the stairs? Oh yes. The world and himself.

He went back into the ward.

'You saw Wieldy?' asked Ellie.

'Yes.'

'It was good to see him,' she said.

'Yes.'

He looked from her face to Rosie's, from the blossom to the bud, and felt that if anything happened here, there was no way to duck responsibility, and no way to bear it either. The world was safe. His rage would have to strike where its shadow began.

'Why don't you take a walk?' he said gently. 'Jill's up

on the roof, having a smoke. Or get yourself a coffee. Go on. I'll stay.'

'OK,' she said, unable to resist the gentle force of his will. 'I won't be long.'

She went out of the room like a woman sleepwalking.

Shit, he thought. She blames herself, too. Which is crazy when it's all my fault. Everything's my fault.

'Even England not winning the Test is my fault,' he said out loud. 'You hear that, kid? Your father may not have a million in share options, but probably even the water shortage is down to him as well.'

This old technique of exaggerating fears till they reached absurdity seemed to work. He sat down by the bed and took his daughter's hand.

'That's right, it's me, dear,' he said. 'But you'd know that anyway. My smooth soft concert pianist's fingers are completely different from those rough, calloused stumps of your mum's. But she will spend all day up to the elbows in soapy water when she's not outside picking sisal.'

He paused. They'd asked if talking to Rosie would help and got a non-committal, 'Can't do any harm.' Great. But could she hear? That was what he needed to know. No. Not *needed*. While there was the faintest chance of the sound of his voice having any effect, he would talk till his larynx was raw. But what to say? He doubted if his introspective ramblings could be all that therapeutic. How could it help for Rosie to know that her dad was a self-absorbed neurotic?

He looked around for the pile of stuff they'd brought in for Rosie, favourite dolls, clothes, books – a great pile to reassure themselves she would soon be convalescent.

At the top was *Nina and the Nix*. He picked it up, opened it and began to read aloud.

'Once there were a nix lived by a pool in a cave under a hill . . .'

FOUR

Hattersley proved to be a large sprawling estate on the south-west fringe of Sheffield. Its design made Hampton Court Maze look like a short one-way street, and confusion was further confounded by the use of the Brontë family as the sole source of street names. Even the inclusion of Maria and Elizabeth, the two sisters who died in childhood, meant there were only seven names to play with, and this deficiency had been overcome by applying each to a street, a road, a way, a crescent, an avenue, a grove, a place, a lane, a boulevard, and a close.

It was, decided Novello, the place that delinquent postmen got sent to.

It took her half an hour to find her way to Branwell Close and when she did, she didn't get out of the car straightaway, not because she was hot and flustered (which she was), but because of the nature of number 9.

Her job had often taken her to houses which looked so neglected it came as a surprise to discover people were actually living there. The Fleck bungalow produced the same effect by opposite means. It looked more like an architect's model than the real thing, with its paintwork so bright, its brickwork so perfectly pointed, its little lawn such an exact square of emerald green, its borders so carefully combed, its flowers so precisely planted, its windows so gleamingly polished, its lace curtains so symmetrically hung, and its wrought-iron gate so brightly burnished that when she finally plucked up courage to make an approach, she hesitated to touch the shining latch and tread on the pastel pink flags of the arrow-straight path.

Then a lace curtain twitched and the spell was broken.

The front door opened before she reached it, presumably to save the bell push from the danger of an alien print.

Winifred Fleck was the kind of thin, straight, pared-down woman who cannot be said to have reached fifty but rather looks as if she has always been there. She wore a nylon overall as sterile as a surgeon's smock, and her right hand held a duster of such a shocking yellow, dust probably flew away at the very sight of it.

'Mrs Fleck?' said Novello.

'Yes.'

'I'm Detective Constable Novello, Mid-Yorkshire CID,' she said, displaying her warrant. 'It's about your aunt, Mrs Agnes Lightfoot. I believe she used to live with you.'

She used the past tense almost without thinking. The glimpse of the interior through the open door confirmed that the gods of geometry and hygiene ruled inside also. No way was an elderly relative being cared for within these walls, not unless she was moribund and pinned down in a straitjacket of starched white sheets.

'Yes,' said Winifred Fleck.

Words too were contaminants, it seemed. The fewer you used, the less the risk.

'So, what happened? Did she die, Mrs Fleck?'

Novello tried to infuse a suitable degree of sympathy into her tone, but felt that she wasn't altogether success-ful. Sympathy seemed a commodity which would be wasted here. Also, if truth were told, she couldn't help hoping that the old lady had passed peacefully away. Then she could abandon this wild-goose chase and get back to the real work going on around Danby without her.

'No,' said Mrs Fleck.

'No?' echoed Novello. This woman clearly needed some form of accelerant to get her going. Coldly she considered the possibilities, carefully selected the best.

'Perhaps we could talk about this inside? It's so warm out here, I'm sweating cobbles. I'd give my right arm for a cold drink and a fag.'

Novello didn't smoke. But the threat of her presence in this temple of hygiene, spraying perspiration and ash all over the place, must be good for a trade-off.

It was.

'She's at Wark House.'

'Sorry?' said Novello, mishearing *workhouse*, and thinking this was a bit blunt, even for South Yorkshire.

'Wark House. The nursing home.'

'Ah, yes. But she did live with you?'

'For a while. Then she got to be too much. With my back.'

'I see. How long was it she lived here then?'

'Four years, nigh on.'

'Four years. And then she got to be too much?'

Mrs Fleck glared as if sensing a slight.

'She had another stroke. We couldn't manage her. Not with my back.'

We. So there was a Mr Fleck. Probably hanging up in a cupboard so's not to crease the antimacassars.

'And she's still alive?'

'Oh, yes.'

That sounded certain, if unenthusiastic.

'You visit her?'

'I look in if I'm up there. I help out sometimes. Just the light work now. With my back.'

Plowright had said she'd been a care assistant in a nursing home. With her back!

Novello reproached herself for lack of charity. The woman had after all taken her aunt in when there was

274

no one else to look after her. And it was one thing taking care of an old lady who was a bit doddery, but quite another nursing a bedridden invalid. Novello wondered how she'd cope, shuddered at the thought, and gave Mrs Fleck a guilt-inspired smile as she said, 'If you'd give me the address, I'll not take up any more of your time.'

She got the address and directions and took her leave.

As she moved away, Mrs Fleck said, 'What's this about?'

At last, curiosity. Novello had been wondering about its absence.

'Just an enquiry,' she replied. 'Nothing to concern yourself with.'

Lovely language, English. One word covering both legitimate anxiety and sticking your neb in!

She closed the gate carefully, resisting the temptation to wipe it with her handkerchief, and got into her car. It was almost a pleasure to be back in that chaotic, unhygienic box, even if it did take a couple of minutes to dig out her map. Mrs Fleck's directions had been typically precise, but Novello was determined to make sure she lost no more time.

In fact, Wark House proved as easy to find as the woman had indicated. She drove along a main road till, with a suddenness which surprised her, she was out of the city and into wild moorland. Away to her right she could see a lone building standing against the skyline like the Bates residence in *Psycho*. She turned off towards it on a steadily climbing minor road and five minutes later found herself passing through a gateway which would not have looked out of place at the entrance to a small walled city.

The views from here were spectacular, mile after mile of rolling moor, attractive now in its golden robe of bright sunlight, but in lowering cloud and driving rain hardly a prospect calculated to comfort the old and the dying.

Inside, she took a deep breath, recalling Father Kerrigan's technique for grading the Old Folks' Homes he visited. 'If you can smell piss in the hallway, start asking questions.'

Wark House passed that test, which was a relief. In fact, looking around she was pleasantly surprised by the contrast with its forbidding exterior.

A nurse came out of a room, spotted her, asked if she could help.

'Could I see the matron, please?'

She was taken to an open-doored, open-windowed office where a small black woman of about forty sat behind a paper-strewn desk. Her dress was nurse-like but not aggressively so, and her smile was natural rather than professional.

'Shirley Novello,' said Novello, taking the outstretched hand.

'Billie Saltair,' said the woman. 'What can I do for you?'

Novello glanced at the door to make sure the nurse had moved out of earshot.

'Close it if you like,' said the matron. 'I keep it open so's people can see how hard I work. Also, this weather, I'd love to create a draught. Usually up here, you open a window and you get hit by a gale that would scatter all this paper round the building in ten seconds flat, which is probably the best way of dealing with it.'

Novello closed the door.

'I'm a police officer,' she said. 'Nothing to worry about, but people can get the wrong idea.'

'Is that so?' said Saltair, mildly amused. 'Better tell me the right idea before I join them.'

'You've got a Mrs Agnes Lightfoot staying here, I believe.'

'That's right.'

'How is she?'

'She's fine, considering.'

'Considering what?'

'Considering she can't walk, is half-blind, has problems with her speech, and hardly ever gets a visitor.'

'Not even Mrs Fleck?'

'You know Winifred?' said the matron neutrally.

'I've met her. She works here, doesn't she?'

'Occasionally.'

'Yes, of course. Her back.'

'Ah, you've met her back too?'

The two women regarded each other deadpan for a moment then began to smile.

'Perhaps I'd better explain,' said Novello, deciding that with Billie Saltair, frankness was likely to provoke frankness.

She outlined the background of the case succinctly, finishing by saying, 'So all you've got to do is confirm Mrs Lightfoot hasn't had any strange man in his thirties visiting her in the past couple of weeks and I can get out of your hair.'

Saltair was frowning and shaking her head.

'Sorry, I can't do that,' she said.

'Oh, come on! It's hardly privileged medical information, is it?' said Novello, irritated, especially as her liking for the matron had led her to strain her own bounds of professional discretion.

'You're getting me wrong,' said the matron. 'What I mean is, I can't tell you Agnes hasn't had any such visitor. There was a man came last week, Friday morning it was. I wasn't here, but I got told all about it when I got back. It was news, you see, Agnes being visited. Unfortunately, it was Sally that met him when he turned up on the doorstep. Sally's our youngest nurse, just started.

Normally any new visitor would be steered along here first, just so's we can run an eye over them, also put them in the picture about whoever they're wanting to see, once we've judged them genuine. But Sally didn't take this fellow to meet my deputy, just led him straight into Agnes's room and left him there. And by the time she mentioned it to Mary, that's my deputy, the bird had flown.'

'Could I talk to Sally?' asked Novello, trying to keep it casual, but with her stomach churning with excitement. Up to now she'd been putting this whole thing down to ultra-cautious Pascoe covering every angle. She'd ignored his reputation for finding corners of an investigation other cops couldn't reach. What was it that one of her friendlier male colleagues, DC Dennis Seymour, had said when he had invited her to have supper with him and his nice Irish wife and they'd lounged around afterwards drinking Old Bushmills? 'Big Andy's easy to follow. He walks through walls and you just pour in after him through the gap. But that Pascoe's something else. He creeps through cracks and you've no idea where the clever sod's taking you.'

Saltair had gone to the door and yelled at someone to ask Sally to step along when she had a moment.

'Anything else you can tell me about this guy?' asked Novello.

'It's all hearsay with me, best leave it to Sally,' said Saltair, which suggested to Novello's sensitive ear that there was.

'OK,' she said. 'So what about Agnes? Were you here when she came into the Home?'

'Sure I was. I've been here from the start. This place used to be the family house of one of the consultants at the hospital I worked at. His wife died, his family moved on, and he was rattling around in here so he decided to move out. But he saw the way things were going back in the eighties, health care for the aged was going to be a major growth industry, so instead of selling up, he turned the place into what you see and made his favourite staff nurse, who happened to be me, an offer I couldn't refuse. That was seventeen years ago. Jesus, where does the time go?'

'And Winifred Fleck?'

'She came along at the start too. As a care assistant. She'd had some experience and she was pretty good. Not over-endowed with human sympathy, maybe, but you may have noticed that when it comes to hygiene and good order, she'd got no equal.'

'It did strike me that her lawn looked shrink-wrapped,' said Novello.

'Yes, well, mustn't mock. Too much. Hygiene's really important in a place like this and having someone like Winifred around really kept us on our toes. Must say, we were all a bit surprised way back when we heard she was taking an invalid aunt in.'

Novello said lightly, 'I suppose we're all inclined to take care of our well-to-do relatives.'

'Indeed. And if that had been a motive, I could have understood it. But Agnes had a few hundred in the bank, no more. I know because when she had her second stroke and came in here, she was on full grant from the start.'

'Sorry, what does that mean?'

'Put simply, the more you've got saved up, the larger your personal contribution to our fees. But if your savings are under what was a fairly modest limit ten years back, then Social Services pick up the tab. The limit's gone up quite a lot since then with a lot of well-heeled people complaining it was a tax on thrift.'

'And the authorities check up on this?'

'Oh, yes. They require sight of bank statements and so on for a couple of years before admission just to make sure there hasn't been some recent large movement of funds in anticipation of care need.'

'Which bank?' Novello surprised herself and the matron by asking. But she looked it up and said, 'The Mid-Yorkshire Savings.' As Novello made a note, she mused, 'So Agnes had nothing or very little when she came here. Of course, that doesn't necessarily mean she had nothing when she went to live with Winifred.'

She saw instantly that she had made a bad move. Billie Saltair's lips puckered like she was sucking a lemon and she said, 'Let's get one thing straight, Detective Constable. Winnie Fleck can be a pain in the arse, and I know she'd stoop a hell of a long way, bad back and all, to pick up a penny, but she's as honest as the day is long. Sure, if old Agnes did have a fortune, Winifred would expect her share of it as her due when the old lady died. But she wouldn't screw it out of her, no way.'

'Sorry,' said Novello meekly, but was saved from further apology by the arrival of a young nurse with short red hair and an anxious expression.

'Sally, this is Shirley Novello,' said the matron, obviously judging that any mention of the police would only increase the girl's tension. 'We were just talking about Agnes. Miss Novello thinks she might know the visitor she had last week and as you're the only one who actually met him, I'd like you to tell her whatever you can remember. It's OK. There's nothing wrong.'

She smiled reassuringly and the girl relaxed slightly and began talking. 'Well he just came in and when I spoke to him and he said he was Agnes's grandson, I got quite excited 'cos I knew Agnes didn't get many visits so I just took him straight along to her room, we usually bring her down to the day room after eleven but she hadn't been feeling too clever so it seemed best to let her lie on and see how she felt after lunch . . .'

The nurse spoke in a flash flood of words which a linguist might have been content to observe from the bank till it died away of its own accord. Billie Saltair, however, bravely plunged in with, 'OK, Sally, we get the picture. Miss Novello?'

'He told you he was Agnes's grandson?' said Novello.

'Oh yes, that's why I took him straight up, he said, Hello, I believe you've got my grandmother Mrs Agnes Lightfoot living here, and I said, Yes . . .'

'Did he tell you his name?' said Novello, following the matron's example.

'No, but when I took him in and said, Agnes, I've got a visitor for you, it's your grandson, she said, Benny, Benny, is that you? I knew you'd come some day, I always knew. And then he took her hand and sat down by the bed and I left them together 'cos I didn't want to intrude . . .'

'You did OK, Sally,' said Novello, smiling. 'You were quite right. They needed to be alone. So, her grandson after all these years. How did he look? Not a short fat chap, was he?'

'Oh no, he was quite tall and very thin, even his face, sort of long and narrow, and brown, with the sun, I mean, well, I know everyone's quite brown just now what with all this heatwave, but his face was sort of leathery like he was used to being out in the sun all of the time which isn't surprising because they get this kind of weather all the time in Australia . . .'

'Hold on,' said Novello. 'Why do you say Australia?'

'Because of the way he talked, he had this accent, you know, sort of cockney but different, like the way they speak in Australian movies and *Neighbours* on the telly.'

'And his clothes?'

'Blue-and-white checked shirt, short sleeves, dark blue cotton slacks, black moccasins,' said Sally with a precision almost shocking by comparison with her customary loquaciousness.

'Age?' said Novello, hoping to stay tuned to this new wavelength.

'Thirties maybe. Hard to say with that leathery sun-burnt look.'

'How long did he stay?'

'Well, I don't know exactly, there was a bit of a crisis with Eddie, that's Mr Tibbett, having a fall and we had to get him into bed and then call out the doctor just to make sure he hadn't done himself any real harm and next time I looked in on Agnes, he'd gone – her grandson, I mean . . .'

Clearly clothes and looks were her special subject.

'You didn't happen to notice how he got here?' said Novello. 'Car? Taxi? Bike?'

'Sorry,' said the girl. 'He was in the hallway when I saw him, I didn't see if there was a car or anything . . .'

This time she tailed off of her own accord, sounding distressed.

'Hey,' said Novello brightly. 'It doesn't matter. You've been a real help. It's not that important. Old Agnes's grandson! I bet she's talked about nothing else since his visit.'

'Not really,' said Sally. 'She doesn't say a lot. It's hard for her, finding the words, you see. I asked her about him, you know, just making conversation. But all she said was, I knew he'd come, he's a good lad, whatever they say. And when I tried to ask a few questions, she just closed her eyes, so I didn't say anything else. I thought she probably wanted to keep the memory to herself. It could be all she's got.'

Novello smiled and said, 'No. She's got good nurses

and friends like you, Sally, and that's a lot. Thank you. You've been really helpful.'

The girl flushed, glanced at the matron who nodded dismissal, then left the room at a lope.

'You handle people well,' said Saltair.

'Thanks. And sorry again for treading on your toes about Winifred.'

'But you'll still check?'

'If I told you one of your patients didn't have a heart condition, would you simply put it on his record?'

'Certainly not. But Winifred isn't one of your patients. I mean, she's got nothing to do with this other business, has she?'

'Not that I can see,' said Novello. 'Not, in fact, that I can see very much at all.'

'So Sally hasn't helped?'

'In one way, of course she has. But sometimes more information just means more confusion.'

'I know the feeling. Like symptoms. They don't always help diagnose the right disease.'

Novello reached out her hand.

'Anyway, thanks for your help. Look, I don't see any point to me bothering Agnes now. Or at any time, from the sound of it. But there may be others who think differently. I'll need to discuss all this with my superiors. They may want to talk to her.'

'They'll need to talk to me first,' said Billie Saltair with an anticipatory smile. 'No one tells me what to do at the Wark.'

'Not even your boss?'

'My boss?' said Saltair sounding surprised.

'The owner. The consultant who made you the offer you couldn't refuse.'

'Oh, you mean my husband?' She laughed at Novello's expression. 'I should have said. *That* was the offer I

283

couldn't refuse. He's retired now.' She grinned rather wickedly. 'I've told him there's a bed waiting for him here the first sign he gives of senility, like trying to interfere with the way I run things. I think he half believes me.'

And so do I, thought Novello as she headed out into the savage brightness of that moorland sun.

And so do I!

FIVE

Wield yawned.

Sergeant Clark, not normally an imaginative man, somehow found himself thinking of a visit to Wookey Hole he'd made on holiday years back.

'You were saying, Nobby?'

Wield's face had resumed its normal blank cragginess.

'Oh aye. She said you rather than the super, if that was possible.'

So DC Novello finds me more user-friendly than Fat Andy, thought Wield. Should I be flattered?

He yawned again. It wasn't just his even earlier than usual reveille that was making him tired. It was the emotional energy he'd used in making the visit to the hospital, plus the hours he'd spent since in that claustro- phobic interview room going round and round in ever- decreasing circles with Ringmaster Hoddle cracking the whip.

Well, it was over now. Dalziel had taken Clark's inter- ruption as the signal to abandon hope even though there were still ten minutes to go on the clock.

He picked up the phone and said, 'Wield.'

He listened carefully to what she told him, making notes in his notebook.

When she finished, he said, 'So what do you do now?'

Surprised, she said, 'That's why I was ringing, Sarge. To get instructions.'

'You're the one hot on the scent,' said Wield. 'How do you see the next move?'

She hesitated, then said, 'I know it's a lousy time and all that, but I wonder if someone shouldn't run this by the DCI. I mean, it was his call, and he may have thought it through a lot further than the rest of us . . . I mean, that's the way he does things, isn't it? Coming at them sort of cock-eyed . . . I don't mean . . .'

'I know what you mean,' said Wield gently. 'You're dead right. Someone ought to run this past him.'

'That's the way I see it,' said Novello relieved. 'So what shall I do till I hear from you?'

'From me?' echoed Wield.

'Or from the super, whoever does it.'

'Into job delegation, are you?' said Wield. 'No, this one's down to you. Got a pen? I'll give you Mr Pascoe's mobile number.'

'Sarge, I couldn't . . . it's not right . . . someone who's a friend maybe . . .'

'That what you're going to say next time you're told off to question some woman who's just seen her husband kicked to death, is it? Any road, if you don't think Mr Pascoe's your friend, then I can't imagine who you think is. So write this down. And keep me posted.'

As he replaced the receiver after dictating the number, it rang again.

'Mr Dalziel, please,' said a female voice.

'Mr Dalziel's . . .' *Busy* he'd been going to say, but as the Fat Man walked into the office at that moment, mopping his brow with a khaki handkerchief like the side of a military marquee, he emended it to, '. . . here.'

'Hello?' growled Dalziel.

'If I were you, I'd take a closer look at Walter Wulfstan.' The line went dead.

'Anything?' said Wield as Dalziel banged the phone down.

'Some nut telling me to take a close look at Wulfstan.'

'And will you?'

'At the moment all I want to take a close look at is a yard of ale. Let's sneak out the back while Turnbull and Hoddle are attracting the press flies out front.'

The Coach and Horses was only a few yards down the street, and seated in its cool dark bar, the Fat Man downed his first pint in a single draught and was well into his second as Wield filled him in on Novello's report.

'And you've told her to ring Pete? That's a bit hard, isn't it?'

'Who for, sir?'

'Both on 'em! Her for having to do it and him for having to answer it.'

This was a new situation, Dalziel playing Mr Nice to Wield's Mr Nasty.

He said carefully, 'When I saw Pete this morning, it seemed to me that what he needs least is being left to himself. I'd say he's not been really right since that business about his great-granddad, and this thing with his lass is . . . could be . . . a last straw. Even if all Novello gets is a blasting, at least it'll have been a diversion.'

'So that's Pete taken care of. What about the lass?'

'Part of the learning curve, isn't that what they say, sir?'

'Is that what it is? Well, women have different curves from men, or mebbe you haven't noticed. Seems to me she's making summat from nothing out of this assignment and she ought to be encouraged.'

'My reading of her is that's exactly what this is. Encouragement.'

'Oh aye? What do you do for reward out there at Enscombe? Kick each other in the teeth?'

Dalziel finished his second pint and signalled for a third. A memory of the one he'd left standing in the Book and Candle flashed across his mind.

'So what do you think, sir?' said Wield, moving the subject on. 'The old lady's visitor: could it be Benny?'

'Who ran off to Oz to join his mum and has now come back on a trip, had a chat with his gran, then decided to come up here and start where he left off, killing little lasses? Make a great book, Wieldy. I'll wait for the movie.'

'But the facts, sir . . .'

'Facts? What a teenage nurse thought she heard a half-blind, half-doolally old woman say?'

'But alongside Mrs Hardcastle's sighting . . .'

'That's a fact now too, is it?' said Dalziel. 'Only fact about that is that it set her plonker of a lad running riot with a spray gun . . .'

He paused, and supped another gill of ale.

'He'd have had to notice it, wouldn't he, Wieldy?' he said. 'If any man on God's earth is going to notice a sign saying BENNY'S BACK, it's Walter Wulfstan. But he never mentioned it. And now we're getting funny phone calls.'

He drained his pot and stood up.

'Where are we going, sir?' said Wield, taking a farewell sip of his shandy.

Dalziel hesitated then said, 'Nay, lad, you get back to St Mike's and make sure George Headingley's not using them computers to work out his pension fund.'

'And you, sir. Where will you be, in case we need you?'

'I think I'll pop round and have another chat to Wulfstan.'

'At the Science Park?'

'Mebbe closer than that.' He raised his voice and addressed the man behind the bar. 'Landlord, I feel a religious fit coming on. How do I find my way to the Beulah Chapel?'

*   *   *

In fact, if guilt is the starting point of religion, Andy Dalziel's jocularity had a grain of truth in it, for he felt slightly guilty as he parted from Wield and went in search of the chapel.

It was true, he had good reason to believe Wulfstan could be there this afternoon, but he also had a feeling, or a hope, or *something*, that Cap Marvell might also be around. Wield knew the woman, knew of their past relationship, and while Dalziel was far too pachydermatous an animal to worry about his colleagues speculating about a relationship, he didn't care to think of them reaching a conclusion before he did.

So giving the sergeant his congé, plus a curiously puritanical self-doubt as to whether in a case like this at a time like this he had any right to such private and personal concerns, left the Fat Man uneasy.

He shook his head to dislodge the feeling like a bear dislodging a bee, and considered his location. Left under an arch, down a ginnel, and the chapel's in yard at bottom, the landlord had said.

There was the arch. He turned under it. By contrast with the bright street the ginnel was a railway tunnel, so when the voice spoke, he had a problem spotting its source.

'I see he's back then.'

'Eh?' said Dalziel, poised on the balls of his feet with his fists lightly clenched, ready for either punching or grappling. Strange voices in dark places didn't always presage trouble, but it was worth an each-way bet.

'Yon mad bugger, Lightfoot. He's back. I'd have thought you'd have known.'

The voice was lightly matter of fact, and had the reediness of age or perhaps adolescence. Dalziel relaxed a little and blinked rapidly till his sight adjusted to the new light level.

He saw a shape first, small enough to be a boy. Then his brain filled in a face and he leapt rapidly to the other end of the scale. It was a hollow sunken face with deep clefts in the skin to mark the cheekbones and split the brow over which hung a few wisps of thin greying hair.

It also had something familiar about it.

'Telford?' said Dalziel doubtfully. 'Joe Telford? Is that you?'

'It was,' said the man. 'Long time no see, Mr Dalziel.'

It was indeed. But not as long as that evidenced by this man's appearance. He must still be in his forties! thought Dalziel. And while he'd never been a large man, surely he'd been taller than this?

He took a few steps towards the sunlight at the end of the ginnel and the man moved back before him, like flotsam pushed up the beach by the tide. Now the reason for the height loss became evident. Telford walked with a stoop, leaning heavily on a thick ashen stick. The dark brown suit he wore, making no concessions to the heat, may once have fitted, but now it hung on his slight frame like a tea towel on a beer pump.

The ginnel ended in an open cobbled yard across which Dalziel saw the Beulah Chapel. It was an imposing building, constructed of dark red brick and looking rather out of place, certainly out of proportion, in this location. A faint buzz came out of it as from a huge hive of bees. The yard itself was littered with a carpenter's bench, several trestles bearing lengths of wood, and plastic carriers stuffed with tools.

Telford had halted, still in the ginnel's shade. He was tidy enough despite the ill-fitting suit, clean shaven, and smelt of soap and sawdust rather than neglect. This was slightly but not totally reassuring. Dalziel had met too many folk in whom cleanliness was next to dottiness, and his inner sensors were telling him Joe Telford was dotty as a dartboard.

'So how're you doing, Mr Telford?' said the Fat Man.

'I get by. It's been a worry, but.'

'Aye, I daresay it has,' said Dalziel.

'Still, wi' a bit of luck, you'll catch bugger this time and that'll be an end on it.'

It was the unremittingly matter-of-fact tone of voice which was perhaps the most unnerving thing about the man. In fact, the premature ageing apart, it was the only unnerving thing about him. So why was he getting that care-in-the-community tingle? Dalziel decided to apply a subtle psychological test.

'Sorry to hear about your missus,' he said. 'Must've been a shock.'

Telford looked at him and scratched his chin reflectively.

'Not so much of a shock as it'll be to our George when he sees what she does to a tube of toothpaste,' he said.

Dalziel smiled approvingly. Flying colours. That was how you expected a down-to-earth Yorkie to react to domestic strife.

'So you're letting the singers use the chapel,' he said.

'Aye. Why not? To tell truth, Mr Dalziel, I don't spend a lot of time down here. And Mr Wulfstan were always a good customer in the old days. Owt needed done at Heck, he always went local, didn't bring in some fancy Dan from town like a lot of them offcomers. He'll be glad of it, too.'

'Glad of having somewhere for his concert, you mean? I expect he will.'

'No. Glad you're close to getting things sorted. He'll be wanting to see his little lass as much as me.'

'See his lass?' echoed Dalziel. 'Aye, I daresay, I daresay.'

He was thinking *remains*. He didn't need any bereavement counsellor to tell him how important it was for a parent's peace of mind to have a proper funeral, a proper leave-taking after no matter how many years.

But Telford's next words sent him reeling back to his initial diagnosis.

'This sun's a bloody nuisance, but. You'll have to take care of that when you find them. Could burn their eyes out after all them years in the dark. Best wait for night afore you fetch them out.'

'Fetch them out? Out of where, Mr Telford?'

'Out of yon hole in the Neb he's been keeping them in all these years. Aye, night 'ud be best. Then let them get used to the light gradual like.'

Oh, fuck, thought Dalziel. The poor bastard wasn't talking remains, he was talking recovery, he was talking resurrection. He thought his lost lass was going to come up blinking out of some dark cave in the hillside where Benny had kept her all these years. Did he think she'd be older or that some magical suspension of time would have kept her the same age as when she got taken? Dalziel didn't want to know. It was that rare thing, a problem beyond his competence. He remembered Telford's wife. A small strong woman who had balled up her apron and stuffed it into her mouth when she heard the news. He guessed she'd have kept her suffering to herself as far as she could, would finally have come to some sort of terms with it. But what was beyond her strength, what she couldn't come to terms with after all these years was the matter-of-fact craziness of her husband, his gentle insistence that little Madge was alive under the Neb somewhere, just waiting to be rescued. So she'd run. Not far, just to George, who bore a strong physical resemblance to his brother. He bet they lived close. He bet they kept a close eye on Joe. And the Danbyians would accept it.

In matters of extra-marital lust Yorkshire rustics could be as unforgiving as a government chief whip, but in terms of domestic practicality, they were often more laid back than Latins.

He said gently, 'We'll do what's right, Mr Telford. Is Mr Wulfstan here now?'

'Aye, him and some others. I'm just waiting for the truck to come. Mr Wulfstan's arranged to have my bits and pieces taken round to store at his place in the Science Park. I told him not to bother, they'd not come to harm in this weather. But he insisted. He's a good man.'

'I'll go and have a word with him then, Mr Telford. You take care now.'

He strode across the yard thinking, this is no place for me. He didn't mean the Beulah Chapel, he meant Danby. Soon as he'd got news of the case, he should have gone sick, taken a holiday, dumped the whole thing in Peter Pascoe's lap. Then he recalled what else had been dumped in his lieutenant's lap and growled to himself, 'Get a grip on yourself, man, or you'll end up daft as poor Joe Telford.'

He glanced back to the ginnel. The man had stepped further back into the deep shade and was only visible now as a gleam of eye white. Perhaps he haunted shadowy places because he felt they somehow kept him in touch with his daughter.

Shaking the depressing thought from his mind, Dalziel pushed open the door of the chapel.

There were several people in there, three of them using suction cleaners which explained the buzzing. The floor space was devoid of pews. Perhaps they'd been removed when the chapel was decommissioned. Or maybe the Beulahites didn't believe in sitting at worship. There was nowt so harmless that some religious sect hadn't made it a sin.

At the far end where presumably the altar (if they went in for altars) had stood, he saw Wulfstan in a little group which included the two singers. Behind them, Inger Sandel was sitting at a piano, plucking out single notes and examining them long after they had ceased to resound in Dalziel's ear. There was no sign of Cap Marvell. He felt a sag of disappointment, then told himself he had no right to be disappointed, not when the man he wanted to see was in place.

Not that his reason for wanting to see him was any stronger than not having anyone else he wanted to see at that moment. Some investigators he knew, when things ground to a halt in an enquiry, got through by sitting down and going over the story so far with a fine-tooth comb. He had two on his team who could do that, in their different ways. But his own way was to make things happen, keep prodding, never let the opposition have a rest, even when you didn't have the faintest idea who the opposition was. When this ignorance had been put to him as a possible invalidation of the technique by Peter Pascoe, Dalziel had replied, 'Doesn't matter. The bugger knows who *I* am and so long as he sees me busy, there's no way he'll rest peaceful in his bed. Push, push, and see what gives.'

'Superintendent,' Wulfstan greeted him. 'I hope you have not decided that you need this hall also.'

'Nay, this is all yours,' said Dalziel magnanimously. 'Standing-room only, is it? Like in the Prams?'

'Proms, I think you mean. Where people do stand, yes, but the majority sit. Here everyone will sit. We're having the chairs brought round as soon as we get the place properly cleaned.'

'Aye, I can see you're giving it a good going over,' said the Fat Man.

'The atmosphere of a carpenter's shop is not helpful to

a singer's throat,' said Wulfstan. 'I'll be having a commercial dust extractor brought down from my works later to complete the job. So, how can I help you?'

'Just a word,' said Dalziel. 'Private.'

He glanced at the others in the group. The three he didn't know drifted away. Krog and the woman remained where they were.

'Please, you may say what you will before Elizabeth and Arne,' said Wulfstan. Dalziel shrugged.

'Up to you,' he said. 'Driving into Danby on Sunday morning you'd have to pass under the old railway bridge. There was a big sign sprayed on it. It said BENNY'S BACK. You must have noticed it. But you didn't mention it to me.'

He'd placed himself so that all three were in his sight line and he saw the woman's intense gaze move from his face to her father's as though curious as to the answer to this question. Well, why not? It was a question to be curious about.

Wulfstan said, 'I did not mention it because it did not seem relevant, and in any case, I did not doubt that you yourself would already have seen it, or had it pointed out to you.'

Reasonable explanation? Or rather, explanations, there being two of them. In Dalziel's maths, this meant reasonableness divided rather than multiplied by a factor of two.

He said, 'Not relevant? After what happened back in Dendale? I'd have thought you'd have felt it relevant, if anyone did.'

'And the shock of seeing that name would have brought everything flooding back?' Wulfstan smiled wearily. 'First of all, Mr Dalziel, it has never been away. Not a day passes without me thinking of Mary. That was how I was able to return to Yorkshire, because I realized that distance made no difference.'

Dalziel clocked Elizabeth again to see if there was any reaction to this unambiguous statement of the order of things, the dead natural daughter still ranking ahead of the live adopted one. There wasn't.

'As for Lightfoot's name,' the man went on, 'there was a time when it caused a reaction. But that was several years ago when I first returned here to Danby. He has entered the local folklore. The children have a skipping rhyme that uses his name, and when they play hide and seek the seeker is called Benny. The men in the pubs describing the speed of some football player will say, "He can move like Benny Lightfoot." Most of them have no idea who they're referring to, of course. With my work-site here, I had to get used to the name. And I did.'

Dalziel nodded sympathetically.

'Aye, grin and bear it, that's the Yorkshire way,' he said.

That got a flicker of amusement from the woman.

Wulfstan said, 'Now if that's all . . . I'm expecting the fire inspector any minute now . . .'

'Sorry, I know you're busy. Yes, that's it . . . except . . .'

Dalziel bowled a good *except*. He gave it plenty of air so the batsman had lots of time to worry whether it was his googly or not.

'. . . except, you've been set up here in Danby for several years now, right? But witness who saw your car parked up the Corpse Road says she's only started noticing it there in the last couple of weeks, and she's been walking her dog up there every morning, come rain or shine, for years.'

Wulfstan looked at him broodingly for a long moment. He looked like . . . something, Dalziel couldn't remember what. Then he gave an exasperated smile and said, 'If your question is, why now? the answer is so obvious, I would have thought even a man in your line of work

296

might have got within hailing distance of it unaided. Morbid curiosity, Superintendent. This heat wave has gone on so long that what remains of Dendale village has begun to re-emerge. I climb up the Neb to watch its progress. And sometimes as I walk up the Corpse Road, I fantasize that when I reach the Neb, I'll see everything as it was, I mean *everything* as it was. There. Now you see the depths of absurdity to which the rational mind can descend.'

'Oh, I've seen minds that have gone a sight deeper than that,' said Dalziel. 'Thanks for being so frank. And I'm sorry to have troubled you.'

'No trouble. And perfect timing. There, I believe, is the fire inspector. Excuse me.'

He headed towards a man who'd just stepped through the door and was looking around with that sceptical have-we-got-trouble-here expression which is the first thing safety inspectors learn at college.

'How about us, Superintendent? You got any *excepts* for us?'

Elizabeth Wulfstan's accent still bothered him even though he'd absolved her of taking the piss.

He said, 'None I can think of, miss. Except, them Kraut songs about dead kids, you still planning to sing them tomorrow?'

'I am. After a complimentary ticket, are you? Well, we might manage one, but I reckon someone as glorrfat as you 'ud need two and I don't know if we can spare that many.'

This was piss-taking in any language.

He said, 'Just thought you might have changed your mind, all things considered.'

The Turnip gave him a nod of approval, but the woman just shrugged indifferently.

She said, 'Kids die, all the time. Show me somewhere I could sing them that no kids have died.'

'We're not talking general, we're talking specific here,' he said.

'I thought the Liggside lass were only missing,' she said. 'Like the others. They're only missing, right? You never found any bodies, did you?'

She spoke mildly, as if they were discussing some minor point of etiquette.

Dalziel said, 'Fifteen years is a long time missing. I don't think anyone . . .'

He paused. He'd been going to say he didn't think anyone was expecting them to come walking back through the door, but his encounter with Joe Telford popped up in his mind. And what did he really know about what Wulfstan and his wife were thinking? Or the Hardcastles. From what Clark had told him it sounded like all that family had gone doolally to some degree or another.

Perhaps he was the only man in Mid-Yorkshire who was certain beyond doubt all the children were dead . . . No, not the only one . . . there was another . . .

He said, 'Any road, it's none of my business. You can sing what you like, luv, long as it doesn't offend public decency.'

'Thank you,' she said seriously. 'But I'll not be singing at all if this place doesn't suit. You done yet, Inger?'

Inger Sandel hadn't once glanced Dalziel's way during the whole of his conversation with the Wulfstans, concentrating on what sounded to his untutored ear like an unnecessary fine tuning of the piano. But he had the feeling that she hadn't missed a thing. Now she sat back and started to play a scale, tentative at first, then expanding till she was sweeping up and down the whole length of the keyboard. The notes filled the chapel. Finally she stopped and listened to their dying echoes with the same rapt attention as she'd paid to the originals. Then she turned to the other woman and gave a barely perceptible nod.

'Let's give it a bash, then,' said Elizabeth Wulfstan.

Dalziel moved towards the door, Arne Krog fell into step beside him.

'I think you are right, Mr Dalziel,' he said. 'Elizabeth should not sing the *Kindertotenlieder*. For the sake of this place. And for her own sake.'

'Her own sake?'

Krog shrugged.

'Elizabeth is strong, like a steel door. You cannot see what is behind it. But as you know, the way the child is shaped forms the adult. Perhaps that's where we should look.'

Before Dalziel could reply, Inger Sandel started playing the piano; an abrupt, rapid, disturbing torrent of notes before the singer came in, with words to match.

> In such foul weather, in such a gale,
> I'd never have sent them to play up the dale!
> They were dragged by force or fear.
> Nought I said could keep them here.

She spat out the words with such power they turned the Beulah Chapel into a self-contained storm in the midst of the bright sunny day outside. As she sang, her eyes were once more fixed on Wulfstan, who at first tried to keep his conversation with the fire inspector going but soon turned his head to watch the singer.

> In such foul weather, in sleet and hail,
> I'd never have let them play out in the dale,
> I was feart they'd take badly;
> Now such fears I'd suffer gladly.

She stopped abruptly and the pianist stopped too.

'Bit echoey,' said Elizabeth. 'But that'll likely improve

once the place is filled with punters. Arne, you know everything, what do you reckon?'

Her voice was not loud but its projection was imperative. Practising to be a prima donna, or does she just not like the idea of me and the Turnip having a cosy chat? wondered Dalziel.

He looked at Krog and waited for his response. A look of irritation passed across the man's face, then he smiled apologetically and said, 'Excuse me. We will talk again perhaps.'

He hurried away to the two women by the piano.

Dalziel, who had noticed that Wulfstan, despite his close confabulation with the fire inspector, hadn't missed a nuance of this exchange, murmured to himself, 'No perhaps about it, lad.'

Then he went out into the sunshine.

SIX

It was, decided Pascoe, like being on a stakeout.

You did your stag, sat and watched, nothing happened, you got relieved, went off and had a wash and a sandwich, got your head down if you could, went back on stag, and the longer it all went on, the more you began to fear it was all no bloody use, all just a waste of time, your info was wrong, your snout had been sussed, and nothing was going to happen, not now, not in a few minutes, not ever . . . never never never never nev . . .

'Everything OK?' said Ellie.

'What? Yeah, sure, fine, I mean, no change . . .'

'You look worse than she does,' said Ellie, looking from the slight form of her daughter to her husband's drawn face. 'Why don't you go and try to get some sleep?'

He shook his head and said, 'Been there, tried that; it's worse than being awake.'

'OK. At least get out of this place, try some fresh air and sunshine.'

'I'm sick of sunshine, couldn't I try some rain?' he said, managing a smile.

She kissed him gently on the lips and he went out of the ward.

The hospital grounds were extensive and had once been a centre of horticultural excellence. But the public purse strings had been drawn much tighter in recent years, and this plus the drought and its attendant hose-pipe ban had turned the gardens into near desert. He walked around for a while, then sat down on a bench

301

and watched the stream of people moving between the car park and the main entrance. Coming, their gait was halting and slow; going, they moved with ease and vigour. Or was his keen detective gaze distorted by fatigue and that rumbling rage which like a storm in a neighbour valley never left him?

Eventually he must have fallen asleep, for he woke suddenly, slumped against the bench, not knowing where he was, then panicking when he worked it out.

But a glance at his watch told him he'd only been away for half an hour. He stood up, stretched, walked briskly back inside, and found a washroom where he splashed cold water over his face.

He got himself a coffee from a machine and went back upstairs. It was, he decided, too early to go back into the ward. Ellie would just get exasperated with him and give him the let's-be-sensible-about-this lecture. Not that he minded the lecture. Like the Mr Nice and Mr Nasty interrogation technique, they took turns at being the tower of strength and the weaker vessel. The lecture was part of Ellie's tower mode.

The waiting-room door was slightly ajar and as he made to enter to finish his coffee inside, he heard Derek Purlingstone's voice. He hadn't seen the man so far today. Maybe Mid-Yorkshire Water needed all their staff out in the sticks, digging for wells. Or maybe he needed to keep busy to stop going mad.

Mad was what he sounded now, more angry than mental.

'You know where I lay the blame, don't you?'

Jill said, 'Please, Derek . . .'

'That bloody school! If only you'd agreed to send her to a decent school, this would never have happened. No! Don't come near me. You smell like an old ashtray. God, did you have to start smoking again?'

Before Pascoe could retreat, the door was pulled wide open and Jill Purlingstone, her eyes full of tears, pushed past him and ran down the corridor.

Pascoe stepped inside. His instinct was to pretend he'd heard nothing, but when he broke the awkward silence, he found himself saying, 'You don't really think the school's got anything to do with it, do you?'

'They had to catch it somewhere,' snapped Purlingstone.

'And you really think there'd have been less chance at what you call a "decent school"?'

Pascoe's intention was still conversational rather than combative. During their few social encounters, usually apropos of the children, he'd found Purlingstone pleasant enough company, with sufficient common ground between them to make it easy to pass a couple of hours without trespass into disputed areas on either side. And when they had touched upon forbidden topics, like the responsibilities of a modern police force or the efficiency and record of Mid-Yorkshire Water, they had both been able to settle for a light, piss-taking touch. Perhaps that was what Purlingstone was straining for now as he said, 'Don't you? You get what you pay for in this life, Peter. OK, I know you and Ellie are card-carrying Trots, but I always got the impression you reckoned what was best for Rosie was worth going after, no holds barred.'

'The best in the system, by all means,' said Pascoe. 'But not buying yourself out of the system.'

'You mean it's OK for you to call in a few favours to get your kid where you want her, but not for me to pay a few quid to do the same?'

'What the hell are you saying? It's a good school and I'm pleased to have Rosie going there.'

'Of course you are, especially as Bullgate Primary's three miles closer to you in the opposite direction. How

303

many parking tickets did you have to cancel to get her on the roll at Edengrove, I wonder?'

The sneer came out so glibly that Pascoe guessed it had been used many times before. So what? he told himself. He wasn't always exactly complimentary about Purlingstone behind his back. Time to back away from this irritable spat between two men who should be united by worry instead of set at each other's throats by it.

That was what his mind was saying, but his voice wasn't taking any notice.

'Oh yes, you're right, a hell of a lot of parking tickets. But that's because I'm not a fat cat with his nose in the trough, so I can't afford the really big bribes.'

Jesus! Where's your self-control? he asked himself. Back off. Back off. He could see the other man too was close to snapping. Here it comes. Whatever he says, ignore it, walk away.

But his feet remained rooted as Purlingstone's strained breathless voice said, 'I don't have to take that from a jumped-up plod. I work bloody hard for my money, mate. I live in the real world and I've got to earn every penny I get.'

'You're joking!' said Pascoe incredulously. 'You're doing the same job you used to do before privatization. And if what they paid you then was peanuts, what's that make you now but a monkey with a bloated bank balance? And you know where that money's coming from? It's coming from us poor sods who can't get decent water pumped into our houses. Christ, if anyone's responsible for our kids being sick, it's likely to be you with your polluted beaches and stinking tap water!'

Purlingstone, his face working, took a step towards him. Pascoe balled his fist. Then he felt himself seized from behind and dragged through the door which was slammed shut behind him.

'Peter, what the hell are you playing at?' demanded Ellie, her voice low but trembling with fury.

'I don't know . . . he said . . . and I just felt it was time . . . Oh shit, it was just stupid. Things came pouring out. Him too. He said . . .'

'I'm not interested in what he said. All I'm interested in is our daughter, and you getting into a fight in the hospital waiting room isn't going to help her, is it? Look, if you can't hack it here, why don't you go out, go home, have a sleep?'

He took a deep breath, reached down inside himself for control, found it.

'No, I'm all right now,' he said. 'I'm sorry. It's just I'm so frustrated I had to lash out. Could have been worse. Could have been you on the receiving end. What are you doing out of the ward, anyway? Nothing's happened, has it?'

'You think I'd be wasting time on this crap? No, no change. I just need the loo, that's all. And I need it even more after this delay.'

'Take your time,' said Pascoe. 'I'll go into the ward, see if I can find a nurse to beat up.'

His weak joke seemed to reassure her and she hurried off. Pascoe looked at the waiting-room door, wondered if he should go in and try to make his peace, decided he wasn't quite ready for that yet and went down the corridor to the room where Rosie lay.

A nurse was checking the monitors. She gave him a nice smile before she left, so perhaps he didn't look like Mr Hyde, after all. He sat down and took his daughter's hand.

'Hi, Rosie,' he said. 'It's me. I've just been having a fight with Zandra's dad. You didn't think fathers had fights, did you? Well, it's just like the school playground out there. One moment you're minding your own business, next, someone says something and you say something back, then you're rolling on the ground trying to bite someone's ear off. That's boys I'm talking about. You girls are different. Got more sense, your mum would say. Maybe she's right. Or maybe it's just that women don't get physical, they get even. Sure, they're all for peace, but I sometimes think that for them peace is just a continuation of war by other means. That's a grown-up joke which you'll understand some day when you're a woman. Won't be too long, darling. You'll be bringing some revolting young man home and hoping your aged p's won't disgrace you by drooling into their teacups or taking their teeth out to remove the raspberry jam seeds. Rosie, be kind to us. That's all the world needs really to keep it going round, kids being kind to their parents, parents being kind to their kids, that's the only family value that's worth a toss, that's the only bit of wisdom I've got to give you. I hope you can hear it. Can you hear it, darling? Are you listening to me deep down there somewhere?'

He leaned over the little girl and stared intently into her face. There was no movement, no flicker of the eyelids. No sign of life at all.

Panic-stricken, he turned to the monitor. There it was, a steady pulse. He looked from the machine to the face, still not trusting. A muscle moved in her cheek like the softest sigh of breeze on a summer pool. He let out the long relieved breath he hadn't realized he was holding.

He started to talk again, but now his monologue sounded self-conscious and forced so he picked up *Nina and the Nix* and started reading where he'd left off before.

'*Outside, sun were so bright, a little bit of light filtered down the entrance tunnel. By its dim glow she saw she were in a cave. The ground were strewn with rocks and stuff. In the middle of the cave was a small, foul-smelling pool, and on its edge sat this thing.*

'Its body was long and scaly, its fingers and toes were webbed with long curved nails, its face was gaunt and hollow, its nose hooked, its chin pointed and fringed with sharp spikes of beard, its eyes deep-set and . . .'

Suddenly there was a mechanical beeping sound which had him staring in terror at the monitor for the split second it took him to realize it was his mobile. Angrily he clicked it on and snarled, 'Yes?'

There was a pause, as if his vehemence had frightened the speaker. Then a woman's voice said, 'Hello. This is Shirley Novello. I was just ringing . . . I was wondering, how is she, your little girl?'

'No change,' said Pascoe.

'Well, that's . . . I mean, I'm glad . . . I hope everything turns out OK, sir. Sorry to bother you . . .'

'That's OK,' said Pascoe, relenting his brusqueness. 'It was good of you to ring. Look, I shouldn't be using this thing in here. They say it can affect things . . .'

As he spoke he looked anxiously at the monitor. Everything seemed to be as before.

Novello was saying, 'I'm sorry. I didn't mean to . . . look, this wasn't such a good idea, sorry, sir. I hope everything turns out OK.'

Not such a good idea? It dawned on him that maybe this wasn't just a sympathy call.

For a second he felt furious. Then he thought, to hell with it! What do you want? The world to stop out there just because it was grinding to a halt in here? And the girl wasn't to know he was actually sitting at Rosie's bedside, watching a machine for reassurance she was still breathing.

He said, 'Give me your number.'

Surprised, she obeyed. He rang off without saying anything further, went out into the corridor and wheeled in a telephone trolley he'd noticed before, plugged it in and dialled.

'Right,' he said. 'You've done the sympathy bit. Now you've got two minutes for the rest.'

It came out fast and slick. This she'd rehearsed, reckoning that if she did get the chance to speak, the faster the better.

He said, 'You got the name of Mrs Lightfoot's bank?'

'Mid-Yorks Savings.'

'That's Willie Noolan. Old rugby club chum of the super's. He'll co-operate if you mention Mr Dalziel's name and smile knowingly. Tell him you'd like to know when the large sum of money paid into Mrs Lightfoot's account fifteen years ago went out and in what form.'

'Yes, sir. Please, what large sum?'

'The compensation money for Neb Cottage. I found out the other day . . . yesterday . . .'

He paused. Novello guessed he was having difficulty matching real and relative time.

'. . . anyway, it seems Agnes actually owned Neb Cottage, so the Board would have had to cough up before the move, otherwise they wouldn't have been legally entitled to shift her. Don't know how much, but certainly tens of thousands, I should think. If the money left the account after she went to live with her niece, contact Sheffield and let them go after Mrs Fleck.'

'But the Social people checked when she moved into Wark House.'

'Yes, but only two years back. Working in the Home, Fleck would know the procedures and make damn sure she kept a hold of Agnes for at least another couple of years after she'd got her hands on the cash. Of course, if it left her account before she had her first stroke . . .'

Now Novello was with him.

'It could be that Benny got it and that's how he managed to finance his escape.'

'Right. With forty or fifty thou in his pocket, it wouldn't

have been too hard for him to vanish right out of the country.'

'You think so?' said Novello dubiously. 'Wasn't he supposed to be a bit simple?'

'Odd, not simple, according to Mrs Shimmings. You said this visitor at the Home had an Australian accent? Well, you've probably been told Australia was where the rest of his family had gone. So where else would someone like Benny head when everything that meant home and security here had vanished? Anyway, it's a lot more likely than the notion that he disappeared into the Neb like a nix or something . . .'

He looked at the book he'd laid on the coverlet. The nix leered malevolently up at him. Not much like Lightfoot from the descriptions in the file.

He said, 'Anyway, check it out, Shirley. Check everything out, no matter how unlikely. It's a funny world, full of surprises . . .'

He sounded very weary.

She said, 'Thank you very much. I'm sorry to have troubled you when . . . I hope everything turns out OK. I lit a candle for Rosie this morning . . .'

She hadn't meant to say that. Pascoe was at best agnostic and as for his wife, if rumour were true, she'd banish all priests to Antarctica bollock-naked. But it was all the hope Novello had to offer, so she offered it.

'Thank you,' said Pascoe. 'That was kind. Thank you.'

He replaced the phone.

'You hear that, Rosie? There's a candle burning for you,' he said. 'Let's hope it's one of those great big ones, eh? Let's hope it goes on burning a long long time.'

He picked up *Nina and the Nix*. Was this any use? he wondered. Could she hear anything at all?

Pointless question. He began to read again.

*   *   *

Rosie Pascoe is lying in a corner where the nix has thrown her. She is very uncomfortable. There are small pieces of rock digging into her back. But she dares not move.

The nix is sitting only a few feet away, staring fixedly at her, as if trying to make up his mind what to do. Is there pity in his eyes? She tries to see it but can't, just a terrifying blankness.

Then somewhere far above her, she hears a telephone ringing.

The nix looks up. She looks up too. And she realizes it isn't a telephone. It is the squeak of the bat who hangs high in the roof of the cave.

The nix is still looking up. He has cupped his pointed ears in his webbed hands and seems to be straining to catch a sound. It is a sight almost comical, but Rosie doesn't feel like laughing. She guesses that any message coming down from the bat will not be for her comfort.

But she takes the chance of the nix's distraction to slide some of the rocks from under her aching body. Only, when she comes to touch them they don't feel like rocks. And when she looks down, she sees that they are bones.

Now she strains her ears too and begins to imagine she can catch those high alien squeaks. How loud they are in the nix's mind she can only guess, but he is nodding his head as though to acknowledge he understands . . . and will obey.

This may be her last chance to escape. The nix sits between her and the cave entrance through which filters that faint light with its promise of the sunlit world above. Is he so rapt by what he hears that she can steal past him and try once more to run up the tunnel? She has to try.

She begins to move, pushing herself up from the bone-strewn ground with infinite care. Then, just as she reaches a crouching position, she feels her left hand seized.

Startled she looks down. The grip is tight but it is no

monstrous paw that holds her. It is a child's hand. She lets her gaze run up the slim white arm and finds herself looking at another little girl like herself. Not quite like herself, for her hair is long and blonde while Rosie's is short and black. But there is a terror on that pale face she recognizes as her own. And the face too she recognizes, or thinks she does. First it is Nina's from the story book. Then it is her friend Zandra's. Then it is another little blonde-haired girl she doesn't know.

'Help me,' says the newcomer. 'Please help me.'

But when Rosie looks back to the nix, she sees it is too late for help. The webbed hands have come down from the pointed ears, the fixed gaze swings back to her face once more.

And the eyes are no longer expressionless blanks.

They are burning, burning.

SEVEN

Shirley Novello had always believed you needed a High Court Order, if not a Papal Dispensation, to persuade banks to break the seal of confidentiality on a client's account.

But now she discovered, as many before her in Mid-Yorkshire, that all seals flew asunder at the Open Sesame of Dalziel's name.

Or perhaps it was the smile that did it, she thought, as she followed Pascoe's instructions to the letter and smiled knowingly at Willie Noolan of the Mid-Yorkshire Savings Bank.

He smiled back, more lecherous than knowing, then turned to a computer keyboard.

'Old Agnes Lightfoot? She still alive? By God, you're right,' he said, peering at the screen. 'Not much there, but. No one's going to get rich when she snuffs it.'

'It's fifteen years back, Mr Dalziel's interested in,' said Novello.

'Before we got computerized,' said Noolan nostalgically.

'So, no record?' said Novello, disappointed.

'For shame! You don't get to be a bank by throwing stuff away. It'll be in the cellar. My lad, Herbert, will soon ferret it out. Herbert!'

Herbert, far from being a lad, was perfect evidence of the bank's reluctance to throw anything away, appearing to a neutral eye more years the far side of a rail-pass than the near side of a requiem.

He moved on nimble feet, however, and in a very short space with even shorter breath he was laying on Noolan's desk a file as creased and dusty as his own suit.

'Thank you, Herbert,' said the manager. 'Go and have a lie down till you get your wind.'

'Isn't he a little old to be working?' said Novello after he'd panted his way out of the office.

'You think so? And aren't you a little young to be asking?'

'Sorry,' said Novello.

'Nay, lass, don't look so crestfallen!' laughed Noolan. 'Herbert's long retired. Only he prefers it here to home. Says his wife makes demands. I can't imagine what he means. Now, let's take a look, shall we? Oh yes. There it is, I thought it rang a bell. Fifty thousand paid in as compensation by the Water Board. That was the end of July. Then a short while after, forty-nine thousand withdrawn. In cash. Aye, I recall it now. Cash withdrawal like that, everyone wants someone else to sign. More signatures here than a peace treaty. It all comes back now. I tried dissuading her, but she told me if I didn't want her business there was plenty as did. And off she went with the loot in a carpet bag.'

'And this was fifteen years ago?'

'So I said.'

'And the money's never come back into her account?'

He checked, right through to the time when Agnes's account was transferred to computer recording.

'Not a thing.'

'Well, thank you very much for your co-operation,' said Novello. 'Mr Dalziel will be pleased.'

'I'm glad of that. Always happy to help the police, but tell him the slate's beginning to look a bit bare. You don't save with us, do you, luv?'

'I don't earn enough to save with anyone,' said Novello. 'Sorry!'

She examined the facts as she left the building. This let Winifred off the hook. Like Billie Saltair had said, she might be greedy but she'd done nothing dishonest. In fact, old Aunt Agnes had rather taken advantage of her cupidity. She probably guessed that it was only the thought of the compensation money that had made her niece take her in. And for all the years she'd spent in Branwell Close, she'd made damn sure Winifred never got a look at her bank statements. But her guard had dropped when she'd had her second stroke and once Winifred saw the state of her accounts, the road to Wark House had been opened. Or rather, the road back from it had been closed.

So now the crazy scenario in which Benny Lightfoot, with the help of his gran's money, fled to Australia whence he had returned to start killing children again took another step towards realization.

This meant someone had to talk to Agnes. *Someone*! It meant *she* had to talk to the old lady.

Which meant first of all talking to Billie Saltair.

She rang rather than making the journey back to Sheffield. It was a wise move.

'Not today,' said the matron firmly. 'We've just put her to bed. She's not at all well, very feverish. If she gets any worse, we'll call in the doctor. Ring me in the morning.'

Would the Holy Trinity have insisted? Novello wondered. Big Andy was quite capable of interrogating a frail old woman on her deathbed, but was even he capable of pushing past Billie Saltair?

It would have been a battle worth paying ring-side prices to see.

Novello knew better than to fight outside her weight unless forced by dire necessity.

'I'll ring you tomorrow,' she said.

As if mollified by this ready compliance, the matron said, 'One thing might interest you. Probably nothing to do with Agnes's visitor, but one of our handymen I was chatting to recalled seeing a white van, like a camper van, he said, bumping down the drive that Friday morning.'

Novello smiled. Detective work was contagious. Even Billie Saltair wasn't immune.

'Thanks a lot,' she said, putting some warmth into her voice this time. 'I'll be in touch.'

She put the phone down, picked it up again and got through to the Danby incident centre. Wield was around somewhere but not immediately visible, so she left her update with DI Headingley, who thanked her avuncularly like she was a little girl tolerated in the adult world for her lisping voice and golden locks. But to some extent this was preferable to the anticipated response of the sergeant who, she felt, would rather she didn't come up with any more evidence to support a Benny's Back scenario.

And was he back? she wondered. Certainly someone was back.

She stood at the window of the CID room, wide open in hope of encouraging a cooling draught. All she got, however, were fumes and noise from the traffic in the street below. She raised her eyes to the Madonna blue sky above the Franciscan grey roofs and said, 'So where are you now, my wild colonial boy?'

If she'd been a little humbler and cast her eyes down instead of up, she might have seen the 'boy' in question pause outside the main entrance of Mid-Yorkshire Police Headquarters and peer up at the old blue lamp which still hung there. She might have observed that for a moment it looked as if he was making up his mind to

315

enter and share whatever was troubling him with those within.

Then the moment was past. He turned away and in a few steps was lost from view.

EIGHT

Dalziel dipped his biscuit into his post-coital tea, got it to his mouth before it collapsed, bit it, and said, 'Bloody hell,' soggily.

'Bad tooth?' said Cap Marvell sympathetically.

'No,' he replied. 'This is a Grannie's Golden Shortie.'

'Is that a problem?'

'It were for my dad,' said Dalziel. 'It were his recipe.'

It occurred to Cap she knew nothing of Dalziel before he became a policeman, and very little of him before he became the Detective Superintendent who had incredibly eased his bulk into her bed and her affections.

He was back in the former now because when he'd turned up at her flat door earlier that evening, she'd realized he'd never left the latter.

He'd been to the hospital to visit his colleague's sick daughter. There'd been some sort of crisis that afternoon but the child was stable again. The parents had naturally been in a state and Dalziel, she guessed, had exerted all his energies in the line of optimistic reassurance. Standing on her doorstep, he looked absolutely drained, which was as shocking as visiting Loch Lomond and finding it empty. He'd talked about the sick child, talked about the missing child, talked about the Dendale children, in an uncharacteristically disconnected way, till it was difficult to separate one from the other. What was clear was that he seemed to feel responsible in some way for all of them, and the pain of their parents weighed so heavily that even those broad shoulders were close to bending.

She'd given him whisky, refilling his glass three times as he talked, and it wasn't till the third glass was emptied that he paused, licked his lips, sniffed, and said accusingly. 'This is Macallan. Twenty-five-year-old Anniversary.'

'That's right.'

During their old itemization, a major point of friction had been her indifference to the subtleties of single malts and her predilection for the purchase of what he termed 'rubbing whisky'.

'You got someone important coming?'

'Not yet,' she said. 'But a girl can hope.'

Upon which *double entendre* Dalziel had acted.

It had been an encounter more marked by ferocity than tenderness, but that had suited her to such a degree that when he got his breath back and said with passionate longing, 'Ee, I could murder a cup of tea,' she had slipped meekly out of bed and mashed it for him.

There were times even in the best regulated of households when the Old Adam got the vote over the New Man.

The Golden Shortie had been a treat which looked like paying dividends.

'Your father was a baker, then?' she said.

'Aye. Master. Came down from Glasgow for his health, got took on at Ebor.'

The Ebor Biscuit and Confectionery Company was one of Mid-Yorkshire's principal businesses.

'For his health? He was an invalid?'

'Don't be daft,' said Dalziel, scornful at the idea that the loins whose fruit he was could be in any fettle but fine. 'He fell out with some folk in Glasgow it wasn't healthy to fall out with. Misunderstanding about a loan. He were just a lad. If it weren't for gravity, he'd not have known to crap downwards, that's what he used to say.'

'I see where you got your silver tongue,' observed Cap. 'So what about the Golden Shorties?'

'He used to make his own shortbread at home from his gran's recipe and often took a piece in his snap. One day the general manager stopped for a chat during tea break. He noticed Dad eating this shortbread and he said, "That's not ours, is it?" sort of reproachful. My dad, being a cheeky bugger, said, "No, it's not, and I doubt you could afford it." Manager broke off a bit and et it. Then another bit. And another. Then he said, "Right, lad, why don't you tell me just how much it is you think I can't afford?" Dad, knowing all his mates' lugs were flapping, thought he'd pitch it real high and said, "Next bit'll cost you five hundred nicker," which were a lot of money in them days. "In that case," said the manager, "you'd best come to my office." And fifteen minutes later, Dad were back with his mates, flashing the biggest bundle of notes most on 'em had ever seen.'

'So, a happy ending,' said Cap.

Dalziel sucked in the rest of his biscuit.

'Not really,' he said. 'Made him a big man on the bakehouse floor right enough. And when the first batch of Grannie's Goldens came out, he felt right proud. Then it became Ebor's best-selling line. And forever after when he went into a shop, and saw the packs piled high, he felt sick to his stomach. He were an easy-going man, my dad, but whenever he'd had a couple of drinks and started on about selling his birthright for messy porridge, us kids 'ud take cover 'cos he were likely to start breaking things. It all came back just now when I took a bite.'

'So, more than just a biscuit,' said Cap, mentally noting *us kids* for future investigation. 'A madeleine. Now all you've got to do is write a novel about your life and loves in seven volumes.'

'Not enough,' said Dalziel. 'And what's Madeleine got to do with it? Weren't she the lass who got bedded in that mucky poem?'

'I don't think I recall the mucky poem in question.'

'Course you do. If I did it at school, every bugger did it. By that pair of puffs, Sheets and Kelly – one of 'em anyway. Sort of poem you had to work at afore you realized just how mucky it was.'

'That is an incentive to learning I don't think they've grasped at Cheltenham Ladies,' said Cap, who suspected that much of Dalziel's philistinism was a bait to lure her into the trap of patronage.

Or perhaps not.

She observed him carefully and found herself carefully observed in return.

As they were both in that state most perilous to the consumer of crumbly biscuits and hot tea, and both in a condition which marked them as enthusiastic consumers, there was much to observe.

'So what's to become of us, Andy?' she asked.

Dalziel shrugged, and said, 'You screw a bit, scream a bit, then you die.'

'Thank you, Rochefoucauld,' she said. 'I was meaning specifically rather than generally.'

'Me, too. No one I'd rather do both with than you, lass.'

'Is that a compliment?'

'You need compliments?'

'*Like*, yes. *Need*, no.'

'Then it's a compliment. Oh, fuck, where'd I leave me trousers?'

This was in response to a muffled shrilling he recognized as coming from his mobile phone.

'I think we started in the kitchen,' said Cap. 'I hate those things.'

'Could have been worse. Could have rung fifteen minutes back,' said Dalziel, rolling off the bed.

She watched him pad out of the room and recalled a monograph she'd read in one of the Sunday supplements on 'The Sumo Wrestler as Sex Object'. She hadn't taken it very seriously at the time, but maybe after all . . .

In the kitchen, Dalziel was listening to Wield's account of Novello's latest finding with the unenthusiasm she had foreseen.

'So this means the bugger could have had nigh on fifty thou in his pocket when he took off finally. Great!'

'Gets better, or worse,' said Wield. 'I thought about this camper van that was seen at Wark House. We've been trawling all the hotels and B and B's in the area with no luck. But if he's camping . . . so I took a trip into Dendale.'

'No camping, caravans, or unauthorized motor vehicles on Water Board land in Dendale,' quoted Dalziel. 'They don't like the idea of folk pissing in our drinking water.'

'Yes, I know, sir. But back a ways down the valley, there's a farmer lets out a field to campers and such. Fellow called Holmes. Wild-eyed bugger with a tangle of beard like a briar patch, he'd as lief shot me as helped me, I reckon. But his wife's a tidy body and she sent him to muck out the pigs or something while she told me, yes, there was a camping van, and the fellow on it spoke with what could have been an Aussie twang . . .'

'These Holmeses, they local?'

'Meaning, would they have known Lightfoot? Holmes, yes, but he never saw this guy. Camping's his wife's business, nowt to do wi' him, long as they shut his gates and don't scare his stock. Wife's an offcomer from Pateley Bridge.'

'So when did matey with the twang arrive?'

'Late last Friday. Left yesterday morning.'

'Damn,' said Dalziel. 'Bloody cool if he's our man, but. Owt else, Wieldy? Van number's a bit much to hope for, I suppose?'

'Mrs Holmes thought the plate had a C and a 2 and a 7 in it. Not much, but I've got Traffic working on it. But she did get a name for the guy. Slater.'

He said it with unnecessary significance. Dalziel was there instantly.

'As in Marion Slater, you mean. Benny's mam's new married name when she took off to Oz? You ever get a reply to your enquiries to Adelaide?'

'Nothing yet.'

'Well, let's not get excited. It's a common enough name.'

'Yes, sir. Not all that common a face, but.'

'What do you mean? You said this Holmes woman were an offcomer . . .'

'That's right. But I got an old photo of Benny from the file, ran it through the copier, touched it up a bit to put a few years on in, and showed her that.'

'And?'

'And she said it were him. Mr Slater. No doubt at all.'

Cap watched Dalziel come back into the bedroom carrying an armful of clothes which he dumped on the bed prior to starting dressing.

'You're going then? I hoped you'd stay the night.'

'Me too. Sorry. Something's come up.'

'Something you can tell me?'

'Nowt to tell really. Just a possible.'

'And you've got him?'

'No. Bugger's still out there somewhere. But if he's the one, we will get him, never have any doubt about that!'

He spoke with such vehemence, she had a vision of being pursued with extreme prejudice by this relentless man, and shuddered.

He observed the effect of the shudder on her breasts with undisguised interest.

She said, 'Well, take a key, just in case you feel like dropping in later.'

'I'll see what I can manage,' he said.

After he left, she put on a robe and poured herself a scotch, digging out the bottle of supermarket blended she'd hidden in the kitchen. It was a gesture. No getting away from it, the single malt was infinitely superior, but sometimes gestures needed to be made.

Things were moving faster than she'd anticipated – the bedding, the key. Too fast? How to say? She was playing this by ear and her ear was not as reliable as once it had been. What she needed was a sign, or better still a sound, something for her to fix her fine-tuning by.

The telephone rang.

Well, that was a sound. Was it an answer?

She picked it up and said, 'Hello? Beryl, hi! Yes, it's fine. No one here, not at the moment. No, that doesn't mean . . . well, perhaps it does . . . My God you've got a disgusting mind . . . but if you've got an hour to spare, and as you're paying for the call, relax, and I'll tell you all about it.'

NINE

'Don't imagine just 'cos you don't show it, I don't know you think this is a waste of bloody time,' snarled Dalziel.

Wield, by his side, viewing with his customary impassivity the overgrown hedgerows reducing the already narrow road along which they were moving at a perilous speed, did not bother to reply.

They were on their way from Danby to Nether Dendale to talk again with Mrs Holmes, and though the sergeant was certain he'd got all there was to be got out of the woman, and that he'd done all there was to be done about it, viz put out an alert for a white camper with a C, 2, and a 7 in its plate, arranged for copies of his updated picture of Benny Lightfoot to be distributed to all reliefs, and sent a fax to Adelaide saying their previous enquiry about the Slater family was now urgent, he didn't think this revisit was a waste of time. This enquiry was building up a head of frustrated energy in the Fat Man which a wise subordinate took every opportunity to release. And besides, the very sight of the Fat Man at full throttle was often a remarkable *aide-mémoire* even to the most co-operative of witnesses.

In fact, in terms of Mrs Holmes, it did turn out to be non-productive. She had given Wield her all. Dalziel kept on pressing till finally her husband growled through his tangle of beard, 'Enough's enough. You buggers got no beds to go to? You missed him last time, what meks you think all this durdum's going to get you any closer this?'

'What's that you say?' demanded Dalziel rounding on him.

Holmes didn't flinch.

'I said, my missus has told you all she's got to tell and it's about time . . .'

'No, no,' said Dalziel impatiently. 'You said, all that durdum, right?'

'It means fuss, or noise,' Wield interpreted helpfully.

'I know what it bloody well means,' said Dalziel. 'Mrs Holmes, I'm sorry to have kept you up late. You've been a great help. Thanks a lot. And Mr Holmes . . .'

'Aye?'

'I seem to recollect it's a farmer's responsibility to keep his hedges from blocking public roads. You should get them seen to afore there's an accident. Good night.'

They got back in the car, but instead of heading back to Danby, Dalziel drove up the valley till they reached the locked gate across the reservoir road.

'Fancy a walk?' he said.

They took torches but didn't need them. There was an almost full moon hanging like a spotlight in the inevitably clear sky. By its light they climbed the steps up to the top of the dam wall and stood there, looking across the silvered waters of the shrunken mere to the sharp silhouette of Lang Neb and Beulah Height.

'Search is knackered over Danby side,' said Dalziel. 'And Desperate Dan wants his plods back. Mebbe we should have spent more time looking on this side, eh? At the very least, we should have looked in the mere. I'll have a team of mermaids over here first thing in the morning. What do you think?'

'Good idea, sir,' said Wield. 'I'll see to it if you like.'

Privately he thought that trawling the mere was a waste of time, but he knew that the Fat Man was being driven by more than duty here, so he looked up at the magnificent sweep of stars and held his peace.

Nor did he complain when back at Danby, though there was nothing more to be done, Dalziel kept him from his bed for another half hour or more with fruitless speculation. But finally they were done and took leave of each other, and drove their separate ways home. Or rather, Wield drove home, but Dalziel drove back to Cap Marvell's flat.

He didn't know whether he'd have gone in if a light hadn't been showing, but it was, so he did.

Cap was waiting up. She looked at him enquiringly and said, 'Anything?'

He said, 'Nowt that makes sense. If it is Benny back, it needs a wiser head than mine to suss out why.'

As on his first arrival, the revelation of vulnerability touched her deeply and she went to him and took him in her arms.

This time their love-making was slower, deeper, though its climax was as explosive as ever.

'Jesus,' she said. 'That was like . . . like . . .'

'Like what?' he said.

'I don't know. Like as if someone had shaken a bottle of bubbly up in heaven and popped the cork, and we were in one of the bubbles streaming out across the cosmos.' Then she laughed at her own floweriness and went on, 'Sorry about the purple prose, but you know what I mean, don't you?'

'Oh aye,' he said. 'But likely it were just God farting in his bath.'

She pushed herself far enough back from him to beat his insensitive breast, then let him pull her close again.

'How on earth have I let myself get involved with a Neanderthal like you, Andy?' she asked.

'It's the uniform,' he said.

'You don't wear a uniform.'

'I'm speaking metabolically,' he said. 'It's the authority turns you on. I've had snouts like you before. It's my body they want, not my money.'

'I'm not your snout,' she protested.

'No? Then it must be my natural charm. Am I to keep the key in case I can get tomorrow night?'

'I suppose it's marginally better than having you kick the door down. But tomorrow night I shall be busy myself till quite late. In Danby, oddly enough. It's the first concert of the festival.'

'I'd not forgotten,' he said. 'The Turnip and yon Wulfstan lass. I've been thinking about her.'

'Me too,' she said. 'In fact, I've been doing more than thinking. I've been talking. My friend, Beryl – you remember, the headmistress who had Elizabeth in her school . . . ?'

'Oh aye. One of your spiders on the worldwide web.'

'Thank you for that, Andy. Well, she rang, and during the course of our conversation, I quite naturally mentioned Elizabeth Wulfstan . . .'

'You pumped her!' exclaimed Dalziel delightedly. 'I always knew you were a natural!'

'In its Elizabethan sense, I think I must be,' said Cap. 'What she told me was of great interest. And as I cannot see how it can be relevant to your enquiries and therefore qualifies as simple gossip, I shall not hesitate to pass it on. Of Elizabeth's early history, Beryl knew nothing, except that she was in fact distantly related to Chloe Wulfstan . . . What's the matter?'

'Durdum,' said Dalziel.

'Sorry?'

'Durdum. Means a lot of noise and fuss. I heard this farmer use it tonight. He's from Dendale. It rang a bell. That's the only place I've heard it used.'

'Philology now,' said Cap impatiently. 'Shall I go on?'

'The Wulfstan girl used it too,' said Dalziel. 'And glorrfat. Another Dendale word. She called me glorrfat. Either she's really turning the screw or she's from Dendale! And related to Chloe, you say?'

His mind was trying to superimpose an image of a tall slim woman with shoulder-length blonde tresses on an image of a small chubby child with cropped black hair. Nothing matched . . . except mebbe those dark, unblinking eyes . . .

'Shall I go on?'

'Yeah. What happened?'

'Well, it was all very sad really, though happily it seems to have worked out more or less all right. It seems that when she first came to the school, Elizabeth was a rather unprepossessing, chubby child with short black hair . . . Andy, I wish you wouldn't twitch? Is it a revival of sexual passion or merely the DT's?'

'Just keep talking,' he urged.

'Best offer I've had all night,' she said. 'But a change took place. Tell me, was the Wulfstans' real daughter, the one who went missing, a slim, blonde child?'

'Aye, were she,' said Dalziel. 'Pretty as a picture.'

'Well, it was that picture which probably got into Elizabeth's head. That's what they all guessed she was trying to do. Turn herself into the child her adoptive parents had lost. She started to lose weight, but no one paid much heed. Adolescent girls do go through all kinds of changes. And she let her hair grow. Only of course it was the wrong colour. And that's where the tragedy, or near tragedy, happened. It seems one night she shut herself in the bathroom with a bottle of bleach and set about trying to turn her hair blonde. The results were devastating. Fortunately, Chloe heard her screams and got her under the shower. But her scalp was badly damaged. She was lucky not to have got any in her eyes. And while she was in hospital they realized that far from just losing puppy fat, the girl was severely anorexic.'

'I knew it!' exclaimed Dalziel. 'From the start. First off I thought she were taking the piss with the way she spoke. Even when I realized she weren't, I still had this feeling she were having a secret laugh. It were because I didn't recognize her.'

'You knew her? When? How?'

'Back in Dendale,' said Dalziel. 'She were the last of the girls to get attacked, the only one to get away. She were little Betsy Allgood.'

TEN

Like I said, I thought everything were going to be all right forever.

If things worked out, sheep would have gumboots, my dad used to say.

But they don't. And Dad didn't get Stirps End either.

When we heard that Mr Hardcastle had got it, Dad wanted to rush off and speak to Mr Pontifex straight off. But Mam got in front of the door and wouldn't let him pass. She didn't often stand up to him when he were ireful, but this time she did, and told him he'd best sleep on it, and she knew it weren't right and Stirps End had been good as promised, but she reckoned Mr Pontifex had given it to Cedric Hardcastle out of guilt.

'Guilt over what?' yelled my dad.

''Cos he thinks it were him selling land to the Water Board that set things off back there in Dendale, so he's given Ced the farm 'cos they lost Madge, which makes us the lucky ones, 'cos we might not have Stirps End but we've still got our Betsy!'

And when she said this, I saw my dad's eyes turn to me, and they were black as grate-lead, and I knew he were thinking he'd rather have the farm.

Well, he held off seeing Mr Pontifex till next morn, but it didn't do much good from all accounts, and he came back saying we'd best pack as he'd told Mr Pontifex to stuff his job, and

330

likely the old sod would be coming with the bum-bailiffs to turns us out of our cottage afore nightfall.

Mr Pontifex did turn up later that day, but he were on his lone and he talked a long while with my mam first, 'cos Dad went out into the back yard when he came through front door, then he talked to them both together, and upshot was, Dad stayed on as his sheep man with a bit more brass besides and the promise of first refusal on the next farm to come up. But that would be like waiting for a drink from a methodee, said Dad, seeing as all the farms on the Pontifex estate were let to families who'd got sons to carry on the tenancies. And though he didn't look at me this time, I knew he were thinking of me again.

So everything were spoilt now. I thought for a bit after we left Dendale that it was all going to be all right, but now it were back to what it had been before only worse, with Mam taken badly again and Dad walking round like he had come to the end of things but just couldn't stop moving.

That's how it were, you see, for all of us, I mean. It's funny how you can know inside that everything's knackered, that there's no point in owt, but outside you just carry on living like nothing was different, like it made some sense to be going to school and doing your lessons and learning stuff by heart to help you for the future.

I don't know how long this went on. It could have gone on forever, I suppose. Some folk have been dead forty years before they get buried, Dad used to say. I know I were in the top class and next year I'd be moving on to the secondary. I remember thinking mebbe that would change things somehow for me. They gave us a lot of stuff about it at school one day and I went home with it to show Mam.

And I found her dead.

No, I don't want to talk about it. What's to talk about? She'd lived, now she were dead. End of story.

Which left me and Dad.

They wanted to take me away and put me with someone. They wanted to write to Aunt Chloe straight off and see if she could help.

But I said no, I were going to stay at home and look after Dad. Someone had to look after him now, didn't they? And what with Mam being so ill for such a long time, I'd been doing most things round the house anyway, so where was the difference? They said we'd need to have someone from Social who'd come in to help and I said that would be OK even though I didn't want them, 'cos I could see this was the only way they were going to agree.

So that's what we did and it was OK for a bit, and it would have been OK forever if only Dad could have got his farm and if only Mam hadn't died like she did and if only . . .

Any road, he went off one morning and I never saw him again. They said he went up over the Corpse Road and down into Dendale, and over to the far side of the reservoir closest to where Low Beulah used to be. Then he filled his pockets with rocks and walked into the watter so that when the divers found him, he were lying close by the pile of rubble which they'd made out of the old house.

I said it weren't so, he weren't dead, he'd just gone away and he'd come back for me one day. They wanted me to look at his face afore they closed up the coffin and buried him, but I wouldn't. Of course, I know that he's dead, but that's not the same as knowing for sure, is it? That's what Dad used to say. There's knowing and there's knowing for sure and there's space between the two of them for a man to get lost in. That's where he is for me, in that space. Lost.

And after that? After I came to live down here with Auntie Chloe? I had to do something, you can see that. Things don't just stop and start again, like nothing had happened before. But things can be changed. I read in this book about yon singer called Callas, how she changed herself from being plain and glorrfat, so that's what I was aimed at, changing myself; that's how come I burned my head and all. To be like Mary? Oh yes, I wanted to be like Mary. And Madge. And Jenny. I wanted to be like any of them as were wanted and missed . . .

That's all. You said I just had to talk about the old days, I needn't talk about now if I didn't want. Well, I don't. And I don't want Aunt Chloe to hear this, that's definite. But him, oh aye, you can show it to him if you like, let him hear what it's like to be me, I'd like him to understand, that's for sure. Because who else is left in the world to understand?

Songs for Dead Children

ONE

Lieder are usually sung in their original German, but the young mezzo-soprano, Elizabeth Wulfstan, feels strongly that something essential is lost to an English-speaking audience, the majority of whom have to get the sense of the songs from a programme note. Unable to find a satisfactory performing translation of the cycle, she has made her own, not hesitating from time to time to use her own Yorkshire demotic.

The original texts were the work of the German poet, Friedrich Rückert (1788–1866) who had reacted to the death of his son by writing more than four hundred poems of lament, some specific to his loss, many more general. Mahler used five in his song cycle. His interest in setting them was primarily imaginative and artistic. He was unmarried and childless when he started working on them in 1901. By the time he completed the cycle in 1905 he had married Alma Schindler and they had two children. After their birth, Alma could not understand his continuing obsession with the Rückert-based cycle which superstitiously she saw as a rash tempting of fate. The death of their eldest daughter of scarlet fever in 1907 seemed confirmation of her worst fears.

Here are the poems in Elizabeth Wulfstan's own translation.

(i)

And now the sun will rise as bright
As though no horror had touched the night.
The horror affected me alone.
The sunlight illumines everyone.
You must not dam up that dark infernal,
But drown it deep in light eternal!
So deep in my heart a small flame died.
Hail to the joyous morningtide!

(ii)

At last I think I see the explanation
Of those dark flames in many glances burning.
Such glances! As though in just one look so burning
You'd concentrate your whole soul's conflagration.
I could not guess, lost in the obfuscation
Of blinding fate which hampered all discerning,
That even then your gaze was homeward turning,
Back to the source of all illumination.

You tried with all your might to speak this warning:
Though all our love is focused on you,
Yet our desires must bow to Fate's strict bourning.
Look on us now, for soon we must go from you.
These eyes that open brightly every morning
In nights to come as stars will shine upon you.

(iii)

When your mother dear to my door draws near,
And my thoughts all centre there to see her enter
Not on her sweet face first off falls my gaze,
But a little past her seeking something after
There where your own dear features would appear
Lit with love and laughter bringing up the rear
As once my daughter dear.

When your mother dear to my door draws near,
Then I get the feeling you are softly stealing
With the candle's clear gentle flame in here,
Dancing on my ceiling! O light of love and laughter!
Too soon put out to leave me dark and drear.

(iv)

I often think they've only gone out walking
And soon they'll come homewards all laughing and talking.
The weather's bright! Don't look so pale.

338

They've only gone for a hike updale.
Oh, yes, they've only gone out walking,
Returning now, all laughing and talking.
Don't look so pale! The weather's bright.
They've only gone to climb up Beulah Height.
Ahead of us they've gone out walking
But shan't be returning all laughing and talking.
We'll catch up with them on Beulah Height
In bright sunlight.
The weather's bright on Beulah Height.

(v)

In such foul weather, in such a gale,
I'd never have sent them to play up the dale!
They were dragged by force or fear.
Nought I said could keep them here.
In such foul weather, in sleet and hail,
I'd never have let them play out in the dale.
I was feart they'd take badly.
Now such fears I'd suffer gladly.
In such foul weather, in such a bale,
I'd never have let them play out in the dale
For fear they might die tomorrow.
That's no more my source of sorrow.
In such foul weather, in such a bale,
I'd never have sent them to play up the dale.
They were dragged by force or fear.
Nought I said could keep them here.
In such foul weather, in such a gale,
In sleet and hail,
They rest as if in their mother's house,
By no foul storm confounded,
By God's own hands surrounded,
They rest as in their mother's house.

TWO

On the morning of the fourth day of the Lorraine Dacre enquiry, Geordie Turnbull rose early.

He had a hangover, not the sort that makes you turn over in bed and burrow under the sheets in search of masking darkness and the sanctuary of sleep, but the sort that sends you stumbling to the bathroom to void the contents of your gut one way or the other, and wish you could do the same with the contents of your head.

Ten minutes under a cold shower set at maximum force brought him closer to the possibility that there might be life after coffee.

It had been a long time since he felt like this. His release from custody and return to Bixford hadn't brought him the relief he'd hoped for. First off, there'd been the press who both in person and on the phone had pestered him all day. Then there'd been the attitude of his fellow villagers. Fifteen years ago in Dendale it had taken him aback to see the speed with which he'd declined from good ol' Geordie to the Fiend of the Fells. But there he'd been an offcomer, an outsider tolerated because he was pleasant company and would soon be gone. Here in Bixford he thought he'd set down roots, but the taint of being questioned in a child abduction case soon showed him how shallow those roots were. Not that anything had been said, but an overheard whisper, a turned-away glance, even the over-sympathetic tone in which they'd asked about his ordeal down at the pub, had been enough to send him home early to his thoughts and his own whisky bottle.

Now, towelling himself vigorously, he wandered from the bathroom to the kitchen. His brain was clawing its way painfully to normal consciousness level, but how far it had to go was evidenced by the fact that he'd filled his kettle before he registered that the back door on to the patio was wide open.

This jolted him several steps further up the slope, and when he heard the footstep behind him, he twisted round, flailing with the kettle at the intruder.

The man swayed back, easily avoiding contact with anything other than the lash of water whipped out of the spout. Then he stepped forward and brought his forehead crashing against Geordie's, paused to examine the effect, before driving a vicious punch into the unprotected belly and raising his knee to receive the man's face as he doubled up. Finally he strolled round the retching figure, pushed a kitchen chair against the back of his legs and pulled him down on to it by his hair. Blood from Turnbull's nose and split eyebrow spattered his naked belly and thighs. The intruder pulled some sheets of kitchen roll and tossed it on to his bloodstained lap.

'Blow your nose, Mr Turnbull,' he said. 'I think there's something you want to get off your conscience. When you're ready, I'd like to talk with you about it.'

THREE

On the morning of that fourth day, Elizabeth Wulfstan rose early too.

She slipped out of bed and flung back the curtains on the deep sash window, drenching herself luxuriously in the light which flooded in, heedless of the fact that she was naked and the window fronted directly on to Holy-clerk Street.

Hail to the joyous morningtide! The words formed on her lips but she did not speak them, much less sing them.

Below her the street was empty, not even a milkman to enjoy the spectacle she offered. Not that hers was a classically voluptuous body. She had a singer's good chest development, but her breasts were small, almost adolescent, and there wasn't enough spare flesh to hide her ribs' corrugations. Indeed, what was most likely to have caught a prurient milkman's eye was the complete absence of hair from her head and her pubes.

What caught her eye were two spaces in the line of residents' cars parked along the kerb. As she stood there, going through a sequence of breathing exercises, she checked to left and right and couldn't spot either Walter's Discovery or Arne's Saab.

She finished her exercises, crossed the room, opened the door and, with the same total indifference to the possibility of being seen, strolled down the corridor to the bathroom.

Here she brushed her teeth, then gargled gently with a mild antiseptic mouthwash, rinsed, and examined the moist pink interior of her mouth with critical interest.

Now she sang the words, *pianissimo*.

'Hail to the joyous morningtide.'

Finally she showered in lukewarm water so there wasn't too much steam, towelled vigorously, and returned to her room.

Inger Sandel, dressed in shorts and suntop, was sitting on the bed.

Elizabeth didn't break stride but went to her dressing table, sat down and began to make up her face. It was a slow delicate process. Her skin was naturally sallow and it took meticulous work to transform it to the flushing fairness of her preference.

Satisfied at last, she met the other woman's eyes in the mirror, then spun slowly round on her stool to face her and said conversationally, 'You an active dyke or do you just like gawking?'

Inger said, 'Am I a practising lesbian? Yes.'

'Always? Sorry, that's daft. I mean, when did you suss it? When you were a lass, or not till later?'

'Always.'

'So you never tried it with a man? Not even Arne?'

Inger gave one of her rare smiles and said, 'Of course with Arne. Once. He wanted. I wanted to work with him. It seemed necessary, and once out of the way, it has stayed out of the way. And you?'

'Not with Arne, no way.'

'But someone?'

'A tutor at college. Thought I'd best try it to get it over with.'

'And?'

'And I got it over with.'

'So there was no relationship after between you and this tutor?'

'No way.'

'You are sure of yourself, I see. But what about him? Did he not want something more?'

'Well, I left a fiver on my pillow next morning and went off early. I expect he got the message.'

It was a moment when, if they were ever going to share a smile, they might have done so. But it passed.

'Any more questions?' asked Elizabeth.

'Why do you shave your bush?'

'To get a match with this,' said Elizabeth, patting her bald pate. 'Turns you on, looking at me, does it?'

'It is . . . pleasing, yes.'

'Pleasing?' She stood up, yawned, stretched. 'Well, don't get your hopes up, luv.'

She slipped into a pair of pants and pulled a black T-shirt over her head, careful not to touch her face. Then, taking the blonde wig off its stand, she fitted it on to her head and studied herself in the dressing-table mirror.

'I had no hopes,' said Inger.

'Best way to be. It's always midnight somewhere, my dad used to say. So if it weren't hope that brought you here, how come you're squatting on my bed end?'

'It is the *Kindertotenlieder*. I agree with the others. I think you should not sing them.'

'Which others?'

'Arne. The fat policeman. Walter.'

'Walter's said nowt.'

'When does Walter ever say anything in contradiction to you? But I see the way he is when you sing them.'

'Oh aye. That's a clever trick when you're banging the piano. Got eyes in the back of your head, have you?'

The woman on the bed didn't answer but just sat there, monumentally still, face impassive, her unblinking gaze fixed on Elizabeth who made some unnecessary adjustments to her wig.

'So what're you saying, Inger?' she asked finally. 'That you're going to take your piano and play in some other street?'

'No. We must all make our own choices. I will not make yours for you. If you will sing, I will play.'

'Then everything's champion, isn't it? Ist'a coming down to breakfast or what?'

Without waiting for an answer, she left the room and ran down the stairs. In the kitchen she found the back door open and Chloe standing on the patio, drinking a mug of coffee. The garden, long and narrow, flanked with mature shrubs and shaded at the bottom by a tall pear tree, showed the effect of the drought everywhere, with the rectangle of lawn looking as cracked and ochrous as an early oil painting.

'Morning,' called Elizabeth, switching on the electric kettle. 'Wet the bed, did you?'

'That's an idea. If we all peed on the lawn, do you think it would help?' said Chloe. 'Walter went out very early and woke me, so I got up. And I've come out here in hope of seeing a bit of dew, but even that seems to have stopped.'

'Mebbe it's been banned, like hose-pipes. I'd not try a pee. Likely that's been banned too.'

Chloe came back inside, smiling. There could never be a mother/daughter closeness between them, but sometimes when alone together their bond of Yorkshire blood allowed them to relax into an earthy familiarity which threatened neither.

Just as common were the times when she felt she'd given houseroom to an alien.

'I've been talking to Inger. She reckons I oughtn't to sing the Mahler cycle. What do you think?' asked Elizabeth suddenly.

Chloe pretended to drink from her empty mug and

wondered how someone so direct could be so inapprehensible.

'Why are you interested in what I think?' she prevaricated.

Elizabeth chewed on a handful of dried muesli then washed it down with a mouthful of black coffee.

'She said Walter and Arne and yon glorrfat bobby thought I shouldn't. But she didn't mention you. So I thought I'd ask if them songs bother you.'

'Because of Mary, you mean? The part of my mind which deals with that has long been out of the reach of mere songs,' said Chloe.

'That's what I thought,' said Elizabeth. 'Oh, by the way, thanks.'

'For what?'

'For bringing me up.'

Chloe opened her mouth in a mock-gape which wasn't altogether mock. Before she could say anything, the door opened and Inger came in. Elizabeth finished her coffee, grabbed a handful of fresh grapes, said, 'See you,' and left.

Inger said, 'Does she eat enough?'

'For a singer, you mean?'

'For a woman. This morning I saw her naked. She has strong bones so I had never realized before how little flesh is on them. She was anorexic once, I think?'

Another member of the unreadably direct tendency, thought Chloe wryly. The only way to respond was either silence or a directness to match their own.

She sat down and said, 'After Betsy had been with us some time – she was still Betsy in those days – she was diagnosed as being anorexic. She had treatment, both medical and psychological. Eventually she recovered.'

There. How easy it was to be completely direct and yet give next to nothing away!

'So she went through a phase many modern children go through, you spotted it, had it treated. Why do you feel so guilty?'

Give nothing away! Who was she fooling? Not this sharp-eared woman, that was for certain. She'd once asked Arne what made Inger tick. She'd been a little jealous of her in those long ago days when the young singer had surprised her body on to levels of pleasure her experience with Walter had hardly even hinted at.

Arne had laughed and said, 'Inger is gay, so no need to feel that kind of jealousy, my love. But don't feel superior either, which, though they will deny it, is how straight women feel about lesbians, because they think they offer no threat. Inger hears more in the silence between the notes than most of us hear in the music itself.'

Perhaps also she had heard things from Arne that should not have been spoken, or at the least listened carefully to the silences between his words.

Ironically, it had been the crisis with Betsy which brought Arne back into her bed. After Mary's disappearance she had broken off relations with him for reasons too incoherent to merit the term, but which included a sense of being punished for her infidelity and a revulsion against anything which even threatened to dilute her pain.

But the Betsy crisis had been different. This time she needed escape from herself, and had found it in the singer's company and caresses.

She couldn't remember now exactly how much she'd revealed of her feelings to Arne. But, if he'd spoken of it to Inger, then even a little was probably enough.

So let her have it from the horse's mouth now, why not? The human heart can only shut so much away, and her dark cavern was full.

She said, 'I never wanted Betsy to come to us, you

347

know. We'd moved away to the south, I had used every ounce of my will to close a door on Dendale and the past, and now here was this child threatening to open it all up again. I'd never really liked her, she was such a plain child, dark and fat, and strange too, you'd get this uneasy feeling and turn around and there Betsy would be, watching you, waiting till you noticed her, then asking if Mary was coming out to play. We put it down to her mother, Lizzie, my cousin, who'd always been highly strung, and had the baby blues after Betsy was born and never seemed truly to get out of them. It didn't surprise most people, I think, when she took an overdose. The inquest said it could have been accidental, but I think they were just being kind. Jack, that's Betsy's father, was much more of a shock. He was real down-to-earth Yorkshire, hard as nails, he'd see off anything, so most people thought. So when he drowned himself . . .'

'There was no doubt this time?' asked Inger.

'Not a lot of people go swimming with their pockets full of rocks,' said Chloe. 'So there was Betsy. Eleven and a half years old. An orphan. Without a relative in the world, except for me.'

'So you took her in?'

Chloe shook her head.

'I took to my bed. I screamed and shouted and blubbered gallons of tears every time the possibility of her coming to live with us was mentioned. It was Walter who persuaded me . . . no, not persuaded . . . that implies an appeal to rationality . . . he just worked on me, you know the way the sun can still be burning you even when you think you're protected by a thick layer of cloud? Well, I put up my layer of cloud, but all the time Walter was up there, burning through. And in the end, he won.'

'You think he was right?'

'Of course he was right. The child needed a home. And

when she came, it was a lot easier than I thought. Far from bringing a pressure to open that door I'd worked so hard to shut, the girl showed no desire to talk about her parents, or Dendale or anything in the past. In fact, she talked very little at all, and less and less as time went by, and I thought (if I thought at all), oh good, she's closed a door on the past too. And it seemed to me we could co-exist very well in this untroublesome silence.'

'She was a child,' said Inger in a neutral tone that was none the less judgemental.

'I know. I should have ... but I didn't. She seemed fine to me. OK, she lost a bit of weight, but that pleased me. I used to tell her sometimes she shouldn't eat so many sweets and cakes and stuff, and I thought she was just growing out of a puppy-fat stage.'

'How old was she when you realized there was a problem?' asked Inger.

'Realized?' Chloe laughed bitterly. 'I never realized. One night there were these terrible screams from upstairs. I rushed up to find Betsy in the bathroom. Her head ... Oh, God, what a mess. She'd decided to turn her hair blonde, and she'd mixed a hideously strong solution of bleaching powder ... I got her under the shower and screamed at her to keep her eyes closed and held her there far longer than I should have done, because all the time I was holding her there, I felt I was doing something right and I didn't have to start thinking about what I had done wrong. But finally I got her to hospital. They sorted her out, said she had damaged part of her scalp so badly that her hair would probably fall out and might grow back in patches, but that wasn't what they were worried about, it was her anorexia, and they wanted to know what treatment she was getting for it.'

'And you had no idea of this?'

'I don't know. Perhaps I did, deep down, but just didn't

349

want to let her be a trouble to me. Walter had been away on a long trip, a couple of months. Perhaps he would have noticed. He was always closer to her than I was.'

'It does not seem so now,' said Inger.

'No?' Chloe smiled to herself. Perhaps after all the pianist by listening so closely to the silences missed some of the notes. 'Ah well. Certainly back then, it must have been very clear. She was treated by a child psychiatrist, Dr Paula Appleby – you may have heard of her. I believe she's quite well known. Walter never settled for anything but the best. Dr Appleby treated Betsy for eighteen months, two years, I don't know how long. I sat back and let Walter take care of all that. I felt guilty now, yes, but I still didn't want to get involved. I had closed a door on Dendale to shut it out. Betsy too had closed a door, but it seems she had shut herself in with it, and I didn't want any part of opening all that up again. And when Dr Appleby said that the business with the hair and the anorexia was her attempt to turn herself from a little fat dark-haired girl into a slim blonde so that she'd be like Mary and we'd love her, I just felt sick. Do I sound like a monster?'

'You sound like you needed help as much as Betsy. I am surprised that Walter did not understand this.'

'He was too busy seeing Betsy through her trouble. Dr Appleby got her talking about the past and wanted us to see the transcripts. She said it was a family problem, we all needed to know all about each other. I refused point-blank and I don't think I'd have let myself be persuaded, but it turned out Betsy herself said she didn't mind Walter seeing them, but she didn't want me to have to read them. I think when I heard that, for the first time I felt something like affection for her.'

'Because she wanted to save you pain?'

'That was the only reason I could see. After the treatment was over and she was back to normality, if that's the right word, we got on much better. I think we both felt that even if she could never be a daughter to me, on the other hand there was a tie of blood between us which couldn't be denied.'

'But despite being *normal*,' said Inger, 'she kept on dieting and took to wearing a blonde wig?'

'Her hair wouldn't grow back properly. She needed a wig. She asked if I would mind if it was blonde. I said, why should I? As for the dieting, I did get worried about this and used to fuss her at meal times. Then one day she showed me a chart with all the calorific values of the stuff she ate carefully worked out and said, "No way am I going to stuff myself with cakes and such fodder. This is what I eat, and it's enough, and I don't go off to the lavvy to stuff my finger down my throat and spew it all up either. So never rack thyself, I'll be fine." After that I stopped worrying. She started taking the singing seriously about then. She'd always had a voice, that you know. Now she said she wanted to find out if it was good enough to make her living with. It was about this time we formally adopted her. We'd called her Elizabeth from the start, and when she went to school, it had seemed easier to say her name was Wulfstan.'

'She didn't mind?'

'Who knows what goes on in Elizabeth's head? But she said nothing. And when Walter suggested we made it legal, she seemed almost pleased.'

'And you?'

'I didn't mind. Somehow it made her less of a reminder of the past. I think that was why I quite welcomed the blonde wig and the change of shape too. All that remained of Betsy Allgood out of Dendale was the accent.'

'That bothered you?'

'No, but I thought it might cause her trouble, with her classmates, I mean. And later, as she grew up. I once suggested she had elocution lessons. She said, "Why? There's nothing wrong with my voice, is there?" And I realized she was speaking perfect BBC English. Then she went on, "But I'll not be shamed to crack on like Mam and Dad, and them as don't like it can bloody lump it!" That was the last time I brought the subject up.'

'So you became friends.'

'I'd not put it strong as that,' said Chloe. 'But as I said, we're blood, and you don't need to like your relations all the time, do you? She helped me, I think. Or perhaps it was just time that helped me.'

'To get better, you mean?'

'Not really. Like Elizabeth's scalp, there's no cure for what was damaged in me. But you learn to live with a wig. Whatever, four years ago when Walter seemed to be spending more and more time up here at the Works, I heard myself say, wouldn't it make more sense for us to live up there? It took him by surprise. Me too. He said, "You're sure?" And I said, because I am after all a woman and we must seize our chances, "Yes, but only if we can buy a house *in the bell*." And here we are.'

'You did not want to live in the country?'

Chloe's face went dark and she said softly, 'No. I'm a country lass born and bred, but now I can't even bear to look out of the train or car window when we're passing through empty countryside. Now, is that all, Inger? Have I quite satisfied your curiosity?'

'Like sex, only till the next time,' said Inger.

FOUR

Edgar Wield wouldn't have minded a lie-in that morning.

His own sense of guilt had got him up early the previous morning, and the Fat Man's sense of guilt had kept him up late the previous night. But he'd missed his morning visit to Monte in order to get to the hospital, and to miss it again would just add guilt to guilt, so he slipped out of bed at his usual ungodly (Edwin's epithet) hour.

Not perhaps all that ungodly, however. For as he strolled through the churchyard, the church door opened and Larry Lillingstone, the vicar, came out. A handsome young man, his present unclerical garb of singlet and shorts made him look more Apolline acolyte than Anglican divine.

Wield ran his gaze appreciatively over the suntanned limbs and said, 'Morning, Larry. This what they call muscular Christianity?'

'Just off for my jog,' said Lillingstone smiling. 'This truly is the best time of day. You can't believe there's much wrong with the world on mornings like this, can you?'

Wield thought of the Dacres waking from whatever chemical sleep they'd managed, of the Pascoes keeping their desperate vigil by Rosie's bed. But joy was as rare and refreshing as rain these past few days, so he returned the smile and said, 'Dead right. Specially if you've been lucky enough to get yourself a bonny lass like Kee Scudamore. I gather congratulations are in order.'

'How on earth . . . we only decided yesterday and I've

not told anyone . . .' Then Lillingstone laughed and went on, 'What am I saying? This is Enscombe! Yes, Kee's going to marry me, and I'm the happiest . . . Bloody hell!'

This impious ejaculation was caused by the sudden descent from the branches of the old yew under which they stood of a small furry figure on to Wield's head, where it clung, gibbering.

'How do, Monte,' said Wield, gently drawing the little monkey down into his arms. 'What's up, Vicar? Think the devil had come for a visit?'

'It's strange how medieval the mind can be in moments of stress,' admitted Lillingstone.

'Never fear. I missed my visit yesterday morning and he's obviously made his mind up it's not going to happen twice so he's come looking for me, right, Monte?'

'Well, certainly if you ever became Enscombe's second missing policeman, there'd be no need to mount a search party, would there?' said Lillingstone, referring to the event which had first brought Wield to Enscombe.

'No,' said Wield thoughtfully. 'No. Likely there wouldn't. Excuse me, Vicar, but I think I'd best be getting to work. Enjoy your run. And you, you little bugger, enjoy your nuts.'

Putting the muslin bag of peanuts into Monte's paws, he launched the tiny animal up into the yew and watched as he commenced his aerial route back to his tree house in the grounds of Old Hall. Then, with a wave of his hand which comprehended both man and monkey, he set off back the way he'd come.

The first person he saw as he got off his motorbike in Danby was Sergeant Clark, who had the faintly self-important look of a man who knows more than you do.

'Super around?' asked Wield.

'Been and gone,' said Clark.

Wield waited, not asking more. 'No wonder the

bugger's such a good interviewer,' Dalziel had once observed. 'Face like that's worth a thousand clever questions.'

'He's gone to Bixford,' said Clark. 'Word came this morning, Geordie Turnbull's been attacked.'

If he'd been looking for oohs and ahs, he was disappointed.

'Tell us,' said Wield impassively.

'Local patrol car were driving by his place early on. Seems the super had said to keep a close eye on Turnbull. Well, the big gate were open. It's always kept shut, save when he's got machinery coming in and out, that is. They went in to check and found Turnbull looking like he'd gone three rounds with Tyson.'

Wield, who abhorred imprecision above all things, said impatiently, 'Just how bad is he?'

'Looked worse than it was,' admitted Clark almost reluctantly. 'Few cuts and a squashed nose, they say. Turnbull were trying to patch himself up, and he didn't want to make it official. But the lads called it in anyway.'

'Very wise,' said Wield.

'So what do you think? There's a lot of folk round here said when we let him go that best thing would have been to kick the truth out of him.'

'I hope you got their names then, 'cos likely Mr Dalziel will want to talk to them,' said Wield heavily. 'One thing's for sure, if that *was* the aim of the exercise, he's off the hook.'

'How's that?' asked Clark, puzzled.

'If he'd admitted owt, they wouldn't have left him nursing his wounds, would they?' said Wield. 'Something you can do for me, Nobby. That vet I read about, Douglas, is it? Where's he hang out?'

Clark told him. Wield put his crash helmet back on and flung his leg over the bike.

'You not going inside?' demanded Clark. 'What shall I say if anyone asks after you?'

Wield grinned, like a fissure in a rock.

'Tell them I've gone to see a man about a dog,' he said.

Andy Dalziel was meanwhile standing over Geordie Turnbull, looking minded to start where the intruder had stopped.

'You're not helping anyone, Geordie, least of all yourself. He could be back. So why not tell me who it was, what he were after, and I'll sort it?'

'I've told you, Mr Dalziel. I never saw his face. He jumped me, knocked hell out of me, then took off.'

'You're a bloody liar,' said Dalziel. 'You'd have been straight on the phone to us, in that case. But you're so keen to keep it quiet, you don't even bother with getting treatment in case someone reports it. That eye needs a couple of stitches, I'd say. And your nose could do with being lined up with your gob again.'

'Maybe so, but at least I keep it out of other buggers' business,' retorted Turnbull spiritedly.

'I think this *is* my business, Geordie,' said Dalziel. 'I think this is about them missing lasses.'

'Do you think if I knew anything about that, I'd not tell you?' demanded Turnbull. 'Now, if you'll excuse me, I'm going to take your advice and go down to the surgery. As everyone in the place'll know what's happened by now, I might as well save them the trouble of thinking up excuses to come and gawk.'

'I'll find out in the end, tha knows that, Geordie,' promised Dalziel.

'I don't doubt it, Mr Dalziel,' said Turnbull. 'But as it could take you another fifteen years, I won't hold my breath.'

It was a parting shot that not even the adamantine defences of the great Andy Dalziel could parry.

He went out to his car, glaring up at the already ferocious sun as though thinking about tearing it out of the sky. But the eye of God beamed benevolently back, knowing that this fiery fury was nothing but the inflamed swelling round a deep wound of despair.

The eye of God which makes no distinctions of persons was beaming with equal benevolence on Police Constable Hector as he left Mid-Yorkshire Police Headquarters and began his slow perambulation through the centre of town. His gait was not exactly majestic; in fact he moved as if under the control of a trainee puppeteer who'd got his strings tangled. This was also an apt metaphor for how his superiors felt. Finding a niche for a man of his talents had been difficult. For a time the conventional wisdom was that the public weal would be best served by keeping Hector hidden in the bowels of the building, 'helping' with records. But the increase in computerization had put an end to that. Though specifically forbidden to touch anything that had switches, buttons, lights, or made a humming noise, Hector's mere presence seemed somehow perilous to the proper function of electronic equipment. 'He's a human virus,' declared the sergeant in charge. 'Get him out of here else he'll be into the Pentagon War Room in a fortnight!' A spell on the desk had brought complaints from the public that they got better service from Mid-Yorks Water. Finally, when the *Evening Post* supported a local campaign to get bobbies back on the beat with a piece of research from the Applied Psychology Department of MYU showing that life-sized cardboard cut-outs of policemen in supermarkets reduced the incidence of shoplifting by half, the ACC said, 'Well, we can manage *that* at any rate,' and Hector was returned into the community.

But not without some necessary fail-safes. He had to radio in every thirty minutes, else a car was sent out to look for him. If his assistance was required in any matter more serious than a request for the time, he had to contact Control for instructions. And in particular, he was strictly forbidden to make any attempt to direct traffic, as his last venture in that area had resulted in a gridlock which made the Chief Constable miss a train.

But when the copies of Wield's modified photo of Benny Lightfoot had been handed out that morning, Hector had taken his with the rest and registered that they were being instructed to ask people if they had seen this man. The instruction was, in fact, aimed at patrol car officers who were advised particularly to check garages in the district in case the camper van had been filled up with petrol. Door-to-door enquiries were being concentrated on the Danby area. But Hector, delighted to have a task he comprehended, thrust the photo in front of any pedestrians he encountered, demanding, 'Have you seen this man?' but rarely staying for an answer as his eager eye spotted yet another target who might pass him by unless he hurried.

It was with some irritation that he felt himself tapped on the shoulder as he blocked the way of a young man on a skateboard. He turned to find himself looking at the woman he'd just questioned.

'What?' he demanded.

'I said, "Yes,"' she said.

'Eh?'

'You asked me if I'd seen that man and I said, "Yes."'

'Oh.'

He scowled, partly in puzzlement, partly because he'd just noticed the skateboarder had taken the chance to glide away.

'Right,' he said. 'So you've seen him then?'

'I said so, didn't I?'

This was undeniable.

He said, 'Hang on, will you?' and looked at his personal radio. One of the buttons had been painted fluorescent orange by a kindly sergeant who had then written in Hector's notebook, 'Press the bright orange button when you want to talk.'

Hector actually remembered this, but checked in his book just to be quite sure.

'Hello?' he said. 'This is Hector talking. Over.'

He had an official call sign, but no one was foolish enough to insist on it.

'Hector, you're ahead of yourself, aren't you? You're not due to check in for another ten minutes.'

'I know. It's yon photo you gave me. I showed it to this woman and she says she's seen the man. What do you want me to do?'

'The pho . . . ? Hector, where are you?'

'Hang on.'

He turned his head slowly, looking for something to locate himself by.

The woman said, 'You're in Braddgate. Can you hurry this up? I'll be late for work.'

'She says we're in Braddgate, Sarge,' said Hector.

'She's still with you, is she? Thank God for that. Stay there, Hector. And whatever you do, don't let her leave, right?'

'Right,' said Hector. 'How shall I stop her?'

'You're a policeman, for God's sake!' yelled the sergeant. 'Just keep her there!'

'Right,' said Hector again.

He switched off his radio and replaced it with great care. Then he turned to the woman.

'So what's going off?' she asked.

He said, 'You are under arrest. You do not have to say

359

anything, but I have to warn you that anything you do say will be taken down . . .'

'This is crazy,' she said angrily. 'I'm off.'

She turned to walk away. Hector with some difficulty pulled out his new-style long baton, and set out after her.

Fortunately his first swing missed entirely and the patrol car had turned up before he could get into position to try a second.

The car officers got the woman into the back seat and calmed her down, then listened to what she had to tell them.

She finished with, 'And I've got to get to work now. With the cutbacks we're short-staffed as it is, and if I'm not there to get things started, there'll be real trouble.'

'Someone from CID will need to talk to you,' said the driver. 'But from the sound of it, it's best they do that at work, anyway. So let's be on our way.'

Through the window, open against the morning heat, Hector said, 'What shall I do?'

The woman told him.

'Couldn't have put it better myself, luv,' said the driver, grinning broadly as he drove away.

That morning of early rising, Shirley Novello slept in.

Sparing only enough time to make herself look as if she hadn't just fallen out of bed, she drove to Headquarters with a disregard for speed limits and road courtesy which she would have found deplorable in a civilian.

By the time she parked her car, she was awake enough to find it deplorable in herself. Two minutes she might have saved, if that. And for what? Dalziel and Wield and all the *important* people would be clocking on at Danby. It was only the supernumeraries like herself who were kept on the perimeter of the enquiry, tidying up. She herself was faced with the possibility of another tedious trip down to Sheffield if old Mrs Lightfoot had revived sufficiently to be interviewed.

Still, even if the big guns were away, no need to give the little pistols ammunition.

She opened the door of the CID room and strolled in trying to look as if she'd been researching down in Records for the past half hour.

Dennis Seymour looked up from his desk and said in a loud voice, 'Morning, Shirley. You're looking gorgeous today. But then why shouldn't you be, with all that beauty sleep you're having?'

She glowered at him, angry that someone she thought of as a mate should be pointing the finger like this. Then it dawned on her that Seymour was the only person in the room.

'Where's everybody?' she asked.

'Busy,' he said. 'Things don't stop just because you're asleep. All our suspects have been in the action. Geordie Turnbull's been attacked and there's been a definite sighting of Benny Lightfoot in Dendale. We even have a good likeness, thanks to our own Toulouse Lautrec.'

He tossed Novello a copy of Wield's updated picture.

She said, 'I wish I'd had this yesterday when I was down at Wark House.'

'Never heard of the fax, Detective?' said Seymour. 'Or take it with you. Didn't you say someone would have to talk to the old lady?'

'Yes. I'd have done it yesterday, only she wasn't up to snuff.'

She must have sounded a touch defensive, because Seymour said, 'But you think a hard insensitive man might have insisted? If you're thinking of a hard extremely fat insensitive man, you're probably right. But no harm done. Much better to chat when the old girl can chat back. They're up and down like a fiddler's elbow,

361

these old folk. She'll probably be bright as a button today.'

'I hope so. But I'll fax the photo, anyway. Sooner we get confirmation, the better.'

She scribbled a note to Billie Saltair asking her to show the accompanying picture to the nurse, Sally, and get her reaction, if any; also enquiring how Mrs Lightfoot was this morning and stressing the necessity for an early interview.

Even her note lacked the true CID masculine assertiveness, she thought. But whatthehell? Some of her male colleagues would still be questioning Winifred Fleck!

The reply came back ten minutes later.

'Great!' she said, reading it as it crept out of the machine. 'Spitting image of the man who came to see old Agnes.'

'Another triumph,' mocked Seymour. 'They'll be letting you lie in bed all day if you go on like this.'

'Oh, shit,' said Novello, the complete fax in her hand.

'Sorry. Didn't realize you were quite so sensitive.'

'Not you. It's Agnes Lightfoot. She died in the night. I knew I should have talked to her yesterday!'

'Hey, what could she have told you that you don't know?' asked Seymour.

'I'll never know, will I?' said Novello savagely, grabbing the phone and dialling the Wark House number.

'Saltair,' said the matron's husky voice. 'That Detective Novello? Thought you'd be ringing.'

'What happened?'

'Nature happened,' said Billie Saltair. 'It was her time. I think she'd just been waiting for a signal, and her visitor last week seems to have been it.'

'Did she say anything before she died?' asked Novello without much hope.

'She did, as a matter of fact,' said the matron. 'She took my hand, looked up at me bright and hard. And said, "I knew he'd come. I knew. Benny's back." Then she died. That's it. Anything else I can help with?'

Novello thought hard.

'Yes,' she said. 'If anyone rings up asking about Agnes, don't say she's dead, OK? Just say she's pretty ill, too ill to talk on the phone. Can you do that?'

There was a pause, then Saltair said, 'Yes, in this case, I think I can stretch to that. But only because no one's rung up asking about Agnes for so many years, I think the chances of causing distress are minimal. Anything else?'

'Yes. I think it would be a good idea if we had one of our people at the Home, just in case Benny turns up in person to have another chat to his gran.'

'Fine. But have you got anyone old enough to fit in?'

'We'll send a master of disguises. Thanks a lot. And I'm really sorry about Mrs Lightfoot.'

'Me too. Happens all the time, but you never get used to it. Bye.'

Novello replaced the phone.

'So,' said Seymour. 'And who's this master of disguises?'

'There's only two of us here, and what is it you macho men are always saying, that putting the cuffs on a young, fit and dangerous criminal's no job for a woman?'

'I've never said that in my life,' said Seymour indignantly. 'Bernadette would have my guts for garters if she thought I said things like that.'

'OK. Sorry. But someone's got to go. I'm sure if we could track the Fat Man down, he'd give the go-ahead. Lots of Brownie points for initiative on offer here, Dennis.'

'I'm sure. So why aren't you rushing to collect them?'

'Because I think I need to talk to the DCI,' said Novello unhappily.

'Mr Pascoe? But he's . . .'

'Yes, I know. But this is *his* line of enquiry. I spoke to him yesterday and he was very helpful. I need to bring him up to date and check whether there's anything I'm missing. This time I think I'd better go round and see him in person.'

'To the hospital, you mean?' Seymour whistled and rose to his feet. 'You're right, I reckon, Shirley. I've got the easy job. In these nursing homes, it's only the old who die.'

FIVE

'Wieldy, what the hell have you got there?' said Maggie Burroughs.

She was standing on the shady side of the caravan on Ligg Common, drinking a cup of tea.

As if in answer to her question, from the basket strapped to the sergeant's pillion came a sharp yap.

'This is Tig, ma'am,' he said. 'Lorraine's dog. Vet says he's fit enough to go home.'

'You think the Dacres'll want it?' said Burroughs doubtfully. 'Every time they look at it . . .'

'Yeah,' said Wield. 'No telling how it'll take people.'

'There's always the RSPCA,' said Burroughs with the indifference of a non-animal lover. 'So why've you brought it here?'

'Just thought it might be worthwhile taking him up the valley.'

She looked at him doubtfully and said, 'Might have been a good idea two days ago, but I can't see what you can hope for when men, dogs, and thermal-imaging cameras haven't come up with anything more interesting than a dead sheep. You know the search has been scaled down? Super's got a frog team diving in the reservoir. Worth a look, I suppose. But this side, we're done. The caravan will stay for a couple of days just to show willing, maybe jog someone's memory. But that's it.'

Does she think I'm asking permission? wondered Wield. Technically, she was in charge of the search, that was true. But now there wasn't any search for her to be in charge of.

'So you reckon I shouldn't bother?' he said.

It was the old put-up-or-shut-up technique. But Maggie Burroughs was up to it.

She took a long sip of tea, then smiled at him.

'Not up to me to tell CID how to pass their time,' she said. 'No, Sergeant, you take your walk. But do me a favour. Write it up for me. It'll round the search report off. Show we tried everything.'

Show *you* tried everything, thought Wield, who had no doubts about, or problems with, the extent of Maggie Burroughs' ambition.

He said, 'Thank you, ma'am,' revved up, and sent the bike bumping up the dusty path running alongside the creeping beck.

Burroughs watched him go. In her eyes, a middle-aged queer on a vintage motorbike was not the image of modern policing she wanted to project. But he was close to Dalziel, and she didn't reckon that falling out with the Fat Man's favourites was any way for an ambitious officer to get on in the Mid-Yorkshire force.

Wield took the bike as far as he could before the path became too steep and rocky for comfort. He was almost at the spot where Tony Dacre had found Tig that Sunday morning, and assuming the frightened and injured animal had headed for home, the attack must have taken place upstream from here.

'Right, lad. Walkies,' said Wield.

At first he put the little animal on a lead, frightened it might simply run away. But when it showed no inclination to do anything but trot up the familiar path with occasional stops to cock its leg or bark at a bird or butterfly, Wield took the risk of letting it run free.

They were now high up the valley where it narrowed

considerably. Westward rose the steep side of the Neb, while to the east the ground sloped a little more easily to the Danby–Highcross Moor road. Here Ligg Beck ran through a steep sided ghyll, no Grand Canyon, but deep enough for a bone-breaking fall. In spate, there must have been fine cascades here, but this summer all that remained of the water which over a thousand years had etched this crack in the bare rock was a trickle of damp in the depths where ferns drooped and mosses clung.

Wield took a breather. He'd brought a bottle of water, and after taking a swig himself, he poured some into the palm of his hand and let the dog have a drink.

Likely, Burroughs was right, he thought. This was a waste of time. Except that in his methodical mind, even negatives needed to be tested before you put them to one side.

He'd also brought a pair of field glasses. He put them to his eyes and slowly scanned the valley. Not a sign of life, except for the odd sheep. If he stood up, he could get a good view of the rooftops of Danby. The Highcross Moor road was visible in glimpses lower down, but immediately above him, the folds of ground kept it out of sight, though he could see the back of a square plaque on a metal post which he worked out must be the NO LITTER sign at the viewpoint young Novello had had such high hopes of.

Mebbe her theory wasn't so daft, after all. If he could see the sign so clearly, anyone up there with glasses would easily be able to pick out a small girl walking her dog along this path.

There'd been no glasses in Turnbull's car, but there had been a powerful pair in his bungalow.

He lowered the binoculars and let his naked eye take in the proper scale of the thing. The slope was steep but not too steep, and mainly grassy. Man in a hurry could come down here in four or five minutes, he reckoned.

Going back up, carrying a child, that was something else. Twenty minutes . . . probably thirty, depending how fit you were. Turnbull looked strong enough in the shoulders to carry the girl, but how much exercise did those legs get?

In any case, it was a hell of a risk to take.

But, seeing the girl down here, alone and vulnerable, what would such a sick mind as this man must have reck of risk?

Wield was brought out of his reverie by the sound of Tig barking.

It seemed to be coming from the bowels of the earth and his first thought was that the daft animal had gone down a rabbit hole. Then he realized the noise was coming from the ghyll.

Tig was down there somewhere, and he sounded as if he'd found something.

Getting down the ghyll proved fairly easy. A narrow sheep-trod angled down the slope, offering little problem to a man who kept himself in trim. He soon found himself in shade, but any hope that this would be better than the heat of the sun soon vanished. It was like descending into a sludge of warm air, and what was worse, the atmosphere was foul with the stink of corruption.

Dogs, men, thermal-image cameras – they couldn't possibly have missed this, thought Wield.

And now he saw that of course they hadn't. The trod ran across the bottom of the ghyll and up the other face till it was blocked by a slab of rock resting at an angle of about thirty degrees, where it turned back on itself and zigzagged up the remaining slope.

Across the path by the slab lay the remains of a sheep. The scavengers had been here and there were bones lying apart from the main carcase. But decay had been rapid enough in this heat to quickly rot the flesh to a state not even a hungry fox found appetizing, and the body had been left to the depredations of flies, which rose like a wind-tugged pall each time Tig barked.

'Come away, boy!' called Wield.

The dog turned, took an uncertain step towards him, then turned back.

'For Christ's sake, didn't that vet feed you?' demanded the sergeant. 'You've got to be desperate to want to stick your gob into that lot!'

He took a deep breath and held it as he crossed the stream bed and started up the other side, planning to grab Tig and keep going to the top.

The dog struggled as it felt Wield's hands seize it and whimpered piteously as he lifted it up to his chest.

Got to be desperate . . . His own words echoed in his head.

He stopped and had to take a breath. But now he ignored the stench. He was looking at the spot where the carcase lay. Directly above it, the side of the ghyll was almost sheer. It was easy to see how the sheep, grazing too near the edge and stretching down in search of the not so sun-scorched vegetation growing between the rocks, could have lost its footing and plunged to the bottom, breaking its back.

But surely it would have been to the *bottom* of the ghyll, not this angle of the trod which was barely more than a six-inch ledge on the steep slope?

The dog lay dormant in his arms now, as if sensing that he was no longer the object of reprimand.

Wield went back down to the stream bed. There was a rock there with some wool on it and a brown stain which might be blood. He looked up towards the carcase. The grass on the bank of the almost dried-up stream was slightly flattened and some of the ferns were snapped. As

369

if something had been dragged. And here were more traces of wool up the rocky slope to the trod.

He put the dog down and climbed back up to the carcase. The ground was too rocky to bury anything here. But that rock slab, the way it lay, there could be a space beneath in the angle it made with the ghyll wall.

He would need to move the sheep to see.

Not even the heat of the chase could make him contemplate taking his hands to that task. He found a large flat piece of stone which he used as a shovel and, gagging from the foulness directly beneath his nose, he began to lever the rotting corpse away from the slab. It came to pieces as he pushed, and fell in stinking gobbets to the stream bed below. Flies rose in a foetid humming spiral around his head which he shook like an irritated bullock. Tig, dodging the descending bones, was now by his feet as the gap beneath the slab was revealed. Only, there wasn't a gap. It was choked with stones and turf and wads of heather. But that hadn't got there naturally, that hadn't grown there. Using his hands now that it was just good honest rock and vegetation he had to deal with, he began to unplug the hole. Suddenly his hand was through into space. He withdrew it. The hole was big enough to admit a rabbit. Or a small dog. Before Wield could grab him, Tig was through, barking fiercely for a moment; then, perhaps the most terrible noise Wield had ever heard, the bark died to an almost inaudible whimper.

Wield tried to proceed systematically, but despite himself he found he was tearing at the remaining debris with a ferocity which brought sweat streaming down his face and blood from his fingernails.

Finally he stopped. He hadn't got a torch. Mistake. Man should never go anywhere without a length of string, a cutting blade, and a torch.

He knelt on the trod, heedless that his knees were

resting on ground stained by the juices of the decomposing sheep.

He kept his head a little way back from the hole to permit as much light as possible to enter. And he waited.

At first he could see nothing but the vaguest of shapes. Then gradually, as his eyes adjusted, he saw the light gently run over the outlines of things. As he'd guessed, there was a triangular space in here, almost tent-like, about two and a half feet wide, three feet high and six feet deep. In the middle of it, a hump, difficult to make out perhaps because his mind didn't want to make it out. The first thing he really identified was the gleam of Tig's eyes, and then his teeth as his lips drew back in a soundless snarl.

The dog was lying up against something. Wield knelt there, straining his eyes, till slowly, inexorably, he was forced to see what he had known for some minutes he was going to see.

He rose unsteadily to his feet and reached into his pocket. Torch he might not have, but he hadn't forgotten his mobile.

'Stay, Tig,' he said unnecessarily.

Then, telling himself it was to improve reception, but knowing that he wanted above all things to be out of this dark and noisome canyon and back into the bright light and fresh air, he climbed up from the ghyll, pressed the necessary buttons, and began to speak.

SIX

The woman's name was Jackie Tilney. She was over-weight, overworked, over thirty, and so pissed off with having told her story to three different sets of cops that she was ready to tell the fourth to take a jump.

Only the fourth wasn't a set, though possessed of enough flesh to make two or three ordinary bobbies, and if he'd taken her putative advice and jumped, she feared for the foundations of the public library where she worked.

So she told her story again.

She had definitely seen the man in the photograph. And she had spoken with him. And he had an Australian accent.

'The first time was . . .'

'Hang about. First time?' said Dalziel. 'How many times were there?'

'Two,' she retorted. 'Don't your menials tell you anything?'

Dalziel regarded her thoughtfully. He liked a well-made feisty woman. Then he recalled that in Cap Marvell, he'd got the cruiser-weight Queen of Feist, smiled fondly and said, 'Nay, lass, I don't waste time with tipsters when I can go straight to the horse's mouth. Go on.'

Deciding there had to be a compliment in there some-where, Jackie Tilney went on.

'The first time was last Friday. He came to the reference desk and asked if we had anything about the building of the Dendale Reservoir. I told him that he could look at the local papers for the period on our microfiche system. Also this book.'

She showed him the volume. It was called *The Drowning of Dendale*, a square volume, not all that thick. He remembered it vaguely. It had been written by one of the *Post* journalists and contained more photographs than text, basically a before-and-after record.

'He asked me to do a couple of photocopies,' Tilney went on. 'These maps.'

She showed him. One was of Dendale before the flooding, the other, after.

'Did you chat to him at all?'

'A bit. He had a nice easy manner. Just about the weather and such, how it was a lot cooler back home this time of year and how he'd packed three raincoats for his trip to England because everyone told him it rained all the time.'

'Was he trying to chat you up, do you think? Good-looking lass like yourself, it 'ud not be surprising.'

'Am I meant to be flattered?' she said. 'No, as a matter of fact, he didn't come on at me at all. It made a nice change. World's full of fellows who think, just because you're on the other side of a counter, you're sales goods. I got the impression he had other things on his mind, anyway.'

'Such as?'

'Look, mister, I'm too busy trying to keep an underfunded understaffed library system going in this town to have time to develop my psychic powers. I wouldn't be spending this amount of time with you if it didn't have something to do with that missing girl.'

'Now, what makes you think that, luv?'

'I read the *Post*, don't I?'

She produced the paper and spread it before him, open at an article about the investigation with photos of

373

Lorraine Dacre and her parents, of the Hardcastles and Joe Telford, of Geordie Turnbull and his solicitor, and one of Dalziel himself, caught at what looked like a moment of religious contemplation.

With that subtlety and taste for which British journalists are universally famed, the editor had opted to print on the page opposite a feature about the Mid-Yorkshire Music Festival, highlighting the facts that the opening concert was in Danby, featuring 'Songs for Dead Children' sung by Elizabeth Wulfstan, who as a child in Dendale fifteen years back had been the last and only surviving victim of the uncaught abductor of three local girls.

There was a full-figure picture of Elizabeth looking inscrutable, a close-up of Walter Wulfstan looking irritated, and a mid-shot of Sandel on a piano stool looking bored, with the Turnip by the piano looking charming.

Without being actionable, the combined effect of the two pages was to suggest that the police were as out of their depth now as they'd been fifteen years ago.

'Sounds like you need all the help you can get,' said Jackie Tilney.

'I'll not quarrel with that,' said Dalziel. 'So that's the first time you saw him. What about the second?'

'Yesterday afternoon, he were back. He went through the papers again. And then he went through the book. He was noting things down. Then I noticed he'd left the table where he'd been sitting and I thought he'd gone. But I glimpsed him over there, behind that stack.'

'And what's kept over there?' asked Dalziel.

'Business directories, mainly,' said Tilney.

'Oh aye?'

Dalziel strolled over and took a look. She was right. Why shouldn't she be? He returned to the desk.

'And then?'

'And then he left. He was going somewhere else in

town, I think. I saw him looking at one of those town maps you get from the Tourist Centre. And that was the last I saw of him till that constable of yours stuck that picture in front of me this morning. By the by, is he fit to be let out by himself? The bugger came after me with his stick!'

'He's an impulsive young lad,' said Dalziel. 'But good-hearted. I'll have a fatherly word with him.'

He gave her a savage smile suggesting the father he had in mind was Cronos.

'Are we done?' she asked.

He didn't answer. When you've caught a bright witness, don't let it go till you've squeezed it dry, was a good maxim. A uniformed constable approached and was not put off by Dalziel's Gorgon glare.

'What?'

'You're to ring Sergeant Wield at the caravan, sir.'

Meaning, use a land line not your mobile for extra security. Meaning . . . Jackie Tilney said, 'There's a phone in the office. You can be private there.'

She'd caught the vibes of his reaction. Sharp lady.

He went through and dialled. Half a ring and the phone was answered.

'It's me,' he said.

'We've found her, sir.'

The tone told him, dead. His head had long since given up hope of any other outcome, but a tightening of the chest told him his heart had kept a secret vigil.

He said, 'Where?'

'Up the valley.'

Where he himself had ordered the abandonment of the search the previous night. Shit.

He said, 'I'm on my way. You got things started?'

Unnecessary question.

'Yes, sir.'

'And quiet as you can, Wieldy.'

Unnecessary injunction. Born of his own sense of missing things.

'Yes, sir.'

He put the phone down and went back to the desk.

'That'll do for now, luv,' he said. 'Thanks for your help.'

Her eyes suggested his efforts to stay casual were failing.

He picked up *The Drowning of Dendale*.

'All right if I borrow this?'

'Long as you pay the fine,' she said. 'Good luck.'

'Thanks,' he said.

He strode out of the library. Suddenly he felt full of energy. The pain at the confirmation of the child's death was still there, but alongside it was another feeling, less laudable and best kept hidden from others, but unhideable from himself.

After fifteen years, he finally had a body. Bodies told you things. Bodies had been in contact with killers at their most desperate, hasty, and unthinking moments. Mere vanishings were the mothers of rumours, of false trails, of myths and imaginings. But a body . . . !

He might hate himself for it, but he could not keep a spring out of his step as he headed for his car.

SEVEN

Tuesday's bright dawn had brought little but the blackness of contrast to the Pascoes, but Wednesday's brought a glimpse of hope.

Mrs Curtis, the consultant, was still several watts short of optimism, but when she said, 'For a while yesterday we seemed close to falling through, but now it seems more likely we were simply bottoming out,' Ellie didn't even register the medically patronizing *we* but simply embraced the embarrassed woman.

She knew there was no question yet of celebration. Rosie was still unconscious. But at least and at last the sunshine brought with it the hope of hope. And with hope came space for her mind to relax its relentless focus on a single object.

Halfway through the morning, Ellie was in the wash-room regarding herself critically in the mirror. She looked a wreck, but that was nothing to the way Peter looked. He looked like a wreck that had had another couple of accidents. Which, she thought, was not all that far from the truth.

They were both in the wrong jobs, she'd often thought it. He should have been basking on the fringes of the life academic, trying his hand at the novel introspective, running Rosie back and forth to school, keeping the house ticking over . . . no, more than ticking over; on the odd occasion when he'd taken over the ironing, she'd found him pressing underpants, for God's sake! With Peter in charge, they'd have crisp new sheets *every* night.

And herself? She should have been out there on the mean streets, riding the punches and taking the bumps, moving on from one case to the next with nothing to show but the odd bit of scar tissue, none of these deep bruises which keep on haemorrhaging around the bone long after the surface flesh has apparently recovered.

Trouble was, though they shared great areas of social conscience in common, the spin that nature and/or nurture had put on hers made her regard the police force as a cure almost as bad as the disease. Peter, on the other hand, though not blind to its flaws, felt himself duty driven to work from within. A right pious little Aeneas, *Italiam non sponte sequor* and all that crap. Which made her ... Odysseus? Fat, earthy, cunning old Odysseus? Hardly! That was much more Andy Dalziel. Then Dido? Come on! See her chucking herself on a pyre 'cos she'd been jilted. Helen? Ellie looked at herself in the mirror. Not today. So who?

'Me, myself,' she mouthed in the mirror. 'God help me.'

As she returned to the ward, a nurse came towards her, saying, 'Mrs Pascoe, we've got someone on the phone for your husband. She says she's a colleague and it's important.'

'She does, does she?' said Ellie. 'I'll be the judge of that.'

She went to the phone and picked it up.

'Hello,' she said.

There was silence, then a woman's voice said, 'I was trying to get hold of DCI Pascoe ...'

'This is Mrs Pascoe.'

'DC Novello, Shirley Novello. Hi. Mrs Pascoe, I was so sorry to hear ... how is she, the little girl?'

'Hanging on,' said Ellie, not about to share her hope

of hope with a woman she'd only met once briefly. 'So tell me, D C Novello, what's so important?'

Another silence, then, 'I just wanted a quick word . . . Look, I'm sorry, this is a terrible time, I know. It's just that there's this line of enquiry he started, really, and it would be useful, the way he looks at things . . . I'm sorry . . . it's really insensitive, especially . . . it really doesn't matter Mrs Pascoe. I do hope your little girl gets better soon.'

She meant, especially because it's about the child who'd gone missing from Danby, thought Ellie. This was the woman who'd rung yesterday. Peter had mentioned her, provoking an outburst of indignation at such crassness. What had Peter replied? *She lit a candle for Rosie.*

Ellie had no time for religion, but no harm in hedging your bets with a bit of good old-fashioned magic.

'That candle still burning?' she said.

'Sorry?'

'Never mind. What precisely do you want, Miss Novello? No way you get to tell Peter without telling me first.'

Five minutes later she re-entered the ward.

Pascoe looked up and said, 'Still nice and peaceful. Hey, you going somewhere?'

Ellie had brushed her hair and used her minimalist make-up to maximum effect.

'No. You are. I want you to go home, have a bath, get a couple of hours sleep in a real bed. No, don't argue. Come here.'

She led him to the window and swung the panel so that it acted as a mirror.

'See that antique wreck standing next to that gorgeous woman? That's you. If Rosie opens her eyes and sees you first, she'll think she's done a Rip Van Winkle and slept for fifty years. So go home. Sleep with your mobile under your pillow. Slightest change and I'll ring till you waken, I promise.'

'Ellie, no . . .'

'Yes. And now. I've fixed a lift for you, that nice young girl from your office called . . . Shirley Novello, is it? She said she'd be delighted to run you home. She's down in the car park waiting.'

'Shirley? Again? Jesus . . .'

'She's in touch with him, too, I gather. Listen, she wants help and she must think you're the only one if she's willing to come after you here. Perhaps she's delusional, but I think in this case, if you can help, you ought to.'

He shook his head, not in denial but in wonderment.

'You are . . . ineffable,' he said.

'Oh, I don't know. I'm looking forward to being effed quite a lot when this is over,' she said lightly. 'Now go.'

'Only if you'll promise to do the same when I get back.'

'Drive around with a DC? You must be joking. Yes, yes, I promise.'

They kissed. It was, she realized, the first intimate non-comforting contact they'd had since this began.

She watched him go, hoping her homeopathic theory would work, if that was the right way to describe putting him in the way of other parents' woe at the loss of a child. No, it wasn't the right way, she told herself, turning now to look down at Rosie. They weren't going to lose their child. There was a candle burning for her. And, like Dido, after all, her mother would make a candle of herself if that's what it took.

'Hello, sir.'

'And hello to you, too, Shirley,' said Pascoe, getting into the car. 'Kind of you to drive me home. You've got between here and there to tell me what you want to tell me.'

Novello thought, if you want to know what a man will look like when he's old, put him by his child's sickbed for a couple of nights.

But she responded to his crisp speech, not his wrecked appearance, and ran off the résumé she had prepared with a Wieldian conciseness and lucidity.

He offered no compliment. Indeed, he seemed to offer little attention, apparently more interested in the crackling air traffic of her car radio which she'd left switched on.

She reached down to turn it off, but he grasped her hand and said, 'No, leave it.'

It was the first time they'd made physical contact and in other circumstances with other officers she'd have suspected it was the preliminary to a pass and prepared for defensive action.

He held the hand for a second, then she had to change gear and he released it.

'So,' he said. 'Benny's been seen in Dendale and in the Central Library by a reliable witness. Agnes drew the money out of the bank. And Geordie Turnbull's been attacked.'

Novello, who'd included the latter piece of information only in the interests of comprehensiveness, said, 'Yes, but that'll probably be some local nutter, someone like this Jed Hardcastle, perhaps . . .'

'Geordie Turnbull's been living in Bixford for years and making no secret about it, not unless you think having your name printed in big red letters over a fleet of bulldozers is being secretive. Why wait so long?'

'Because of the Dacre girl going missing,' said Novello, stating the obvious, and wondering whether this had been such a good idea. 'That started it all up again.'

To her surprise, he laughed. Or made a sound which had a familiar resemblance to laughter.

'Shirley, you should get it out of your mind that what happened to those families who lost their daughters is something that needs starting up again. It's a permanent condition, no matter how long they survive. Like losing an arm. You might learn to live without it, but you never learn to live as if you've still got it.'

He spoke with a vehemence she found disturbing and when he saw the effect he was having on her, he took a breath and made himself relax.

'Sorry,' he said. 'It's just that in a case like this you share in the woes of others only insofar as they relate to, or underline your own. When I heard Rosie was ill, the fact that the Dacres' child was missing, probably abducted, possibly already murdered, may not have gone out of my mind altogether, but it certainly dropped right out of my consciousness. Understandable initial reaction, you think? Perhaps so. And the perspective will return. But never the same. I know now that if I was within an arm's length of fingering the collar of Benny or any other serial killer, and someone said, "Rosie needs you," I'd let him go.'

He realized that his laid-back confidentiality was troubling her as much as his previous vehemence. He recalled a long time ago in his early days with Dalziel, the Fat Man in his cups had come close to talking about his broken marriage, and he'd shied away from the confidence, unwilling to know what his superior might regret telling.

'In other words, I think we need to look beyond the Dendale families for Turnbull's attacker. And you say he didn't want to report it? That's interesting.'

'Yes, sir,' she said, aware that the distance between the hospital and Pascoe's house was growing shorter. 'But

I'm not really concerned with that bit of the investigation any more.'

But you've not forgotten it was you who got the lead in the first place, thought Pascoe, detecting resentment.

He said gently, 'I know that being mucked around can be a real pain sometimes. But you've got to keep the whole investigation in view. That's what the people you think are mucking you around are doing. Don't get mad, get promoted. Mr Dalziel has thought from the start that Lorraine Dacre's disappearance was connected with Dendale fifteen years back. I didn't agree, but the more I see the way things are working out, the more I think he may be right. So, don't create connections, but don't overlook them, either.'

'No, sir,' said Novello. 'They do keep on jumping up, don't they? I read the old files. You recall that girl, Betsy Allgood, the one who got away from Benny? Well, seems she's back too!'

She reached into the back seat, picked up the *Post* and dropped it in Pascoe's lap.

Not such a clever idea, she thought, as he spent the next couple of minutes studying both pages, the one on the case and the one on the concert.

'Betsy Allgood,' he murmured. 'There was a photo in the file. She didn't look much like that.'

'We grow up, sir,' she said. 'We start looking the way we want, not our parents, as you'll likely find out.'

He glanced at her sharply, then smiled his thanks for this oblique reassurance.

'Well, it's certainly an improvement,' he said. 'She was, if I recall, a rather unprepossessing child.'

It was her turn to give him the sharp glance. He thought, that was pretty crass, Pascoe, in your situation being snooty about other people's kids.

But the photo continued to bother him. Or rather the

photos, because while Betsy/Elizabeth who he'd seen before looked totally unfamiliar, Walter Wulfstan whom he'd never seen rang some kind of bell. But why not? Local dignitary, the kind of man you were likely to see on the top table at some of the civic occasions he'd been delegated to attend as what Dalziel called the 'smart-arse face of policing'.

And something else was bothering him too . . .

He said, 'Pull in here, will you? By that phone box.'

She obeyed, puzzled, but had the wit to sit in silence while Pascoe listened, frowning to the air traffic on her radio.

'Something's happening,' he said.

She said, 'I didn't hear anything, sir . . .'

'No, it's not what anyone's saying, just now and then a pause, an inflexion . . . Maybe I'm way off beam, but do me a favour, Shirley. Check with the incident room at Danby.'

'OK,' she said, pulling out her mobile.

'No,' he said, pointing to the phone box. 'If I'm right, you won't get anything unless you're on a land line.'

She flushed at her slowness, and got out of the car.

Pascoe studied the paper again, then twisted round to place it on the rear seat. Novello had the same attitude as Ellie towards her car, he observed. You kept the driver's seat free and used the rest as a mobile litter bin. He frowned as he saw a couple of plastic evidence bags amidst the debris. Things like that you kept locked in your boot till you could hand them in for examination or storage as soon as possible.

He picked the bags up and set them on his lap. They both had tags indicating their contents had been examined by the lab. The larger bag contained a cigarette packet, two Sunday papers and a stained tissue, the smaller one a camera battery and a silver earring in the shape of a dagger.

He was still looking at this bag when Novello got back into the car, but her words put any questions he had to the back of his mind.

'They've found her,' she said in a flat controlled voice. 'I spoke to Mr Headingley. Not formally identified yet, but it seems Sergeant Wield's sure. He took her dog up the valley . . .'

'Clever old Wieldy,' said Pascoe. 'Doesn't explain how everyone else missed her. Dogs, thermal imaging . . .'

'There was a dead sheep. In this weather . . .'

'Clever old killer,' said Pascoe, trying to keep the image of the dead girl at arm's length. 'Anything on cause yet?'

'No sir. The SOCO team's up there with the doctor now. This knocks my notion about abduction on the head.'

She too was trying to cope with it by losing the child's body in a heap of detective abstractions.

Pascoe said, 'I bet the super's pleased.'

'Sir?' Her indignation couldn't be hidden.

'Because he's got a body,' said Pascoe. 'He'd given her up long since. From the very first moment he heard she'd gone missing, I think. But to get after the killer he needs something concrete. Otherwise you're just punching air. So, anything else?'

'Yes, the super briefed the DI before he went off up the valley.'

She passed on the results of Dalziel's interview with Jackie Tilney, with an amount of detail that surprised Pascoe.

'You must have a lot of influence with George Headingley,' he said.

The DI belonged to an old school who believed that telling DCs too much only confused them and telling

385

female DCs anything other than how many sugars you took was a complete waste of breath.

'Told him I was under instructions from you, sir, and you wanted a blow-by-blow. He sends his best wishes, by the way, for . . . you know . . .'

'Yes, I know,' said Pascoe. 'This book . . . *The Drowning of Dendale*. Ellie's got a copy lying around somewhere. She's into this local-history stuff. But why would Benny want to see it? And what would he need photocopies of the maps for? By all accounts, he knew the valley like the back of his hand.'

'That was fifteen years ago, before the valley was flooded,' said Novello.

'With the drought it's pretty well back to what it was,' objected Pascoe.

'Except that all the buildings have been bulldozed,' said Novello, starting up the car and pulling away from the kerb.

'I suppose so,' said Pascoe. 'Tell me, these evidence bags . . .'

She had noticed the bags in his lap and anticipated his reprimand.

'It's OK, sir,' she said. 'They're for dumping not storing. It's stuff I got out of the litter bin at the viewpoint on the Highcross Moor road when I was thinking abduction. The lab found nothing, not surprising now the girl's been found in the valley. I'll stick them back in a rubbish bin next time I have a clear out.'

'Fine,' he said.

He sat in silence for the rest of the journey. Not the best idea she'd ever had, thought Novello. But what had she expected? He'd been useful last time, probably because his mind had already taken a couple of hypothetical steps ahead before his personal crisis intervened. But since then, as he said himself, the Dacre case had been relegated to a very low place in his mental priorities.

When they reached his house, he got out, still clutching the plastic bags.

'Sir,' she said, pointing.

'What? Oh, yes. I'll stick them in our bin, shall I? Look, come inside for a moment.'

She followed him inside. He headed straight upstairs, leaving her wondering whether she was meant to follow. Not that she cared what was meant. Down here by the open door was the place to be. Pascoe was neither a verbal nor a physical groper, but men under stress could behave strangely, and being assaulted by a popular senior officer with a kid on the danger list was not a good career move for an ambitious woman police officer.

A few moments later, he came back down, clutching a book.

'Here we are. I knew we had a copy. *The Drowning of Dendale*. Let's see if we can find what so interested Lightfoot.'

'It was the maps, sir. We know that,' she said patiently, like an infant teacher.

He caught the intonation, smiled at her, and said, 'Thank you, nurse, but that was the first time. He had photocopies of them. So what brought him back to take another look?'

He went into the lounge, sat down and began to flip through the book. Novello stood behind him, looking over his shoulder.

He supposed he must have glanced through the volume some time in the past, but apart from the first panoramic view of the dale which Mrs Shimmings had shown him, he could remember nothing of it. In any case, what would any previous examination have meant to him? But now he had looked down at the dale as it had become, and he had seen several of its old inhabitants as they had become, and these pictures brought the past to life in a way that, unaided, his imagination could never have managed.

Here were all the buildings he knew only as heaps of rubble scarcely distinguishable from the stony fellside on which they lay.

Here was Heck, a solid, rather stern house even in the bright sunlight which filled all the photos. No one in sight, but a child's swing on an oak tree in the garden had a twist to its ropes as if some small form had just stepped off and slipped quietly away.

Here was Hobholme, one of those old farms which had grown in linear progression, with barn tagged on to house, shippen to barn, lambing shed to shippen, and so on as each need arose. A woman was caught walking purposefully along the line of buildings with a pail in either hand. In the delicate young profile, Pascoe had no difficulty in identifying the features of Molly Hardcastle. Here she was going about her business with the dutiful stoicism of a hillfarmer's wife, not happy exactly, her mind perhaps preoccupied with contrasting the hard expectations of her husband with the softer approaches of Constable Clark. Were these just the idle dreams of a hard-worked wife? Was her love for her three young children, and perhaps the memory that Hardcastle too had once been tender, enough to have kept her anchored here at Hobholme? Or was she seriously contemplating braving her husband's anger and her neighbours' gossip and making a break for happiness? Idle dreams or positive planning, how she must have felt she had paid for either so soon after when little Jenny walked away alone from the bathing pool . . .

A few pages on was The Stang, with the carpenter's shed bigger than the whitewashed cottage, smoke pouring out of its chimney to remind the onlooker that fire was a necessary workmate even when the sun was hot enough to bake apples on the tree. Outside the shed stood two men, stripped to the waist with runnels of sweat down their forearms and pectorals, one clutching a saw and the other a plank, both smiling at the camera, clearly relieved at this excuse to pause and take a well-earned breather. There was a strong family resemblance. One was doubtless Joe Telford, the other his brother George, but an unfamiliar eye couldn't tell the difference between them. Doubtless anybody could now.

The church was here too, St Luke's, with a newly-wed couple emerging, all smiles and happiness; the Holly Bush Inn with folk sitting outside, enjoying a drink in the evening sun, looking as used to these al fresco pleasures as any Provençal peasant; Low Beulah, where the Allgoods lived, with a slim dark-haired man emerging, his leathery face creased into a Heathcliffian frown as though about to give the photographer a piece of his mind.

And here was the village school.

Pascoe's heart contracted, and he felt Shirley Novello stiffen beside him. All the valley's children were here, about two dozen of them, posed in three rows, front sitting on the ground, middle kneeling, back standing with their teachers, Mrs Winter and Miss Lavery, at either side. His eyes ran along the rows. There had been photos of the missing girls in the file and he picked out their little blonde heads and smiling faces one by one. The dark solemn features of Betsy Allgood were easily spottable too. And another face which looked familiar among the bigger girls on the back row . . . now he made the connection . . . this must be Elsie Coe, age ten or eleven, unmistakable to anyone who'd studied the police hand-out photo of her daughter, Lorraine Dacre.

The school photo had the caption *Smiling on a bright future, but not in Dendale*!

No. Not in Dendale.

There were other landscape pictures – of the mere with someone swimming in it; of Beulah Height with the old sheepfold built from stones of the even older hill-fort; of White Mare's Tail in full spate, which meant it was probably taken earlier than the others, before the drought took hold. Then he reached the second section, 'The Drowning', with the epigraph:

> Oh, unexpected stroke, worse than of Death!
> Must I thus leave thee, Paradise?

Now followed photos of the building of the dam and the clearing of the valley. Here were people loading possessions into vans or on to trailers pulled by tractors. Here were sheep being brought down the fellside by the Heathcliffian character who was probably Mr Allgood; here was the churchyard with graves gaping wide and an anxious-looking vicar watching the disinterment of a coffin. Here was the Holly Bush with the landlord removing the sign. Here was the schoolroom, empty of children and desks, with only a few remnants of artwork stuck to the windows to show what this place had once been. And here was the village hall, a man coming out, his arms weighed down with box files, back-heeling the door shut behind him.

The face was unmistakable. Sergeant Wield. The police, too, had had to pack up, though the text made no reference to the other tragedy being played out in Dendale that long hot summer. Probably right for this kind of book. Those involved in the investigation would need no souvenir.

Pascoe flicked on, wondering what the hell, maps apart, Benny Lightfoot – if it were he – could have been interested in?

In the first section there had been only one glimpse of

Neb Cottage seen distantly, but here there was another, much closer. Yet not the kind of shot the returning native would want to pore over. It showed the cottage at the very moment of its destruction. It was a dramatic picture with evening sunlight setting everything in bold definition. A bulldozer with the name TIPLAKE clearly legible down the arm of its shovel was climbing up the side of the building like a rapacious dinosaur, the walls were collapsing like a shot beast and the chimney stack had cracked above the gable and was leaning back like a mouth gaping to let out an agonized death cry.

He went on to the end. The second-last picture showed the release of the Black Moss waters from Highcross Moor over the col between the Neb and Beulah Height. It was a dark and dismal picture, with the skies heavy with cloud and the air dense with the downpour which had broken the drought.

And the last picture of all showed the new dale, in sunshine again, with the reservoir brimfull, a scene as quiet and as peaceful and as lifeless as a crematorium Garden of Remembrance.

He looked up at Novello. She met his gaze hopefully, but not, he was glad to gauge, expectantly.

He said, 'He goes to see his gran, he visits the Central Library and studies old newspapers and this book, he takes photocopies of the maps and camps out in Dendale till yesterday morning when he packs up and comes back to town and the library. This we know. What more do you want to know?'

Her expression changed from vague hope to bafflement.

'Well, I want to know what he's up to, I want to know why he . . .'

'Yes,' he interrupted. 'But why do you want to know why?'

'Because . . . because . . .' Then suddenly she was with him.

'Because knowing might help us catch him soon as possible so we can question him about his possible involvement in the killing of Lorraine Dacre,' she said.

'That's right. *Might* help us catch him. Frankly, it's much more likely we'll pick him up through the camper van, or because he calls in again at Wark House. You've got that covered, I take it?'

'Yes, sir.'

'So don't beat your brains out on this clever detective stuff,' he said wearily. 'Curiosity's fine, but there comes a time when you've got to rejoin the team, even if it means pouring the tea, OK?'

'I just thought . . .'

'No harm in thinking. Here. Take a look yourself before you go. Just slam the door behind you. But not too loud, eh?'

He rose and left the room. She heard him going up the stairs again.

She sat down, opened the book at random and found herself looking at the picture of the bulldozer destroying Neb Cottage.

Significant or not, this is one picture Benny Lightfoot would spend time over, she was sure. She tried to imagine herself looking at a similar photo of the destruction of the suburban semi where she'd been brought up. Even though it had none of the individuality of Neb Cottage, it would rend her heart to see the rooms where she had felt uniquely secure ripped open to the sky.

But Pascoe was right, she thought, closing the book. You shouldn't confuse idle curiosity with good CID work. Time to head out to Danby, see what new assignments were being dished out following the discovery of the body, play in the team even if you ended up pouring the tea . . .

'Fuck that,' she said aloud. Opened the book again. Looked again. Went to the foot of the stairs and called, 'Sir? You still awake?'

There was a pause, then Pascoe's voice said, 'What?'

She went up the stairs, previous doubts forgotten, and stood at the open bedroom door. Pascoe was sitting at a dressing table on to whose surface he had spilled what looked like the contents of a jewel box. He glanced up at her and said again irritably, 'What?'

'Have you got a magnifying glass?' she asked.

She half expected some sarcasm about Sherlock Holmes, but all he said impatiently was, 'Bureau. Left-hand drawer,' and resumed his sorting out of the shining baubles.

She went downstairs, found the bureau, found the glass, and returned to the book.

'Bingo,' she said.

'Still here? Good.' Pascoe was in the hallway.

'Sir, take a look . . .'

'Yes, yes, tell me all about it in the car. I need a lift back to town.'

'But I thought . . . Mrs Pascoe said . . .'

'Just take me back.'

'Yes, sir. To the hospital, sir?'

'No,' he said. 'You can take me to the offices of Mid-Yorkshire Water plc.'

EIGHT

The police doctor's preliminary on-site report was brief.

The child's skull was fractured, which was probably the cause of death. She was fully clothed and there was no immediate sign of sexual interference.

'Anything more, you'll need to wait till they've had her on the slab,' he concluded.

Dalziel recognized this brutal brevity as a familiar way of dealing with a child's death. No way of keeping it out of those areas of sensibility which surface in the dark hours of the night, but here and now there was no time for mournful meditation.

'Right. Let's get her down there,' he said.

Once the body had been removed from the rocky chamber, it became clear that this must have been the 'secret place' Lorraine's friends had talked about. A candle, some comics, a tin containing biscuits and bearing the inscription *Emerjensy ratoins*, a rubber bone pocked with Tig's teeth marks, these told the tale. There was some evidence that she must have contrived her own screen door of grass and brushwood, but the bung of rock and earth which Wield had removed had almost certainly been put there by the killer.

'Then he dragged the sheep's body up from the ghyll bottom,' said Wield. 'That was enough to confuse the dogs and the thermal-imaging cameras alike. Tig knew where to come, but. He weren't following a scent. He just knew.'

The dog had had to be removed from the chamber by a dog handler wearing protective gauntlets, but once out and in Wield's care, he had allowed himself to be put on his lead and tied up without protest. He stood up when the corpse was removed and watched the body box being carried down the fellside to the nearest spot the vehicle could reach. Then he subsided as if knowing that this part of his life was over.

'We'll need formal identification,' said Dalziel.

Meaning, the Dacres had to be told. Whatever small ember of hope they still kept glowing in their hearts had to be put out beyond all doubt.

'I'll sort that,' said Wield.

They both knew it was Dalziel's responsibility. But something in the way he spoke had been the nearest to a plea for help the Fat Man was ever likely to utter.

'My job,' he said, reluctant to confirm weakness.

'Your job's catching the bastard responsible,' said Wield. 'You can tell 'em when you've done that.'

He didn't wait for an answer but untied Tig and set off down the path with the little dog at his heels. He glanced back once before he turned out of sight and saw Dalziel still standing there, watching him go. One huge hand rose slowly to shoulder height in a gesture which might have passed for benediction but which Wield knew was the only thank you he was likely to get.

Back at his bike, he found the dog reluctant to get into the carrying basket, but when Wield straddled the saddle and patted the petrol tank before him, Tig leapt up as if he'd been using this form of travel since birth.

He didn't hurry. What was to hurry for? He tried to blank out all thought and just let himself relax into the rush of cooling air on his face, the feel of the land's twists and contours rippling up his thighs. Down to Ligg Common, the ground levelling off. Past the police cara-van, D I Burroughs standing there, waiting for him to stop and fill her in. He went past her without a glance.

And finally he drew to a halt in front of 7 Liggside.

Even before he could switch the engine off, Tig had jumped from his perch and rushed in through the open doorway, barking.

Oh, shit! thought Wield. Shit shit shit!

He hurried after the animal, but it was already too late. Tony and Elsie Dacre were on their feet, staring towards the doorway, their eyes bright with desperate hope in reaction to Tig's noisy arrival, which must so often have presaged Lorraine's return home.

'I'm sorry,' said Wield, helplessly. 'I'm sorry.'

He was apologizing for letting the dog run in, but his words did the harder task too. The woman cried, 'Oh no. Oh no!' And collapsed weeping into her husband's arms.

'Where . . . ? How . . . ?' choked the man.

'Up the valley, along the beck where it runs through that deep ghyll,' said Wield. 'Tig found her.'

'What happened? Were she . . .'

'Can't say how for certain till they get the chance to . . . But the doctor says she was fully clothed. No signs of interference.'

All this was more than he ought to be saying before the post mortem, but he couldn't sit and see this pain without doing the little in his power to ease it.

'We'll need to ask someone to do an identification,' he went on.

Elsie's head snapped up. Hope was a black beetle. Stamp on it hard as you liked, it still scuttled on.

'It's not sure, then?' she pleaded.

'Yes, it's sure,' he said gently. 'The clothes she was wearing. And we had the photo. I'm so sorry. Look, I'll come back later, talk about arrangements. You'll need some time . . .'

He turned and left, feeling shame at his sense of relief to get out of that room where something had finally died.

A woman was coming through the front door. It was Margaret Coe, Elsie Dacre's mother.

She said, 'I saw you go in. Has summat happened?'

Wield nodded.

'We found her.'

'Oh, Christ.'

She pushed past him into the living room. Wield went outside. The sunlight had never seemed so cruel. He felt many eyes upon him. Ignoring them all, he mounted his bike. Tony Dacre came out of the house with Tig in his arms.

'Can you take him with you?' he said. 'It's going to be too much having him around. Every time he barks, it'll be like . . . Any road, he seems to have taken a fancy to you . . . I don't mean have owt done to him, you understand . . . just see he's taken care of while . . . look, were you telling truth back there? He'd not done anything to her?'

'As far as they could tell without a full examination,' said Wield.

'Well, that's something,' said Tony Dacre. Then he looked up at the rich blue sky and shook his head wonderingly.

'Nowt so funny as folk, eh? Here's me, just heard my daughter's dead, and I'm trying to feel comforted she weren't raped. For God's sake, what kind of creatures are we, Sergeant? What's the use of us, any of us?'

'I don't know,' said Wield. 'I just don't know.'

He set the dog before him and rode away thinking, oh you bastard, you bastard, whoever you are, it's all of us you kill because you kill our faith in each other, in ourselves. We don't just recoil in horror from what you do, we recoil in horror from ourselves for being part of the same humanity that produced whatever it is that you are.

A rasping noise rose from between his legs. Tig had

fallen asleep with his head on Wield's thigh and was snoring.

And what the hell is Edwin going to say when he sees you? Wield asked himself.

And then, as he felt the ease with which he'd made the leap from cosmic despair to domestic problem, he didn't know whether to laugh or cry.

NINE

The half of the woman visible above the reception desk of the Mid-Yorkshire Water company was welcoming and fair, but her implacability towards those seeking entrance to the world behind her hinted the presence of a cry of hell-hounds below.

Pascoe looked easy meat. During the past couple of years, as complaints about drought, pollution and directors' perks had multiplied, she had become adept at repelling much heavier onslaughts than promised by this slim, pale, dishevelled figure.

'I'm afraid Mr Purlingstone is unavailable today. If you leave your name, I'll see he's told you called.'

'Just tell him I'm here now. Pascoe's the name. Pascoe. Just tell him.'

He saw her right hand move and guessed it was on its way to a security button. With a sigh, he produced his warrant.

'Chief Inspector Pascoe. Tell him.'

She picked up the phone and moments later Pascoe was floating to the top floor in a scented musical lift.

Purlingstone was waiting for him when the door slid open.

'What?' he demanded. 'What's happened? Why've you come?'

'It's OK,' said Pascoe. 'Nothing to do with Zandra. Really. It's OK.'

He felt a huge pang of guilt. He wasn't thinking straight, coming round here like this. Just because the man was dealing with his trauma by fleeing from its centre to the place where he still had power and control didn't mean he wasn't in pain. And what else would he think on hearing of Pascoe's arrival but the worst?

The two men hadn't spoken since their quarrel, and this, thought Pascoe, is no way to build bridges.

'Derek,' he said. 'I'm sorry. I should have rung. Everything's fine at the hospital. They'd be in touch direct if anything was wrong, wouldn't they?'

This appeal to logic seemed to work, as worry was replaced by suspicion.

'OK, so what the hell are you doing here?' demanded Purlingstone.

'I'm sorry,' repeated Pascoe. 'There are just a couple of questions I'd like to ask.'

'You sound just like a policeman,' sneered Purlingstone.

It was true, thought Pascoe. His phraseology was straight out of a telly cop show. But so what? We are what we are.

He said, 'Where did you stop on Sunday?'

'What?'

'Rosie said you stopped for a breakfast picnic on your way to the coast. I just wondered which way you went and where . . .'

He faltered to a halt, not because the other man was looking angry, but because his annoyance was visibly fading and being replaced by a sort of wary pity.

He thinks I've cracked, thought Pascoe. He thinks I've lost it entirely.

It might have been clever to use this wrong impression as a basis for winning both sympathy and information, but he wasn't able to go along with that. What he felt about his sick daughter was his business, not communicable to anyone save Ellie, and certainly not usable in this kind of situation to gain an advantage.

He said sharply, 'Come on. It's a simple question. Where did you stop to picnic?'

'On the moor road out of Danby,' replied Purlingstone. 'I prefer to go that way to the coast. It's a bit further, but it misses a hell of a lot of the traffic. Look, what's all this about? I can't believe it's police business . . . but it is, isn't it? Jesus Christ, how insensitive can you get, Pascoe?'

No pity now, just anger.

'No, not really, well, in a way, but . . .' Pascoe was stuttering in his effort to offer an explanation and avoid another open quarrel. He saw from Purlingstone's face that he wasn't making much headway either way.

'It's just that Rosie lost this cross she wore, well, it wasn't really a cross, one of Ellie's earrings shaped like a dagger, actually, and one of my DCs found one like it in a waste bin, and I wondered how . . . It is it, you see . . . I checked . . . I mean, it's probably just coincidence, but . . .'

A phone had been ringing in a room behind Purlingstone. It stopped and a young woman came out.

'Derek,' she said urgently.

'What?'

'Sorry, but it's the hospital. They said, can you get back there straightaway?'

'Oh, Christ.'

The two men looked desperately at each other, each hoping for a reassurance the other couldn't give. Pascoe was thinking, they could be ringing home, and I'm not there, and I've had my mobile switched off . . .

He said, 'Can you give me a lift? Please.'

'Come on.'

Ignoring the lift, together the two men ran down the stairs.

* * *

They could have rung from the car, but didn't. The pain of ignorance can end. The pain of knowledge is forever. As they entered the waiting room and saw the two women clinging together, they knew it was very bad. On sight of her husband Jill Purlingstone broke loose and rushed to his arms.

'What's happened?' demanded Pascoe, going to Ellie.

'Exactly what, I don't know, but it doesn't sound good,' said Ellie in a low voice.

'Oh, Christ, and she was doing so well. I should never have left . . .'

'It isn't Rosie,' hissed Ellie in his ear. 'She's doing fine. It's Zandra.'

For a moment his relief was so strong he could have laughed out loud. Then his gaze went to the other couple, locked in an embrace which looked like an attempt to crush out all feeling, and shame at his joy came rushing in.

'Should I go and try to find out something?' he asked Ellie, his voice as low as hers.

'No. They said they'd let Jill know as soon as there was anything more to tell.'

The door opened. Mrs Curtis the paediatric consultant came in. Ignoring the Pascoes, she went towards the Purlingstones, who broke apart like guilty lovers surprised. Only their hands remained in fingertip contact.

'Please,' said the consultant. 'Shall we sit down?'

'Oh, God,' breathed Ellie, for the woman's voice had the ring of death as sure as any passing bell.

Pascoe took her arm and drew her unresisting body out of the room.

In the corridor she looked up at him pleadingly, as if in hope of finding contradiction in his face. He had none to offer. There was a hush about the wards, and the set look on the faces of two nurses who went quietly by which confirmed what they already felt.

Ellie turned back towards the door, but Pascoe tightened his grip on her.

'Jill will need me,' she said fiercely.

'No,' he said. 'We're the last people on earth those two will want to see at the moment.'

From inside the waiting room a voice – it could have been either male or female – screamed, *'Why*?'

It was the universal cry of loss; but it contained in it the particular question, *Why my child? Why not someone else's?*

Ellie heard it at all its levels and ceased her efforts to pull away.

'Let's go in and see Rosie,' said Pascoe.

They found the attending nurse full of excitement.

'She opened her eyes just now. I think she's beginning to wake up,' she said. 'I've been talking to her, but it's your voices she'll be wanting to hear.'

They stood on either side of the bed, leaning over the small still figure of their daughter. Ellie tried to speak, but there were too many conflicting emotions squeezing at her throat.

Pascoe said, 'Rosie, darling. Come on now. This is Daddy. Time to wake up. It's time to wake up.'

In the gloomy cave, the nix has made his move. No pursuit round the pool this time; instead he comes running straight across it, splashing through the black waters so that they part on either side like the water in the tank at the fairground when the roller coaster comes hurtling down.

Taken by surprise, Rosie and her companion break apart and take flight, one to the left, one to the right. The air is filled with noise, the animal roar of the nix, the high spiralling squeaks of the bat, the screams of the two little girls – and something else, a voice, her father's voice, calling Rosie's name.

403

Her flight has brought her round the pool to the mouth of the exit tunnel. Here the voice is clearer. She looks up into the brighter light, then looks round to see where the nix is.

He is on the far side of the pool once more. He is standing over the other girl who has stumbled to the ground.

Her hair has fallen over her face so that all Rosie can see are her eyes, which might be Nina's, or Zandra's, or some other child's altogether, peering at her so fearfully, so pleadingly, she hesitates for a moment.

Then her father's voice again. *Come on, Rosie, time to wake up!*

And she turns her back on the cave and the pool and the dark world of the nix, and goes running up the tunnel into the light.

TEN

Shirley Novello was not a natural liar. During childhood, both parental and religious influences had urged upon her the primacy of truth.

Her parents had believed, or pretended to believe, anything she told them. At first, this had seemed fun. You could eat your ice cream then tell them you'd tripped and dropped it in the sand, and they'd give you the money for another. Or you could blame your little brother for some breakage you'd done yourself and sit back and watch him get a spanking. It had seemed easy to reconcile this with the standard of absolute truth in the confessional which she accepted without question. After all, what was the point of lying to God who knew everything, especially when by confessing all the lies she told at home, she could get absolution for them?

Then one day after confession, the priest had asked, 'Why do we tell God the truth, Shirley?' And she'd replied, 'Because He would know if we were telling lies.' And he'd said, 'No, that's not it. It's because of the pain we give those who love us when they know we're telling lies.'

That was all. But she knew he was talking about her mum and dad. And that was the end of lying.

Except, of course, when it was absolutely necessary. Adolescence taught her that truth was not always an option, a lesson confirmed most forcefully by work in the CID. Far too much of your time was spent on the slippery slopes of ends justifying means.

And with colleagues almost as much as criminals.

'Let me get this straight,' said Detective Inspector Head-ingley. 'The DCI has assigned you to watching Geordie Turnbull?'

'Yes, sir.'

She'd been both lucky and unlucky to find Headingley in charge of the incident centre when she reported to Danby. While he was the least likely of the CID hierarchy to authorize her 'poncing about' (his epicene usage) on her own line of enquiry, he was also least likely to question the alleged authority of a senior.

'You're seeing a lot of Mr Pascoe,' he observed.

'The super's had me following up some of his lines of enquiry, and now things are looking a bit better at the hospital, he wants to be sure I'm doing things right, sir.'

Headingley nodded approvingly. This he could under-stand. Even at moments of great personal crisis, any self-respecting CID officer wants to keep an eye on any airheaded female who was getting her painted fingernails into his . . . the metaphor tapered out, but he knew what he meant.

'All right,' he said. 'I'll put it in the book, DCI's assign-ment. And don't take all day over it.'

But all day looked like what she was going to have to take, and each succeeding minute made it more likely that she would have to explain herself to at best Wield, at worst, the Fat Man.

The truth of her 'assignment', which she'd wrapped up so imposingly for Headingley, was that Pascoe had listened, or half-listened, to her assertion that, prompted by the name TIPLAKE on the bulldozer in the Neb Cottage photograph, she had examined the driver through the magnifying glass and was almost certain she could identify him as Geordie Turnbull. Then he had said, 'So what?'

Good question, but one she'd hoped he might try to answer rather than simply ask.

Not that she wasn't willing to give it a go.

'Well, Benny would know him, wouldn't he? I mean, he was around the dale all that summer. And suppose the reason Benny's come back is to clear his name . . . Yes, that could be it. Benny's innocent and he's trying to work out who really did it, and he recalls that Turnbull was taken in for questioning back then, and he sees in the papers that he's been questioned again . . . then he spots him in that photo, and you can see the name of the firm on the bulldozer, the old name, I mean, Tiplake it was. So Lightfoot checks in the business directories at the library and finds the address, only it's Turnbull's now of course . . .'

'And goes out there this morning to try and beat the truth out of Geordie?' Pascoe concluded for her. He didn't hoot with laughter. Even if his present situation hadn't put so much ground between himself and amusement, he probably wouldn't have openly ridiculed her. But his serious expression and even tone didn't conceal the fact that he thought she was being ridiculous.

'It's possible,' she said defiantly.

'If he'd read what's been written about Turnbull in the local papers this week, why would he need to go burrowing among the business directories?' asked Pascoe. 'No problem about finding him after he read that lot.'

Even with half his mind on her hypothesis, he could see the gaping cracks in it, she thought bitterly.

'No, sir,' she said, trying not to sound like a sulking child.

'So what did you think might be your next move?' Pascoe enquired courteously.

They had reached the Water Company building and she brought the car to a halt by the main entrance.

'Well, I had thought maybe a watch on Turnbull might be a good move,' she said for the want of anything better.

'In case Lightfoot comes back to try what another beating might do?'

This time he did manage a faint smile, and with a great effort she matched it.

'Yeah, well, now I think about it, doesn't seem all that likely, even if I'd managed to get it right, which seems even less likely.'

He opened the car door.

'So why not do it?' he said.

'Sorry?'

'Keep an eye on Geordie.'

'But you said . . . I thought you said . . .' Time for truth, long past time for pussyfooting around. '. . . you did say, not in so many words, but what you meant was, it was a bloody stupid idea!'

He got out, closed the door, and leaned in through the open window.

'No,' he said mildly. 'If I meant anything like that, it was that your reasons for doing it were . . . flawed. But the heart has its reasons that reason wots not of. I, for instance, have only the faintest notion what I'm doing here, but here I am. But it might be wise while you are keeping your watch to think up a better reason than the one you've offered me for doing it. Nor would I fall back on a French philosopher. Mr Dalziel is more a Nietzsche man. May I borrow your *Post*?'

He plucked the paper from the rear seat, managed the faint smile again, and walked away.

She stared after him without gratitude. All that crap about the heart's reasons. The clever sod had some clever notions in his noddle that he didn't have the time or maybe the inclination to waste on her. Or likely he'd say it was part of the learning process to make her work things out for herself. Who the fuck did he think he was? Socrates?

Now here she was, parked within sight of Turnbull's bungalow, working out reasons for her presence, each ten times dafter than the last.

Turnbull was at home. Through her glasses she'd glimpsed him moving around inside. It had been early afternoon when she arrived, so whether he'd been out that morning or not, she had no way of knowing. Certainly there was only one digger remaining parked in the compound, so presumably the others were out on a job somewhere. Perhaps after the assault he didn't feel well enough to go out to the sites himself.

Fortunately, Novello had had the sense to grab a pre-packed sandwich and a bottle of water from the incident room fridge. Even so, with the sun burning down and time ticking by, she guessed she was going to end up baked, parched and hungered before the day was out. And still nothing happened. The good part of the nothing was that nobody was trying to raise her with angry queries as to what the hell she thought she was doing. The bad part was that after an hour or so without further sight of Turnbull through the wide-open windows of the bungalow, she began to fear that he might somehow have slipped out of the back and away across the fields. Had there been a rear gate in the compound security fence? She tried to recall, and failed.

Perhaps she should take a stroll. Even if he clocked her, he'd only seen her the once, no reason he should remember.

Except of course that he was Geordie Turnbull. She recalled that unashamedly appreciative gaze which flattered rather than offended. Part of its power was that it seemed to be registering you as an individual, not just as an arrangement of tits and crotch. Once your face was filed in Geordie's memory, she betted it was retrievable for ever.

But just as she thought both professional necessity and personal comfort made such a stroll essential, something happened.

A vehicle transporter turned into the compound. A flabbily fat man slid out and sat on the running board, gasping with the effort. He was wearing football shorts and a string vest through whose meshes glowed diamonds of red flesh. Flayed, you could have used him to decorate an Indian restaurant. Finally he recovered enough to reach into the cab, take out a plastic carrier bag and head to the bungalow, the door of which opened before him. He went inside. Twenty minutes later he re-emerged, minus the bag and plus a can of lager. Novello watched in envy as he squeezed the last drops into his mouth and handed the can to Turnbull who dropped it to the floor behind him. The two men now manoeuvred the digger on to the transporter, made it secure, and shook hands. Turnbull watched as the vehicle drove out of the compound, then turned back into the bungalow.

Novello made a note of the transporter number, called up Control on her radio and asked for a vehicle check. It was registered to Kellaway Plant Sales, proprietor Liberace Kellaway. Novello gave details of the transporter's likely present location and asked if it could be stopped, ostensibly for a check on stability or something, but in fact to find out anything they could about the origins of the digger. When the sergeant i/c Control came on to enquire who it was requesting this misuse of hard-worked car officers' time, with the implication that it had better not be anyone low as a DC, Novello thought of sheep and lambs and said, 'Mr Dalziel would be grateful.'

In Mid-Yorkshire police circles, this was the equivalent of a Royal Command, and half an hour later the word came back. The transporter, which was being driven by Mr Kellaway himself (Liberace! thought Novello. What a fan his mother must have been. What a disappointment little Lib probably was!) had passed all tests satisfactorily. As for the digger, it had just been purchased from the firm of G. Turnbull, (Demolition & Excavation) Ltd of Bixford, and he had the papers to prove it.

Novello uttered her thanks, plus a request that no further reference be made to this matter on open air, hoping thus to delay the moment when the Fat Man discovered his name had been taken in vain.

Now she settled down again to wait, still hungry, still hot, but refreshed by hope as her mind began to get an inkling of what that smart-ass Pascoe had probably worked out several hours before.

ELEVEN

In fact, Shirley Novello was both overestimating Pascoe, and underestimating Dalziel.

The former it was true had glimpsed the outline of a sketch of a cartoon of a possible picture when he advised her to follow her heart, but no more than that, and in the hours since he had found little leisure or inclination to essay bolder strokes and finer shadings.

The awaking of Rosie was both huge joy and piercing pain.

She had opened her eyes and been instantly aware of her parents. Initially she showed no curiosity about where she was but babbled on – not deliriously but merely out of her customary eagerness to tell everything at once – about caves and pools and tunnels and bats and nixes.

Then she paused and said, 'Where's Zandra? Is Zandra back too?'

That was the pain. The pain of her loss to come. And the infinitely greater pain of Derek and Jill Purlingstone's loss, which Pascoe shared by empathy as his heart and imagination showed him how he would have felt had it been Rosie, and which was joined by guilt as he found himself offering up thanks to the God he didn't believe in that it hadn't been her.

'It wasn't a choice, Peter,' urged Ellie when he explained this. 'There was no moment when someone, or some thing, decided, we'll take this one and let that one go.'

'No,' said Pascoe. 'But if it had been a choice, and I had to make it, this is what I would have chosen without a second's thought.'

'And that makes you feel guilty?' said Ellie. 'If you'd needed a second's thought, *that* would have been something to feel guilty about.'

Rosie had fallen asleep now, as if the excitement of recovery was as exhausting as the illness itself, but now her rest was recognizably the repose of sleep, with all the small grunts and changes of expression and shifts of position which her watching parents knew so well.

They sat by the bed hand in hand, sometimes talking quietly, sometimes in a shared silence full of pleasurable memory of times past, and in pleasurable anticipation of times to come; but always if the silence went on too long, they would finally look at each other and register that each had drifted in his and her reverie to that other place in the hospital where a small form lay and two other parents sat in their own silence as profound and unbreachable as that beneath the sea.

As for Andy Dalziel, it was some time since he had turned his attention to the disposition of his troops and first of all he asked, 'What's Seymour on?'

Wield, who made it his business to find out in rapid retrospect what he had failed to know in long advance, said, 'He's at Wark House in case Lightfoot shows up there.'

'Oh aye? I thought that were Ivor's assignment.'

'No. It were her idea to send Seymour.'

'*Her* idea?' said Dalziel making it sound oxymoronic. 'And where's *she* at?'

'She's watching Turnbull.'

'And whose idea were that?'

'She says the DCI's.'

'*She says*! Meaning she's doing it off her own bat, I suppose. Dear God, Wieldy, you've got to watch these women. Give 'em an inch and they're black-leading your bollocks.'

'You want I should call her up?'

'Nay. Let her be. There's nowt for her to do here and if she turns summat up, she'll be a hero.'

'And if she doesn't?' said Wield.

'Then likely she'll be sorry she ever troubled the midwife,' said Dalziel balefully.

The superintendent was in a bad mood. So far the fresh lines of enquiry he'd anticipated from the finding of the body hadn't materialized. The post mortem had confirmed the on-the-spot diagnosis. Death following a skull fracture caused either by being hit by an irregular-shaped object, probably a piece of rock, or by falling heavily against same. No sexual assault. Forensic examination of the clothing had so far come up with nothing. In fact the only opportunities for Dalziel to exercise any of his many skills came from being required by first the Chief Constable and secondly the press to explain how come an extensive, and expensive, search over the same ground had failed to turn up the child's corpse.

Desperate Dan Trimble, the CC, had been relatively easy to deal with. Despite their occasional differences, they had a lot of respect for each other, which is to say Trimble accepted that Dalziel's regime was good for the area's crime figures, and Dalziel accepted that, as far as was possible, Trimble protected his back. Also Dan liked the way Dalziel made no effort to offload responsibility on to Maggie Burroughs or any other of the officers on the ground. 'Shifting dead sheep and paying special heed to the area round about was my shout,' said the Fat Man. 'I missed it.' And the question rose in his mind as to whether he might have missed it fifteen years ago also.

If this were the same killer, why should he have bothered to learn new tricks?

At the press conference summoned in late afternoon in a classroom at St Michael's school, the ladies and gents of the press were another kettle of fish. The locals, knowing that keeping on the right side of Dalziel was good survival technique, were relatively kind, but the national pack had no such inhibitions. After they'd worried the police incompetence hare to death, they turned their attention to their second perceived prey, the Dendale connection. This was a two-pronged onslaught with the sensationalist tabloids eager to tell their readers this was the same killer come back to start again (which meant that police incompetence fifteen years ago was now coming back to haunt them), while the rest were pursuing the line that the two cases were probably not connected but Dalziel was letting his obsession with Dendale contaminate the contemporary investigation.

The Fat Man bit back the word, 'Bollocks!' and said, 'Nay, we've got an open mind to all possibilities, and we hope you gents will keep an open mind too.' . . . And I'll be happy to help open it with a hatchet, his thoughts ran on.

A smarmily sarky sod from one of the heavyweight Sundays said, 'I presume it's in pursuance of this openminded approach that you still have a diving team searching the Dendale Reservoir?'

Shit! thought Dalziel. So much had happened today that he'd forgotten to call the mermaids off.

'In view of the discovery of the lass's body,' he said portentously, 'we are of course now re-searching the whole area for traces of the assailant.'

'Think he got away by swimming, do you?' called someone to laughter.

'Water's a good place for getting rid of things,' said Dalziel stonily.

'Like a murder weapon, you mean?' said the sarky sod. 'Which I understand, is likely to have been a rock? You mean, you've got a team of divers searching the bed of a reservoir in a Yorkshire dale for a rock? Tell me, Super-intendent, have they managed to find one yet?'

More amusement. This was getting out of hand.

He waited for silence, then said, 'I see the serious questions are over, so I'll get back to work now. I know I don't need to remind you folk that there's people suffering out there, and there's people frightened, and the last thing they need is for what's gone off to be sensationalized or trivialized.'

He let his gaze run slowly over the assembled faces, as if committing each one to memory, then spoke again.

'Up here we judge folk not only by the way they keep the Law but by the way they treat each other. And we don't take kindly to intrusion or harassment. So think on.'

He rose, ignoring the attempts to continue the questioning, and walked out.

'You were good,' said Wield.

'I were crap,' said Dalziel indifferently. 'Wieldy, get on the line to them mermaids and tell them to start towelling off.'

The sergeant went away. He was back in a couple of minutes, looking – so far as it was possible to tell from those craggy features – unhappy.

'All sorted?' said Dalziel.

'Not really,' said Wield. 'When I got through they were just on the point of contacting us. Sir, they've found some bones.'

'*What*? You mean, human?'

'Aye. Human.'

'Champion,' said Dalziel, looking out of the window at the infinite blue of the sky. 'Like my old dad used to say, it never bloody rains but it pours!'

TWELVE

At five o'clock, Geordie Turnbull was on the move.

Novello had been driven by a call of nature to leave the car in search of seclusion. This enforced exploration had led her to a small copse in a field almost opposite the compound where, relief achieved, she discovered that with the aid of her glasses, she was able to get a view clear through the length of the bungalow's living room, from open front window to open French door.

She could see Turnbull's head and shoulders as he slouched in an armchair, occasionally taking a sip from a glass. Then he straightened up, reached out and picked up the telephone.

He didn't dial so it had to be an incoming call. It didn't last long. He replaced the receiver, drained his glass and stood up.

Then he moved out of sight. Novello didn't hang about but headed back to her car fast.

Her instinct proved right. A minute later, Turnbull came out of the bungalow carrying a bag. He got into the Volvo estate and drove out through the compound gate, turning eastward. It was a fairly empty B-road and Novello hung well back. But six or seven miles beyond Bixford, the B-road joined the busy dual carriageway to the coast and she had to accelerate to keep him within sight.

A few miles further on he signalled to turn off into a service area. She thought it must be fuel he was after, but he turned into the car park, got out, still carrying the bag, and headed for the cafeteria.

Novello followed. She hung back till several more people joined the queue behind him, then took her place. He bought a pot of tea and carried it to a table by the window overlooking the road. She noticed he took the seat which gave him a view of the entrance door.

She got a coffee and found a seat a few tables behind him. Someone had left a newspaper. She picked it up and held it so that, if he should happen to glance round, half her face would be covered. If his roving eye was keen enough to identify her from the top half alone, tough.

He was waiting for someone, there was no doubt about that. He poured his tea and raised the cup to his lips with his left hand, his right never letting go of the handle of the bag on the chair next to his, and his head angled towards the doorway.

This went on for twenty minutes. People came and ate and left. A clearer-up tried to remove Novello's empty cup, but she hung onto it. She had turned the pages of her paper several times without reading a word or even identifying which title she was holding. He likewise had squeezed the last drops out of his teapot. More time passed. Whatever reason he had for being here, he was determined his journey should not have been in vain.

Then finally he froze. Not that he'd been moving much before, but now he went so still he made the furniture look active.

Novello looked towards the entrance door.

She knew him at once from Wield's doctored photograph.

Benny Lightfoot had just come into the cafeteria.

Andy Dalziel was standing at the edge of Dender Mere, close by the pile of stones which marked the site of Heck Farm. On the sun-baked mud at his feet lay a small selection of bones. He stirred them with his toe.

'Radius, ulna, and we think these could be carpal bones, but being small, they've been a bit more mucked about,' said the chief mermaid, whose everyday name was Sergeant Tom Perriman.

'Age? Sex? How long they've been there?' prompted Dalziel greedily.

Perriman shrugged his broad rubberized shoulders.

'We just pulled 'em out,' he said. 'Adult, I'd say, or adolescent at least.'

'And the rest?'

'Still looking,' said Perriman. 'Funny really. Not much in the way of current here. You'd expect them to stay pretty much together even after a fairly long time. Pure chance I found them. We weren't really interested in searching near the side where it's so shallow . . .'

'Where exactly?' demanded Dalziel.

'Just here,' said Perriman, disgruntled at having his narrative flow interrupted.

He indicated a spot on the watery side of the exposed pile of rubble and went on, 'I was just coming out, stood up to walk the last couple of yards and felt something under my foot. Of course it would have been a lot deeper here before the drought. But where's the rest, that's my question.'

'Perhaps there is no more,' suggested Wield.

'What? Someone cut off an arm and hoyed it into the mere?' said Dalziel. 'Still means there's the rest of him somewhere, or some bugger caused a bit of comment by going out for a stroll with a full set of arms and coming back one short.'

'Some very secretive folk in Mid-Yorkshire, sir. Any road, chances are it's nowt to do with our case.'

'Oh aye? So what are you suggesting, Wieldy? Chuck it back and if any bugger asks, tell 'em it got away? Listen, even if it's not our case, it's certainly another of our cases.

Bag this lot and get them down to the lab, Tom. And keep looking.'

The Fat Man turned and headed toward his Range Rover, Wield following.

'There's been a few suicides up here, sir,' he said.

'Aye, I think of them every time I mash my tea, Wieldy,' said Dalziel. 'But we usually trawl them out, don't we?'

'The ones we know about,' agreed the sergeant. 'But anyone could come up here and take a walk into the middle with a pocketful of stones and end up a statistic on our missing persons list.'

'I may have to give up tea,' said Dalziel. 'You know, I never liked this water from the first time I saw it. Something about Dender Mere always gave me the creeps. Here, that sounds like George Headingley laying an egg on the car radio. What's woken him up, I wonder?'

'Soon find out,' said Wield, picking up the mike and responding.

'Is he there, Wieldy?' demanded Headingley. 'Tell him we've just got a message in from DC Novello. She says she's sitting in the cafeteria of the Orecliff Services on the coast road watching Geordie Turnbull having a chat with Benny Lightfoot. You see what this means? They could be in it together! Two of them, not just the one. That 'ud explain a hell of a lot, wouldn't it?'

Dalziel reached over and took the mike.

He said, 'It wouldn't explain what you're doing telling the world and his mother this on the open air, George. So shut up unless you're sending the four-minute warning. We're on our way!'

'So what do you think, sir?' said Wield as they drove away. 'Two for the price of one?'

'I think George Headingley got his brain on the National Health and his immune system's rejecting it,' said Dalziel. 'But if yon Ivor really has got us Benny Lightfoot, I think I might have to marry her.'

At about the same time, Rosie Pascoe woke again and announced she was hungry. When she was only allowed a very light amount of liquid intake, she started to complain bitterly and her parents looked at each other with broad smiles.

'Am I very ill?' the little girl asked suddenly.

Pascoe's heart jolted for a second, but Ellie's ear was much more attuned to the note of calculation in the question.

'You've been *fairly* ill,' she said firmly. 'But now you are much better. And if you're completely better in time for the Mid-Yorks Fair, Daddy will take you and you can go on the Big Loop. Now, Mummy's got to go out for a little while, but I'll be back shortly.'

Pascoe followed her to the door.

'What was all that about?' he asked.

'The trick is to make the reward for getting better, not for being ill, otherwise she'll spin the invalid state out for months,' said Ellie patiently.

'Yes, I got that. I meant about the Big Loop. You know it makes me sick.'

'Peter, though I'll deny ever having said it, sometimes a little more Schwarzenegger, a little less Hugh Grant, would be a useful corrective.'

'OK. Where the hell do you think you're going, babe?'

'That is pure Cagney,' she said. Then, more serious, 'I'm just going to check on Jill. OK, I understand what you said before, and I'm not going to push myself on her. She'll be at home now anyway, I should think. But I wanted to talk to someone about her and try to work out what's best for us to do.'

'OK,' said Pascoe. 'I'll entertain the monster.'

After a fairly short spell of 'entertainment', the monster looked ready to go back to sleep again.

'That's right, sweetie. You have a nap, get your strength up,' said Pascoe. 'In hospital you need to be fit to keep an eye on all the visitors trying to steal your grapes.'

'Will I get a lot of visitors?' asked Rosie sleepily.

'Depends on the quality of your grapes.'

'Will Zandra come?'

Pascoe made a huge effort to keep his voice light.

'If she can,' he said.

He didn't know when the time would be ripe to tell her, but he knew it wasn't now.

'I haven't seen her since Sunday. Not to talk to, anyway. She might have the photos Derek took by now.'

'Yes. Darling, remember when you had your breakfast picnic on Sunday?'

He felt guilty about asking but assured himself he wouldn't have brought it up if she hadn't mentioned Zandra herself.

'Yes. And I saw the nix taking Nina,' she said.

It was as if he'd somehow conveyed the trend of his thought to her.

'That's right. You were using Derek's binoculars, weren't you?'

'Yes. They make things a lot bigger than yours, you know,' she said seriously.

'I'm sure,' he said, smiling. 'And you saw Nina down in the valley. By herself was she?'

'Yes. No. She had a little dog.'

'Then the nix came.'

'Yes. He came running down the hill and he threw her into a hole in the ground. I expect his cave is down there somewhere.'

Her voice was very faint and weary now.

Pascoe pulled Novello's *Post* out of his pocket and

unfolded it so that the double-page spread at its centre showed.

'Just before you drop off, darling, anyone here you recognize?'

She peered through half-closed eyes, then smiled and stabbed with her finger.

'That's Uncle Andy,' she said.

'Hello. What's this game you're playing?' said Ellie's voice.

She had come in undetected and her tone was light and playful. But something in her husband's manner as he looked up must have alerted her, for now she asked suspiciously, 'What is that you're showing her, Peter?'

'Just a photo of Uncle Andy, that's all,' said Pascoe, starting to fold the paper.

But before he could do this, the little hand reached out and the finger stabbed again.

'And that's the rotten old nix,' said Rosie Pascoe.

Then she yawned hugely and fell asleep.

THIRTEEN

The Summer Festival Concert was due to start at seven o'clock.

After a light lunch, Elizabeth went into the garden, stretched out on a lounger shaded by a parasol and fell asleep.

She was woken by a sound and opened her eyes to Arne Krog looking down at her.

'I was moving the umbrella,' he said. 'The sun's moved round. I didn't think you'd want to sing with your face looking like a partial eclipse. And you have such delicate skin, don't you?'

'No, I've got skin like a cucumber, but I like it to look delicate,' she said. 'As you, of course, know.'

'I do?'

'Aye, you don't miss a lot, Arne. Especially when it comes to watching women. Not that it's just women you watch.'

'What on earth do you mean?'

'What did you see when you followed Walter this morning?' She laughed as he looked taken aback. 'Gotcha! I guessed that's what tha were up to.'

'You are a clever girl, Elizabeth. Or perhaps I should call you Betsy when your accent is as broad as this?'

'Please yourself,' she said, swinging her legs off the lounger.

'Not if, as I observe, it doesn't please you. You were asking about Walter. I saw him park his car in the usual spot and take his walk up the Corpse Road to the top of the Neb where he stood looking down into Dendale. I had a look myself after he'd gone. It's quite fascinating to see how the valley has been resurrected by the drought. Have you been to take a look, Elizabeth?'

'Got the wrong word, I think, Arne. Resurrected means fetched back to life. And no, I haven't been.'

'I think you ought to. I'll be happy to accompany you, if you feel the experience might be too arduous.'

She stood up and stretched, yawning widely.

'Going with you might be too arduous, I reckon you're right there,' she said. 'But it might be interesting to take a look.'

She went into the house. The Wulfstans were sitting in the lounge, Walter studying some papers, Chloe reading a book.

'Walter, I wouldn't mind going off to Danby a bit early,' she said. 'I thought you and me could take a walk up the Neb. You too, Chloe, if you fancied it.'

'I don't think so, dear,' said the woman, not looking up from her reading.

'You don't want to rest before the performance?' said Wulfstan.

'I've rested. Any road, you said you've fixed up a room at the Science Park for me to change and smarten up in. I might as well be there as here.'

'I suppose so. What about you, Arne . . . ?'

'Arne can bring Chloe and Inger when they're ready,' said Elizabeth firmly. 'Right. I'll just get my stuff and we'll be off.'

They didn't speak at all on the journey to Danby, but when Wulfstan slowed down as they approached the entrance to the Science and Business Park, Elizabeth said, 'Can we go straight on to the Corpse Road and come back here after?'

'As you wish,' said Wulfstan.

Passing through the streets of Danby, Elizabeth stared out of the window and said, 'Funny. I felt nowt when we came yesterday, but I thought it might just be a sort of numbness. It's not though. I really do feel nowt. It's not like coming home. I weren't here long enough for that. Three years, was it? Four? And with what happened and all, it were never home.'

They drove past the school and the church. She looked at the police vehicles parked outside St Michael's Hall, but made no comment. When they'd bumped up the Corpse Road as far as the Discovery could take them, Wulfstan parked and they got out.

'You are sure you want to do this?' he asked.

'Why not?'

'It's very hot. And steep. You do not want to tire yourself out.'

She laughed and said, 'Don't talk daft. I'm a country lass, remember? When I went out on the fell helping Dad fold his sheep, I could cover more ground than these hikers do in a hard day's walk, and never notice it.'

He looked at her without speaking then set out up the track.

She matched him stride for stride and wasn't even breathing hard when they reached the crest.

She stood in silence for a while looking down into the sunlit valley, then she said quietly, 'Now I'm home.'

He said harshly, 'How can you say that? What is there down there for any of us to call home?'

She said, 'The buildings, you mean? They were nowt but heaps of rock to start with and that's what they are now. Couple of months' hard work and you could raise them up again. No, this is it for me. Full circle.'

'Full circle implies completion,' said Wulfstan.

'Is that right? Time for a fresh start, eh? You and Chloe never really managed a fresh start, did you? I mean, you

426

went off, but back you came to Yorkshire eventually, which is a bit of a full circle. But I don't see the fresh start.'

'There are things you cannot leave behind, not without amputation,' said Wulfstan.

'Mary, you mean? Little Mary. She'd be same age as me, right? But she'd never have had my voice. That's something, eh? She'd never have had my voice. Except, of course, if what happened hadn't have happened, I'd likely never have had the chance to use it. Singing down the pub. Karaoke. That would likely have been the limit. 'Stead of which in a hundred years they could be looking back to me like we look back to Melba. First great diva of the new millennium. Could be a plan, eh? You might almost think it could have been a plan.'

He looked at her with an intensity almost tangible, but all he said was, 'You are planning to raise your register?'

'What? Oh, Melba. Yeah, mebbe. I could do it, I think. We'll see what that old woman in Italy says next year.'

'That old woman in Italy is one of the finest voice coaches living,' said Wulfstan. 'And not cheap.'

'Oh aye,' said Elizabeth indifferently. 'When she hears me, she'll likely work for IOUs and know her money's safe. What's going off down there, do you think?'

There were men standing in the shallows close by the ruins of Heck. One of them moved out of the water and went to a parked Range Rover and took a long crowbar out of the back. As they watched, he returned to the water's edge and began to probe in the rubble.

'It seems they are looking for something,' said Wulfstan.

'Oh aye? And is there owt to find, do you think?'

He looked at her for a moment, then said, 'I saw him, you know.'

'Who?'

'Benny Lightfoot. I was up here and I saw him.'

'Down there?'

'No. Up here on the ridge. Walking towards the Neb.'

'And what did you do?'

'I followed him, of course. Isn't that why evil spirits visit us, so they can lure us to our destruction.'

'And did he?'

'Of course. It wasn't a long journey. Elizabeth . . .'

'Yes?'

'One thing remains. If . . .'

'Yes,' she said. 'I think mebbe it's time we made a start.'

'That fresh start, you mean?'

'Aye, that too. Though mebbe that's been made for us. Walter, I'm sorry.'

'For what? How is anything your fault?'

'Nay, but I always thought everything was, and I can't be altogether wrong, can I? Let's talk. But not till after I've sung, eh?'

She took his hand and turned him away from the valley and hand in hand they began to descend the Corpse Road.

FOURTEEN

It had been a risk but a small one for Novello to leave the cafeteria to ring in for back-up. She had spent enough hours in the police gym to feel fairly confident about confronting one unarmed man, but two was pushing things. And while Turnbull with a weapon other than his charm seemed unlikely, she couldn't be sure about Lightfoot.

Moving back to the entrance, she saw that she'd just been in time. The two men were rising together and making for the door. She noted that Lightfoot was carrying the leather bag, which meant he had one hand occupied. She retreated before them to the car park.

No sign yet of any help, but it should be close. The coast road was well patrolled. She wouldn't hear it coming as she'd asked specifically for no siren. Sometimes she suspected some of her male colleagues learned more from cop shows than police college. No one on the telly seemed to have worked out the advantages of sneaking up on a suspect. They either rang a warning bell or simply shouted, 'Oy! You!' from a distance of fifty yards. Of course this meant you got an exciting chase or lively shoot-out, which was a visual plus. In real life, you wanted to be neither seen nor heard till you'd got within half-nelson distance.

Anyway, close or not, she couldn't wait. A suspect in a car was an arrest problem squared.

She turned away as they approached, watching them in the window of a parked Peugeot. Then, as they drew level, she turned, smiled widely, and said, 'Geordie, how're you doing? Why don't you introduce me to your lovely friend?'

Turnbull instinctively smiled back before recognition began to dawn. She reached out her hand to Lightfoot. Instinctively he took it. She twisted his arm sharply, at the same time pulling him off balance and driving her toe cap into his shin.

He fell forward against the car, setting its alarm off, and Novello forced his arm up between his shoulder-blades till he yelled with pain.

Into his left ear she told him he was being arrested on suspicion of murder and advised him of his right to remain silent, but he carried on yelling all the same. She glanced sideways to see how Turnbull was taking all this. To her surprise he was standing watching with an expression in which resignation warred with admiration.

'I hope you and me are going to stay good friends, bonny lass,' he said. She smiled. He had the great gift of making you smile, but in this case half her pleasure came from the sight over his shoulder of a police car nosing into the car park. Attracted by the alarm and also a gathering group of spectators, they came straight to her, and two young constables got out.

'You Novello?' asked one of them.

'That's right. Cuff this one, I'll take care of the other.'

Relieved of Lightfoot, she bent down and picked up the bag he'd dropped. She pulled open the zip.

It was full of money.

Lightfoot, upright now with his hands cuffed behind his back, was glaring in angry disbelief at Turnbull.

'Why the hell'd you do this, you stupid bastard? You think this is going to get you anywhere but jail?'

He spoke pure Strine.

'Get him into the car,' said Novello. A crowd was

430

forming. She didn't want anyone to have the chance to recognize Lightfoot and warn the media pack.

They pushed him into the back seat of the police car and she turned to the onlookers.

'OK,' she said. 'Show over. Nothing to bother your-selves with.'

They looked unconvinced.

The owner of the beeping Peugeot arrived, pressed his remote key and silenced it.

'Did he get inside?' he demanded, examining the body-work for damage.

'No, sir, it's fine. Good alarm you've got.'

'Look, I'm in a hurry. Do I have to make a statement?'

'No, thank you, sir. We've got enough and we've noted your vehicle number if we need you.'

'Great. Hope they hang the bastard.'

The man got into his car and the onlookers drifted away. Just another car break-in, nothing worth boasting that you'd seen.

'Clever,' said Turnbull. 'You did that really well, petal.'

'Mr Turnbull, I am not your petal,' said Novello wearily.

She stooped to the window of the police car. Lightfoot was looking more angry than afraid. He said, 'What the hell are you talking about, murder? OK, I gave the guy a pasting, but the money's mine. Tell them, you stupid bastard! The money's mine!'

'Where do you want him, luv?' enquired the driver.

She said, 'First I need his keys.'

The constable sitting beside Lightfoot dug his hand into the prisoner's pocket and came up with the keys.

'Where are you parked?' asked Novello.

'Over there,' he said, jerking his head. 'You're making a big mistake here, girl.'

She spotted the top of the white camper a couple of

431

rows away. At the same time with relief she saw two more police cars turning into the car park. This meant she had enough personnel to take care of the prisoners separately, plus both their vehicles. She made a quick calculation. They'd make quite a little procession, but there shouldn't be anyone alerted yet to take notice of it.

'Danby,' she said. 'I think we should all go to Danby.'

FIFTEEN

In the company of their friends, Peter and Ellie Pascoe mocked the kind of well-heeled people who lived 'within the bell', but privately they both lusted for a house here. This was the nearest you could get in Mid-Yorkshire to *rus in urbem*, all the peace of the countryside in your lovely back garden, all the pleasures of the city outside your front door.

Or, to put it more crudely, you could get pissed out of your pericranium in your favourite pub and not need to rely on a sourly sober spouse to drive you home.

So usually when he had occasion to be 'in the bell', his imagination was as active as an oil sheikh's in Mayfair, selecting this property and discarding that with reckless abandon.

Today, however, despite the fact that Holyclerk Street looked at its most seductive in the cidrous aureola of the early evening sun, the springs of covetousness were quite dried up within him as he walked along looking for the Wulfstan residence.

Ellie had told him she knew that being a policeman rotted your soul, but when you considered the Wulfstans' tragic history, not to mention the fact that his own daughter was just recovering from a serious illness, he was breaking all known records of insensitivity, illogicality, and irresponsibility . . .

'Listen,' he said. 'It's because of Rosie I'm doing this . . .'

'Because of what an over-excited kid thinks she saw?

433

Because of a fucking picture book?' she'd interjected. 'Now I've heard everything!'

'No,' he said with matching ferocity. 'Because we nearly lost her. Because in my head I did lose her, and I got to understand what I've often observed but never really fathomed before, why all those poor sods who do lose a kid run around like headless chickens, organizing protests and pressure groups and petitions and God knows what else. It's because you've got to make some sense of it, you've got to juggle with reasons and responsibilities, you've got to know the whys and the wherefores and the whens and the hows and the who's, oh yes, especially the who's. Listen, you want to find out what you can do for Jill, and when you think you've found it, nothing will stop you doing it. Well, that's how I feel about Mr and Mrs Dacre. *Knowing* is all that's left for them; I'm not talking justice or revenge at this stage, just simple *knowing*. I may be right off line here, but I owe it to them, I owe it to whatever God or blind fate gave us back Rosie, to check this thing out.'

She had never seen him, certainly never heard him, like this before, and for once in their life together, she let herself be beaten into silence by his flailing words.

All she said as he left the hospital where Rosie had fallen into a deep peaceful sleep which looked set to last the night, was, 'Softly, softly, eh, love?' then kissed him hard.

He had gone on his way, not exactly triumphing, but with that glow of righteousness which springs from winning a heated moral debate.

But now, as he stood before the door of number 41, it suddenly seemed to him, as so very often in the past, that though Ellie might not be right in every respect, she was right enough to have got the points decision.

This was crazy. Or if in its essentials, which were that

something had come up in connection with a serious enquiry that needed to be investigated, not altogether crazy, certainly in this way of going about it totally bonkers.

He took a step back from the door, and might have fled, or might not, he never knew which, for at that moment the door opened and he found himself looking at Inger Sandel.

They had never met, but he recognized her from the photograph in the *Post* which he was carrying in his briefcase.

She said, 'Yes?'

He said, 'Hello. I'm Detective Chief Inspector Pascoe.'

She said, 'Mr Wulfstan is already gone to Danby with Elizabeth, but Chloe is still here if you want to talk to her.'

'Why not?' he said, though he could think of reasons.

He stepped into the hall. There were several boxes full of compact discs standing on the floor.

'We poor troubadours must be our own merchants too,' she said, catching his glance. 'They are to sell at the concert.'

'Oh, yes?' He picked up the *Kindertotenlieder* disc. 'Interesting design. The bars of music are Mahler, I presume?'

'Yes. But not from the *lieder*. The Second Symphony, I think.' She paused as if waiting for a response, then went on: 'You would like to buy one?'

'No, thanks,' he said, putting it down hastily. 'My wife's got one already. Mrs Wulfstan's in, you say?'

'Yes, she is,' she said, smiling as if at some private joke. 'Goodbye, Mr Pascoe. Nice to have met you.'

She stepped outside and began pulling the door to behind her.

'Hold on,' he said anxiously. 'Mrs Wulfstan . . .'

'It's all right,' she reassured him. 'I must go out for a little while. Just shout.'

He'd have preferred that she did the shouting. As he'd once explained to Ellie, being a cop isn't a cure for shyness, it just makes it rather inconvenient on occasion, as when for example you find yourself in a strange house without any visible authority.

He first coughed, then called 'Hello' in the small voice, at once summons and apology, he used for waiters.

He strained his ears for a response. There was none, but he thought he detected a distant murmur of voices.

Dalziel would either have bellowed 'SHOP!' or taken the chance to poke around.

He opened his mouth to shout, then decided that on the whole, for a man of his temperament, being caught poking around was the lesser of two embarrassments.

He pushed open the nearest door with an apologetic smile ready on his lips.

It opened on to what looked like a gent's study of the old school. He ran his eyes over the glazed bookcases, the mahogany desk, the oak wainscoting, and thought of the converted bedroom which he used as a home office. Perhaps he should start taking bribes?

The room was empty and even his decision to follow one of the Fat Man's paths didn't mean he could go as far as poking through the desk drawers.

He went back into the hall and tried the door opposite. This led into a small sitting room, also empty, which had another door leading into a nicely sized dining room, very Adam, with an oval table so highly polished it must have been a card-sharper's delight.

In the wall opposite the door he'd come in by was a serving hatch, partially open. The voices he'd heard before were now quite distinct, and he went forward and peered through the hatch without opening it further.

He found he was looking into a kitchen, but the talkers weren't in there. The back door was wide open on to a patio with one of those lovely long luscious 'bell' gardens beyond, and he felt the stab of covetousness once more. He could see two people out there. One, a woman, visible in half-profile, was seated in a low-back wicker chair. The other, a man, was leaning over her from behind with his hands inside her blouse, gently massaging her breasts.

The man (again identified from the *Post*) was Arne Krog. The woman he assumed to be Chloe Wulfstan, a deduction quickly confirmed.

Krog was saying, 'Enough is enough. Some day you will have to leave him. If not now, when?'

The woman replied agitatedly, 'Why will I have to leave? All right, yes, you're probably right. But it's an option. Like suicide. Knowing you can, knowing one day you probably will, is a great prop to endurance.'

'You mean, knowing one day you'll leave gives you strength to stay? Come on, Chloe! That's just a clever way of using words to avoid making decisions.'

She gripped both his wrists and forced his hands up out of her blouse.

'Don't talk to me about avoiding decisions, Arne. Where's the decision you're making in all this? Are you saying if I left Walter today, you'd fling me over your saddle, gallop me away into the sunset, and make sure I lived happily ever after?'

Arne Krog fingered his fringe of silky beard sensuously. Likes to have his hands on something soft, thought Pascoe.

'Yes, I suppose that's more or less what I'm saying,' he said.

'More? Or less?'

'Well, less the saddle,' he said, smiling. 'And I'm not

sure if anyone should promise ever after. But as far as is humanly possible, that's what I'd do.'

He spoke the last sentence with a simple sincerity that Pascoe found quite moving.

Chloe stood up and regarded him fondly, but with the kind of fondness one feels for a lovable but untrainable dog.

'So you love me, Arne. Enough to want to spend the rest of your life with me. My very perfect, gentle, and chaste knight. You would be chaste, wouldn't you, Arne? I mean, when we're not together, you don't go putting it around your little groupies on the concert circuit, or in the opera chorus, do you?'

Krog's fingers stopped moving in his beard.

'Let me guess,' he said softly. 'The lovely Elizabeth, the Yorkshire nightingale, has been singing?'

'I talk to my daughter, yes.'

'Your *daughter*.' Krog smiled. 'I remember your daughter, Chloe. And not all the wigs and cosmetics and diets in the world can turn Betsy Allgood into your daughter. If that is what she is trying to be, of course.'

'Why do you hate her so much, Arne? Is it because she's going to have the kind of career you always dreamt of? A huge fish in the big ponds, not just a smallish one in the puddles?'

'That shows how close we really are, Chloe. I cannot hide my disappointments from you.'

The woman smiled sadly.

'Arne, you don't hide them from anybody. No one can be so laid-back unless he's seething inside. Perhaps you should have let some of the anger show in your singing.'

'Ah, a music critic as well as a psychologist. Perhaps you are right. Just because I appear calm doesn't mean I'm not angry. By the same token, just because I screw around doesn't mean I don't love you. Always follow your logic through, my dear. And just because I'm not flying into a despairing rage doesn't mean I'm giving up on you. If you won't leave, I'll wait until you are left, as you will be, believe me. Everyone will go: Elizabeth to her career, Walter to . . . God knows what. And one day you'll look around, and there'll be nobody left but good old laid-back Arne. Better to run now, I say. You notice pain far less if you're running than if you're standing still.'

It was, Pascoe decided, time to make his move before Inger Sandel returned and wondered why he'd been in the house all this time without making contact with Chloe.

He went back into the hallway, walked towards the kitchen door, pushed it open and shouted with Dalzie-lesque force, 'Shop!'

Then he went into the kitchen, put on his apologetic smile as he saw their surprised faces turned towards him, and advanced on to the patio, flourishing his warrant and saying, 'Hello, sorry to intrude, but Miss Sandel let me in. Chief Inspector Pascoe. Mrs Wulfstan, I wonder if I might have a word.'

Krog was looking at him frowningly. Pascoe thought, this clever sod is thinking it's at least five minutes since the woman left, so what the hell have I been doing in the meantime?

He said, 'It's Mr Krog, isn't it? The singer? My wife's a great fan.'

He recalled hearing a writer say during a radio interview that when men told him their wives loved his books, he ran his eyes up and down the speaker and replied, 'Well, no one can be indiscriminating all of the time.'

All Krog said was, 'How nice. Excuse me.' And left.

Chloe Wulfstan said, 'Please sit down, Mr Pascoe. I'm afraid I don't have too much time.'

'Yes. Of course. The concert. Your husband's gone

already? Actually it was really him I wanted to see, so I don't need to delay you any longer.'

Once more his mind supplied the smart reply. 'I don't see why you needed to delay me at all.' And once again the opportunity was missed.

'You're sure it's nothing I can help you with?' she said. 'Has it anything to do with that poor child out at Danby? I heard on the news they'd found her body.'

'Yes, it's terrible, isn't it?' said Pascoe. 'I can guess how painful it must be for you, Mrs Wulfstan.'

'Oh, you can guess, can you?' interrupted the woman contemptuously.

He thought of the past few days and said quietly, 'Yes, I think I can. I'm sorry. I'll go now and let you get ready for the concert. It's OK, I'll see myself out.'

He left her sitting there, staring fixedly into the garden. What she was seeing he didn't know, but he suspected it was more than grass and trees and flowers.

As he moved along the entrance hall, the door of the study opened and Arne Krog stepped out.

He had a sealed A4 envelope in his hand.

'Leaving so soon, Mr Pascoe?' he said.

'Yes.'

'Though not perhaps so soon as it seems.'

So the clever sod had worked it out.

Pascoe said, 'I was brought up to believe it was rude to interrupt.'

'Which must also be convenient in your adult profession. You heard something of the discussion between Mrs Wulfstan and myself?'

'Something,' said Pascoe, seeing no point in lying.

The man nodded, but there was as much uncertainty in the gesture as affirmation. He was close to doing something, but not absolutely committed to the final step.

'Then you will see a part of my motive in giving you

this, and may mistake it for the whole. But please believe in the other larger part which has to do with justice.' He smiled his attractive smile which made him look ten years younger. 'As with your eavesdropping, sometimes even a virtue may also be convenient.'

He handed over the envelope, gave a stiff, rather Teutonic bow, and went up the stairs.

Pascoe opened the front door. Inger Sandel was coming up the steps.

'Just leaving?' she said. 'You must have had a good talk.'

Her eyes were fixed on the envelope.

'Yes. I hope you have a good concert.'

'You are coming?'

He shook his head and said, 'No, I don't think so.'

But five minutes later as he sat in his car with the contents of the envelope on his knee, he had changed his mind.

He rang the hospital and finally got hold of Ellie.

'How is she?'

'Sleeping soundly. You coming back?'

'Not directly.'

He explained. It took a deal of explanation, but finally her disapproval faded, and she said, 'OK, Aeneas, off you go and do what you've gotta do.'

'Aeneas?'

'Private joke. I love you.'

'I love you, too. I love you both. More than any of this.'

'Which is why you've got to do it, yeah, yeah. Pete, remember way back in one of our more heated debates, you told me I was neglecting my family so that I could play at being a left-wing revolutionary?'

'Did I say that? Sounds more like Fat Andy on a good day.'

'That's what really bothered me. But all I want to say now is it's a good job you never got the revolutionary bug, because there'd have been no playing. Kalashnikovs and Semtex all the way. Take care. And if you look back and see a light in the sky, don't worry. It's only me.'

Pascoe switched off his phone, smiling. Through the open sun roof of his car he said to the delft-blue sky, 'I am probably the luckiest man alive.'

Then he set off north.

SIXTEEN

The arrival of Shirley Novello's convoy at Danby police station was observed through an upper window by Andy Dalziel with great satisfaction.

'That's what I like, Wieldy,' he said. 'Bit of swank. Like the Allies rolling into Paris in '44. We should be throwing flowers. You've not got the odd poppy or lily in your pocket have you?'

Wield, who was just relieved the D C had had the sense not to have lights flashing and sirens blaring, said, 'How do you want to do this, sir?'

'Let's see what they say about briefs,' said Dalziel.

'Duty solicitor's on stand-by,' said Wield. 'And I daresay Turnbull will be yelling for Hoddle again.'

'Yon death's head. Well, it'll almost be a pleasure to see him. I doubt if he can pull Geordie out of this one.'

Wield frowned superstitiously at this display of confidence. He felt they'd a long way to go before they were out of this wood.

The Australian police had still come up with nothing useful about the Slater family. The myth that modern technology made it almost impossible to vanish in the civilized world was one that most policemen saw exploded every day. Even without making any huge effort to cover their tracks, people dropped out and the waters of society closed over their heads with scarcely a ripple to show the spot. All they did have now was a record that a B. Slater, Australian citizen, had landed at Heathrow ten days earlier.

It took Novello a little while to book her prisoners in, then she came up to report.

Dalziel greeted her beamingly.

'Well done, lass. I always said you were a lot more than just a pretty face, though I've got nowt against pretty faces when you see some of the ugly buggers I've got to work with.'

Novello avoided glancing at Wield. One thing she had to give Andy Dalziel, he was an equal opportunity employer. He was bloody rude to everyone.

'So what's the crack, Ivor? Fill us in,' continued the Fat Man.

She made her rehearsed report, succinct and to the point, and got an approving nod from Wield.

'Grand,' said Dalziel, rubbing his hands in anticipation of the interviews to come. 'Yelling for their briefs, are they?'

They weren't.

Turnbull had shrugged and said, 'I reckon I'll play this one solo, bonny lass.'

And Slater/Lightfoot had said, 'What the fuck do I need with a fucking lawyer? Just fetch the bastard who's in charge of this shit-pile, will you?'

She told them this verbatim.

'And there's something else,' she added, seeing that Dalziel's expression had lost some of its previous manic sparkle, and deciding that bad news was best spilled out in a single bucketful. 'Slater gave his name as Barney, not Benny. And it's there on his passport. Barnaby Slater.'

She waited to be assured this meant nowt, but from the Fat Man's face she saw it meant more than she knew.

'The younger brother,' said Wield. 'The one who stayed with his mam. He was called Barnabas. Benjamin and Barnabas. The old lady's choice, I always thought. From the sound of it, Marion were none too religious.'

'So, Benny's not going to come back using his own name, is he?' said Dalziel. 'Helps himself to his brother's passport. Mebbe he had to. Mebbe he never got round to changing his own name.'

He sounded less than convinced.

Wield said, 'One way to find out, sir.'

'Aye. Let's get to it. Ivor, you sit in on this too. Don't gab on, but don't be afraid to speak up if you see the need.'

So this time she wasn't going to be dumped after doing the donkey-work, thought Novello. Great!

Unless, of course, Dalziel simply wanted a sacrificial victim handy if things started turning sour. Which they gave every sign of doing from the moment they entered the tiny interview room.

Slater looked from Wield to Dalziel without the slightest sign of recognition and said, 'Jesus, what's this? *You* gonna sit on my legs while he frightens me to death?'

'A joker,' said Dalziel. 'I like a laugh.'

'Yeah? And just who the hell are you, mate?'

'Me? I'm the bastard in charge of this shit-pile,' said Dalziel. 'But you know that, don't you, Benny? We've met before.'

The man looked at him blankly. Then he said, 'What was that you called me?'

'Benny. Benjamin Lightfoot as was.'

A grin split the man's face.

'The name's Barney. You think I'm Benny, is that what this is all about? Jeez, what a screw-up.'

If it was an act, it was a great one. But Wield, studying the man's face, was almost sure it wasn't. The man certainly looked very like the photo of Benny which he himself had doctored, but seen in the flesh, there were too many differences.

It wasn't a question of physical characteristics, all of

which fitted well enough. It was a matter of expression, a glint in the eyes, a twist of the lips, a watchful cocking of the head to one side, little things like this. OK, so people could change a lot in fifteen years, but there was no way Wield could imagine that repressed, shy, fey youngster turning into this assured, aggressive, self-sufficient man, any more than (he now admitted fully to himself for the first time) he had ever been able to believe that Benny Lightfoot had the nous to get himself safe out of the country. Not even with fifty thousand pounds. He'd have had it taken off him by the first con man he met!

He said, 'When did you last see your brother, Mr Slater?'

'Before Ma took us to Oz,' said the man. 'We went up the valley to see Granny Lightfoot. Ma said he could still come with us if he wanted, but he just shook his head and clung on to the old lady like someone was going to try and drag him free.'

Dalziel groaned, like thunder over the sea, but he didn't speak.

'You keep in touch? Letters and such?' said Wield.

'Nah. Christmas cards was the limit. We're not a writing family. Not till the old lady's letters when Benny had his spot of trouble, and then there was only the two.'

'You knew about the Dendale disappearances?'

'Heard something. Didn't pay it much mind. Troubles of our own. Things started falling apart for us soon after we hit Oz. Jack, that's Jack Slater, my stepfather, turned out a wrong 'un. Nothing crooked – well not so's you'd notice. But the horses, the booze, the sheilas. I left school soon as I could, lot sooner than I should, that's for certain. Someone had to earn. To start with, Ma tried to keep up with Jack, in the boozing at least. Only she didn't have the constitution. By the time Jack up and left, she was real ill with it. That's when the letters came, I guess.'

'The letters from your grandmother, Mrs Lightfoot?'

'That's right. Look, telling you all this stuff is going to get me out of here, right?'

He addressed his words to Dalziel.

The monkey might be doing the talking, thought Novello, but this guy knows who's grinding the organ.

'I'm starting to think the sooner I see thy back, the better,' said Dalziel with feeling. 'But I reckon I can thole thy face till you've answered all our questions.'

'No need to turn on the charm, mate,' said Slater. 'OK. These letters. I didn't pay them any heed till years later when I was tidying up after Ma passed on. First one said the old girl had changed her address and was living with some relative in Sheffield and if we saw anything of Benny, would we let her know. Second said she moved again to this nursing home, Wark House, and asked about Benny again. That was it.'

'Your mother write back?' asked Wield.

'How would I know?' said Slater. 'Could be, but like I say, she wasn't much in control for a helluva lot of the time. Talked about Granny Lightfoot sometimes, hated her guts as far as I could make out, and I gathered the feeling was mutual. But one thing Ma always did say about her was she was a tidy old bird with her head screwed on, and if anyone in our family could hang on to a bit of dosh, Agnes was the girl.'

'Wasn't she concerned about Benny?' Novello heard herself asking.

Slater shrugged and said, 'Who knows? Didn't talk about him much and when she did, it was usually to say he'd made his bed and could lie on it. I think she was really pissed when he chose to stay with his gran rather than take off with her.'

'But he was her son, her first born,' Novello persisted.

'So? That just made getting the old heave-ho from him

447

worse. Sometimes when the booze had got her to the weepy stage, she'd say she'd like to see Benny before she died. Then she'd get past it and say he'd probably got the old girl's dosh by now and was living high on the hog, so why the hell should she worry about him when he didn't worry about her?'

Wield was looking over his shoulder at Novello to see if she had anything else to say. She gave a small shake of her head.

'So after your mother died, you thought you'd come back to England and check whether in fact the old lady was seriously rich and see if you could squeeze some of it your way?' said the sergeant.

'Not so,' said Slater, unperturbed by the provocative question. 'Ma died, and suddenly I was footloose and fancy free, no one to please but myself, no one to spend my money on but me, and I thought, the only relatives I got in the whole wide world are back there in Pommerania, so why not take a trip and see what there was to see.'

'But you made a beeline for Wark House, right?' said Wield accusingly.

'No way, mate. Touched down on Monday. Dossed down with this mate of a mate in London. He had this old camper he let me borrow for a few quid. Lot cheaper than hotels and I'm a real open-air boy. I drifted north taking in the sights. Hit Yorkshire Friday morning and thought, no harm in checking Gran Lightfoot out. It was good to find her still alive. Mind you, she was pretty crook. And confused. Thought I was Benny. I tried to put her straight, then she said something which really made my ears prick and I stopped trying. Something about she knew I'd have found the money and used it to get away safe.'

'Thought you weren't interested in money,' said Wield.

'Didn't say that, mate. What I said was, that wasn't why I came back. But I wasn't going to look the other way if it looked like some dosh might be due to me. Especially when she let on in her ramblings it was fifty thou in cash, and she'd put it in a tin chest up under the eaves where Benny knew she always hid her valuables, so that's where he'd have looked after she went into hospital.'

'And she believed Benny had got the money?' said Wield.

'Yeah, that's clearly what she reckoned when he vanished from sight. And now that she knew for certain he'd got it – because she'd seen me, thinking I was Benny – she said she could die happy. Now I did try telling her again, no need for her to die just yet, happy or not, as I was Barney not Benny, but she was pretty flaked out by now and I could tell she wasn't taking it in. So I left. Look, no need to sit there looking all po-faced. I want her to know who I really am. I'm going to call in again on my way back south and hope I get her when she's a bit more with it.'

He stared defiantly at Wield and the others, then it came to him that it wasn't just disapproval he was seeing on their faces.

'What?' he said.

'Bad news,' said Dalziel. 'Or mebbe good, depending how you look at it. After your visit, she died happy. Last night.'

'Ah, shit, you're jossing me? No, you're not, are you? Shit. I really hoped . . .'

He appeared genuinely distressed.

Novello waited for someone to suggest a break in the interview, but all Dalziel said was, 'Never fret, lad. Tha's still in good time for the funeral. And now there's the money to make it a good 'un. Sooner we get this sorted, sooner you can start seeing to all that. So let's get on, shall we? Just take it from when you leave Wark House.'

The implication that soon as Slater had told them this, he would be free to go, came close to being an inducement, thought Novello. Not that it mattered. She reckoned she could have told most of the man's story for him anyway.

'I headed on north 'cos that was the way I was pointing,' he began. 'But all the time I was thinking, like you do when you're driving. And what I thought was if Benny *had* picked up the dosh and taken off, why'd he never tried to contact Gran? I mean, he loved her more than anyone else in the world, right? So what had happened to him? And the sixty-four thousand dollar question, had it happened to him before or after he got his hands on the money?'

'So you got to wondering if mebbe the box were still where Agnes put it, up in the attic of Neb Cottage,' said Dalziel.

'That's right. Seemed a long shot, but what the hell, I had nowhere else in particular I wanted to be. Only, when I got to Dendale I discovered there was no Neb Cottage any more. I had a wander round, but it was so long since I'd been there, I couldn't even be sure I was looking at the right heap of stones! But by now I was getting to feel stubborn. If that money was still around and Benny wasn't, then I had as good a claim as anyone, right? So I headed into town and tried the library. Lady there was truly helpful. I was able to read all about what happened back there in the old papers. Also she showed me this book which had before-and-after maps in it which I got photocopied.'

'Hold on,' said Wield, ever the stickler for detail. 'Let's get the timing sorted. You arrived in Dendale when?'

'Saturday morning. Got myself a pitch at this farm, then walked up the dale and started looking. When I realized I was getting nowhere, that's when I drove into town. Was in the library till closing, which was also close to opening so I had a few beers and a spot of grub, then back to the dale. Sunday I was up with the lark. This time I boxed clever and first off I climbed up to the ridge of the Neb and wandered along there a while, getting a bird's-eye view. Best way to get your bearings, made more sense of the maps than working out mileage and such on the ground. Once I was sure I'd located the right heap of rubble, I went down there and started digging.'

'Let's hold it there,' said Dalziel. 'You're up on the ridge. Just looked down one side, did you? Into Dendale? Never looked down the Danby side?'

'What? Hey, you're not still trying to tie me in to that missing kiddie, are you? Come on! It's clear from what the papers said that you're running around like headless chickens, pointing the finger at poor Benny who no one's seen for fifteen years. You try to keep it in the family and you'll look a real load of assholes!'

Pascoe at this point would probably have said something about headless chickens not having fingers, thought Novello.

Dalziel just looked longingly at the tape machine as if trying to switch it off by force of will so he could have a real heart-to-heart.

Then he said gently, 'Not *missing* kiddie. *Dead* kiddie, Mr Slater. Just tell us. Please.'

'Yeah. Sure. Sorry. You've got a job to do. I hope to hell you get the bastard,' said Slater. 'No, I don't believe I did look down the Danby side. I was concentrating on locating what I hoped might be the site of fifty thousand quid, remember. Soon as I was sure I'd located the cottage ruins, I headed on down there.'

'You mean you returned to the col and went back down the Corpse Road?' said Wield.

'Nah. Headed straight down. Crazy really, it's bloody steep. I went arse over tip and nearly did my ankle. In the end I dropped into this ghyll, White Mare's Tail, they call it. The going was a bit easier there, though I'd not have liked to try it if the fall hadn't been all dried up with the heat.'

'And did you see anyone else?'

'In the valley? Not a soul for a long time. Oh, yeah, there was someone on the ridge, I think. I glanced back and think I saw some guy on the col where the Corpse Road crosses. But he was a long way off and the ridge took a dip just then and I didn't see him again.'

'But there were people in the valley later?' said Wield.

'Yeah, sure. Hikers, families having picnics, all kinds of folk wandering around the bits of the old village that the drought's brought back up. I didn't want an audience to what I was doing, natch, but by then anyway I was pig sick of the business. I'd done all I could with my hands and found nothing. There were blocks of stone there I'd need a crow or pickaxe to shift. So I gave myself the rest of the day off, went to get a wet and see if I could find any action.'

'Any luck?' asked Dalziel.

'Not sure. All I know is I woke in my camp bed next morning with my Y-fronts on back to front and a mouth like a pig man's bucket. All I could think was, when I finally stop shaking, I'm out of here. But by midday when I'd got a few pints of tea inside me and could think of taking solids without spewing my ring, I got a little more upbeat. So I drove off to get some tucker, and afterwards, I found one of these big DIY superstores and bought myself a pick and a crow. I waited till late evening when I had the valley to myself before I started work. It was almost pitch black by the time I gave up. By then I knew for certain that wherever the money was, it wasn't there.'

'But you still didn't accept the obvious conclusion that Benny had got it?' said Wield.

'Did at first,' said the man. 'Then I got to thinking, you jokers were after him, right? So one place you'd be watching day and night till it was 'dozed would be Neb Cottage, 'cos that's where he'd most likely make for. So if he'd shown, you'd have spotted him. And as you didn't, maybe he had never come back for the money.'

'Maybe he did come back,' said Novello. 'Maybe that's what he was doing by the ruins when he attacked Betsy Allgood. Looking for the box.'

'Could be,' said Dalziel. 'Had a bad night, didn't he? So you started wondering who else might have got the money?'

'Right,' said Slater. 'First off, I thought it might be one of you lot. Well, you were on the spot, right? And fifty thou in used notes is a helluva temptation even for virtuous gents like yourselves.'

He smiled at Novello as if to exclude her from the slur. She didn't smile back.

'But once you'd put such a daft notion out of your head,' said Dalziel genially, 'you still didn't give up. Once a Yorkie, always a Yorkie, eh? So it was back to yon bonnie lass in the library, eh?'

'Right,' grinned Slater. 'I just didn't want to leave before I'd made damn sure I'd not missed anything. And this time I found myself staring at the pic of the 'dozer demolishing the cottage.'

They were all as far ahead of him now as Novello had been from the start, but it was necessary for him to spell it out for the tape.

He'd made out the name painted on the bulldozer, checked it in the local business directories, and discovered

453

that for the last several years Tommy Tiplake had been trading as Geordie Turnbull out of the same address. And he recalled reading in the local paper the day before that this same Turnbull had been helping the police with their enquiries just as he'd done fifteen years ago in Dendale.

'Coincidence? Maybe,' he said. 'I almost dropped it in your laps then, got as far as the cop shop, but thought, what the hell, with all this stuff in the paper about Benny Lightfoot fifteen years back, once you jokers get your hands on Benny's brother, you're going to be more interested in fucking him around – pardon my French, miss – than following up some half-baked gumshoe work I'd been doing. So I went off to Bixford and had a drink in the pub and got chatting to some of the locals. All the talk was about Turnbull, and I soon heard enough to make me wonder how come a 'dozer driver like him had suddenly got enough put by to buy into his boss's firm way back. It made me think it was worth having a quick talk with Geordie.'

'Talk?' said Dalziel. 'If that's what you do to any poor sod you have a quiet talk with, I shouldn't like to see anyone you fancied having a quiet snog with!'

'There was a misunderstanding,' said Slater. 'But we soon got on the same wavelength. I'll give him his due. Once he saw the way the wind was blowing, he didn't mess around but put his hand up straightaway. Said it had been bothering him for years, but he just hadn't been able to resist the temptation when he pushed over the old cottage and saw this tin box lying in the rubble with tenners spilling out of it. Can't say I blamed him. Would probably have done the same myself.'

'I get the impression, Mr Slater, that you have done much the same yourself,' said Wield.

'The money, you mean? Listen, mate, I got that money fair and square. You ask Turnbull. Like I said, once he understood who I was, he co-operated of his own free will. Wanted to get it off his conscience. Also he's done all right, our Geordie. Fifteen years ago, fifty thou was big money still. Now it's a down payment on one of those earth movers of his. I told him, get me the dosh in readies today and I'll forget the fifteen years interest I'd be entitled to. He agreed. If he says different, he's a liar. Why the hell he wanted to get you people involved, I don't know. He's the only one committed a crime here, not me.'

'Blackmail's a crime,' said Dalziel softly. 'Extortion's a crime. And don't give me any of that kangaroo crap about this being your money. It was your gran got robbed, not you. It's *her* sodding money if it's anyone's.'

'Yeah, and that's where I was heading, straight back down to Wark House to give it to her,' said Slater.

He gazed openly at them with what was either wide-eyed sincerity or you-prove-different complacency.

Novello said quietly, 'That's good to hear, Mr Slater. The Social Service Department that's been picking up your grandmother's tab at Wark House for the past several years will be pleased to hear it too. You see, they've been dishing out taxpayers' money on the understanding she was penniless, and now they'll be able to get most of it back.'

Slater looked shocked for a moment then smiled ruefully.

'Hell, perhaps I should talk to Turnbull about interest after all!'

Dalziel stood up so suddenly his chair rattled back and almost fell over.

Slater shoved his chair back a few inches as though anticipating assault. But the Fat Man's tone had more of resignation than aggression in it.

'Interview terminated,' he said, flicking off the tape

switch. 'And no, you won't talk to Turnbull, Mr Slater. We'll talk to him instead. We'll need a written statement of all this, OK?'

'Yeah. Sure thing,' said Slater. 'Then that's it?'

'Unless my sergeant here can thumb through the big book and find summat tasty to charge you with.'

'Assault on Mr Turnbull?' said Wield hopefully.

'Not much hope of that if we've just been listening to the truth. I think we're done here. Wieldy. Ivor?'

Wield shook his head. Novello said, 'What do you think happened to your brother, Mr Slater?'

'Benny? I don't recall much of him, miss, except that he was the nervous type, always scared of his own shadow. My bet would be, with his gran gone and the cottage wrecked, the poor bastard topped himself, God rest his soul.'

It seemed a suitable note to finish on. The station didn't run to two interview rooms, so Slater was returned to his cell with pen and paper to write his statement and Geordie Turnbull was brought out.

He had had time to recover most of his old bounce. In fact, the feeling that emanated from him was of euphoria that at last things were out in the open.

'Daft to say, but when I saw your face, bonny lad,' he said to Wield, 'I thought it had somehow come out then and I was almost relieved when you started asking about the poor little girl instead. Makes you think, doesn't it. Fancy preferring to be suspected of something like that! No, I'm glad it's out.'

Probably the first time in his life Wield had been addressed as *bonny lad*, thought Novello. Or was that just mental queer-bashing? Could be this boyfriend out in the sticks everyone gossiped about thought he was lovely.

The story he told confirmed in every significant respect that offered by Slater.

He should have had his lawyer, thought Novello. The hideous Hoddle would have made him keep his mouth shut. With old Mrs Lightfoot dead and only Slater's hearsay to set against him, there was no way the CPS would have entertained a charge.

But this had less to do with legality than guilt. It soon emerged that simple down-to-earth happy-go-lucky Geordie had a strong streak of religious fatalism. If he hadn't kept the money, Tommy Tiplake's business would have failed and he, Geordie, would have been long gone and well out of the way of this second round of child molestation enquiries. This was his punishment. Anything the CPS could throw at him would merely be almost welcome public evidence of his lack of culpability in the larger case.

Novello found herself totally in sympathy with him by the time the interview was finished. If his innate and unselfconscious charm hadn't done the trick (which, she assured herself firmly, it wouldn't have done), his final words would have won her over.

'What really bothers me now I know the whole story is the thought of yon poor lad, Benny, coming back in the rain and searching through the rubble of Neb Cottage for the money his gran had promised him. Poor sod.'

'Poor sod?' said Dalziel incredulously. 'Yon poor sod might be responsible for kidnapping and killing three young girls, and afore you say that's not proved, there's no doubt he attacked Betsy Allgood that same night you're talking about.'

'You think so? Well, that's the way you're trained to look at things, Mr Dalziel,' said Turnbull with some dignity. 'Me, I knew the lad and I could never see any harm in him. I never believed he had anything to do with those lasses disappearing any more than I did. As for attacking the Allgood girl, I'm sure he gave her a nasty fright. Little kid lost on the fell in a storm at night suddenly sees the man everyone's been telling her is the bogeyman, naturally she's going to be scared out of her wits, isn't she? I daresay if you'd been the one she met on the fellside that night, she'd have been just as frightened, poor little lass.'

'Interview terminated,' said Dalziel. 'Nowt turns my stomach more than listening to a Newcastle United supporter who's got religion.'

'Is that right, bonny lad? Well, one thing's for sure, despite all them signs you told me about, Benny's not back, is he? And I had nothing to do with little Lorraine, and nor did Barney Lightfoot from the sound of it. So I'll get back to my cell, shall I? And let you lot get back to your work. From the sound of it, you've still got a hell of a lot to do.'

SEVENTEEN

The three detectives sat in silence after Turnbull was removed from the interview room.

Finally, Novello said, 'Could he be right, sir? Could Betsy Allgood have got it wrong? She was so frightened at seeing Lightfoot, she panicked, and when he tried to reassure her, she thought he was attacking her.'

'For a lass her age she were one of the best witnesses I ever came across,' said the sergeant approvingly. 'We'd talked with her several times afore this, and this time she were just the same, nice and calm and precise. All that stuff about her cat, you're not saying she just imagined that? Rang true to me then, rings true to me now. You've read the file? Then you'll know what I mean.'

Yes, thought Novello. I know what you mean. But I'm not sure I know what I mean, which is maybe something more than you know. Or can know. Something about the way little girls think. About the way they can be frightened into the most fanciful inventions . . . the way they rearrange reality to suit their own needs and desires . . . the way they observe and analyse the adult world . . .

Her mind ran back over the Dendale file, highlighting it not as a record of an investigation but as a sort of patterned tapestry, with its intricate design based on the thrice-repeated motif of a vanished child. Suddenly looked at like this, she saw something she had only been dimly conscious of before.

She said, 'Sir . . .'

The door opened and Sergeant's Clark's head appeared.

He said, 'Sorry, sir, but compliments of Mr Pascoe, and would you care to join him at Dender Mere, which is to say, the Dendale Reservoir?'

'Pascoe?' said Dalziel, looking towards Wield with astonishment. 'What's yon bugger doing back on the job? You know owt of this, Wieldy?'

'No, sir.'

'What about you, Ivor? You were the last to see him.'

'Yes, sir. Well, like I told you, his daughter was doing much much better, they thought she was out of danger. And he seemed to be quite excited about something, I don't know what, something about an earring . . .'

'So what's he say to you, Nobby?' demanded Dalziel.

'Nothing more than I've told you, sir. Compliments to Mr Dalziel and would you care . . .'

'Aye aye, I can hear them prissy tones without the club impressionist act,' he said testily. 'Well, I don't think there's owt else to do round here this night except go to yon bloody concert, so let's go and see what our resident intellectual has got laid on for us. But it had better be good!'

It was.

Peter Pascoe, on his way to Danby, had rung the incident room at St Michael's Hall. Here he got George Headingley sitting in solitary state. He had given a detailed account of everything that had been happening that afternoon. The DI's demob-happiness had rendered him something of a liability when it came to active policing, but he was an excellent man to leave in charge of the shop, if only because, though reluctant to initiate action in case something went wrong in a manner which might adversely affect his pension, this same preoccupation made him an assiduous collator of the minutiae of other people's activities, to avoid the fall-out if any of them went wobbly.

'So His Fatship and Wieldy are down the local nick with wet towels at the ready?' said Pascoe, knowing how even jokes about police impropriety made old George tremble.

'They are interrogating the suspects, yes,' said Headingley.

'But this fellow Lightfoot they've caught says he's Barney, not Benny?'

'That's what Nobby Clark says. And he agrees. He knew Benny well and says that this fellow might have a family resemblance, but no way is he the real thing.'

'Interesting,' said Pascoe. 'Tell me, George, the frog team at the mere, they still there?'

'Just had them on asking if Mr Dalziel had left authority for overtime. I said no, so they're packing up for the night.'

Pascoe thought, then said, 'Do me a favour. Get on to them and say . . . no, on second thoughts, give me their number.'

George was quite capable of staging a breakdown of all communication equipment rather than risk getting involved in an unauthorized overtime scandal.

Pascoe dialled the diving team's mobile and was pleased to hear Tom Perriman's voice answer. They were old acquaintances and got on well.

'Pete, how are you? I heard about your trouble. How're things going?'

'Fine,' Pascoe assured him. 'Hairy while it lasted, but I think everything's going to be OK now. Listen Tom, I'm on my way to join you, so don't rush off.'

'Oh, come on!' protested Perriman. 'We've just got all the gear packed.'

'It's all right. It's not diving I want you for. Listen, you can get started while I'm on my way.'

He explained what he wanted. When he finished, Perriman said, 'And it's your signature on the overtime authority?'

'It's more than my signature. It's my neck,' said Pascoe.

'I'll come to the execution,' said Perriman. 'OK, see you soon.'

'Great,' said Pascoe. He turned off the Danby road and, using the sun as navigational aid, wove a path along quiet country lanes until he found himself on the road running into the mouth of Dendale.

The reservoir gate was still open and he drove all the way to where the USU van was parked. He could see the men down at the water's edge, wielding picks and shovels. Tom Perriman detached himself from the group and came to meet him.

'Who's a clever boy, then?' he said. 'I poked around with a grapple and came up with half a ribcage. I'd say it's pretty definite the rest of our guy's down there. It must have been a cellar, and when the house was 'dozed the slabs on the floor above cracked open to leave a space you could get down through. Somehow this poor sod got himself trapped. Probably got up far enough to get an arm through the gap, then his efforts brought the slab down on him. Water rose. He died, then decomposed till eventually his arm bones broke free and washed out a metre or so into the mere.'

'Great. So you've got the rest of the skeleton up?'

'Give us a chance,' said Perriman. 'It's still full of water down there and badly silted up. Also, I'm not too happy sending someone down into gunge a body's been decaying in.'

'Thought this was the same gunge we're drinking and cooking with?'

'Not quite in this concentration. But I see you're in too much of a hurry to wait till we get a pump set up. Is it something identifiable you're after? Like a jawbone? OK, I'll give it a whirl, but it'll cost you several large disinfectant scotches.'

Pascoe stood and watched the operation. The slab they'd moved had left a space just wide enough for a diver to drop through. The water was dark and murky. Not even the warmth of the evening air could make the prospect of dipping into those depths attractive. Perriman had to work by touch. He sank out of sight and groped about the bottom till his fingers felt something. A femur emerged, then a scapula. Then a skull.

Pascoe took it and washed it in the cleaner waters of the mere. When he saw the gleam of a metal plate, he said. 'This'll do nicely. You can get out now before you catch your death of something.'

'Gee, thanks for your concern,' said Perriman. 'But I like it down there. Besides, there's something else . . .'

He vanished again. Thirty seconds passed, then he erupted to the surface, both hands raised high, not in triumph but to display his trophy.

No length of white bone this time, but a coil of rusting chain.

Pascoe took it from him and laid its heavy length on the sun-baked ground. One end had been formed into a narrow noose by a padlock, the other had several large staples rammed into its links.

'Jesus,' said Perriman who'd climbed out. 'Looks like the poor bastard could've been chained up down there. And I think there's a bit more of the stuff lying around.'

'Leave it till you've got the place pumped out,' said Pascoe.

'I was going to. Pete, you don't look too surprised.'

Pascoe looked down at the chain, then raised his gaze to take in the placid waters of the mere, the valley slopes, the long sweep of the fell ridge with the Neb and Beulah Height serenely mysterious against the deepening blue of the evening sky.

It seemed to him there was perfection out there which it would only take an outstretched hand to touch and absorb like an electric current into the very core of human life. It seemed so close that not to partake of it must be deliberate denial, at once wilful and wicked.

Then he thought of his despair in the past forty-eight hours, of the Purlingstones' despair for the next God knows how many years, and finally as his gaze came full circle and took in the chain and the bones once more, of this man's despair as the waters floated him up towards light and freedom, and then drowned him.

'No,' he said. 'I'm not too surprised.'

He rang Danby Station, got Clark and left his message for Dalziel. Then he strolled away along the margin of the lake and dialled the hospital and got them to fetch Ellie to a phone.

'Everything OK?' he said.

'Fine. Looking better by the minute. And you?'

'Making progress,' he said. 'I'm not sure when I'll be done, though.'

'That's OK. Plenty to occupy myself with here.'

'Really? You found a handsome doctor, or what?'

She laughed. It was a good sound to hear.

'No such luck. But I've got my pen. Got a few ideas I'd like to play with.'

'Oh yes' He was thinking, she can't really be thinking of using what we've been through ... not yet ... But how to say this?

He didn't need to. She laughed again and said, 'It's OK, Peter. It'll be a long time before I'll feel able to lay what we've been through on anyone else's plate. But it's not the same old stuff either. If no one will pay the piper, it's time to play a new tune. I think we'll all be ready for some new tunes after this, won't we?'

'I'll second that,' he said fervently. 'Talking of old tunes, but, would you care to whistle me through Mahler's Second Symphony?'

'You what?'

He explained. They talked a little longer. Finally he rang off and looked around. His walk had brought him to the ruins of the old village which the sun had rescued from the deep. He still had the copy of Wield's map that Dalziel had given him. From it he tried to locate individual buildings but couldn't be positive about anything but the church. From what he'd read in *The Drowning of Dendale* it had been built close by the crag under whose shelter the departed of Dendale had lain prior to their journey over the Corpse Road to St Michael's. The rest of the village was just a jumble of stones, needing more local knowledge or archaeological expertise than he had to interpret.

He stood there a long while, feeling all about him the ghosts of the dead, and of the living too, whose departure from this place had been a rehearsal for death. Then he heard a car engine and saw a police Range Rover bumping down to the water's edge where the divers were. Out of it climbed Dalziel followed by Wield and Novello.

By the time he joined them, they'd heard Perriman's account of things, but their first enquiries were after Rosie.

'Spoke to Ellie on my mobile not long back,' he said. 'She's still sleeping sound, I mean really sleeping. It looks good.'

'Great,' said Dalziel. 'And t'other lass, the one with the funny name?'

'Zandra?' said Pascoe. 'She died.'

'Oh, shit.'

There was a long silence, the sort which seems unbreakable. Finally, Dalziel cleared his throat and said brusquely, 'Right, lad. So what's going off here? How come, with all you've had on your plate, you know more than I do?'

'I had help,' said Pascoe. 'From unexpected quarters.'

He led them to his car and took a large envelope from the front seat.

'How much do you know about Elizabeth Wulfstan?' he said.

'Know that she's Betsy Allgood who got orphaned then adopted way back,' said Dalziel. 'Needed a shrink to get her straight in her early teens.'

'Right,' said Pascoe, unsurprised at Dalziel's knowledge, though he might have raised an eyebrow if he'd realized how recently, and how, he'd acquired it. 'The shrink, incidentally, seems to have been Paula Appleby.'

'Her on the telly? Thinks cops should be injected with oestrogen? Jesus!' said Dalziel. 'So what's this got to do with anything?'

Pascoe extracted several sheets from the envelope.

'These are transcripts of Betsy's memories of Dendale and after, recalled and taped during the course of her treatment.'

'You wha'?' said Dalziel taking the sheets.

He ran his eye over them quickly. He might not have Wield's almost total recall after a single reading, but when it came to sheer speed, he was county class.

'So?' he said when he'd finished. 'Lass seems to be saying, bit more grown-up like, what she told us fifteen years back in Dendale.'

'Indeed,' said Pascoe. 'I also have a copy of Dr Appleby's final assessment as prepared for the Wulfstans. She concluded that the girl's condition was the result of her desperate need to feel secure in her new home after

466

the trauma of losing both her parents at a time when she still hadn't recovered from what happened in Dendale, as well, of course, as her family's forcible removal thence.'

'*Thence*,' said Dalziel. 'I've been missing words like that. But what bothers me most is not *thence*, but *whence* did you get all this stuff? You've not been at Wulfstan's desk with a bent hairclip, I hope?'

'It's all right, sir, I wiped my fingerprints,' said Pascoe. Then he grinned and said, 'Relax. Nothing illegal. Not by me, anyway. I was given them, by Arne Krog.'

'Thank God for that,' said Dalziel, relieved not so much that no crime had been committed, but that it hadn't been committed by Pascoe whom he didn't trust not to get caught. 'But why did the Turnip give you them? And what the hell have they got to do with them bones down there?'

'There's more,' said Pascoe. 'A revised version. Or perhaps the authorized version. You decide.'

He took from the envelope three sheets of blue lined paper covered with round flowing handwriting in black ink.

Dalziel took them, laid them on the roof of the car, and began to read.

There was no heading.

I've been thinking about what I said to Dr Appleby and I'm not sure I got it right. I'm alright up to where I got down to the mere and started shouting, 'Bonnie! Bonnie!' Then I think I heard someone shouting back and I know it's daft, but I never thought it were anything but Bonnie. I were wet and frightened and only seven, so I never asked myself how come my cat could talk, and when I shouted again and heard the words, 'Here, here!' I just went towards the sound.

It were coming from right near the water's edge, where the ruins of Heck were. I climbed over the fallen walls, still shouting, and again I heard the reply, and it were coming from a gap half-blocked by a big stone and a lot of rubble but I managed to push some of this aside and there were space enough for me to get through. Only it looked dark and wet down there, and I knew where it was, it was the cellar where Mr Wulfstan kept his fancy wine. I'd been down there with Mary and it was really eery, even with the electric light on. Now it looked like the hole in our yard, I mean the yard at Low Beulah where Dad used to hose all the muck down when Mam started complaining it were like living on a midden. I used to watch muck and watter bubbling down into it and imagine what it ud be like to be down there with the rats and all. So I didn't fancy going into the Heck cellar one little bit, only suddenly I heard not a voice but a long miaow that I'd have known from a thousand others. I didn't hesitate now. Bonnie were down there and he needed my help.

So I climbed through the gap. There were bits of rubble lying around to make a sort of staircase and when I'd got down a bit I found I were stepping into water. It wasn't all that deep yet, just above my knees, and the good thing about it was that the bit of light coming through the hole reflected off the surface and after a while I began to see what there was to see.

I said, 'Bonnie, are you there?' and a voice said back, 'Here I be,' and it was then I made out this shape in a corner of the cellar and realized there was a man there, and I strained my eyes and I saw that it were Benny Lightfoot and he had Bonnie in his arms.

After that it happened more or less like I told Dr Appleby.

Except that when Bonnie scratched his face and he had to let him go and I ran off with the cat, I recall Benny tried to come after me. And he got quite close and I thought he were going to catch hold of me again. I turned to try and fight him off, but suddenly he pulled up short and I could see something stretched out taut behind him, and I saw it was a chain, one end wrapped around his waist, t'other fixed to the wall.

He strained towards me with his hands outstretched, and his eyes were big as saucers 'cos his face were so hungered and waste. And he didn't look frightening any more. No, he looked more frightened than frightening. He looked real sad and lost. And all he said was, 'Help me, please help me.'

Then I turned and scrambled out, and I recall I pushed a lot of stone and stuff back into the gap, and I ran off up the fell hard as I could, I didn't know where, till I had to stop and rest. And it was then that Dad came and found me.

I think this is the truth 'cos Dr Appleby said I'd feel a lot better when I recalled the truth of what happened and told someone, and I do feel better now I've told someone even though it's not Dr Appleby. I don't want to tell anyone else, but, not now, not ever. All I want is to live quietly in London with Aunt Chloe and go to school and do my lessons and be a good daughter like a daughter ought to be.

When Dalziel finished reading, he turned and looked towards the sunlit remains of Heck on the edge of the bright and placid mere. He wasn't a man at the mercy of imagination but, like a movie director, he could let it loose when he chose. Now he chose to turn off the sun and bring the rain lashing down and the mist swirling in. And he chose to see a man chained to a wall under the ground with rising water lapping round his thighs. And he chose to be the man and hear someone calling what he thought was his name and feel hope rise faster than the water that rescue was close . . .

He thrust the sheets into Wield's hand and said to Pascoe, 'All right, clever clogs. Everything was going nice and simple till you got back in the game. Would you like to tell me what *you* think is going off here?'

Nice and simple didn't seem to Novello a possible description of any aspect of the investigation that she'd observed. She looked greedily at the sheets of blue paper in Wield's hands and longed to get hold of them to see what it was that had brought Dalziel to the edge of being gobsmacked.

Pascoe said, 'We'll need dental records for absolute confirmation, but for my money, the plate in the skull's enough. That was Lightfoot down there. Someone chained him up. Most likely candidate is Wulfstan. That would explain why he started climbing up the Neb recently when the drought brought the village back to the surface. Not nostalgia, not grief. Just good old guilt and worry that after all this time he was going to be found out.'

'Explain, too, why he didn't comment on the BENNY'S BACK signs,' said Wield. 'He knew he couldn't be.'

'Why'd yon lass not say anything?' demanded Dalziel.

'A terrified kid answering questions the way she thought the police wanted them answered?' offered Pascoe. 'It happens. Or it used to.'

Dalziel glowered but let this pass.

'And Wulfstan, if it were him, what was he up to? Trying to beat a confession out of Lightfoot?'

'That's one possibility, sir.'

'One? Give us another.'

'Well, it could be he had a vested interest in making sure the chief suspect in the Dendale child disappearances disappeared also.'

'Eh? Come on, lad. You going doolally, or wha'? Tell me one thing which ever suggested Wulfstan could be in the frame for any of them, let alone all.'

'Can't, sir. I wasn't there, remember?'

'So you've got nowt.'

'Not quite,' said Pascoe. 'What I do have is a witness who saw Wulfstan assaulting Lorraine Dacre on Sunday morning.'

No doubt about it this time, thought Novello. Dalziel was definitely gobsmacked. And angry.

'Now listen,' he finally got out. 'I'm making allowances, but if this is one of thy clever games . . .'

'No game, sir,' said Pascoe. 'Though I doubt if it would stand up in court. In fact, I'm absolutely certain I won't

470

be letting this witness get anywhere near court. You see, it's Rosie.'

And the Fat Man was gobsmacked again. Twice in twenty seconds. Plus that earlier near miss. Novello's respect for Pascoe soared to new heights.

And her own mind was sparked by his example to make a connection.

'The earring,' she said, knowing she was right but not why.

Pascoe smiled at her and said, 'Her crucifix substitute, actually. She picnicked early Sunday morning at the viewpoint on the Highcross Moor road. She was looking through Derek Purlingstone's binoculars. And she saw her imaginary friend, Nina, get taken by the nix.'

'The nix?' said Dalziel, clearly still not convinced Pascoe's recent trauma hadn't pushed him over the edge.

'That's right. Nina is a little blonde girl with pigtails, like this.' He reached into his car and produced the Eendale Press volume.

'And that's what the nix looks like. Remind you of anyone?'

Dalziel shook his head, still in denial. But Novello said, 'That photo in the *Post* . . .'

'Right,' said Pascoe. 'I showed Rosie that pageful of photos and she pointed straight at Wulfstan and said, there's the nix. I'm sure she saw him, sir.'

The Fat Man shook his head, more to clear it than express absolute doubt.

'Pete,' he said gently. 'The lass has been through a bad time. You too. Can do funny things to you. On t'other hand, she's the only one in your family I'd trust with two pigs at Paddy's Market. So there's no harm in checking it out.'

With a sudden renewal of energy, he strode down to the mere's edge where the divers were packing up their

471

gear, spoke to Perriman, picked up the length of chain, and dragging it behind him like Marley's ledgers, made for the Range Rover.

'Right,' he called. 'Pete, you travel with us. Esther Williams down there will fetch your car back to Danby. I'm not letting you out of my sight, else God knows how many more *whences* and *thences* you'll be plucking out of the air.'

'Where exactly are we headed, sir?' asked Pascoe, as he climbed into the front passenger seat.

'Where do you think? You like music, don't you? We're off to a concert. And I reckon if we shout *Piss! Piss!* loud enough we might just get some of them buggers to sing us an encore.'

'I think you mean *Bis! Bis!*' suggested Pascoe.

'I know what I mean,' said Andy Dalziel.

EIGHTEEN

The opening concert of the twentieth Mid-Yorkshire Dales Summer Music Festival started late.

This was expected. Despite posters, local press announcements, and word of mouth, news of the change of venue hadn't reached everyone and several patrons had had to be redirected from St Michael's Hall to the Beulah Chapel.

In the circumstances, no one complained. In fact, commercially speaking, it was no bad thing, thought Arne Krog as he observed the throng of people examining the tapes and discs on sale at the foot of the chapel. There were half a dozen on which he figured, though only two on which he was the sole artist. His recording career had paralleled his performing career – a steady effulgence that rarely threatened to explode into stardom.

Elizabeth had only the one disc on offer, but it was the one attracting most attention. Krog wasn't surprised. The clever among them would buy half a dozen copies and get her to sign and date them. Fifteen years on they could be a collector's item. Whereas his voice would hardly even rank as forgotten because it had never really ranked as rememberable. He could smile ruefully at the thought. The trappings of stardom he had always envied, but the possession of the kind of voice that brought them he regarded as a gift of God, and therefore simply to be marvelled at. So it didn't bother him that Elizabeth might be a star, only that her brightening might be at the expense of others' darkness.

But he still wasn't sure he'd been wise to hand that envelope to the detective. It had been a moment's impulse, unlikely to have been acted on had the man been that fat bastard, Dalziel!

He went into what would have been the vestry if the Beulahites had vestries. Elizabeth was in there, looking as calm as a frozen mere. Inger was going through her usual pre-performance finger-suppling exercises. Walter was looking at his watch as though it had disobeyed a direct command.

'I think we must start,' he said.

'Fine,' said Krog. 'I'm ready. Inger?'

'Yes.'

They looked at Wulfstan. There had been a time when, as chairman of the committee, he had acted as a sort of MC, introducing the performers. But there had been something so unbending about his manner that in the end the experiment had been discontinued. 'Not so much a warm-up', Krog had described it, 'as a chill-down.' Now it was his custom to signal to the regulars that things were about to start by simply joining Chloe on the front row.

Tonight, however, he said, 'I will stay with Elizabeth so she is not sitting here alone.'

The singer looked at him and smiled with a kind of distant compassion, like some classical goddess gazing down on the mortal coil from her Olympian tea table.

'No, I'll be fine. You go and sit with Chloe. She'll be expecting you.'

Wulfstan didn't argue. He simply left. He might not be much good on a stage, but he certainly knew how to get off it.

In a broad American accent, Krog said, 'O K. Let's do it.'

He stood aside to let Inger go out before him.

'Good luck, Elizabeth,' he said. 'Or, if you are super-stitious, break a leg.'

She met his gaze with an expression blank beyond indifference and he turned away quickly.

The applause which had begun as Inger took her seat at the piano swelled at his appearance. Small audiences loved him. If he could have performed to the whole world, fifty or sixty at a time, in village halls on summer eves, he would have been an international favourite.

He smiled on them and they smiled back as he bade them welcome with easy charm. As he spoke, his eyes ran along the rows. Many he recognized from previous years, the Mid-Yorks culture vultures who came flapping down to feast, and be seen feasting, on these musical bar-snacks. Then there were the tourists, glad of an evening excursion from musty hotel lounges, or holiday cottages not half as comfortable as home. And scattered among them were other faces he remembered or half-remembered, from those long off days when he stayed at Heck and was a popular customer at the village shop and patron of the Holly Bush Inn.

Wasn't that Miss Lavery from the village school? And old Mr Pontifex who'd owned half the valley? And those wizened features at the back of the hall, didn't they belong to Joe Telford, the joiner, by whose gracious permission they were performing here tonight? And that couple there, she like patience on a monument, and he like the granite it was carved from, were not they the Hardcastles, Cedric and Molly?

His gaze came forward and met Chloe's on the front row, and his voice faltered. His instinct had been right. This was no occasion for the Mahler cycle. Elizabeth had wanted to end the concert with it, but at least his resist-ance had prevented that. He wanted the concert to end on an upbeat note with a rousing encore or two. No one would be calling for encores after the *Kindertotenlieder*. So finally she had agreed to end the first half with it. Now he saw even that as a mistake. God help us, they'd probably all go home!

But it wasn't possible to change now. All he could hope was that the Vaughan Williams *Songs of Travel* which sat ill with the *Kindertotenlieder* but which he'd chosen deliberately for that reason would act as a kind of advance antidote.

By the time he came to the ninth and final song, he knew he'd been wrong. Sometimes an audience creates its own atmosphere, let the artist do what he will. He could feel them turning from the masculine vigour and sturdy independence expressed in several of the songs, and immersing themselves in the fatalistic melancholy which he'd always regarded as their lesser component. Even this last song, 'I Have Trod the Upward and the Downward Path', a sort of middle-brow 'My Way' in its assertion of stoic refusal to be overwhelmed by the vagaries of unfeeling fate, somehow came out positively plangent with despair.

He took his bow, made no attempt to milk the applause, but went straight into his introduction of Elizabeth.

He kept it short and flat, but Walter Wulfstan at his worst would have been hard pressed to lower that overheated atmosphere of expectation. And even if he had, the appearance of Elizabeth would have sent it soaring again. Those who had seen only the photos were rocked back by the reality. And those on whose minds the image was printed of a short, plump, plain child with cropped black hair gasped audibly at the sight of this tall elegant woman with the erect carriage of a model, her slim body sheathed in an ankle-length black gown, with long tresses of blonde hair framing the face of a tragic queen.

Krog turned and walked off, suspecting he could have hopped off backwards, grimacing like an ape, for all the attention anyone was paying him. Someone remembered to applaud, but the clapping was spasmodic and soon done. Silence fell. Outside, sounds swam by like fish seen from a bathyscope, denizens of a completely different world.

Elizabeth spoke, her Yorkshire vowels startling as growls from a skylark.

'Fifteen years back, over the Neb in Dendale, three little lasses, friends of mine, went missing. I'm singing these songs for them.'

Inger came in with the short introduction, then Elizabeth started singing.

And now the sun will rise as bright
As though no horror had touched the night.

It took no more than the first few lines of that first song to show Krog that he had been both right and wrong.

Wrong that she wasn't ready for this cycle. She sang with a purity of line, an uncluttered directness, which made her performance on disc seem strained and affected. And the piano accompaniment was the perfect complement to this version of her voice which could have been buried in the richer textures of the full orchestra.

And right that she should never have been allowed to sing them here. In the silence when the first song ended he heard a stifled sob. And many of the faces he saw from his vantage point to the side were stricken rather than rapt. At the least he should have agreed to her request that the concert finished with the cycle, for after this the second half of the programme with its mix of love duets and popular favourites was going to sound tastelessly bathetic.

He focused on Chloe Wulfstan's face. The pain he saw

there was reason enough to have banned the Mahler even if everyone else in the audience were simply enjoying the performance as a superb example of *lieder* singing. It was nearly twenty years since he'd met her on his very first appearance at the Festival. To a young singer making his way, this kind of engagement was a necessary staging post on the way to heights. And when he saw his host's young wife and felt that familiar tightening of the throat which was the first signal of desire, his instinctive reaction had been to chance his arm because he doubted if he'd be this way again.

He'd given her the full treatment, but she had only smiled – amused, as she admitted later, by his flowery Continental manners – and returned her attention to its main focus, her young daughter.

He had thought about her for a while, but not for long, and when Wulfstan invited him back the following year he had accepted, not because of Chloe, but simply because he wasn't yet in a position where he could afford to refuse.

When he saw her again, it felt like coming home. That summer they became friends. And his relationship with Wulfstan changed too. Another reason for accepting the invitation was that he'd come to realize the man was rather more than just a big frog in the middle of a little northern pool. He had connections all over Europe, not the kind of connections, alas, which oiled the hinges of the doors of La Scala or l'Opéra or the Festspielhaus, but a useful network of local introductions which could help bring work and get himself noticed. At a personal level, he found it hard to warm to the man, which should have made the prospect of seducing his wife that much easier; but now that he saw him as in some degree a patron, self-interest turned its cold shower on his loins, and it was almost pure accident when, during his third festival, while strolling with Chloe under the Neb, he slipped while crossing a stream, fell against her, splashing them both, and they kissed as though there was nothing else to do.

So it had begun. She saw it as 'the real thing', whatever the real thing might be, and this might have worried him had she not made it clear that her daughter's interests came first, and until the girl was fully grown, there was no way Chloe would contemplate leaving Walter. But she was no fool. When he assured her that his love was so strong, he was willing to wait forever, she replied, 'That's very noble, Arne, though it could be of course that you're just delighted to be able to have your cake and ha'penny!'

What would have happened if the tragedy of fifteen years ago hadn't intervened, he could only guess. What he knew for sure was that her pain and their separation had affected him in ways he could not begin to understand, and his life had seemed a walk-on part till in the wake of the Elizabeth crisis, she had come back to him once more.

Now there seemed nothing to prevent her leaving Wulfstan. Instead, she had prevaricated, and finally come back up here to live.

What had made Krog start poking around his host's study, he did not know. He had no particular object in mind, just a vague hope that he might find something to give him leverage in prising Chloe and her husband apart. Inger had caught him searching in there, but in her usual uninvolved way, had said nothing and closed the door. When he had found the transcripts and worked out the implications, his first reaction had been dismay. That a man would wish revenge on his daughter's killer, he understood. That he could chain a suspect against whom nothing had been proved in a hole in the ground and leave him there to drown, baffled his understanding. And the other big question which he didn't want to ask because he was afraid of the answer was, how much did Chloe know about this?

Nothing, he assured himself . . . he could not believe . . . nothing! Perhaps indeed he had got it all wrong and these were merely the crazy ramblings of a disturbed adolescent. Or perhaps Walter had nothing to do with the presence of Benny in his cellar. But when he had followed him up the Corpse Road on Sunday morning, and again today, and seen him standing there looking down on the re-emerging relics of Heck, he had been sure.

Certainty of knowledge did not mean certainty of action. His earlier doubts about the impulse which had made him give the transcripts to Pascoe were now turning to bitter regrets. Why had he made himself an instrument when he could have simply remained an observer? For now, as his gaze moved from the lovely and beloved face of the wife to the ravaged face of the husband, he thought he saw there, as clearly as the returning outline of Dendale village under the searching eye of the sun, the lineaments of guilt and the acceptance of discovery.

There were only five songs in the cycle but each created a timeless world of grief of its own. So rapt were the listeners that no one turned during the penultimate song when the rear door opened and three men and a woman stepped quietly inside.

Don't look so pale! The weather's bright.
They've only gone to climb up Beulah Height.

The local reference turned the screw of pain another notch. And its repetition in the closing lines with their heart-rendingly false serenity in which hope comes close to being crushed out of despair, was too much for Mrs Hardcastle who slumped against her husband's rigid body, silently sobbing.

> We'll catch up with them on Beulah Height
> In bright sunlight.
> The weather's bright on Beulah Height.

Then almost without pause, Inger Sandel launched into the tumultuous accompaniment of the final song.

Krog, from his viewpoint through the partially open door of the vestry, could see the reactions of the new-comers. Three he knew. Dalziel, his face slab-like, show-ing nothing of what was going on behind those piggy eyes. Wield, his irregular features equally unreadable but giving an impression of an intensity of listening. Pascoe, visibly moved, unable to hide his feelings. And the fourth, a woman Krog did not know, young, attractive without being an obvious beauty, her eyes like a policeman's taking everything in, while her ears heard the music with-out responding to it.

The tumult and strife of the song, with its images of foul weather and guilt and recrimination, all began to fade now as the singer emerged from it, like a lost traveller finally achieving peace and shelter.

> By no foul storm confounded

Elizabeth's head was back, her gaze fixed high over the heads of her audience.

> By God's own hands surrounded

Krog couldn't see her face but he knew it would be radiant as a saint's at that moment of martyrdom when the gates of heaven are seen to open.

> They rest

They rest. Let them rest. *Requiescant. . .* That was what this was. A requiem.

> They rest

Perhaps she was right, he was wrong. If only the police weren't there . . . and whose fault was that? Would Pascoe be discreet about the source of the transcripts? Not that it mattered. Chloe would know. Without being told, she would know.

. . . as in their father's house.

Father's? Mother's surely? A slip? Perhaps. But who was noticing?

The piano wound its way through the long melancholy coda which set its seal of calm acceptance on all the turbulence of loss and sorrow which had gone before. When it finished, no one spoke. No one applauded.

This was how it should be. Now they should all simply rise and go home.

Then came a noise like a thunderclap. And another. And another.

It was the fat policeman, the abominable Dalziel, standing there like the Spirit of Discord, bringing his huge hands together in what came close to a parody of applause.

Six times he did this. Heads turned but no one joined in. The young woman in the group looked at the fat man with mingled amazement and admiration. The younger man's eyes closed momentarily in a spasm of embarrassment, then he picked up a CD and found it necessary to examine it closely. Only the third man, the ugly one called Wield, showed no reaction but kept his gaze fixed unblinkingly on Elizabeth.

After the final clap, Dalziel spoke.

'Ee, that were grand, lass,' he said, beaming. 'I do like a good ballad when it's sung with feeling. Is it the tea break now? This weather, eh? I've got a throat like a dried-up culvert.'

NINETEEN

'What is truth?' asked Peter Pascoe.

Sometimes it hangs before you, bright as a star when only one is shining in the sky.

Sometimes like a very faint star in a sky full of brilliant constellations, you can only glimpse it by looking aside.

Sometimes you get close enough to reach out your hand to grasp it, only to find your fingers scrabbling at a *trompe l'oeil*.

And sometimes a simple shift of perspective can turn a wild goose into a trapped rabbit.

The real trick was to recognize it when you saw it and not confuse the part with the whole.

Dalziel was a gut detective, working through animal instinct. Wield used logic and order, arranging and re-arranging things till they made sense. Pascoe saw himself as a creature of imagination, making huge leaps, then waiting hopefully for the facts to catch up with him.

And Shirley Novello . . . ?

In the Range Rover she'd finally got hold of the tran-scripts.

She read through them as the vehicle moved at uncom-fortable speed along the narrow country roads. The blue sheets she read twice.

After the second reading she sat back and closed her eyes tight, as if in darkness she had better hope of illumi-nation.

She was recalling the confused and fragmented feelings of her own early adolescent years. But that had been a period of halcyon calm compared with this. And Betsy Allgood's trauma hadn't just started with the onset of adolescence, but much much earlier. A plain, unloved child, starved of affection by a work-obsessed father and an emotionally unstable mother, with what envy she must have regarded her prettier, happier, cared-for and cosseted friends, and in particular, Mary Wulfstan, who materialized only during holidays to take her place in the Dendale hierarchy like a little princess.

Yet Mary's mother was only an Allgood, like Betsy's own dad. So this special quality, this enviable, desirable 'otherness' must spring from her father, the powerful, enigmatic Walter Wulfstan.

How much did these men understand of this? Pascoe there, after what he'd been through, after all that business of the imaginary friend and the real/unreal nix, surely he must have some inkling of the looking-glass world young girls could wander in and out of without hardly noticing? And Wield, how much did he partake of those qualities of sensitivity and empathic insight conventionally attributed to gays in literature? Or were they just part of a picture as false as that still more prevalent in police circles which painted gays at best as sad and sordid shirt-lifters, at worst as potential child-molesters?

And the awful Dalziel . . . God, he was speaking to her. Let no dog bark!

'You asleep, Ivor, or wha'? I were asking what you reckoned to all this now you've read that trick-cyclist crap?'

Here I am, she thought, stuck in a machine with my three-personed God, sticking out like the fourth corner on a triangle, and they're waiting to hear my opinion! Chance to shine? Or chance to eclipse myself forever? Wise move might be to box clever, check what these great minds think, then go along with them, so that at worst, if they turn out completely wrong, you're all in the same clag together.

Pascoe turned in the front seat and smiled at her.

'No need to worry,' he said. 'No Brownie points on offer here. It's about a dead child, four dead children perhaps, and perhaps one ruined one. It's only the truth that matters. Not personal ambition. Or personal troubles. I know you understand that.'

Shit, thought Novello. The mind-reading bastard's reminding me I went clod-hopping into his life when he was sitting by his daughter's sickbed, and he's saying, that was all right if it was for the job but not if it was just for me. Who the hell does he think this is? Gentle bloody Jesus?

But she knew her indignation was partly based on guilt. And there was something else too, something worse because it ran counter to all her private resolve to make her way to the top of this masculine world without paying the price of becoming part of it. It was a feeling of pleasure that maybe she'd got her geometry wrong, maybe this Holy Triangle was really a Holy Circle which had just been drawn wider to include her in . . . ?

I won't be caught like that either! she assured herself, then gasped as the car went into a skid.

Dalziel had braked to avoid a dog which had emerged from the hedgerow. It was a small indeterminate creature which went on its way with a jaunty indifference to lesser beings whose shortage of legs required them to can themselves like dog meat in order to travel.

The incident took only a moment then the car was back under the Fat Man's control. But Novello found herself thinking of Tig, Lorraine's pet. She hadn't seen the beast. She hadn't seen Lorraine either. Alive or dead.

But Dalziel had, and Wield too.

Suddenly she wanted to cry, but this was a feeling she'd long since got used to dealing with.

She said briskly, 'Clearly, Betsy was very disturbed, but I'm not so sure she was confused. She obviously wanted Wulfstan to know she remembered the real version of what happened that night. In other words, she was protecting him. But suppose her obsession with Wulfstan went back a lot further, and her protection of him, too? I noticed when I read the file that on every occasion it was Betsy who said she'd seen Lightfoot hanging around. Perhaps she'd already started protecting Wulfstan then, so when she saw Benny chained up in the Heck cellar, it was instinctual for her to relocate him at Neb Cottage.'

There, she'd done it, suggested that fifteen years back when she herself was little older than the lost girls, these men had been getting things badly wrong and letting a child run rings around them.

Dalziel said, 'Bloody hell, lass. I know you lot think with your hormones, but could a seven-year-old really be jerking us off like that?'

She smiled to herself, finding the blast of Dalziel's breezy crudities refreshing after the tear gas of Pascoe's pieties.

She said, 'I don't think we're talking carefully worked-out strategies here, sir. She must have been really frightened and confused the night she met Benny. Maybe because she was found near Neb Cottage and everyone assumed that's where Benny had attacked her, she just went along with it, even came to believe it, or at least block off the truth. And it wasn't till Dr Appleby, the psych, got to work on her that it all came back.'

'But she didn't tell her it had come back, did she?' said Pascoe.

'No. Not the psych. By then she was old enough to work out the full implication of what she'd seen. And obsessed enough to grasp that she had it in her power to *force* Wulfstan into the loving father role she'd tried to *persuade* him into by losing all that weight and bleaching her hair.'

There was silence in the car. They were on the outskirts of Danby now. It wasn't exactly a place that throbbed at night, she thought. There was next to no traffic and the few figures visible in the streets moved slow as wreaths of smoke through the evening sunlight.

A ghost town. A town full of ghosts come drifting down the Corpse Road from the Neb. But not to haunt. Rather to ask to be laid to rest.

'So you reckon Wulfstan's in the frame for them all, including his own daughter?' said Dalziel.

'He wouldn't be the first,' said Novello.

'The first what?' enquired Pascoe.

'The first child abuser and killer not to let distinctions of family get in the way of his kicks!' she exclaimed with more vehemence than she intended.

'And Betsy knows he's this monster but still sets her heart on becoming his daughter?' said Dalziel incredulously. 'One thing I'll say about you, lass, is you're not one of them girls-can-do-no-wrong feminists.'

'I'm not talking right or wrong, I'm talking truth,' retorted Novello angrily. 'And it would probably make our job a damn sight easier if only men were as willing to face up to the truth about themselves as women are.'

Oh, shit, she thought, sinking back in her seat. Up there being hallelujah'd with the Trinity one moment, over the battlements and cometing down to hell the next!

And this was the point where Pascoe rifled his storehouse of palliatives and could only come up with, 'What is truth?'

The rest of the journey to the Beulah Chapel passed in a contemplative silence.

Once in the chapel, Pascoe abandoned meditation for observation. He had a sense of things coming to an end. But as in all the best shows, before it was over, the Fat Man had to sing.

A voice cut through the hubbub which broke out after Dalziel's declarations of thirst. It was clear, classy, and came from a well-built, handsome woman whom Pascoe recognized without surprise (he was past surprise) as Cap Marvell, Dalziel's ex-inamorata. She was proclaiming, 'Ladies and gentlemen, it's such a fine night, refreshments are being served out in the yard.'

As the audience began to file out, she approached the Fat Man, put her hand on his arm and said softly into his ear, 'Andy, what's happened?'

'Tell you later, luv,' he said. 'It 'ud be a help if you could get shut of that lot too.'

A few of the audience, motivated by parsimony, curiosity or arthritis, had opted to remain in their seats. Cap Marvell moved among them speaking quietly, and one by one they rose. She shepherded them to the exit, exchanging a smile with Dalziel as she passed.

Perhaps, thought Pascoe, I should cancel the *ex*.

Dalziel glanced his way, and without thinking he cocked his head to one side and made a *hello! hello!* face. Christ, I'm getting bold, he thought.

Marvell closed the door behind the last of the audience. Persuasive lady, thought Pascoe. Or maybe she'd taken lessons from her *petit ami* and simply told them to sod off out while they still had two unbroken legs to walk on.

She rejoined Dalziel and said, meek as a housemaid, 'Anything else, sir?'

He said, 'I've got a feeling the concert's over, so you could always lead them in a sing-song to stop 'em asking for their money back. Seriously, pack 'em off home once they've had their refreshments. Talking of which, I weren't joking when I said I were parched. You couldn't jump the queue could you and fetch us a mug of tea? Better still, make it a pot and enough mugs to go round.'

He looked to the far end of the chapel where the three Wulfstans and Arne Krog stood by the piano at which Inger Sandel remained seated. Like a barber's shop quartet waiting for a cue, thought Pascoe.

'Five of them, four of us, that makes nine,' said Dalziel. 'Wieldy, you're house-trained. Give the lass a hand.'

The lass gave him a submissive smile, trod hard but ineffectively on his toe, and went out followed by Wield.

Pascoe caught a brief flicker of pleasure on Novello's face. Thinks she's forgiven because she's not been elected tea girl, he guessed. Poor sprog. She'd learned a lot. But until she learned that *in re* Dalziel, pleasure was as emotionally irrelevant as pique, she had not learned enough.

'Well, let's not be unsociable,' said the Fat Man.

And beaming like an insurance salesman about to sell annuities on the *Titanic*, he set off towards the group by the piano.

'Now this is nice,' he declared as he approached. 'Family and friends. It'll likely save time if I can talk to all of you at once, but if any of you think that could be embarrassing, just say the word and I'll fix to see you privately.'

Like a wolf asking the sheep if they want to stick together or take their chances one by one, thought Pascoe.

No one spoke.

'Grand,' said Dalziel. 'No secrets, then. That's how it should be with family and friends. Let's make ourselves comfortable, shall we?'

He helped himself to a chair and sat on it with such force, its joints squealed and its legs splayed. Pascoe and Novello brought out chairs for the others and placed them in a semicircle. Then the two detectives took their places behind Dalziel, like attendants at a durbar.

Elizabeth was the last to sit down. As she draped herself elegantly over the chair she pulled off her blonde wig and tossed it casually towards the piano. It landed half on the frame, half off, hung there for a moment, then slithered to the ground like a legless Pekinese.

No one noticed. All eyes were on the singer as she scratched her bald head vigorously with both hands.

'Bloody hot in yon thing,' she said. 'I think I'll give it up.'

'Change of colour, eh?' said Dalziel.

'Aye. I think my blonde days are just about done.'

She sat there like an alien in a sci-fi movie. Pascoe, whose impression of her till now had been of a woman striking in appearance but chilling in effect, surprised himself by having a sudden image of pressing that naked head down between his thighs. She caught his eye and smiled as if she knew exactly what he was thinking. He turned his attention quickly to her CD which he was still carrying.

And that was when goose turned to rabbit.

At this moment Wield reappeared bearing a tray laden with teapot, cups, sugar, milk and a trayful of biscuits.

'Here comes mother,' said Dalziel. 'Funny thing that. When weather's hot and you're really parched, there's nowt cuts your thirst like a cup of tea.'

He spoke with the conviction of a temperance preacher. Pascoe watched with resigned amusement as the Fat Man made a big thing of seeing the ladies were served first before lifting his own cup to his great lips with little finger delicately crooked in the best genteel fashion. Either he was still planning his strategy or he felt that something which had been fifteen years coming deserved a leisurely delectation.

Finally he was ready.

His opening gambit surprised Pascoe, because it repeated his offer of separation, only this time targeted and sounding sincere.

'Mrs Wulfstan,' he said gently, 'this could be painful for you. If you'd rather we spoke later, or at home . . .'

'No,' she replied. 'I'm used to pain.'

Krog, seated to her left, gripped her hand which was dangling loosely almost to the floor, but she offered no return pressure and after a moment he let it go. Wulfstan did not even turn his head to look at her. All his attention was concentrated on Dalziel.

Was the Fat Man's concern for the woman really genuine or just another way of turning the screw on her husband? wondered Pascoe.

Probably a bit of both. Dalziel was long practised at bringing down whole flocks of birds with one stone.

'So it's cards on the table time,' he said with all the engaging openness of a Mississippi gambler who has got pasteboard up his sleeve, down his collar, behind his hatband, and in every orifice known to man. 'Who's going to start us off?'

Silence. Which was what he expected. Pascoe caught Wield's eye and murmured something in his ear. The sergeant nodded and moved quietly towards the exit.

'Stage fright, is it?' said Dalziel. 'All right. D C Novello, why don't you see if you can give us a kick start?'

Jesus Christ! thought Novello, in both oath and prayer.

She had been watching with interest to see how the Fat Man was going to play this. Would he come in at the past or the present? Would he be open about what they'd found out or keep most of it back to trip them up with?

She'd been ready to make critical notes, to give mental marks. Now here she was, at the front of the class, chalk in hand.

Jesus, she repeated, this time wholly supplicatory.

Her mind was spinning between the chained skeleton at Heck, the blue sheets of Betsy's revised recollection, Barney Lightfoot's story, Geordie Turnbull's confession . . .

Then she thought, that's all to do with the past! Sod the past. Fat Andy might be anchored in it, but I'm not. The case I'm working on is the murder of Lorraine Dacre, age seven.

She said, 'Mr Wulfstan, is there anything you'd like to add to your account of your visit to Danby early last Sunday morning?'

She focused hard on Wulfstan's gaunt features, partly in resistance to her desire to glance at Dalziel in search of approval, but also keen to catch any tell-tale reaction. An emotion did move like a mist-wraith across those passive features, but she couldn't quite read it. If anything it resembled . . . relief?

He said, 'As I told Mr Dalziel, I went up the Corpse Road and stood for some time on the col, looking down into Dendale.'

'And then?'

'And then as I turned away to start the descent to Danby, I glanced along the ridge towards the Neb. And I saw a man.'

'A man? What man? You didn't mention this in your statement. Why not?'

She was gabbling too many questions in her eagerness to be at him.

He touched his hand to his face as though in need of tactile reassurance that he was flesh and blood.

Then he said quietly, 'Because it was Benny Lightfoot.'

Novello let out a snort of angry derision. The bastard was going to play silly buggers, was he? He was hoping

492

to hide behind all this *Benny's Back*! hysteria. But she had the wherewithal to chop that frail prop from under him.

Her voice sour with sarcasm, she said, 'You saw Benny Lightfoot? Now that must have been a *real* shock, Mr Wulfstan. Especially as you of all people must have known beyond any shadow of doubt that he was dead.'

If she'd expected shock/horror all round, she was disappointed.

Wulfstan shook his head wearily and repeated, 'I saw him.'

The three women showed nothing, or very little, on their faces.

And Arne Krog said, 'It's true. There was a man.'

And to Wulfstan he said, almost apologetically, 'I followed you.'

This confirmation set Novello back for a second till she grasped its implications. Of course, there *had* been a man, not Benny but Barney, who'd talked about wandering high on the Neb in search of a bird's-eye view of the valley.

Wulfstan was looking at Krog, faintly surprised. Well, a man would be surprised to have his sighting of a ghost confirmed from such an unexpected source.

'So what did you do then, Mr Wulfstan?' enquired Novello.

'I went up the ridge after him,' said Wulfstan.

'And did you catch up with him?' she asked.

'No. He disappeared.'

'You mean, like in a puff of smoke?' she mocked.

'No. There are crags and folds of ground along the ridge. He went out of sight and did not reappear. I assumed he'd dropped down one side or the other.'

She got his drift now. Benny/Barney had dropped down on the Ligg Beck side and there encountered

Lorraine and . . . Good try, Walter. Only it wouldn't wash.

Feeling completely in control, she set about clearing the ground.

'What about you, Mr Krog? You see which way this man went?'

Krog said, 'No. I saw Walter go after him, then I went back down the Corpse Road.'

'And you didn't see Mr Wulfstan again?'

'Not till later that day at his house.'

So now you're on your own, Wulfstan. Just you, and me.

And the child.

'So what happened next, Mr Wulfstan?' she asked gently. 'Did you walk along the ridge, looking left and right in search of this man you thought was Benny Lightfoot? And did you look down at the Ligg Beck side and see someone down there, far below? And was it a little girl you saw, Mr Wulfstan?'

In court this would be called 'leading the witness'. She almost hoped he wouldn't let himself be led, forcing her to drive him with angry scorn.

But there was no defiance in his face, nor denial in his voice.

'Yes,' he said. 'Yes, I looked down. And I saw a little girl. I looked down and I saw Mary.'

'Mary?' Novello was momentarily bewildered. Against her will she glanced sideways at the men. Pascoe gave a small encouraging nod. Wield, who had rejoined the group bearing the Dendale file and the envelope with Betsy Allgood's transcripts, was as unreadable as ever. Dalziel was staring at Wulfstan and frowning.

She too wrenched her attention back to the man. So he was still wriggling, was he? She gathered her strength for frontal attack.

'Come on, Mr Wulfstan!' she said. 'You mean Lorraine,

don't you? You looked into the valley and saw Lorraine Dacre.'

There was a creaking sound as Dalziel shifted his weight forward on his uneasy chair.

'No, lass,' he corrected gently. 'He means Mary. That right, Mr Wulfstan? You looked down towards Ligg Beck and you saw your daughter, Mary? Looking just like she looked last time you saw her, fifteen years back?'

And for the first time in their acquaintance, Wulfstan regarded Andy Dalziel with something close to gratitude and said, 'Yes. That's right, Superintendent. I saw my Mary.'

TWENTY

The sky shimmers like blown silk, the sun staggers drunkenly, the rocky ridge beneath his feet yields like a trampoline. After so many years, after so much pain, she is there, as blonde and blithe as he remembers her, not a day older, not a wit changed. The ghost of the man who took her has led him back to her.

He does not pause to wonder how she has grown no older during all those years. He does not pause to ask why she is in this valley rather than Dendale where she was lost. He does not pause to consider the steepness of the hillside beneath him. Instead he plunges down the slope like a champion fell runner at the peak of his form. Nimble-footed, he bounds from rock to rock. Below, at the edge of the deep ghyll through which the beck runs out of sight, she gathers flowers, heedless of anything but herself and the plants beneath her feet, and perhaps the little dog that circles her, barking at bees and flies and nothing at all.

He calls her name. He is too breathless to call very loud, but he calls it all the same. The dog hears him first and looks up, its excited bark turning to deep-throated growl. He calls again, louder this time, and this time the girl hears him.

'Mary!'

She turns and looks up. She sees, rushing down on her, a wild-eyed creature mouthing strange words, his arms flailing high and wide, his legs tiring now and sending him staggering like a drunkard. The flowers fall from her hand. She turns to flee. He shouts again. She runs blindly. The edge of the ghyll is near. She looks back to see his outstretched hands descending upon her.

And she falls.

'I saw two things when I got down beside her. I saw that she was not Mary. And I saw that she was dead.'

Novello glared at him, trying not to believe, and failing. She had wanted a trapped monster, not a crazed father. She opened her mouth to ask sceptical questions, but Dalziel gave her a silencing glance and said, 'So what did you do then?'

'I picked up the body and began to climb out of the ghyll. I think I was going to carry her back down the valley and seek help, though I knew that for her the time of help was over. Halfway up the slope, on a ledge, the dog attacked me, biting at my ankles. I had to stop to try and chase it away. Finally I kicked it so hard, it fell to the bed of the ghyll and lay there, still snarling up at me. It was now I noticed this gap behind a large flake of rock. When I peered in I saw that this must have been some kind of den for the child. It contained the kind of things a little girl would choose to have around her . . . I remember from the days when . . .'

He looked at his wife whose face had lost all colour. Elizabeth was holding one of her hands and Arne Krog was gripping the other arm.

'I laid her in there, thinking that this would be a good place to leave her while I went for assistance. And then I started thinking of what that meant, of telling people, of seeing her parents, perhaps . . . I found I did not have the strength for that. Over the years I had grown to think I had the strength for anything, but I knew I hadn't got the strength for that. So I blocked the entrance to her little den. All I wanted to do was give myself time to think. I was not trying to hide her forever. I would not do that to her parents. I know all too well what not knowing where your child's body lies can do to a parent's mind.'

'So why'd you cover your traces with that dead sheep?'

It was Wield, who'd been standing in the background unnoticed. 'I'm the one who found her,' he went on accusingly. 'I saw how hard you'd worked to make sure she stayed hid.'

'The dog was still close,' said Wulfstan. 'I chased it off with stones but I was worried that it might come back. I thought the dead sheep might prevent it, or any predator, from penetrating behind to where I'd lain the child. And I went back to the car along the fellside and drove home. I don't think anybody saw me.'

Oh yes they did, thought Pascoe. Another little girl who, thank God, imagined she was seeing a scene from the real/unreal world of her story books.

'And exactly when were you going to come forward and give us the benefit of this information, sir?' said Dalziel with functionary courtesy.

'After the concert. Tomorrow morning,' said Wulfstan. 'I have been putting my affairs, both business and personal, in order for some time now. These last three days have given me time to complete the process, and I thought I would not wish to spoil Elizabeth's . . . to spoil my other daughter's debut at the festival.'

He looked towards Elizabeth now. What passed between them was hard to read.

Affection? Understanding? Apology? Regret? All of these, though in what proportion and in what direction was impossible to say.

'Owt else you want to tell us?' said Dalziel. 'Like for instance why you've been going up the Corpse Road these past few weeks. And why you started putting your affairs in order?'

Wulfstan gave him a distant, almost headmasterly nod of approval.

'I think you know, Mr Dalziel,' he said. 'Fifteen years ago, I believed you were irredeemably stupid; now I see I may have been mistaken. About the irredeemable element at least. I started going up to the ridge of Lang Neb when I heard that the reservoir was shrinking so much that Dendale village was reappearing. I make my living from the sun so I appreciated the irony that it was solar heat that was going to bring that living to an end.'

'How exactly?' said Dalziel. 'Just so's everyone knows what you're talking about.'

He glanced towards Chloe Wulfstan. Pascoe, probably the most advanced Dalzielogist in the civilized world, read the message with little difficulty.

Tell her now, publicly, so that if she knew before, no one will be able to trick it out of her.

An unexpected chivalry? Or just a subtle turn of the screw to make sure Wulfstan kept on talking?

Whichever, it was working.

'You will find, probably have found already, the remains of a man in the ruins of Heck. That man is . . . was . . . Benny Lightfoot. I put him there. I left him there to drown. I am solely responsible for his death. My motive was, I think, obvious.'

Dalziel looked towards Novello who was scowling with concentration as she followed events. Hers was one of those rare faces that look prettier in a scowl.

'Not to them as weren't around, mebbe,' said the Fat Man. 'So if you could just give us an outline . . . You'll have lots of opportunity to dot your p's and q's later.'

As well as studying Dalzielology, Pascoe collected Dalzieliana. He made a mental note of this one.

'After we had all moved out of the dale and the rains started, I found I couldn't keep away. At all hours of day and night, I'd be hit by this irresistible urge to go back there and wander around on the fellside. You might imagine such a compulsion, often involving a long drive from some distant place, would be relatively easy to control. But when I tell you that the form it took was an absolute certainty that Mary was there, wandering lost and frightened, and if I didn't go and find her she would certainly die, you may understand why I always obeyed.

'I never found her, of course. Sometimes I imagined . . .'

He paused and almost visibly withdrew into himself, and Pascoe went with him, to a dark, rain-swept fellside, where every fitful gleam of light seemed to glance off a head of blonde curls and every splash and gurgle of water sang like the echo of childish laughter.

'But one night,' he resumed, 'I heard a noise and saw a figure which wasn't just in my imaginings. It was close by the ruins of Neb Cottage, near where you were found a little later,' he said to Elizabeth, who returned his gaze blankly. 'It was of course Benny Lightfoot.'

Another living ghost haunting the valley, finding what comfort he could in the ruined remains of the only existence he had ever wanted.

But there had been nothing for his comfort in this encounter with a fellow ghost.

'I should have brought him in and handed him over to you,' said Wulfstan to Dalziel. 'But I didn't trust you not to let him go again. No. That's too simple. That's too much of an excuse. I wanted him for myself because I felt sure I could get out of him things about my daughter that you with your more restricted methods never could.'

'You tortured him,' said Novello.

'I beat him,' said Wulfstan. 'With my fists. I never used instruments then or later. Does that make it better? It is your area of expertise, not mine. And when I couldn't get anything out of him and I saw dawn lightening the sky, I forced him down to Heck. I knew the cellar was still accessible because I'd cleared a gap sufficient for my entrance in my search for Mary, in case she'd gone back to her old home and taken shelter there. I bound him tight with strips of cloth I tore from his own jacket, and the next night I returned with lengths of chain, and padlocks, and staples, and made him secure. All I wanted was for him to tell me what he'd done to her, where she was. But he wouldn't. No matter what I did to him, he wouldn't. I thought it was because he believed once he'd told me what I wanted to know, I'd kill him. And I swore by everything I held holy, by the memory of Mary herself, that I'd let him live if only he'd tell me what I needed to know. But still he wouldn't talk. Why? Why? All you had to do was tell me . . .'

He was back there again, and this time they were all with him, in that squalid hole with the rising waters lapping ever higher, and the two faces so close together, both so contorted with pain that perhaps it was difficult to tell in that dim light who was torturer, who victim.

Except that one went back each morning to a world of warmth and light while the other lay bound in chains, surrounded by darkness and lapped with freezing water.

Then it was easy to tell, thought Pascoe.

He said, 'So he never talked. And you let him die.'

Wulfstan said, 'Yes. I'm not sure if I meant to. If I'd have been able to. But I had to go away for a couple of days. I came back on the day that Elizabeth . . . Betsy went missing. When they found her and I heard her story that she'd been attacked by Benny near Neb Cottage, I thought . . . I don't know what I thought, but part of it was relief that he must have got out, that he was still alive. The next night I went down to Heck. The water had risen considerably. I could see at once he hadn't got away but he must have made a superhuman effort to pull the chain out of the wall . . . I could see one of his arms sticking out into the water. A block of stone above the entrance hole had collapsed and trapped it. I reached down into the water and touched his skin. It was cold. I tried to push it back into the cellar but couldn't. So I covered it with bits of rubble and went away.'

'How did that make you feel?' said Pascoe. 'Knowing you'd killed him.'

Wulfstan considered this, his lips pursed as though it were some unusual taste he were trying to identify, or a rare wine.

'Sad,' he said finally.

'Sad that you'd killed him?'

'Sad that he'd died without telling me what I wanted to know.'

Pascoe shook his head, but in sorrow not in disgust. He should perhaps have felt a sense of outrage, but it wasn't there. Not after the past few days.

Dalziel said, 'You done, Peter?'

'Yes.'

'Ivor, you got something more to say?'

Why was he so keen to let the DC have her head? wondered Pascoe. In murder investigations as in motor cars, back seats were not the kind of place you expected to find Andy Dalziel.

'Yes, sir. Just a bit,' said Novello. 'I don't think you felt sad, Mr Wulfstan. Why should you when you'd got what you were after? With the prime suspect mysteriously disappeared, no one was going to waste any more time looking, were they?'

'Looking for what? For my child?'

'No! For the real killer. He was home and free. And that must have made him really happy.'

She spoke with a force born partly of moral contempt,

but mainly of a desire to provoke a response. She's so sure she's right, thought Pascoe sympathetically. She's desperate to be right! This was what Dalziel was at. There were some lessons best learned in public. And one of them was that being a step in front of everyone else was fine until, in your efforts to keep ahead, it became a step too far.

'So how about that, Mr Wulfstan?' said Dalziel pleasantly. 'Any chance of this being a cover-up 'cos it were you took the little lasses all along?'

Not just a lesson then. The Fat Man was making sure this time round no possibility, however improbable, didn't get its airing.

Wulfstan wasn't registering horror or indignation, but sheer incomprehension as if he were being addressed in a foreign language. He looked towards his wife as if in search of an interpreter. She shook her head and said almost inaudibly, 'This is vile . . . Superintendent, this is just not possible . . .'

'Well, some bugger thought it was,' said Dalziel. 'Gave us a ring, said to take a closer look at Mr Wulfstan. Sounded like a woman. Or a man pitched high. How's your falsetto, Mr Krog?'

Krog said easily, 'Too false to deceive an ear like yours, Mr Dalziel.'

Tone, expression, body language, were perfectly right. But it was a role, Pascoe detected. A chosen response, not a natural one. Impossible to prove, but he'd have bet his Christmas bonus the Turnip made the call. Which was pretty safe as cops didn't get bonuses. And he must resist Dalziel's invasive terminology!

Wulfstan, pale before, had turned a dreadful white as he finally admitted the enormity of the accusation. Interestingly it wasn't Dalziel but Novello, its first mover, that he turned on.

'You stupid *sick* child,' he grated. 'What do you know about *anything*?'

She stood up to him.

'I know you've killed one girl,' she snapped back. 'I just want to find out if she was the first.'

She was standing, he was sitting, but it still resembled a David vs Goliath tableau as he strained forward in his chair, his face twisted in anger. Very good likeness to the nix now, thought Pascoe, readying himself to intervene.

'Pay her no heed, Walter. Every bugger knows she's talking a load of bollocks. Every bugger save her, that is.'

The phraseology and accent might have been Andy Dalziel's but the voice was Elizabeth Wulfstan's.

She touched Wulfstan's arm, and he subsided. And turning her attention from Novello to Dalziel with a completeness which was like a door shut in the D C's face, she went on. 'You there, glorrfat, you know this is bollocks. Walter's told you what happened with yon poor lass. It were dreadful but it were an accident. So why don't I call his solicitor, we'll all go round to the cop shop, you take his statement, then we can all go home. I mean, this is a waste of time, isn't it? I haven't heard any cautions, I don't see any tape recorders. I'm off to Italy tomorrow and I'd like to get a good night's sleep.'

Dalziel looked at her, and smiled, and shook his head, and murmured, 'Little Betsy Allgood. Who'd have credited it? Little Betsy Allgood turning into a star.'

She scratched her bald head and said, 'Nay, Andy, I've a ways to go yet.'

'Aye, but you'll get there, lass,' he said. 'You've come this far, what's going to stop you now?'

'You mebbe, if you keep us here all bloody night,' she retorted.

'Nay, you're free to go any time, Betsy,' he said.

'What's to keep you here? You've done what you set out to do. Come back. Sung your songs. Made your peace. But afore you go, there's a little matter you could help us with.'

He held up his hand. Wield, with that almost telepathic sense of cue which was a necessary survival technique for the Fat Man's acolytes, dipped into the files and papers he was carrying and produced the handwritten blue sheets.

Reactions: Wulfstan indifferent, hardly registering; Krog, blue-eyed, blank-faced innocence; Elizabeth, frowning, gaze flickering over the others as if assessing how the sheets had got into Dalziel's hands; Chloe, head back, eyes closed, the position she'd assumed after her faint denial of the possibility of her husband's involvement; Inger Sandel, on the piano stool, apparently more interested in the keyboard than the conversation . . .

'Seems you thought later you might have got a bit confused about what happened that night you went after your cat,' said Dalziel. 'Nice to get the record straight.'

'Should've thought after what we've just heard you'd got the record straight as you're ever likely to get it,' said Elizabeth.

'There's nowt like hearing it from the horse's mouth.'

She flashed one of her rare smiles.

'That's what you think of my singing, is it?'

'I think you hoped you could close things off here with your singing,' said Dalziel. 'That was the idea, wasn't it? Come back, get it out of your system, quick march into the rest of your life? But the past's like people, luv. They need to be properly buried else they'll keep coming after you forever. Benny really is back now, so we can give him a proper send off. But what about them others? You think some miserable Kraut songs in a disused chapel will do the trick? I don't think so. Ask the Hardcastles. Ask the Telfords. Ask Chloe and Walter here who've tret you like their own daughter all these years.'

'And she's been a good daughter to me,' proclaimed Chloe Wulfstan, suddenly fully awake. 'A second chance. More perhaps than I deserved. Grief makes you selfish ... Oh, God, when I think of the pain she put herself through ... Betsy, I'm sorry, I've tried to make amends ...'

She was gripping the younger woman's hand and looking at her with desperate appeal to which Elizabeth, however, responded only with a frown.

Pascoe coughed gently. Dalziel glanced at him with something like relief and nodded. They had worked together long enough to have sketched out faint demarcation lines. In Dalziel's words, 'I'll kick 'em in the goolies if you'll shovel the psycho-crap.'

Pascoe said, 'I don't think you need be too hard on yourself, Mrs Wulfstan. You see, I don't think that Betsy's anorexia and bleaching her hair was really an attempt to turn herself into Mary. Or if it was, it wasn't for your sake, certainly not *just* for your sake. No. It was to turn herself into the kind of daughter she thought her own father would have preferred. Fair-haired, slender, attractive, graceful. Everyone thought the short cropped hair and boyish clothes were sops to her father's disappointment at not having a son. But I don't think so, Elizabeth. I think they were your mother's deliberate attempt to make you as un-girl-like as possible. She wanted to make you invisible to him. But you, what you wanted was visibility. Even after he was dead. Perhaps you thought it was because of the way you looked that he died. You blamed yourself for not being what he wanted. Which brings us to the question, how did you know what he wanted? How your mother knew ... well, I think a wife has an instinct. There may be deep layers of pretence which will never permit a public acknowledgement, but she knows. And sometimes the knowledge becomes unbearable. But a little girl . . . Could be it was your sheer invisibility which was the trick. I bet you followed him around . . . I bet you could spot him half a mile away in a good light. Just the merest glimpse up the fell would be enough. Yes, I bet that was it, Betsy. I bet that was it.'

It wasn't working. He'd kept going at such length in the hope of seeing some cracks appearing, but there was nothing on the woman's face except that same frown of concentration. The others more than made up for it, however, as the implications of what he was saying got through. Wulfstan had emerged from his dark inner world, Krog's features had been surprised by a natural feeling. Sandel looked up from her piano amazed, and Chloe's grip on her daughter's hand came close to being an armlock.

She said, 'Betsy, please, what's he mean? What is he trying to say?'

'Pay no heed,' said Elizabeth harshly. 'Load of riddles. It's the way these buggers talk when they've got nowt to say.'

'Betsy, we can't pursue the dead, however guilty,' said Pascoe. 'But the living need to speak out. Think of the pain your silence has caused. OK, a mixed-up child can't be blamed for keeping quiet, but you did more than keep quiet, didn't you? You misdirected. Think of the consequences. Think of that poor man drowning in a cellar. Think of little Lorraine. All these spring from your silence. There has to be an end.'

'Aye,' she said dragging her arm free from Chloe's grip. 'And I've reached it. I've had enough of this. I'm off first thing in the morning and I'd like a good night's sleep if no one else would. Walter, I'm sorry the way things have worked out, but they can't do much to you for an accident. Chloe . . .'

In one last desperate appeal, Chloe said, 'Elizabeth, if you know anything, please, please, tell us.'

'Know what? What should I know?' cried Elizabeth.

'Where she is. Where my daughter is! Tell me. *Tell me!*'

Last chance, thought Pascoe. But to admit she knew would be to admit everything. Not least that she had let the suffering of her adoptive parents stretch out over all those years. Would she have the strength? He could see it was tearing her apart.

He murmured something to Wield, who delved into the files he was carrying and came up with the map he'd drawn of Dendale fifteen years earlier. He gave it to Pascoe, raising his eyebrows interrogatively. Pascoe took it in his left hand at the same time showing Wield what he held in his right.

Instantly Wield was back on the sunlit fellside, the dale spread out below him like the Promised Land, behind him the fold built from stones first raised into walls here four thousand years before, beside him the dark, wiry shepherd, his dogs obedient at his feet, and in the gloaming air the song of larks and the bleating of the folded sheep . . .

You bastard! thought Wield, recalling his thoughts when he realized the dead sheep had been used to hide the missing child's whereabouts. Different man, but yes, the same trick!

And Pascoe like a conjurer held up the map and CD, then turned the latter through forty-five degrees so that the silhouetted face became the outline of the Dendale fells with a formalized sun arrowing its rays down into what had been the girl's mouth.

He knew now what the notes coming out of her mouth signified. Ellie had recalled the presenters discussing it on the record review programme she had been listening to that Sunday morning which now seemed a million light years away.

'Mahler's Second is known as the Resurrection Symphony,' she'd said. 'It's about the awakening of the dead, and judgement, and redemption. These bars are a quote from the first sounding of the resurrection theme, and there was a lot of speculation why she'd used them instead of a quote from the *lieder* themselves.'

Well, the speculation was over.

He held the disc cover close to the singer's eyes.

'I think you've told us where Mary and the others are already, Betsy,' he said. 'I think you've been longing to tell somebody for ages. You want it to be finished, you want to start moving forward, don't you? But you know there can't be any hope of redemption and renewal without resurrection. That's what you want to tell us, isn't it, Betsy? We'll catch up with them on Beulah Height. In bright sunlight. The weather's bright on Beulah Height.'

And though very little physical change was possible, it was as if they saw Elizabeth Wulfstan shrink to Betsy Allgood as she sat heavily on her chair and began crying.

TWENTY-ONE

Though he'd only heard them once, Pascoe could not get the words of the song out of his mind. They sounded there as he lay in bed and they were still with him next morning as he toiled up the fell.

> Oh, yes, they've only gone out walking,
> Returning now, all laughing and talking.

There was no laughing and talking among the men who laboured up the hillside with him. It was already warm enough to make them sweat under the burden of picks and shovels, even though the sun had not yet risen high enough to fill the valley. But up ahead the eastern flanks of the double peak were already washed with gold.

> We'll catch up with them on Beulah Height
> In bright sunlight.
> The weather's bright on Beulah Height.

Now they were close enough to see the sheep fold, a semicircle of dry-stone wall built against the craggy face of the saddle.

Still no one spoke. Like men in a dream they moved, needing no instructions when they reached the fold, but advancing on the crag as if to some well-rehearsed choreography, and swinging their picks in unison as they probed for the weakness they knew must be present in its apparently solid facade.

Three times they swung and three times they struck, and at the third blow a strange thing happened.

Sparks flew as metal clashed against granite and all at once the air seemed to ignite as a bright lava of sunlight poured down the ridge into the hollow of the fold.

At the same time a huge slab of rock swung open like the gates of a fortress.

The men stepped back, amazed. And fearful too. Only Pascoe held his ground, straining his eyes to see into that black cavern, straining them so much that after a while his fancy created the impression of movement.

Fancy? This was no fancy. There *was* movement in there. He could see shapes in the darkness, small forms advancing slowly towards the light.

And now the first was close enough for the sun to give detail to the uncertain outline. Oh, Christ! It was a child, a girl with long blonde hair, blinking her eyes against the unaccustomed light and bearing in her arms a bouquet of fresh-picked foxgloves. Behind her came another child, also carrying flowers. And another . . . Oh, sweet Jesus. He recognized these children from their photographs. The first was Jenny Hardcastle, the second Madge Telford. And the third Mary Wulfstan, her mother's features unmistakable in the small solemn face.

How to account for this Pascoe did not know. Nor did he care. His heart was swelling with such joy he could hardly breathe. So this was how it ended. All that pain and grief and despair hadn't been for nothing. They were alive, alive, alive . . .

But the miracle wasn't over. Another figure came forward. He looked and did not dare believe. Lorraine. Lorraine Dacre, holding her flowers in one hand and rubbing her eyes with the other, as though just awoken from sleep.

And behind came another . . .

Now it wasn't joy that pumped Pascoe's heart, it was fear. He was choking. Not with fear of the child he was

511

seeing, but fear of the knowledge that came with her . . . the knowledge that she had no place in this wild, high landscape, that it was only his imagination that could have put her there . . .

The fifth figure was Zandra Purlingstone.

He threw back his head and shrieked his rage and despair to the empty sky. For a second it seemed he stood alone on the bare hillside. Then even that illusion was gone. He was lying in his bed with the pearly light of dawn turning his window into a magic lantern screen against which moved the slender boughs of the silver birch which grew at the bottom of his garden.

He rose and dressed swiftly. He had plenty of time to keep his first appointment of the day, but there was something else he needed to do which took him in quite the wrong direction. Not pausing for breakfast, he got into his car and drove through the still empty streets into town.

At the hospital, a security man advanced to challenge him, recognized him, and called a greeting. Pascoe raised a hand but did not pause. Lightly he ran up the stairs, waved a hand at a surprised Sister, and went into the small room where Rosie lay.

Late last night he'd spoken to Ellie on the phone, told her what had happened, where he needed to be the following morning. Dalziel had assured him his presence would not be necessary. Pascoe hadn't argued, simply said he'd be there. Ellie had understood, told him to go home, get what rest he could, assured him that Rosie was doing marvellously well.

Last night Ellie's voice, her reassurance, had been enough. This morning he needed to see for himself.

Ellie had had her bed brought into the room so she could be at her daughter's side. She stirred as Pascoe entered but did not waken. He smiled down at her then tiptoed past to Rosie's bed.

She had thrown the top sheet off and lay there curled with one fist pushed up against her chin, like Rodin's *Thinker*.

Think on, my love. But not too much. Not yet. Time enough to wrestle with life's problems. Time enough.

Gently he drew the sheet over her. It would be nice to kick off his shoes and lie down here with his wife and child, and wake with them in a little while. But there was work to be done. A debt to be paid. What had Ellie called him? Pious Aeneas, always on his way to the Lavinian shore.

How the gods must love irony to let the sight of those he loved most both tempt him from his duty and give him the strength to do it.

He brushed Rosie's brow with his lips, then stooped over Ellie.

A writing pad lay by her side, half-hidden by the duvet. She still clutched a pencil in her hand. She'd started writing again. She was indomitable! For her, a huge crisis endured gave her strength to turn away and confront all the smaller crises put on hold. Indomitable!

Guiltily he peeked at the pencilled scrawl. Suppose it wasn't a new book, but something intensely personal . . . but no, there were the reassuring words Chapter One. He read the opening lines.

It was a dark and stormy night. The wind was blowing off the sea and the guard commander bowed into it with his cloak wrapped around his face as he left the shelter of the grove and began to clamber up to the headland.

Ellie stirred. He looked down at her with love and admiration. Indomitable. A new tune, she'd said. I think we'll all be ready for some new tunes after this. And with typical boldness she'd chosen as her fanfare the corniest opening line in literature!

With a woman like this by his side, a man could go anywhere.

But first he had somewhere to go by himself.

He kissed her gently and went out of the room.

The breeze which had stirred the birch tree at dawn was stronger now, pulling at his hair, portending change. As he sped north he saw for the first time in weeks the smooth blue ocean of sky break against the far horizon in a faint spume of silver cloud.

The gate across the reservoir road was thronged with grim-faced policemen who checked his warrant even though they knew him. Today was by the book.

Despite his efforts at speed, his diversion had made him late and he saw the others waiting for him at the head of the mere. Greetings were short and muted. They watched in silence as he pulled on his boots.

Finally he was ready. At a grunted signal from Andy Dalziel, they turned their faces to the rising fell and went to keep their rendezvous on Beulah Height.